THE SAC'A'RITH: REBIRTH

LOST TALES OF POWER VOL. 7

VINCENT TRIGILI

The Lost Tales of Power: The Sac'a'rith: Rebirth

Written and Published by Vincent Trigili
Copyright 2015 Vincent Trigili

Editors:
Kristi Trigili
Elaine Kennedy (elaine.p.kennedy@gmail.com)

Cover Art by Vincent Trigili
Cover designed by Cormar Covers

ISBN: 978-1508724575

ALSO BY VINCENT TRIGILI

LOST TALES OF POWER

The *Lost Tales of Power* is a collection of novels that describe an immense persistent multiverse. The books are a mixture of standalone and miniseries all set in the same universe with overlapping and intertwining story lines. While the books are a mixture of classic science fiction and pure fantasy, some effort is being made to keep the books in the realm of the possible, or at least theoretically possible given some basic assumptions.

BOOKS IN THE *LOST TALES OF POWER* SERIES:

The Enemy of an Enemy
The Academy
Rise of Shadows
Resurgence of Ancient Darkness
The Sac'a'rith
Spectra's Gambit
The Sac'a'rith: Rebirth
Volume VIII and beyond - TBA

THE SILVERLEAF CHRONICLES

The *Silverleaf Chronicles: Season One* follows the life of Silverleaf, a young dragonmaster who was born into a world without dragons, and doomed to die as a madman alone in the wilderness until a young woman enters his life, and a mysterious army marches across the land destroying all its path.

The Wanderer
Awakening

The Hunters
Traps
Drac'nor
Hope

SHORT STORIES

The Null

LOST TALES OF POWER

SERIES TIMELINE

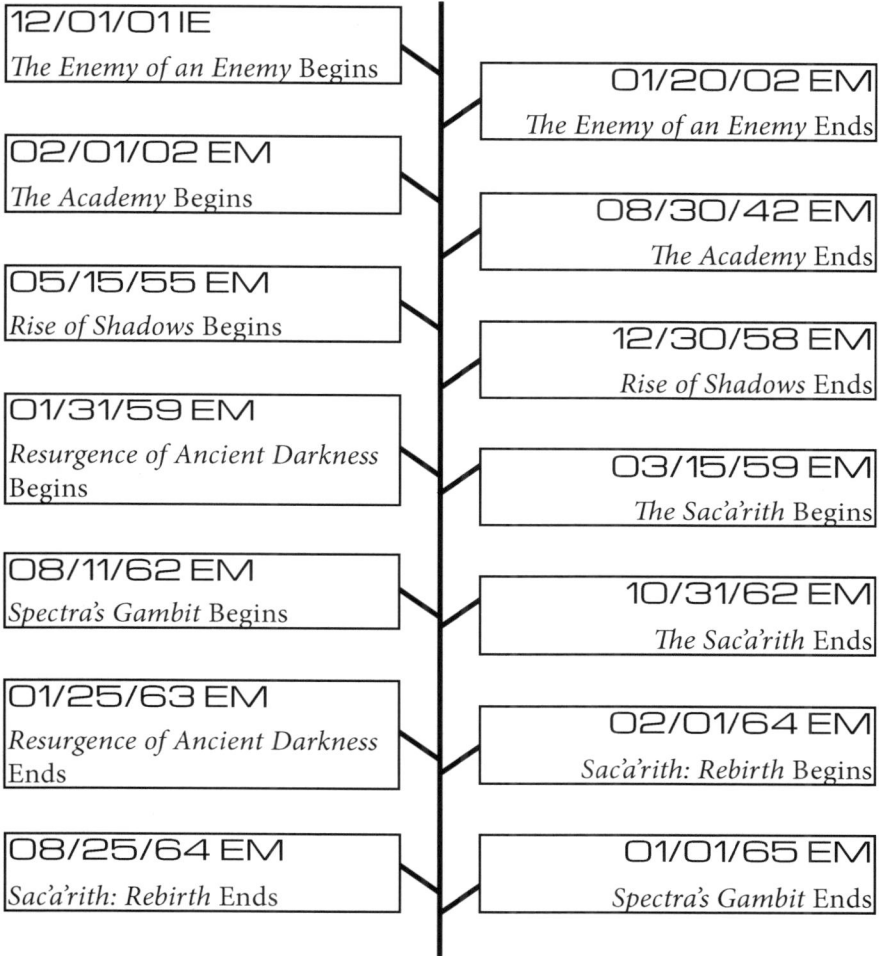

12/01/01 IE	
The Enemy of an Enemy Begins	
	01/20/02 EM
	The Enemy of an Enemy Ends
02/01/02 EM	
The Academy Begins	
	08/30/42 EM
	The Academy Ends
05/15/55 EM	
Rise of Shadows Begins	
	12/30/58 EM
	Rise of Shadows Ends
01/31/59 EM	
Resurgence of Ancient Darkness Begins	
	03/15/59 EM
	The Sac'a'rith Begins
08/11/62 EM	
Spectra's Gambit Begins	
	10/31/62 EM
	The Sac'a'rith Ends
01/25/63 EM	
Resurgence of Ancient Darkness Ends	
	02/01/64 EM
	Sac'a'rith: Rebirth Begins
08/25/64 EM	
Sac'a'rith: Rebirth Ends	
	01/01/65 EM
	Spectra's Gambit Ends

IE = Imperial Era (similar to BC, counts backwards)
EM = Era of Magic

THE

SAC'A'RITH:

REBIRTH

CHAPTER
ONE

"Grandmaster Vydor," said Raquel in greeting as she entered my office. Raquel was tall and carried herself with confidence. There was something in her eyes that told you she was not to be trifled with. The irises were yellow, an eye color I had never seen before. The tips of her pointed ears projected from her auburn hair. She was taller than I, standing at about two meters. Her aura was twisted and bent around her, indicating the burden she carried. When she has learnt to trust us enough to ask for help we will provide it, but that time has not yet come.

She started to bow but stopped herself. When she first joined us, she had insisted on bowing to all the wizards of master level, but I refused to allow anyone to do this. For all our power we were just mortals, unworthy of worship; allowing others to bow before us led to a dangerous path, one I refused to walk.

"Welcome, Raquel! Please have a seat. Would you like a drink?" I gestured at a beverage bar I had had installed in my office. It could make all manner of drinks but was mainly used for coffee. There was something calming about sitting back with a nice warm cup of coffee, just savoring the aroma.

"No, Grandmaster, thank you," she said. She did not sit down and I knew she would not. She had been trained in a different time, when wizards ruled the entire known realm and demanded more formality in their interactions. It was a time which would not have suited me. I hoped that one day she would learn to relax more in my presence, but for the moment I would have to accept her as she was.

I smiled in my most disarming style. "Well, what can I do for you today?"

"Grandmaster, I'd like to use the gate to travel to Hospital Station and find the Sac'a'rith," she said.

"For what purpose?" I asked.

"Grandmaster, with your permission, I'd like to bring them into your … our kingdom and train them," she said.

Interesting slip there. I had hoped she would have seen this as her home by now, but it was probably too soon. "I see. When you first came to us, you mentioned that you wanted to take over from Narcion and restart the 'noble order of the Sac'a'rith'. I assume this is the first step in that plan?" I asked.

"Yes, Grandmaster," she said.

"You have reported five of them currently traveling together," I said. "One of whom is from Korshalemia?"

"Yes, Grandmaster, but only two of them are part of the order," she said.

"What of the others?" I was sure I knew what she would say, but I wanted her to voice it.

"Ragnar and Crivreen are both good candidates to become wizards, Grandmaster, but not Felix," she said.

"Why not?" I asked.

"Grandmaster, Felix owes a large debt to the Assassin's Guild, which makes him untrustworthy."

"Then let us pay it off," I said.

Her eyes widened and she seemed to have difficulty speaking for a moment. "With all due respect, Grandmaster, why would we do that?"

I smiled at her reaction. This could act as an example for her, indicating the true nature of what it meant to be a wizard in this era. "You have yourself reported that he risked his life many times in the quest to find and destroy the table, have you not?" I asked.

"Yes, but – " she began.

I cut her off with a gesture. "And did he not charge in to the necromancer's fortress carrying a backpack full of high explosives, knowing that a dire fate awaited him if he failed?"

"Yes, Grandmaster, but he's a hired mercenary," she said. "And his wages were paid, all of which he has already given to the Assassin's Guild."

"Is he a sorcerer?" I asked.

"No, not yet, Grandmaster," she replied.

"Then pay off his debt and offer him a chance to be a wizard," I said.

"But that would mean giving a large amount of money to an evil organization," she argued.

"In reality, would that amount of money make any difference to their power base?" I asked.

"No, Grandmaster, it wouldn't," she admitted.

"I agree that paying money to the Guild is distasteful, but it is part of the cost of redeeming Felix," I said.

She finally sat down and considered the matter in silence. "Things are so different. I don't understand how to behave."

Finally we were getting somewhere. "What do you mean?"

"I never met your predecessor, Grandmaster. No one could approach him except the other masters. I couldn't even speak directly to any of the masters. I'd pass a message to my superior wizard, and if he thought it worthy he would bring it to one of the masters, who would in all likelihood ignore it. In your kingdom, not only am I allowed to speak directly with you, you even offer me coffee," she said.

Given the size of our domain, I had been forced to split it into six regions and set each master-level wizard over a different section of space in and around our kingdom. Had she been in a different section she would have reported to one of the other masters, but that was nothing like the rigid authoritative structure she was describing. "I see."

"And there was never talk of second chances. Had I come to my superior with this same request, and if it was granted, I would have been told to kill Felix first ," she said, allowing that thought to sink in.

"Well, that is quite unreasonable," I said. She had made similar comments before, and I found them hard to credit. It was not that I thought she was lying; the thought was simply too distasteful to consider.

"I used to agree with them, but I don't know what to think anymore," she said.

"Did you not chase Narcion through the millennia in order to give him another chance?" I asked.

"I was told to kill him," she said. "To prove my loyalty to the council, that nothing would stand in the way of that, I was to kill my own husband. Those were the last orders I received from them."

She had not revealed that information before, and it certainly explained some of her behaviour. "That is why you said you must turn yourself in?"

"Yes, Grandmaster. I disobeyed a direct order from the Wizard's Council," she said.

"And what is the proper penalty for that?" I asked.

"Death," she said.

"For a group of so-called wizards, they seemed to be very focused on killing people," I said. "It is difficult to tell them apart from sorcerers."

"It was a different time," she said. "Nothing is the same."

"Raquel, I gave you full amnesty when you came to me. As the current grandmaster, I have absolved you of all previous crimes," I said.

"Yes, Grandmaster, and I could never repay that kindness, not if I lived another ten millennia," she said.

"Then it should be easy to extend a measure of that same kindness to Felix." I knew that would sting, but it was an important lesson. I did not understand the wizards of her era, but I needed her knowledge of that time in order to succeed in this one, and to obtain that knowledge I needed her trust. If she wrongly saw me as a merciless ruler like her prior masters, it would be hard to extract information from her.

Her head rose and her mouth opened to say something, but she snapped it shut. "Of course you're right, Grandmaster."

"Now, I am fully in support of you assembling these magi and bringing them under our wing, but I think it might be best if you stay out there with them. They would be safer here in our kingdom, but I need them out there."

"Why, Grandmaster?" she asked.

"Right now the only wizards out there are directly connected to the hospital. There are no masters to assign to watch that area, leaving Dr. Leslie as the ranking wizard in the region. For all her skill in medicine, she is not qualified for that position."

"What about Master Dusty and Master Spectra?" she asked.

"They will be leaving that region soon in order to pursue a mission and will not return to that area for a long time, if ever," I said.

"Grandmaster, are you thinking that it would be good to have a few wizards wandering around out there just to keep an eye on things?"

"Yes, but more particularly I am thinking of giving you that region," I said.

"What?"

There was no missing the look of shock on her face. She still saw herself as a disgraced failure, and I had to convince her that her past was long behind her and did not have to determine her future.

"As you know, each region in which we currently have an interest has been assigned to a specific master-level magus. This area is in Kellyn's care, and of course they all fall under me. That region of space is too far away to be added onto an existing area, so it needs a wizard assigned to it. Since you lived out there for a long time and have interests there, it seems reasonable for you to be assigned to it," I said.

"But I'm not a master," she protested.

"No, but you are one of the most experienced wizards in the realm. Nothing needs to be done in a hurry. Travel out there, find the Sac'a'rith, and see where that takes you. I can see change; it is hard to tell in what form, but there is definitely something coming. I need experienced and trustworthy eyes out there, Raquel."

Raquel stood up to reply. "Grandmaster, I am deeply touched. I know I'm not worthy of the honor, but I will strive to become so."

I smiled. I knew she wanted to spin around and leave but her training would not permit it. "Then may the God of Creation bless you and keep you on your journey. I will let the gatemaster know that you are coming. Godspeed, Raquel."

She started to bow again but turned it into a spin, sending her long thick hair flying around her, and left the room. When she was gone I re-filled my coffee cup and sent to Kellyn, *"She still does not fully trust us."*

"No, but she will someday," she replied. *"Then I might be able to save her."*

CHAPTER
TWO

"Special Agent Zah'rak in position. Do we have a green light?" I asked over the comm.

"Special Agent Zah'rak, hold there," came the crackling reply from Command.

Crivreen, Ragnar and myself were just outside a maximum-security prison. Our assignment was to rescue a political figure who had been taken hostage by one of the tribes attempting to take control of this system. They were using the hostage to try to force withdrawal of the Phareon military, but it was about to backfire on them in a big way.

Felix and Shira were back on the Night Wisp in the sensor shadow of the moon, awaiting the signal to sweep in.

"Are we sure about this?" sent Crivreen. Even after all this time serving with me, I could still sense the nervousness in his mental voice. That was good, I supposed; it was certainly better than him being cocky.

"A little late to ask that," I sent back. *"Besides, this is our fourth mission with them. It's not as if we don't know what to expect."*

"Yeah, but we don't even know who we're rescuing; we know very little about the situation," he sent.

"We know enough," I sent back, but I understood his uneasiness. After Narcion died, we had drifted for a bit until Special Agent Byron's handler contacted us and informed us of Byron's death. Apparently, before Byron died he had turned in a report praising our service, and the handler needed someone to replace him and, more importantly, to replace Narcion. Phareon had many magi working for them; what they didn't have was a skilled and experienced team of magi, and that was the niche we could fill.

"Special Agent Zah'rak, move out and good luck," came the order over the comm. It was hard to make out the command over the crackling. Being so close to the prison meant we were getting interference from the scramble field around the base. Once inside communicators would be useless, at least until the attack was underway in earnest and the scramble generators were taken out.

"We're on," I sent. We silently approached the outer wall of one of the prison blocks. It was a massive metal structure, scarred from what I judged to be many failed attacks. In the gloom of the early morning the walls stretched up left and right out of sight. I couldn't see them but I knew from early reconnaissance missions that there were sentry guns spaced out evenly along the entire wall. The area from where we were approaching had lots of natural cover and a narrow pass to a single door, guarded only by two humans and a pair of sentry guns. This appeared to be a weak point in their defenses, one that we planned to exploit.

Somewhere in the distance there was a loud series of explosions that shook the very ground under our feet. *"They've begun their attack! Blast the doors!"*

Ragnar called out a command word and threw a rune at the fortified door. The two guards turned towards him as the rune exploded behind them. The soil on either side of the walkway was thrown into the air by the blast, momentarily obscuring the view. When it cleared, both humans were dead and the doors were destroyed, but the sentry guns were far enough from the blast to have remained intact. They hunted for targets, but we were still under cover just beyond their vision.

"Crivreen, blast them!" I called out.

Crivreen drew his wands and unleashed a wave of lightning. The electrical energy arced back and forth across the open doorway between the guns. The power cells that drove the guns overheated under the barrage and exploded, destroying both guns and a large section of the walls. Overhead, fighter craft raced back and forth defending bombers which were pummeling the colony in seemingly random places. The ground shook and the sky lit up brighter than midday as more and more bombs were dropped. The prison's anti-aircraft defenses were failing to do more than annoy the naval fighters.

Our target was several levels underground, which should be safe for a little while, but we had been warned: Phareon planned to leave no survivors. We had to get out before they broke through the upper level defenses or we'd be destroyed with the base. Phareon intended to show everyone the foolishness of taking hostages, even if they had to kill the hostage themselves which created an unforgiving deadline for us.

I waved my team forward and ran into the fortress with my rifle in hand. I couldn't throw lightning around like Crivreen nor make rocks explode like Ragnar, but my trusty assault rifle was more than capable of dealing death and destruction at the speed of light.

"Which way, Ragnar?" I sent. Ragnar's uncanny sense of direction and unerring memory of maps made him immensely valuable on these missions. In some ways he was the most valuable man on the team, but his lack of understanding of modern technology proved a big hindrance.

"Left at the next junction, and then take the second shaft down," he replied without the slightest hesitation.

Most of the prison guards were heading towards the firefight at the other end of the colony, but alarms were undoubtedly sounding at this end and I knew it was only a matter of time before troops were sent to deal with us. There would be constant confusion throughout the battlefield, and

I was counting on that to create enough delay for us to get in, make the rescue and get out.

We had almost made it to the shaft before coming under fire from some soldiers in heavy armor. *"Don't stop! Make a break for the shaft! I'll cover you,"* I sent. I was pretty sure my rifle couldn't penetrate their armor, but that same armor was heavy and would dramatically reduce their speed of movement. That should give us enough time to make the run, but I was too experienced to count on it.

Crivreen and Ragnar made a mad sprint along the last few meters towards the shaft as I tossed two concussion grenades over their heads at the enemy troops. The force from the blast threw the soldiers back and bought us the time we needed to jump down the shaft. Their armor might have protected some of them from the blast, but those closest would have been killed. More importantly, the rest would move more cautiously now and that would give us more time to gain a good lead on them.

The thrusters on our armor were intended for zero-g maneuvers but were sufficient to slow our twenty-meter descent just enough so that we could hit the ground running.

"Getting back out should be fun," called out Ragnar as we sprinted down the corridor.

I hadn't attempted to make an escape plan as there was no way to guess in advance what options would be open to us, but Ragnar had been insistent that we should have one; he felt strongly enough about it to have probably worked one out himself.

We came to another junction and stopped a moment to catch our breath. I looked around and realized I had no idea where we were. "Which way?"

Ragnar chanted a divination as he wrote something on the floor with his finger. "We're close; this way!" He took off at a jog down one of the corridors and I sent Crivreen after him. I wanted to take the rear, as I was sure those soldiers would figure out which way we'd gone soon enough, unless they had more than one Phareon hostage. It must be obvious why we were here. I was sure that if we allowed them breathing room they would have guards around our target, locking him down tight.

Weapon fire erupted from somewhere ahead of us as we ran, and Ragnar returned fire with one of the wands Crivreen had made for him, but we didn't slow down. Time was completely against us and it was a merciless and tireless enemy.

We managed to stay ahead of the troops sent to stop us and made it to the cell where the target was being held. A few quick blasts from my rifle took care of the locked door, and we found him chained and unconscious in the back of the room. He looked badly beaten and starved. He was probably some ranking politician or, more likely, the son of a politician.

"No time to rouse him," said Crivreen.

"No need," I said as I lifted him onto my shoulder, preferring that he stay asleep. As a Zalionian I was probably at least fifty per cent more massive than the puny human, so his weight was not a hindrance. "Fastest way out?"

"Up," said Ragnar. "Crivreen, barricade the door and then find cover."

Crivreen dragged what little furniture there was in the room over to the door, in an attempt to jam shut what was left of it, and then hunkered down behind the pile. I covered the human we were rescuing with my body as Ragnar tossed one of his runes up to the ceiling. There was a large blast and then I felt hot debris bouncing off my armor.

As soon as the dust had cleared enough I saw that Ragnar had fired up a grappling cable and quickly ascended. "Crivreen, take the rear." I climbed up the rope as quickly as I could without dropping the human. Below, Crivreen cast another wave of lightning to slow down the approaching troops. Once I was out of the hole, I signaled to Crivreen to follow.

Crivreen didn't bother with the cable. Instead, he teleported up into the air in a direct line of sight from where he was and used his jump jets to push him the rest of the way onto the ledge. Below us the prison guards were rushing towards the opening. "Crivreen, grenades - now!" I called out. *You must remember you can do things like that!* I chided myself. Teleportation would have been faster and safer than lugging this fellow up the rope.

Crivreen pulled out two of his explosive grenades and tossed them down after the guards. Ragnar had already started to leave, so Crivreen and I ran to catch up with him without waiting to see if the grenades were effective. Somewhere behind us I heard them explode, and hoped they had at least slowed down our pursuers.

"Felix, we're on our way out," I said over the comm., hoping that the scramblers had been taken out according to plan.

"On our way," he said. His message was crystal clear, which was good since it meant that the scramblers had been taken out, but also bad in the sense that it meant time was running out.

We fought through several more corridors, staying just ahead of the troops, who were scattered and uncoordinated. It seemed Phareon's forces had successfully disrupted their communication network, making our escape much easier. Still, we must be running low on time, and either the guards would rally and overpower us or Phareon would destroy the place around us very soon. Neither outcome was acceptable.

"There's a clearing up ahead; it should be big enough," said Ragnar.

"Okay, make haste!" I said. I activated the homing signal on my armor so that Felix could quickly locate us. All we had to do was reach somewhere with clear line of sight to the sky.

"He's going to have a hard time getting close under all that fire," said Crivreen.

"He doesn't have to get too close, just enough to see us," I said.

As we approached the clearing, the Night Wisp flew by and Shira jumped into the air from the airlock. She spread out her arms as if she thought she could fly and glided away from the Night Wisp. Once she was clear she teleported to the ground. "Hurry!" she called out as she cast her gate spell. "He can't keep the ship in range of my gate for long!"

Overhead the Night Wisp was making a second pass as a two-dimensional blue oval opened in the air in front of us. Ragnar charged through first, followed by Crivreen and myself. Shira came last and closed the gate behind us. *"We're on board, Felix! Get us out of here!"* I sent. Safely on board the Night Wisp, exhaustion set in and I had to lean against the wall for support as the powerful engines of the Night Wisp pushed hard against the planet's atmosphere and gravity.

Once I had caught my breath, Ragnar helped me secure the still-unconscious human as the Night Wisp completed its banking maneuver and accelerated out of the atmosphere. When we were clear of danger, Crivreen and Ragnar moved the human into sickbay and placed him in a hyberpod where he would stay in medical stasis until we could deliver him to the nearest Phareon base. He would need medical expertise I did not have to recover, but the pod would keep him safe until we got there.

"Anyone get hurt this time?" asked Felix over the ship's comm.

"No, we seem to be getting better at this," I said. My instincts told me the training and practice we were getting by running these missions would be critical for our future survival, but I didn't understand why. I could not see into the future, and that was a problem for another day. "Call our contact and arrange for the drop-off."

CHAPTER THREE

Zah'rak! There's a call coming in on our private channel," called out Crivreen.

"Odd," I said. "Put it through to my station." We'd just dropped off the hostage we'd rescued and I wasn't expecting a call for a new mission just yet, so I was a little concerned about getting a call on that channel.

A man appeared on the screen whom I didn't recognize; he appeared to be the same species as Ragnar, and there was something familiar about his features that I couldn't place. Something nagged at the back of my mind. I should know this person. Was it his eyes? No, they seemed unfamiliar too. My instincts told me I knew him, yet I couldn't figure out who he might be.

"Hello, old friend," he said.

The way he said that confirmed our previous acquaintance, but his voice was no more familiar than his face. Still there was that nagging feeling that I should know him. "Who are you?"

"Zah'rak, it's Byron. I know I look different. Is Ragnar there? I am sure he can verify my identity for you with his magic," I said.

That was surely impossible. "I was told Byron was dead."

"My race was discovered, and I had to fake my death to protect some people," he said.

I turned away from the screen and called for Ragnar. Whoever this was had private command channel codes that only Byron should have had and he knew Byron's secret. That could mean he was involved in Byron's death.

When Ragnar came up, I sat him in front of the screen and turned back towards it. "Who is that?"

"I am not sure. I cannot see his aura through this device," said Ragnar.

"Zah'rak, you picked up Ragnar in Korshalemia after using the gate in Narcion's room." The stranger then went on to tell us the details of the fight in which Narcion died. "What more proof do you need?"

"Who are you?" asked Ragnar.

"Special Agent Byron," said the stranger.

"I knew you weren't dead!" shouted Ragnar.

"Are you sure it's Byron?" I asked.

"He talks just like him, his recollection of events matches what Byron would have remembered, AND he has Byron's command codes. Who else could it be?" asked Ragnar.

"Thanks, Ragnar," said the stranger. "I am known as Greymere now. The Byron identity must remain dead to protect those who helped me."

"Understood," said Ragnar. "Where are you?"

"I am on board the Nemesis with thirty or so magi and we need Zah'rak's help," he said. "We are near Hospital Station. Are you close by?"

"Ragnar, are you sure this is Byron?" I sent privately. I wanted to believe our old friend was still alive, but it would be a dangerous mistake to be wrong about this.

"Like I said, I can't read his aura through this device, but it sure seems like it to me," he sent back.

"But why doesn't it look or sound like him?" I sent.

"If it is he, then he can't risk being discovered in this body any more than

he could in his previous one. Remember that everyone out here wants to kill him because of his race," he sent.

"How can we be sure?" I asked.

"If I see him with my own eyes, I will know the truth," he sent.

I turned my focus back to the comm. "We can meet with you in two days at the following coordinates. Then Ragnar can read your aura and we will know the truth of this matter." I then sent him our current coordinates.

"Master Dusty, does that work for us?" Greymere asked of someone off-screen.

"Yes," came the answer.

"Okay, Zah'rak; see you in two days," said Greymere.

"Did he say 'Master Dusty?'" asked Ragnar.

"Agreed," I said and Greymere cut the channel.

"I believe so, why?" I asked.

"If he means THE Master Dusty, that is big news!" he said.

"Who is this Dusty?" I asked.

"Master Dusty is third in command of the Wizard Kingdom's naval force," he said.

"Would that mean that Byron, or whatever he's called now, is aboard a naval craft?" I asked.

"Most likely," said Ragnar.

"Crivreen, can you hide us from them?" I asked.

"If we shut down most of our power systems and give the ship time to cool before they arrive, we will look like just another piece of space debris and their sensors should automatically filter us out of their reports," he said.

"Do it, then," I said.

"Why are we going to hide if we intend to meet them here?" asked Ragnar.

"I want the option to abort if we need it." I left the bridge and went down to the room I had converted into my shop. We had just picked up some more supplies and I was experimenting with new materials, trying to improve our armor. The basic combination of leather, spider silk and cotton worked well to enchant our battle suits, but I wanted to know if there were other things I could use for different effects.

It was the perfect project to work on with the Night Wisp running on lower power, as the process of enchantment would only work if I used all natural tools and only my bare hands. Any power tool or artificial part in the process would ruin the enchantment.

The two days passed without event. Ragnar and Crivreen were excited about the prospect of meeting real wizards, but Felix was cautious. He had a real problem with authority and didn't trust any military craft, even if the 'dead' Byron was on board.

It was hard to tell what Shira thought of the whole thing. She worked hard to help out around the ship, but showed very few signs of emotion. I knew she was plagued by nightmares, but she refused to talk about them. Her years of service as a slave to a necromancer must have left a terrible legacy, and I could only imagine what haunted her at night.

Eventually the time came for our meeting with Greymere and we agreed for him to fly over solo. If it really was Greymere, then crossing the hard vacuum of space should be easy for him, as his race was born and lived out its life in deep space.

We all gathered at the airlock to greet whoever this was. I set the exterior door to open, and a man floated into the airlock without a space suit.

"Only Byron could do that," remarked Crivreen.

"Or any other of his species," added Felix.

"Be ready," I said and cycled the airlock to let him in.

As he walked onto the Night Wisp, Greymere asked, "Okay, satisfied?"

"It is definitely Byron," Ragnar said.

Crivreen, Ragnar and I had a flurry of questions for him, and eventually we extracted from him the information that his race had been discovered by an underling who wanted his job. He knew that exposure of his race would lead to the discovery of those who had helped him, and that could land them in jail or worse.

After a short while he steered the conversation to the situation at hand. "Over there, cloaked, is the Nemesis, with magi on board who range from new apprentices to highly-trained wizards. More to the point, they have spell books for all the major spell lines."

I felt as if I could jump out of my scales. "Even mine?"

"Yes, and that's why we are here," he said. "In a recent trip to the Spirit Realm my armor was destroyed and I need a new set. Master Dusty and Master Spectra, my superiors, would like to barter for new armor for me and also some spares. So what do you say, knowledge for armor?"

"Hold on," interjected Ragnar. "Did you just say 'Master Dusty and Master Spectra'?"

"Yes," he said. "Do you know them?"

"Master Dusty is third in command of the Wizards Kingdom's Navy, and Master Spectra is his wife. I never met them, but they are famous," he said.

"Would you like to meet them?" he asked. "We can dock the two ships together and our cloak will more than cover the Night Wisp." The Night Wisp was a much smaller ship than the Nemesis, so the additional mass and energy that the cloak would need to cover it was relatively small.

Crivreen almost jumped out of his armor when he said that. "You mean we can meet real wizards?"

"As real as you are," he said.

"I'll go right up to the bridge!" responded Crivreen. "Just ask them to contact me so we can interlink our computers, and we can be docked in no time."

As Crivreen ran off Greymere turned to me. "Just to warn you, Nemesis is a special kind of ship and, well, not all its occupants are what you would describe as normal; but they are all my friends, so don't be afraid."

"What would I have to be afraid of?" I asked.

He just smiled and said, "You'll see."

Crivreen worked with someone on their side to dock the Night Wisp to the Nemesis and came down to join us at the airlock. Felix stated that someone should stay behind and make sure the Night Wisp was secure and headed towards the bridge. I assumed that meant he was volunteering for the job.

Master Dusty and Master Spectra met us at the airlock and, once he'd been introduced to them, Ragnar bowed deeply and said, "I am honored to meet you both. I have heard many tales of your adventures, but never expected to be fortunate enough to come into your presence."

A human woman with red hair walked into the room and said, "Ragnar? What are you doing here?"

"Shea? I should ask you the same!" he said.

"So you two know each other?" asked Greymere.

"Ragnar used to buy potions from me back in Korshalemia, but I have not seen him in many seasons," she said.

"How is your brother? Is he here, too?" asked Ragnar.

"No, he stayed behind," she replied and they wandered off to catch up on old times.

Greymere gave us a tour of the Nemesis and introduced us to Nanny and Nemesis himself. Once that was finished, we left Shira and Criveen in the mess hall with Nanny while Zah'rak, Master Dusty, Master Spectra and I moved into a conference room.

"A ghost cook and a living ship," I commented. "No wonder you warned me!"

"Masters, Zah'rak and I used to hunt wraiths together," Greymere informed them and then related some of our adventures.

"A table?' exclaimed Master Dusty. "Describe it to me."

When he had done so, Master Spectra said, "I found none out this way. How long ago did you destroy it?"

"It was sometime in November of last year," I said.

"That was before we went searching for the others," said Master Dusty. He explained that they had found and destroyed several of the tables.

"So our fates have been intertwined for some time now," I said.

"It seems so," said Greymere.

"As for armor, I only have two sets ready right now; they are not quite as good as what you are wearing," I said.

"That's fine," said Master Dusty. "I will give you a datapad that contains instructions on how to make not only these suits but also the jewelry we use as standard equipment. We will take what you have now, and when you have more sets of armor ready we will pick those up."

"How many are you looking for?" I asked.

"Three dozen," he said.

This was a much bigger undertaking than I had ever previously considered. I didn't even know how to estimate the work it would involve. "That will take a lot of time and materials."

"The instructions in the book will help with that, I am sure," said Master Dusty.

"*Ragnar?*" I sent, probing for his mind. Ragnar could not start up a telepathic conversation, but if one of us initiated it he could then communicate with us.

"*Yes?*" he replied.

I informed him of the offer made by Master Dusty and asked him, "*What do you think?*"

"*Take it. If nothing else, befriending people so high up in the Wizard Kingdom will be very beneficial to our future dealings,*" he replied. "*While I have you here: I think I have found some help for Shira. Shea has taken on the role of counselor for the Wizards and she is meeting privately now with Shira.*"

Before I could ask him more Master Spectra said, "We hope to make this an ongoing deal. As we grow we will need more and more magical supplies, and Greymere trusts you so we are happy to give you the business."

"*Tell me later; I must finalize this deal, but that sounds great!*" I sent privately to Ragnar and then said, "This datapad: may I see it?"

Master Dusty slid the datapad over to me and said, "It is all on that."

I flipped through the screens for a few moments. I would guess there was more information there about magic than in all the rest of the region;

not only complete instructions for how to make armor, but also what looked like the basics for many different powers which Crivreen and the others had started to teach me. "It would take me a lifetime to learn all this."

"Then, if you don't mind, start with the armor," said Master Dusty with a grin.

"Do we have a deal, then?" asked Master Spectra.

"Absolutely," I said.

CHAPTER
FOUR

After making arrangements with Master Dusty to report on the progress of the armor and arranging for delivery, I met Ragnar and Crivreen at the airlock. Apparently Master Spectra wasn't concerned about the possible distance between our ships, and would pick up the armor in person when I had the sets ready.

"Where's Shira?" I asked as we boarded the Night Wisp.

"She's still with Shea and will be along shortly," said Ragnar.

"Shea?" I asked.

"Yeah. As I mentioned, Shea and I spent some time together back home. She is apparently serving as their counselor, so I asked her to speak with Shira."

"She know we're leaving?" That was good. Shira had been withdrawn ever since we'd killed her former master. She was a hard worker and dedicated member of the team, but it was obvious she was deeply wounded by her time as a slave to a necromancer. I had served as a slave myself for most of my life, but that was to mundane humans, not a lord of the dead.

"Not sure, but Shea will make sure she gets back to us," he said. "Did you get the spell books?"

Before I could answer, I heard the airlock cycle behind us to let Shira onto the Night Wisp. She was carrying a large box that I didn't recognize.

"What's that?" I asked.

"Oh, just a gift from Shea," she said. "I'll look through it later."

"Felix, detach us and pull away," I said over the comm.

"Sure. What heading?" he asked.

"Um, how about one-two-three mark four," I said.

Ragnar rolled his eyes at that and Crivreen chuckled.

Shira seemed a bit brighter, but it might have just been my imagination. She had put the box down and was sitting on it.

"Yes, Ragnar, I got the datapad," I said.

"What datapad?" asked Crivreen.

Felix came down from the bridge and said, "Okay, course to nowhere set, and we're making great time."

"I agreed to make them some armor in exchange for spell books," I said.

"Real spell books?" asked Crivreen.

"Well, as real as this datapad here in my hands. On it is the basic information for all spell lines, including mine. They lost their armor vendor and want me to take over."

"Their armor looks different to the type you make. I would assume it's better?" queried Crivreen.

"Yes. On this pad are the instructions for making it," I said, swiping through the screens until I brought up the correct formula. "Looks like I need diamond and gold dust to make it, in addition to what we already use."

"Well, diamonds are easy enough to make from common carbon, and gold is pretty cheap, so that should be easy to get," said Felix.

"That won't work," said Ragnar. "The diamonds have to be natural."

"Natural diamonds? I wouldn't even know where to look for them," said Felix. "I'm sure they would be extremely expensive if we could find them, and how would we know if they were real?'

"I'd be able to tell, as would Zah'rak," said Ragnar.

"Great; still, though, how will we find any?" asked Felix.

A quiet voice spoke, so out of place that I almost missed it. "I know where."

I looked over to where Shira was sitting looking down at her feet. Normally, by now she would have wandered off to be alone. I summoned up my most gentle voice and said, "Where, Shira?"

"Under the castle we destroyed," she said. "He was collecting gems and other natural materials."

"Do you think they were kept deep enough to survive the blast?" I asked.

"Yes, more than deep enough," she said. "He was terrified that someone might find them, so he forced slaves to dig deep caverns and sealed them in with rock."

"Well, it sounds like we have our answer," said Felix. "I'll set a course to the Siden System."

"Wait, who owns the planet?" asked Ragnar.

"Who cares?" asked Felix.

"If someone has a claim on it, they might not take too kindly to us mining there," said Ragnar.

"No one seemed to care that we leveled a large section of their forest and destroyed a castle," retorted Felix.

"That was different," cut in Ragnar.

"Even if it belongs to someone, we have a right to salvage," said Felix.

"That sounds more like a right to steal," said Ragnar.

"Hold on," I said. "Crivreen, check the database. Does anyone lay claim to it?"

Crivreen walked over to a terminal and started searching. While he did that I turned to Shira and asked, "You said they are sealed in; will we have to blast through the rock, then?"

"No," she said. "I know a way in. I used to hide down there when he was really angry."

"Well, it's in Phareon space, but there's no record of any claim on it," said Crivreen.

"Then it's ours," replied Felix. "Let's go before someone else thinks of it."

"All right, then; lay in a course and let's get this done," I said. I could tell that Ragnar was still a bit uncomfortable, but in this case I agreed with Felix; it was ours by right of salvage.

"We need to stop for some supplies first. Our fresh water and food stores are running low," said Crivreen.

"What would it take to start up those gardens we have?" asked Ragnar.

"The hydroponics? I believe they work but have never been used," I said.

"Yeah," said Crivreen. "I looked them over a while back. I think they are fully functional, and it would be good to get them going. Not only would they provide food, but they would help the air scrubbers."

"What would it take to get them going?" I asked.

Crivreen scrolled through a list on his terminal. "With regards to materials we need some seeds, seedlings, organic compost and a few other things, but none of that should be an issue. The real problem, of course, is that we need someone to tend to them. They will need regular care and maintenance."

"I could do it," said Shira, "if someone shows me how."

I looked at Crivreen who shrugged, then I said, "I'll take you back there. I'm sure that there are manuals in the database. We can figure it out as we go."

"Okay, so we head to Zenfar for supplies, then over to Siden?" asked Felix.

"Yes," I said.

Felix went to the bridge to set the course and I led Shira back to the hydroponics bay. The bay was filled with empty racks and silent equipment.

When Narcion was alone on this ship there had been no need for it, so I was pretty sure the equipment had never been used.

"Wow," said Shira. "It looks far more complex than I expected."

I was about to say something to let her back out, but then I remembered that the most important thing for a former slave was to find their own identity. This would be the perfect time for her to grow. "We can stop over in Zenfar for a few days and see about training you or getting someone from the station to help get this thing fired up, if you want."

"No, I'll figure it out. How long till we get to Zenfar?" she asked.

"At least a week," I said. "Once Felix has the course laid in, we will be able to work out our arrival date."

She looked around the room, stiffened her shoulders and said, "I will have this ready in time."

"Well, let's fire up these terminals and make sure you have all the access you need." I poked around for a while but couldn't figure it out, so I contacted Crivreen on the comm.

"You need to add 'Garden Master' to her profile," he said.

"Garden Master?" I asked.

"Yep," he said. "Whoever set it up named the security profile for hydroponics 'Garden Master.'"

"Okay, thanks," I said as I added the role to her profile and then turned to Shira. "Congratulations, Garden Master."

Her eyes seemed to expand to fill her face as she quietly whispered, "Garden Master."

"Looks like there's a ton of information in here; do you want help to go through it?"

She shook her head, walked over to the terminal and started paging through the information. "I have this."

"Well, just call if you need anything," I said and left her to work. On my way out I could hear her saying, "Shira, Garden Master," quietly to herself.

CHAPTER FIVE

Zah'rak, we are cleared to dock," said Felix.

"Great. Once we're docked you and Crivreen head over and get whatever supplies the ship needs, and Shira and I will look for what we require for the hydroponics," I said.

"Nah, Crivreen should take Ragnar," said Felix. "I'll stay with the ship."

I knew he would say something like that. He always did. I didn't know why, but he never went onto any stations that weren't mission objectives; or at least not since Narcion died. "Very well," I replied. Once we had docked, the four of us headed over and went our separate ways.

Shira walked close to me with her head down and didn't say much. She would respond to direct questions with as few words as possible, and seemed to have lost ground in her recovery. I wished we could have taken Shea with us, or at least kept in communication with her. It was obvious that she'd helped Shira in a big way.

"Shira, you've done wonders with the hydroponics. I'm very impressed!" I said, attempting to brighten her mood.

"Thank you," she said.

"Besides the organic supplies, is there anything you want?" I asked.

"No," she said.

"More training manuals, perhaps?" I asked.

"No."

"Would you like to see their hydroponic gardens while we're here?" I asked.

"No."

"Anything for yourself?" I asked.

"No."

I sighed and continued to walk towards the shops that would have what she needed. In each shop she silently searched for and gathered the various supplies that were required. She didn't interact with anyone except me but we got through it.

What could I do to help her? She had gone through a very dark time, but that was behind her now. She was young, healthy and free; she could make anything of herself now, but mostly she just moped around.

Once everything was ordered and we had arranged for it to be delivered to our cargo hold, I decided to try to lighten her mood by taking her to a nice restaurant. I figured it was likely that she had never been in one before, as slaves were not welcome.

When we were seated she seemed to collapse into herself even more. The server had to coax an order out of her, and I was starting to doubt my judgment in bringing her on board the station. It seemed that my good intentions weren't enough and it wasn't working out.

The meal passed in silence and I was about to take her back home when into the restaurant walked someone I hadn't expected to see again.

"Raquel!" I said as the warrior walked up to the table. In the harsh station lights her hair looked redder than I remembered it, but it was definitely the same person. She no longer wore the hooded cloak that used to be her signature outfit; instead she wore sleek, modern purple-and-grey battle armor that faintly pulsed with power.

"Hello, Zah'rak," she said and sat down at the table.

"We were just leaving," I said. Shira was deathly afraid of Raquel and I didn't think it would be good for her recovery to have to deal with this fear right now.

"Zah'rak," said Raquel. "We need to talk."

"What about?" I asked.

"It would be better if we moved this conversation onto the Night Wisp," she said.

"Ragnar, Raquel is here," I sent.

"That's wonderful! Bring her aboard. It will be great to catch up with her," he sent.

That was not the reaction I was hoping for, but I suspected he was right. There were so many unanswered questions left from the time we had spent with Narcion, especially relating to that final battle. *"Okay, we'll be back soon, but don't forget about Shira,"* I sent.

"She will probably hide in hydroponics with her new supplies," he sent, *"but sooner or later she needs to start facing her fears."*

Raquel was the widow of Narcion, the man who had freed me from slavery and led us until his recent death, but I didn't know her at all. For a while we had thought her an enemy, and I still had a hard time shaking that. She had tried to break up our team and turn us against Narcion, but in the final battle with the necromancer she had fought by our side and Narcion had fully trusted her.

I was about to say something to Shira, when I noticed she was gone. *"Shira, where did you go?"*

"I'm in hydroponics," she sent.

"Seems that Shira went ahead," I commented.

"Yes, she transported herself away as I approached," said Raquel. "Shall we head to the Night Wisp, then?"

"Are you sure about this, Ragnar?" I sent.

"Yes! We have many questions which only she can answer. We need to take advantage of this opportunity," he sent.

I had to admit he was right; she had inside information we were lacking. I stood to my full height, head and shoulders taller than Raquel, but I knew better than to think that would intimidate her. "Sure, let me take care of the bill and we can be off."

As we left, I noticed that she was wearing an armored backpack. "Travelling light?"

"Always," she said. "Why is Shira afraid of me?"

"Among other reasons, she did try to kill your husband several times," I said.

"I see. She thinks I'll seek vengeance, then," she said.

"Yes," I said. It was a reasonable conclusion, and having seen Raquel in battle I wasn't confident that even our entire team could stop her. Over the months since that fight, Ragnar had insisted several times that Raquel was not hostile to Shira, but Shira either wouldn't or couldn't believe him. So far Ragnar had never been wrong in his predictions, and my instincts told me he was right this time too.

"Neither I nor Narcion ever saw her as an enemy. She was merely a pawn forced to play a role until you freed her. She has nothing to fear from me," she said.

Her answer was logical and reasonable, but logic and reason failed in the face of deep-seated emotional wounds such as those Shira bore.

We walked the rest of the way to the docking port in silence, and out of habit I headed towards the security bypass line which my status as a special agent allowed me to use. "Oh, sorry; I guess I need to take you through the public access."

"No, this will be fine," said Raquel.

As I approached the security checkpoint one of the guards said, "Hey, Zah'rak. Where's Shira?"

"She found her own way back," I said.

As usual, they let me pass without even checking my ID, which was foolish on their part but convenient for me so I never reported them. I was about to mention Raquel when I noticed she was gone. *Raquel?* I sent.

"I'll meet you at the Night Wisp's airlock," she sent back.

When I reached the ship she was there, waiting for me.

"I prefer not to deal with security gates," she said.

I didn't blame her. If you didn't have special access like I did, they were a royal pain and would be worse for her because I was sure she was armed. "They don't bother me much anymore."

I led her onto the Night Wisp and asked everyone to meet us in the common room. Shira didn't want to come, claiming she was busy. Instead of arguing with her, I turned on the comm. system so that she could listen in. When everyone had settled in, I said, "Raquel, the last time we saw you, you said you had to turn yourself in."

"Yes, and I did so; but that's not why I'm here," she replied.

"I think we need some answers first," interjected Felix. "For a while, you were trying to break up this team and turn us against Narcion. You warned us of great doom if we stayed on course, but then helped us complete his task. Now you're back, after supposedly turning yourself in to the authorities?"

She sighed. "Yes, all of that is true. It's complicated. Narcion and I are from a different era, one that has been long forgotten."

"I think you'd better start at the beginning," said Felix.

"Very well," she said. "When the wizards of old were conspiring to tear the weave and put an end to the current great war of magic, Narcion designed the tables as an escape plan."

"That table we destroyed was Narcion's?" I exclaimed.

"Yes," she confirmed.

"But that would make him a sorcerer!" said Crivreen.

"Please let the lady speak," said Ragnar.

"I need to go back a little farther. When I first met him, Narcion was a minor wizard who did his best to stay out of the wars. He was never a gentle person, but his dark side was well under control at that time. He often took people in randomly and helped them get started in life. That was the way he was," said Raquel.

33

I smiled at her comment, as that was just how this team had been formed. Narcion might have been the most ruthless and merciless warrior I had ever heard of, but he poured himself into this team and made us what we were today.

"The wars found him; they found everyone eventually. It was a very dark time. The wars forced him to fight, and all the death and destruction he had to take part in changed him into the cold and calculating man you knew. He turned to necromancy in order to gain the power he needed, but the evil art twisted his soul and turned him darker."

Raquel had to pause there, choked up with emotion. I started to say something but Ragnar stopped me. She had previously confided that he had turned to necromancy to obtain vengeance for someone close to him, but this remark about the war was new. I wondered if that person close to him had been Raquel herself.

After a moment she continued. "The master sorcerers devised a plan to use Narcion's tables to come back after all the wizards were gone and the weave had been healed."

"By the gods! That would have put them in control before anyone could stop them," said Ragnar.

The incident she was referring to had happened ten thousand years previously. At that time, the wizards thought they could stop the sorcerers by rending reality itself. They had hoped it would remove from the sorcerers the ability to do magic by denying them access to the weave, but it did much more: it prevented everyone from working magic until recently.

"Yes, a new age of evil would have risen," she said. "Narcion knew that once the wizards tore the weave, we would all die. I tried to warn them, but they didn't believe me and said I had been duped by my husband. I have often wondered what they might have thought, what excuses they might have come up with, if they hadn't been consumed in the casting. They never had time to realize that their mistake would wipe out the magi, good and bad alike, for eons.

"So, before the wizards could tear the weave, Narcion and I fled to another realm where we pretended to be mundanes. He brooded about creating the tools that would turn this realm into a living, waking nightmare, and over time the guilt drove him mad. The only saving grace he could come up with was that we had survived and might be able to find a way to return to this realm before the sorcerers could, to destroy the tables. In order to do that, Narcion devised a timeless state for us to sleep in, tied to this realm's weave. The plan was that we would wake once the weave had healed enough for us to operate in this realm again."

Ragnar brought a drink over for her and she paused to take a long swig before continuing. "It worked. He woke first and started his hunt without me. I eventually awoke and followed him out here. He was working hard to complete his mission, throwing all caution to the wind and embracing the very powers that had twisted him."

She paused for another swig and Ragnar asked, "Then the doom you warned us of was the expected result of Narcion's use of necromancy?"

"Yes. It was what I believed inevitable, but somehow he managed to stay focused on the mission until the end. Had he not – " she paused for a moment, took a deep breath and continued. "Had he not, it would have ushered in an era ruled by the undead."

It had not been very long since Narcion had died in that final battle and she obviously mourned him deeply. Even Felix was quiet for a moment.

"He redeemed himself," said Ragnar. "Whatever he had once been, he gave his life to save the realm and will always be remembered as a hero of this era."

"Thank you," said Raquel.

"So why did you have to turn yourself in?" asked Felix.

"I failed the Wizard's Council, the one from my era," she said. "They had ordered me to kill Narcion when they found out about the tables, hoping to stop him before it was too late. I told them I would, but I was never able to bring myself to actually do it."

"That seems very cruel, to order you to kill your own husband," I said.

"It was a different time with different rules," she replied.

"What was the penalty for failure?" asked Felix.

"Death," she said. "But the Wizard's Council of today is very different to that which once ruled this realm. Grandmaster Vydor gave me a full pardon even before learning the whole story, and he posthumously reinstated Narcion as a full wizard of the realm."

"And you?" I asked.

"Yes, me too. I'm fully reinstated and back on active duty, serving the Council," she said.

"Then what are you doing way out here?" asked Felix.

"I came to find you," she said.

"Me?" asked Felix.

"Well, everyone, but particularly you." She rummaged around in her pack and pulled out a datapad. "This is a gift from the Wizard Kingdom in gratitude for your recent service."

He took the pad, read it and almost dropped it in surprise. "But why?"

"What is it?" asked Crivreen.

"A second chance at life," said Raquel.

"Freedom," whispered Felix. "I could never repay this."

"No, you couldn't, because it's a gift," said Raquel with a slight smile.

"What do you mean by 'a second chance'?" I asked.

"Grandmaster Vydor cleared up a debt which has kept Felix in chains for longer than you have known him," said Raquel.

"A gift? Truly?" he asked. His face bore a look of shock. He was not the trusting type, and this gift seemed to rock his world.

"Yes. We are in space dock; you can walk out that door a free man, or stay on board and hear the offer I plan to make to the others," she said.

Felix looked in the direction of the airlock and then around the room. "I think I'll stay to hear this offer."

Raquel smiled and looked at Ragnar. "Ragnar, as you know, you are a criminal in your own land for illegally traveling to this realm."

"Yes. I suppose as an official representative of the Council you have to deport me?" he asked.

"I could, but Grandmaster Vydor has asked me to offer you full citizenship of the Wizard Kingdom instead. This is a standing offer to all wizards who have come over, but it would have to be permanent. Relations have broken down between the realms and it is unlikely there will ever be an option for you to return without incurring wrath from their council," she said.

"Full citizenship?" he asked.

"Yes, and full status as a wizard of the kingdom," she said.

"Would I have to return with you to the Wizard Kingdom?" he asked.

"No, and that brings us to the main reason I'm out here. I'm authorized to offer all of you full citizenship and training. I plan to pick up where my husband left off. I am recreating the Sac'a'rith and hope all of you will join me."

CHAPTER SIX

"Are you saying we would be full-blown wizards?" asked Crivreen.

"Yes," said Raquel.

"We already have a contract with Master Spectra," Felix pointed out. "How would this be any different?"

"What contract?" asked Raquel.

"We made an agreement with them a couple of weeks ago. I guess you haven't heard the details," I said and told her about the arrangement.

"Ah, yes. We need armor, but that makes you merely a merchant rather than a full citizen," said Raquel.

"Right, but if we join you then we'd be expected to provide the armor for nothing, since it would be our job. Seems like we lose," said Felix.

Raquel chuckled. "You always focus on the short-term and miss the larger picture. You are welcome to turn down my offer and stay as you are, running errands for the Phareon government until they grow tired of you or some department head changes and they throw you out like yesterday's leftovers."

"What would be expected of us?" I asked.

"Zah'rak," she said, "it would be like it was under Narcion, with the added benefit of having citizenship in the Wizard Kingdom and all the protection that comes with that."

"You said we wouldn't return to the Wizard Kingdom, though?" asked Ragnar.

"Correct. The council needs us out here while they form a presence in this region. We are to try to build goodwill with the locals while I train you."

"*What do you all think?*" I asked privately via our telepathic network.

"*We should accept her offer,*" sent Ragnar without hesitation.

"*Absolutely!*" sent Crivreen. "*How could we pass this up? We always talked about flying across the galaxy to join them. Here's our chance!*"

"*Felix?*" I asked.

"*I don't know. I mean, you guys should do it; like Crivreen said, it's what you've always wanted,*" he sent.

"*What about you?*" I asked.

"*I don't know, I just don't know,*" he sent.

"*Shira?*" asked Ragnar.

"*Whatever Zah'rak thinks is best,*" she sent.

"*What's the problem, Felix?*" I asked.

"*For the first time in ages I have a choice, and I'm not sure I want to give up my freedom now that I've just got it back,*" he sent.

I didn't want to see him go, but I did understand his point. "*Well, Felix, the choice is yours, but I presume if we accept her offer you'll have to leave if you don't join us.*"

"*Yes, I will,*" he sent and then said aloud, "It has been great, and I appreciate everything you have all done for me, but I think it's time I headed home. I haven't seen my family in years."

"I am sorry you're leaving," said Raquel. "Contact me if you ever change your mind. In the meantime, the Phareon government might not take too kindly to your departure, so you should be careful."

"No worries. It's not like 'Felix' is my real name, anyway," he said. After a brief stop in his quarters to gather his gear, he moved to the airlock.

Crivreen began to stop him, but I grabbed his shoulder. "Let him go."

Crivreen sighed. As the airlock cycled to let Felix off, he asked, "But why?"

"Felix never wanted to be part of the team. Narcion and I knew he was only tagging along until he was sure you were safe, and now you are," I said.

"Does this mean you accept my offer?" asked Raquel.

I wasn't convinced yet that I should turn over leadership to her. Narcion had left the Sac'a'rith in my care, and I didn't want to dishonor his memory. "We'll see, but first we have to pick up some supplies to fill Master Spectra's order. Crivreen, undock and lay in our course. Raquel, please come with us and we can talk more en route."

She smiled. "Sure."

"By the way, how did you find us?" I asked.

She stood, gestured to me to follow, and took me up to Narcion's room. "I will show you. Please open this."

I placed my hand on the scanner and gave the command to unlock the door. The room had been sealed since Narcion's death and I let no one enter, but as his widow I felt she should have access.

"What's in that chest?" she asked.

Narcion's room looked essentially unused. The furniture and trappings were what one would expect to find in a brand-new unused room. It had always been that way, with two exceptions. The first was a large, thick curtain which covered the back wall, and the other was an old wooden chest in the middle of the floor. It was made of real wood, not the synthetic manufactured wood that was used throughout the galaxy. It was the only real wood I had ever owned and in that way it was special to me, but not nearly as special as the contents would be to Raquel.

"That chest contains what Ragnar and I rescued from Narcion's home in Korshalemia. I suppose you should have it now," I said.

"Korshalemia? How long did he live there?" she asked.

"I'm not sure. The stories I heard were unclear about his coming and going, but best guess is fifteen to twenty years," I said.

"He never mentioned that. He must have awoken long before I did," she said quietly. Raquel knelt by the chest and slowly moved her hand across the intricate carvings on its top and side. It was made of some local wood from the forest in Korshalemia and the writing and symbols were a mystery to me.

It had two large metal hinges that I assumed were hand-forged, as Korshalemia didn't have any machines to make them. The chest was held shut by a large latch in the front with a loop in it for a lock, although it had never been locked.

Inside the chest was everything I could find that would fit inside. Narcion's house was slated to be destroyed and at the time I had hoped to find him alive, so I'd tried to save what I could of his personal belongings. I had no idea what was important to him, so I had had to guess. Now that the chest was passing into his widow's possession, I worried that I might have chosen poorly.

I sighed deeply. There was no going back. "I'll leave you to it."

"No, wait." She rose and walked over to the curtain.

This depicted a wonderful and hauntingly realistic forest scene. I never found out which forest was depicted, or why he had chosen this one. It was beautifully made from completely natural fibers and seemed to be one large continuous print. It was large enough to cover the entire wall from floor to ceiling. Even having done some sewing, I could not begin to guess how long it would take to weave something like this by hand, as I was sure this one had been woven; perhaps years or even decades.

She pulled it aside, revealing the gate. "This is how I found you."

"What?" I asked.

"You didn't lock the gate after you used it last. Anyone with the dimensional line, like myself and Shira, can track an unlocked gate wherever it goes."

I looked over at the rune-covered ring in the wall. It was a large stone affair; far too big to have fitted through the door to the room, its presence therefore a complete mystery. The ring was unbroken and there seemed to be no way to take it apart. It was massive enough to allow two Zalionians walking shoulder to shoulder to pass through without ducking. When we had activated it it created a doorway to another realm, Korashalemia, where we found Ragnar, Narcion's house and all the items that were in the chest.

I had used it to search for Narcion when we had thought he had been captured but hadn't given it any thought since then. "How do I lock it?"

She placed her hand over the rune at the topmost part of the ring and said a command word. The center of the ring briefly pulsed with azure light. "Only the Sac'a'rith can operate this gate," she said.

"That's why Crivreen couldn't?" I asked.

"Yes, and the reason I pulled you in here alone. Crivreen and Ragnar are not Sac'a'rith, as you and I are," she said.

"What do you mean?" I queried. Narcion had often talked about the noble order of the Sac'a'rith and insisted I was the first of a new generation, a rebirth of the order; but he'd never told me what the Sac'a'rith were, or what I was supposed to do after his death.

"Just as one has to be born a magus, one has to be born a Sac'a'rith," she said.

"But Narcion invited me in and said that the others could join one day, too," I said.

"Narcion wasn't a member of the order," she said. "That invitation wasn't valid. You and I are the only living members of the order of the Sac'a'rith that I know of. I accepted your nomination when Narcion offered it to you, so you are a member, full and true."

I sat down on Narcion's bed and tried to get my mind around it. "Then he lied to me?"

"No, not intentionally. Narcion believed he could restart the order and invited you in good faith, but it was not his place." She looked back at the ring and ran her hand over the runes. "Which one did the chest come from?"

I pointed to one. "That one, but it doesn't matter. They planned to destroy the gate after Ragnar and I came through, and that's why we took the chest. Ragnar's people were worried that the Korashalemian Wizard's Council would be angry with them if the gate were discovered. He slipped through and convinced me to let him stay."

"I see. That makes sense except that the rune is still connected, so they never destroyed the gate," she said.

I knew that was an important piece of information, but my mind was still reeling over what she had revealed of Narcion. "What does this all mean for us now?"

"The reason the Sac'a'rith fell the first time was due in part to the dilution of the order, allowing in members not born with the gift. Crivreen and Ragnar do not have the gift, and we should learn from our past mistakes."

"What do you mean to do?" I asked.

"Nothing. You're still in charge of your ship and team, and I would welcome the others as fellow wizards, just not as brothers in the order," she said.

"What about Shira?" I asked.

"That poor girl," she said with a deep sigh. "The necromancer who enslaved her knew she was gifted with the powers of a Sac'a'rith and rubbed it in her face constantly. He used it frequently to tear down her will. That's why she follows you around so closely; she knows you are family and doesn't know who else to trust."

"This is an awful lot to take in at once," I said.

"Then let's start small. We'll work together to get this armor order filled, I'll push through the forms to obtain your citizenship of the Wizard Kingdom, and we'll see where that takes us."

I needed time to think on this. She brought too many changes with her at once. Then there was Shira to consider: if I couldn't find a way to resolve the fear she suffered, then Raquel would be a destabilizing force on the ship. Just two days previously, I knew what was expected of me as a special agent for Phareon. I had missions, objectives and goals. It was not a great life, but it was simple and I could feel that I was trying to do something good by upholding the law. Raquel's offer was just too much for me to take in.

"Hold off on the citizenship, but I agree to the rest. Now I'll leave you alone so you can open the chest. I hope we chose well, but it was mostly random selection dictated in part by what would fit," I told her.

"It's a window into a part of his life I never knew," she said quietly. "Whatever you chose, it's more than I could have had if you had not chosen it."

"If you have any questions, ask Ragnar. Narcion lived with Ragnar's tribe for at least part of his time there."

"Thanks, I will," she said as she knelt back down in front of the chest. "Where is our next stop?"

"The Siden system. The necromancer had a storehouse of natural materials and Shira knows the way in," I said.

I noticed a tear in her eye and then it occurred to me that this was also the burial site of her late husband. Quietly I left her and closed the door behind me.

CHAPTER
SEVEN

Henrick was busy working at his terminal when Curetes walked into his office. Henrick was dressed in an expensive suit, the kind only the upper echelon of businessmen wore. Everything about him and the room spoke of precise control. Everything in the office appeared to be placed perfectly, and there did not seem to be anything there without a purpose.

Curetes was dressed in metallic body armor that seemed to flow with him as he walked. It was impossible to tell where his body ended and the armor began, giving the impression that the armor might actually be part of his body, a shiny exoskeleton of metal. His piercing steel-grey eyes took in everything as he approached and stood before Henrick's desk.

"News?" asked Henrick.

"Raquel is on the move," said Curetes.

Henrick was an older-looking human and his features were those of a man who had seen many generations come and go, but he was by no means frail. He had a presence that spoke of perfectly-controlled power.

His eyes had ancient depths and spoke of deep understanding and wisdom. He slowly looked up and locked gazes with Curetes. "Where?"

"We aren't sure, but someone just locked the gate on the Night Wisp, and one of our men on Zenfar said he had seen Zah'rak leaving the station with an unusually tall woman in battle armor."

"She's hiding herself somehow. I wonder if she's using an artifact that she brought with her from the past," mused Henrick.

He stood and activated a holographic map of the Phareon region. "She was last seen here," he said. "Which exit lane from the station did they use?"

Curetes smiled, but it did not generate warm feelings in the observer. It was more like the smile of a predator as it closed in on its prey. "One that puts them on the jump route to Siden."

Henrick smiled back. "She might be from a day gone by, but she is just as wonderfully predictable as the rest of them."

He walked over to a window and waved his hand before it. The scene changed from idyllic pastures to a view of the stone table which had recently been used for Narcion's funeral pyre. Plants had started growing nearby as the forest began to reclaim the land, but the table showed no signs of being disturbed.

"We have people watching it around the clock. When the Night Wisp arrives, we'll know," said Curetes.

"Not if she uses whatever artifact she has to hide the ship also," said Henrick.

"Our people saw her on the station. Whatever it is that's hiding her from scrying doesn't seem to block normal vision. We watched the Night Wisp leave, so it must be beyond her power to hide the whole ship. We will see her come in, one way or another."

"See that you are personally on hand when they are expected to arrive," said Henrick as he made to return to his desk.

"One more piece of news you might be interested in," said Curetes.

"What?" asked Henrick.

"Felix stayed behind in Zenfar," replied Curetes.

"Really? What is he up to?" asked Henrick.

"We don't know, but he's destroying his Felix identity as quickly as he can and is converting all his funds to credit sticks," said Curetes.

"Sounds like he's getting ready to leave the region," said Henrick. "I wonder why, and where he's headed."

"Yes, it's a shame. He was our best chance of placing a man inside Zah'rak's team," said Curetes.

Henrick was quiet for a moment as he looked across the room to the landscape visible in his window. His face was hard and cold when he turned to Curetes and said, "Bring him in for questioning."

"With pleasure," said Curetes.

CHAPTER
EIGHT

A week had passed since Raquel had come on board. She had taken Narcion's chest into the quarters we'd alloted her and suggested we dedicate Narcion's quarters to the gate. I agreed and removed the locks from the room so that we could go in and out as needed. That chest held all of Narcion's personal belongings apart from the curtain and gate. We decided to leave the curtain up to cover the gate for the time being.

Shira was still afraid of Raquel and would only come out of hydroponics when I was nearby. I didn't know what it would take to heal that relationship but it had become my priority to fix it, even if it meant kicking Raquel off the ship. Shira was my responsibility, and Raquel could take care of herself if need be.

Ragnar, Raquel and I were eating our morning meal and I was thinking of broaching this issue when Raquel said, "Today, Zah'rak, we have a trip to make."

"What?" I asked. We were in deep space between jump points. I couldn't guess what she meant by that.

"There's something I want to show you. Ragnar can handle things here for a while without us," she said.

"Where?" I asked.

"Through the gate, and I want Shira to come with us," she said.

"But - " I began.

"Zah'rak, Shira needs this more than you. I'd offer to take her alone, but I doubt she'd come," said Raquel.

She was right about that. Not even I could convince her to go, and I'm sure I wouldn't let her. "But where are we going?" I asked.

"As I understand it, you found Narcion's house in a large forest. Is that right?" she asked.

"Yes, but we would not be welcome back there," I said.

"That's understood, but do you remember what that forest felt like? Smelled like? Tasted like?" she asked.

I sighed slightly. I had never felt more alive than when I had been there. It was as if I were decades younger and not carrying the weight of a lifetime of hard slave labor. I could still smell the air, how alive it was. I touched my neck where the scars from my slave collar had healed completely. There was nothing like the feeling of being surrounded by life, and I would jump at the chance to go back. "Yes, very much so."

"Then help me bring Shira to a place like that," she said.

"We can't go to Korshalemia," I said. The idea of returning to the woods was very enticing. I wanted to jump up and go, never to return, but I had to consider my responsibilities to the team and especially to Shira.

"Well, we could but it would be unwise," she said. "I have a different forest in mind."

I looked over to Ragnar who said, "Go, we'll be fine."

Ragnar trusted Raquel, Shira feared her, and my mind wasn't made up. I wanted to believe she was being honest with us but felt there was something behind it. It was as if there were always plans within plans in her mind. She had given me no solid reason to think that, but still that nagging doubt preyed on my mind.

"You really think it will help her?" I asked. I wanted to believe it would. It had helped me so much, although I didn't know why.

"Without question, it will; how much it helps will be up to her, though," she said.

It was worth a shot. If there was any chance that this could help Shira to overcome the darkness that had infested her life, then I couldn't pass up the opportunity. "Okay, meet us at the gate in a few minutes. I'll try to convince her to come," I said.

"Excellent. I'll gather the supplies the three of us will need, but you'll want to take your swords just in case," she said as she left the common area and headed towards her quarters.

I took my swords from the equipment closet and headed to hydroponics where I found Shira sitting and reading a datapad. She was dressed in her typical black jumpsuit and had recently changed her hair and eye color to pure black, matching her clothing choice. She was sitting in a corner where she could easily watch all the entrances, but was too engrossed in her reading to notice me walk in.

"Shira," I said softly, hoping not to startle her. She sprang to her feet and drew a wand almost faster than I could see. I was sure it was trained on me before the datapad she had dropped even hit the floor. "Easy, it's just me."

"Sorry," she said, embarrassed. She put her wand away and picked up the pad.

I looked around at her handiwork. There were lights and tanks everywhere and the quiet hum of machinery doing whatever it did. "Well, I must say, I have no idea what I'm looking at but it looks like you're making great progress."

"I should have self-sustaining oxygen production ready soon. The plant matter just needs some more time to reproduce and mature. Food production is some time off yet."

"Remarkable," I said. "You have really done well!"

"I don't understand how. It was so overwhelming at first, but soon it all seemed so natural," she said.

I walked over and admired the tanks. I could feel the life growing. The plant matter didn't look much like plants, more like green goo, but it was very much alive. Its voice was weak but it was definitely there. "I can feel them. They're small in number but strong and healthy. You really are good at this!"

"Thanks," she said. "The organic mash that handles the carbon-dioxide and oxygen exchange is remarkably easy to grow, but I guess that's because it has been engineered that way. I haven't started the food yet; I was just reading up on our options, but it seems a bit more complicated."

"Will we be able to be completely self-sufficient?" I asked.

"No, we don't have enough space for that, but we can supplement our stores with fresh fruit and vegetables at least."

"We need to go on a field trip. Will the tanks be okay if left alone for a little while?" I asked.

"Sure," she said. "The system is designed to take care of the mash, and there's not much to do so early in the life-cycle."

"Great, let's go then," I said, leading her up to the gate room. We arrived to find Raquel there with two backpacks. I noticed that the smaller one was completely black.

"Here. These should have everything we need for a couple of days," she said.

Shira didn't say a word but took the smaller pack and moved behind me. I couldn't see her, but I suspected she was carefully watching Raquel, ready to bolt.

"A couple of days?" I repeated.

"Yes, we'll have to hike a bit. I can explain as we go," she said and then sent to me privately, *"Zah'rak, you must appear to support this fully if it's going to help her."*

I silently sighed. She was right, but I didn't like not knowing what was going on. "Did we let the others know how long we'll be gone?" I asked.

"Yeah, I told Ragnar," she said. "He'll take care of everything."

"Okay, then lead on," I said.

"First, let me show you how to unlock and relock the gate." She pointed to the symbol on the top of the gate. "That's the lock rune." She placed her hand over it, which was a bit of a stretch for her, and said a command word. The center of the gate pulsed with azure energy. "You can tell it's unlocked by touching the gate. You should feel the energy flowing through it."

I nodded. I had felt it months ago when I activated it the first time. "But that would mean Narcion had left it unlocked for me to find."

"Yes, he did," she said. "To lock it you do the same thing again. The gate can only be used when it's unlocked."

"But that means we have to leave it unlocked to get home?" I asked.

"No, it's part of a system of interconnected gates." She pointed to a different rune. "This one is where we're going. By placing your hand on it and saying the same command word it will unlock the other side and link the gates."

"So anyone can unlock this gate from a remote location?" I asked.

"No, only natural-born Sac'a'rith who are bound to it," she said.

"So I'm bound to it, then?" I said.

"Yes. Why don't you activate that rune and lead us through?"

I wondered how I had become bound to it, but decided to leave that question for another time. At the moment, I was more interested in learning how to use the gate.

I activated the rune she had pointed out. In the center of the ring a small azure dot appeared and grew until it filled the ring. As had happened on the last occasion I used it, when I touched the rune I had a vision of a great forest and wildlife. It was a different forest from the one I had seen in my previous trip. I scooped up my pack and walked through the gate. Shira followed closely behind me, and Raquel came through a few steps behind her.

We stepped out of a rock face into a densely wooded area. There was a small clearing in front of us. I inhaled the fresh air deep into my lungs and could almost taste the life force that was surrounding me. Strength returned to my muscles, and my mind was more alert than it had been in a long while.

My life as commander of a special forces team operating in deep space had brought weariness on me; this lifted and once again I felt I was where I belonged. I wished we could just stay here and forget all the responsibilities we had back in Phareon, but I knew that wasn't possible at this time.

"Yes," said Raquel. "Let the power of nature flow through you and re-store you."

I looked back and saw the gate still open behind her. "How do we lock the gate?"

"First you activate the rune where we came from, and then activate the rune where we are," she said. "Go ahead, you try it."

I locked the gate as per her instructions and turned to catch a slight smile on Shira's face as she looked up into the trees. She was lost in the moment, just taking in the air and life around her. She seemed to be as much at home here as I was.

"*She feels the same thing you do. Let her enjoy it for a while,*" sent Raquel privately.

The last time I had traveled through the gate, coming out in a lush forest like this, I had felt the same way. There was something about being surrounded by nature that seemed to bring vital energy to me. I could even tap it for healing physical wounds.

I watched Shira for a while as she drank in the life around her. There was a tear in her eye, but her face had a hint of joy in it for the first time since I had met her: real, genuine happiness. It was slight but it was there. It seemed that Raquel was right: Shira did need this.

"These woods won't be safe after dark, but we should be able to make it to shelter by mid-afternoon," said Raquel.

I couldn't see any obvious trails. "Which way?"

"We need to keep the rising sun on our left shoulder. Eventually we'll hit a roadway, but we won't be on it for long. Do your best not to leave a trail as we move through the brush," she said.

"*Shira, can you find this place again if we get separated?*" I sent privately.

"*Yeah, I'll mark it so I can gate back if need be,*" she sent.

"Let's go," said Raquel. "We can follow the game trails to make movement easier."

She led us down some very narrow breaks in the bush. We didn't speak much, and Shira kept me between herself and Raquel the entire time. I still didn't know why we were here, but I couldn't deny the uplifting effect the walk was having on Shira. That made it all worthwhile and easily convinced me to stick with whatever plan Raquel had.

It was good for me too. It had been too long since I had breathed fresh air filled with the taste and scent of life. I inhaled deeply as we walked and tried to pick out each variety of life that I scented. There were so many of them and my knowledge of nature was so limited that I didn't even have enough names to choose from. I wondered if Raquel knew them all. *No, probably not,* I thought to myself. Her nose was too tiny to be of any use, and she couldn't use her tongue to taste the air properly. Heck, I didn't think she could get her tongue more than a centimeter past her lips, nowhere near far enough to work properly. I wondered if she could smell much at all.

"There will be a river ahead soon," said Raquel. "I'd like to break there and top up our canteens, but we'll have to approach it carefully. It's the only fresh water for quite a distance, so we'll need to be careful and not hang around."

"Are there people out here we need to avoid?" I asked.

"Among other things, yes," she said.

We walked on for a while longer until she gave the signal to stop. I reached out to place my bare hand on a tree and stretched my mind through it. "I see the river. On the far bank some people are drinking; they look like Zalionians but smaller, closer to human size."

"How many?" asked Raquel.

"Six, all armed with swords and shields. They don't appear to be very attentive to the area around them."

"They aren't Zalionians, and they are trouble. We'll head downstream to the bend. That should place us out of sight," she said.

We turned off the game path she had been leading us down and slowly made our way through the bushes until she felt we had gone far enough and turned back towards the river. "What do you see?" she asked.

Using the trees again, I reached out and looked around. "We are at the bend and just past the bend looks clear, but the trees are uncomfortable, so we'd better be careful."

"Spread out, but keep visual contact with everyone. If there is a trap, it's better if at least one of us is far enough away to avoid it," she said.

"How dangerous is this place?" I asked.

"Dangerous enough," she said and moved off.

Looking back, I saw Shira shrug. She said, "Really, do we ever go on safe trips?"

I had to concede that point and set off after Raquel. She made it to the river without incident and quickly filled her canteen. I kept Shira back in the woods and waited to see if anything would happen. Just when I assumed I'd misread the trees, several of the miniature Zalionian-looking creatures jumped out of the water and reached for Raquel.

CHAPTER
NINE

"Felix, are you sure about this?" sent Crivreen privately as I packed my gear and headed to the airlock.

"Yeah," I sent back. "The wizards bought my freedom. I can return to the life I had before all this started."

"I thought you said, 'What's done cannot be undone,' and all that?" he asked.

"Let's just say it's time to test that theory." The airlock finished its cycle and I walked onto the station. "Don't worry about me, I'll be fine."

"Then let me come with you," he sent.

"No, you have a great thing going there. Stick with Zah'rak and you'll do well," I sent and then cut off the communication. Sadness set in as I watched them undock and launch. I assumed that meant that they were going to take up Raquel's offer. I hoped that was true; it was the best thing they could do. Joining the Wizard Kingdom would give them support and a cause to fight for. That's what they needed more than anything. This wandering around doing the bidding of the government paid well, but it wasn't a good life; it was too limited, with no opportunity to stretch and grow.

The first order of business was to ditch my Felix identity and return to my real self. I went down to a less respectable section of the station and withdrew all my money as credit sticks. I slipped into a public bathroom which was thankfully empty and changed my clothes, altered my hair and eye color, pulled the fake skin from my hands, and removed the contact lenses that I had been using for years to fool sensors.

After removing all my cosmetics, I looked into the mirror and forced myself to concentrate on what I really looked like. I chanted the slow verse that I used to help focus my mind on the task of picturing my real self. It was hard and a little painful, but slowly my skin darkened to an off-blue shade, my ears grew and changed shape, fanning out, my hair grew darker and longer, and my voice changed slightly. Within moments I looked completely different. Anyone who had seen me walk into the rest room would never recognize me on the way out, even if they used biometric scanners.

I knew from testing that even my DNA shifted slightly when I made these changes. The fake skin on my hands and the contact lenses allowed me the option of altering my appearance without having to go through the ordeal of changing my base identity, but a full change meant that there would be no way to connect Felix to my real self. In any way that mattered he just ceased to exist, and if Lady Luck smiled on me he would never rise again.

I took a few minutes to breathe deeply, steadying myself after the effort. It was painful and tiring, but it was the only way I could walk away from this life. I had considered doing this when I was on the run from the Assassin's Guild, but Crivreen had needed me. Now that Crivreen was safe I could leave it all behind.

I doubted if Raquel really understood how much the gift had freed me. For the first time in longer than I could remember, I was my own man. All my debts were paid off, and with Felix gone I could finally make a run at the life I had dreamed about since I was a child.

Once I had packed everything used to create Felix's identity into a separate bag, I left the bathroom and headed for a recycling center. I tossed the whole bag directly into the recycling vat and watched to make sure it had been completely broken down into its raw materials. There would be no undoing that destruction. *Farewell, Felix. It's been fun.*

Once I was sure that all connection between myself and Felix was gone, I headed to the travel hub. I needed to find a way off the station without leaving any trace that I'd been here. It would be best if I were far from here before my real ID was scanned for the first time.

The hub was busy with crews refitting ships and various people looking for work. I knew that if I hung around with the rest of the job seekers I would eventually get something, but I was looking for a slightly higher caliber of work than that which the random pool of workers would obtain.

I passed by all the smaller ships; they would have much fewer crew members and it would be harder to blend in and coast out of this region.

As I continued through the hubs, I finally came across what looked like the perfect opportunity: a large luxury liner which was being loaded with supplies. The crew near one end was yelling back and forth, trying to get some robotic equipment to work and failing miserably. It was the perfect setup for me to step in and be the hero they didn't know they were looking for and didn't particularly want.

"Need a hand?" I asked as I walked over. I knew they'd say 'no,' and had already planned not to accept that answer. I had already been covertly looking over their machines and selecting one that looked easy to repair so that I could impress them by walking up and fixing one, seemingly at random.

"We're busy, move along," said one of them.

I ignored them and moved to the robot that I figured was the best target for my plan. I knew I was pushing my luck. Workers like these could be a rough lot, and I wasn't a match for them physically. "Mark III? Not exactly the quality of machine I would expect."

They looked at each other and one said, "Perhaps you didn't hear –"

"Looks like the secondary servo under the left tire is dragging on the belt. That's causing it to heat up and fail," I said.

"You know how to fix it?" a smaller man said as he pushed to the front.

"I'm a certified level three technician, but have done my share of level four," I said. That was not entirely true: Felix was certified, I was not, but I didn't figure that really mattered. If all went well they wouldn't ask for any proof. I would have to recertify myself as soon as I could manage it if I really wanted to make my dream happen. This time, I wouldn't skimp on the prep and would go for my master repair certification.

"Yeah, right!" said one of the men. Several of the others laughed or made similar comments. Some of them noted my race and made rude comments about my ears. I had forgotten how much prejudice I used to face. My people were not known for being smart, but it was a reputation unfairly earned.

"He's just wasting our time," said another.

"You weren't exactly making any progress before I arrived." I grabbed some of their tools and went to work on the unit in question. The men started to move to stop me, but the smaller man gestured for them to step back. It took about twenty minutes but I soon had the problem fixed. My original diagnosis was correct, so all I really had to do was take the drive train apart and put it back together properly. The repair was simple but looked impressive.

"There," I said. "It needs some more work before I could call it 'good as new,' but it should get you through loading now."

One of the men activated the robot worker's control interface and gave it commands. It efficiently went about its work as designed.

"What's your name, mister?" asked the small man.

I caught myself just in time before I said 'Felix' and told him, "Purwryn."

"Can you service all of these?" he asked, waving his hand towards a pile of disabled machines.

"Yes, for a price," I said.

"And that would be?" he asked.

"Food and passage out of here, with no questions," I said. Ships like this liner needed large crews and were away from their homeport for many years at a time. They often picked up strays and discarded them along the way. It kept costs down and kept their crew fresh. Very few would be permanent members and most would come and go from port to port. This was of course illegal, but the law was rarely enforced. The government was more concerned with the tax money coming from these cruise liners than with tracking down drifters.

He stuck out his hand and said, "Deal."

I shook his hand and went to work on the remaining robots. The rest of the crew was skeptical for a while, but as more and more of their robots returned to functional status they warmed up to me. It was as I had expected. These were working men and women; they cared little for talking or boasting and were more convinced by actions than words.

It took several days to get the liner loaded with gear and to perform the maintenance that the massive vessel needed, during which time I lived on the vessel and worked on all of the ship's robotics. They had a virtual army of robots to maintain the large vessel and it seemed that some were always breaking down. There would be no shortage of work for me on this trip.

On the fourth day since leaving Zah'rak's team, I finally left the station on the liner. It was a Resden-chartered vacation cruise liner headed to the Phineary region, which was perfect. I could finally start over with no ties to my past. I dreamed of setting up a small robotics repair shop in a high-class town where fine dining and entertainment were readily available. After years of living in the underground, I wanted out and I wanted it badly.

The trip through the first jump was uneventful. Thanks to my skill at robotics, I was becoming well-liked by more and more crew members as time went on. I bartered priority order on my repair list for favors and special treatment. The kitchen staff let me eat the food that was normally reserved for the paying customers, and in general the staff treated me like royalty. It felt good to be wanted and liked. All I had to do was stay out of trouble for a few months and I was home free. That should be easy; the *Paradise* was, after all, a high-class vacation cruise liner and not a war ship or pirate vessel like so many of my previous stations.

The liner was massive and could cover great distances in a single jump, but took days between jumps to recharge the drives. During one of these recharge times, I was relaxing in my quarters looking at a movie on my computer terminal when a man appeared in my room.

Instinctively I sprang to my feet and jumped away from him. He was dressed in body armor which appeared almost liquid in texture. The armor moved with him as if it were a second skin. His steel-grey eyes seemed to bore right through me and threatened to drain my will even to stay upright.

"Who are you?" I demanded.

"Come with me," he said.

"No!" I said. "Get out of my room!" There was something about him that sent icy fear through my veins. It wasn't logical, but I had no time to question that feeling just then. My mind searched frantically for options. All of my weapons were securely hidden, so there was no way to retrieve them without giving him plenty of time to stop me.

"My master wants to speak with you," he said emotionlessly. "You will come with me."

I decided I had to risk blowing my cover and exposing myself as a magus. As fast as I could, I cast my mage bolts, sending fire towards him. He didn't even flinch as the bolts came his way but to my horror he seemed to absorb them, completely and effortlessly.

"Very well," he said, raising his hands and pointing at me.

I threw a shield wall between us just as a beam of energy left his hands and headed towards me. The wall held, but I knew it couldn't take much more. I wrapped myself in as much protection as I could and teleported behind him.

Before he could turn I cast a mage bolt again, this time aiming at his back, but he absorbed this also. He turned to fire his beam weapon again, but I switched tactics and used telekinesis to throw a table at him. It caught him off guard and sent him flying into the wall.

While he was still down, I ran out the door into the hallway where several crew members were talking. Before I could shout at them to run, the stranger came out of my room and fired another bolt at me.

This one hit me square in the back and my shielding absorbed most of the energy, but the force of the impact knocked me down. I hit the deck hard. Yelling in pain, I started to get up and saw the men running for cover. Then another bolt hit me, and my world faded from red to black.

CHAPTER
TEN

"Zah'rak, wait!" sent Shira as I started to get up and run to Raquel's aid. Down by the river, the lizard creatures were about to grab Raquel when she disappeared.

"What happened?" I asked.

"Look across the river, up on the bank," sent Shira. There was Raquel, just where Shira had indicated. "She's a traveler, like myself. They'll never catch her."

"Zah'rak, Shira, head downstream until you find a place to cross unseen, then turn back so that the setting sun is behind your right shoulder. I'll catch you up soon, after I've led these away," sent Raquel.

The lizards had swum back across the river and were heading up the bank towards her. They were not much bigger than humans and looked no more dangerous. I couldn't see why Raquel was so worried. "But there are only three of them," I protested.

"Go," she sent. "This is their woods and soon we will be vastly outnumbered."

"Okay," I replied.

Shira and I fell back a bit deeper into the woods and slowly made our way downstream. *"Do you think she'll be okay?"* I sent.

"Yes, she's a traveler," Shira sent. She said that as if I should know what she meant and be comforted by it. I decided not to question it right then, as it was good to keep a positive tone. Besides, if Raquel was lost there was nothing to do but go home, and I didn't want to do that just then.

We stopped and I made use of the trees to see the river. *"Looks clear here. Let's take some water and cross quickly."* We turned toward the river and as we came out I sent, *"You top up the canteens, and I'll keep watch."*

She moved to the riverbank and I followed her, tasting the air with my tongue and sweeping the vicinity with my eyes. The river was deep and appeared to have a strong current. Tree limbs, leaves and other forest debris went floating by at a good speed, but there was no sign of trouble.

The strength of the current made it unlikely that there would be anyone hiding in the river, but if the small lizards were amphibious they might be able to arrive quickly, using the current to cover their movements. That was probably how they'd surprised Raquel earlier.

"Okay, that's done," she sent and then teleported across the river.

I joined her on the other side and we slipped back into the woods. *"What do you mean by: 'she's a traveler'?"*

"It appears that her primary spell line, the one we've seen her use, is dimensional, just like mine," she sent.

"Okay, but what does that mean?" I sent.

"Well, as an elite traveler she can always get away," she sent.

"You weren't able to get away from us," I sent. When she was still a slave to the necromancer and under his complete control, we had trapped and captured her. Ragnar had used some of his runes to put her to sleep, and we kept her in stasis until we could remove her slave implants. It was a gamble; she might have run right back to her old master, but it had paid off.

"I'd hardly call myself an elite magus," she sent.

I suspected she was underestimating herself quite a bit, but I didn't know what justified the title 'elite.' Raquel was by far the most powerful magus among us, but I suspected Shira could easily take the number two spot if put to the test.

We traveled on for a while without talking, using the sun as our guide. Eventually we came out of the forest into a large clearing. This stretched out for quite a distance, but in the direction we were heading it slowly turned into rolling hills.

I had started to speak when I heard something behind us. I turned and saw a green hand emerging from some bushes, reaching for Shira.

I caught that hand, pulled it out of the bushes and threw it to the side. It belonged to one of those small Zalionian-looking creatures. He went tumbling and sliding across the ground, too surprised by my action to catch himself.

Shira teleported away from the forest into the clearing as another one of those creatures came out of the forest. This one had a sword and came at me. I drew my own swords and easily parried his first attack.

"Behind you!" yelled Shira.

The lizard I had thrown was charging towards me with his own weapons. I couldn't disengage from the lizard who was pressing his attack in front of me, so I let the one behind me get close, then used my tail as a whip and spun around quickly.

These two, having tails of their own, must have recognized the move as they merely jumped out of range and then rushed back in, but it allowed me to get out from between them. My superior reach allowed me to keep them at bay, but it was apparent they were more skilled in swordplay than I was. They were able to keep me on the defensive despite my greater reach.

"More coming!" called out Shira and I looked to the forest to see several more coming out with swords drawn. "Teleport away!"

I had to admit I was outmatched and retreat seemed to be the only option. I swung my tail around again to buy some time, and as they jumped back I was able to focus and teleport to Shira.

Shira cast a gate spell and tried to push me through it. I took her hint and went through the gate. She followed me and we came out in the forest again.

After she'd closed the gate I asked, "Where are we?"

She gestured for me to be quiet and sent, *"Less than a half-hour walk from the clearing."*

From the woods nearby I could hear something crashing through the brush. I placed my hand on a nearby tree and expanded my awareness of the area. *"There's a large group of those lizards between us and that clearing. They appear to be searching for us."*

"Now what?" asked Shira.

"Let's swing wide and try to circle back to those hills. Maybe by then they will have moved on to search another area."

Using the sun as our guide, we walked parallel to the clearing for an hour and then turned back towards it. As we approached, I checked with the trees and made sure the area was clear.

"We're losing light, we should hurry," sent Shira.

"Sure, but hurry to where?" I asked as we entered the clearing.

"I think into those hills would be best," she sent back.

We moved quickly towards the hills, not knowing what we were looking for. Raquel's warning about the danger of night travel spurred us on. After we'd crested the second one, we found her waiting in a valley between two hills.

"This way," she said. She touched a spot on the side of the hill and a doorway opened. She gestured to us to enter, and when all three of us were inside she closed the door.

Beyond the door was a room with enough space to fit us and several more people comfortably. The walls were covered with a softly-glowing moss, providing ample light once my eyes had adjusted. The back wall was lined with boxes which I assumed contained supplies. Scattered around the area were what appeared to be sleeping mats.

"We'll spend the night here and press on come morning," said Raquel. "Sorry the accommodation isn't as nice as home, but we'll be safe here."

"Where is 'here'?" I asked.

She went over to the boxes, pulled out some jerky and shared it with us. "We're still in Vydoria, but a long way from anywhere you've ever been. Get some rest. It's summertime, so the night will be short and I want to leave at first light."

I looked over at Shira, who merely shrugged and picked out a mat near the back wall. "I've slept on much worse for years," she said.

"Do we need to set a watch?" I asked.

"No, the door and walls are sufficiently enchanted to protect us," said Raquel as she prepared a mat on the opposite side of the back wall.

I took more jerky from the box and stretched out near Shira. Taking a bite brought a very pleasant sensation to my taste buds. "Hey, this is real meat!"

"Glad you approve," said Raquel.

As I lay down and savored the spiced meat, Shira slid her mat closer to mine. She was small, even for a human, and only about as tall as my waist. My two-and-a-quarter-meter frame must have seemed enormous from her perspective. Raquel was fairly tall for a human, assuming she *was* a human, but still only reached about midway up my chest, making me the giant among the group.

Shira curled up in a tight ball and fell into a fitful sleep. I shuddered to think what kind of nightmares she might be having. I reached over and placed my arm around her, and that seemed to calm her. I lay there wondering what we were doing and why. I could see the changes in Shira and I knew it was helping her so I intended to go along with Raquel's plan, but I'd have to talk to her soon about sharing her plans more fully in the future. Eventually I drifted off to sleep myself, to a night of dreams about life as a tree.

I was woken sometime later by the sound of Raquel slipping out of the cave. Shira had curled up against my side at some point, but everything else was just as it had been when I had fallen asleep. Carefully extracting myself from Shira, I got up and ate some more meat for breakfast.

I slipped outside as quietly as I could and took a deep breath, filling my lungs with the early morning mist. Around the entrance to the cave I saw a large number of tracks, but couldn't begin to guess what manner of creature had made them. Something had come looking for us in the night.

I walked to the top of the hill and looked around. Off a little ways I saw Raquel doing some kind of workout. Her movements were smooth and flowed into each other in a manner similar to the way Narcion had always moved.

Watching Raquel reminded me that Narcion had urged me to do similar exercises every morning, but I'd fallen out of the habit since his death. I stood and began to work through what I could remember of his lessons. My joints felt stiff from spending the night on the floor, but with a little time I began to work them loose. Shira came up the hill and sat to watch as I worked through the last of the routines Narcion had taught me.

Raquel joined us and said, "I'm glad to see you haven't forgotten Narcion's teachings. If you're finished, we have only a few more hours of travel before we reach our destination."

"Where are we going?" I asked.

"We'll keep the rising sun at our back for the rest of the morning. The hill country is safe during the day, or at least it was the last time I was here," she said without acknowledging the question.

We went back to the cave to clean up and gather our gear, and then headed out. As we walked Raquel told us stories from her childhood, a childhood lived ten thousand years before we were born.

CHAPTER ELEVEN

My head hurt, my back hurt and I couldn't see at first. Slowly my vision started to return, but I couldn't shake the cloud that seemed to cover my mind and blur my thoughts. With some pain … no, with great pain, I slowly sat up and looked around. It was hard to see. It was as if I were in a light fog or maybe a smoke-filled room.

I was lying on a couch in a modern office, in the center of which an aged human sat behind a desk with a holographic terminal. He was dressed in formal work attire and looked like the quintessential rich businessman. The room itself was neat and proper with everything precisely in place. I knew the fog was all in my head, but I suspected that, if it were real, every molecule of it would be as perfectly placed as everything else in the room.

"Where am I?" I asked hoarsely through the pain and mist. The words hurt my throat.

"Easy, Purwryn; you had a nasty fall," said the man. His voice was perfectly even and betrayed no feelings.

"Fall?" I repeated. I tried hard to remember how I'd got here or where

I might be, but I just couldn't think clearly. Every time I tried, my mind became cloudier instead of sharp.

"Yes," he said. He waved his hand to close the display in front of him, then stood and walked towards one of the walls. "May I get you something to drink?"

"Water, please," I said. As much as I wanted something stronger, I had to keep what was left of my wits about me until I figured out what was going on. There was a dread growing slowly inside me. Somehow I knew I was in great danger, but I couldn't work out how or why. I was sure I was either hung over or drugged, and with my history I wasn't sure which was worse. Drugged meant I had been taken captive by some hostile force, but hung over meant I had lost control and anything might have happened. I wondered briefly if having been captured and drugged was actually the better alternative.

"Here," said the old man as he held out a cup of water.

I took a deep drink of the water and almost choked on it. As the liquid hit my throat it felt like acid burning its way down. The pain gave my mind a moment of clarity. "I was attacked in my room!"

"Go easy with the water. You almost choked to death on your vomit and we had to clear your air passage with a tube," he said.

"What?" I asked. The moment of clarity had passed and I was struggling to remember what I had just said.

"Your throat is irritated from the tube we used to clear your lungs," he repeated.

"Where am I?" I asked again.

"My office. Now, you took a bad blow to the head and I need to ask you some questions to assess what damage has been done. First, say your name for me," he said.

"Purwryn," I said.

"Good, and where do you work?" he asked.

"Um, just a sec," I said as I raked my clouded mind for the answer. "Robotics! I'm the lead robotics engineer on the *Paradise*."

"Excellent. For how long have you had this job?" he asked.

"I guess a week or so?" I said.

"Good, good. And what was your job before that?" he asked.

Instantly memories of Zah'rak and his team came to mind. "I was working with – " I started to say but some internal alarm went off, stopping me from finishing the thought. I couldn't think through the cloud, but something told me I shouldn't answer that question.

"Yes? Go on," he said.

I tried to stand, but a wave of dizziness caused me to fall back onto the couch. My back screamed in protest, and my legs felt as if ants were crawling up and down them, throwing a party to end all parties.

"Easy; I don't think you are quite ready for that," he said.

Where was I? Why wasn't I ready to stand? What had I just been talking about? My mind struggled against the fog, trying to make sense of my world. Was I in trouble?

"My head is so cloudy," I said.

"Cloudy? How so?" he asked.

"It's hard to think and to remember. There's something important I need to recall, but I can't seem to focus on it," I said.

"I see," he replied.

Might he be a doctor? I was in pain, and maybe he could help. If I could just think, I could figure this out.

"Can you give me something to clear my head?" I asked.

"No, it's probably just the medicine wearing off. It should pass soon. Now, what was the last thing you repaired at your job?"

"Um, I'm not sure," I said. I struggled to remember my day at work. "Oh, I think it was a food transport. Its wheels were sticking; easy job, but it yielded me some chocolate cake."

"Yes, cake is good, especially chocolate. What about your first repair for them?" he asked.

"A Mark III loader," I said as some of my memories started coming clearer, but nothing that helped explain why I was here.

"Excellent. And what were you doing before that?" he asked.

"I was looking for work, so I was wandering the maintenance hub," I said.

"I see. What happened to your previous job?" he asked.

"I quit," I said.

"Why?" he asked.

An image of Raquel came to mind, and her offer to join the Wizard Kingdom. I started to answer, but again I caught myself. There was something I shouldn't tell him, but I couldn't think of what it was. I noticed I was still holding the water and took another deep drink. Fire ran down my throat, but this time I was ready for it; I embraced the pain, as it brought clarity to my thoughts. "I was jumped!" I called out. That meant I was a prisoner, and this was an interrogation!

I forced myself to stand. The room was spinning around me, but I was sure I could correctly time my move to reach the door as it swung by. I took another gulp of water and teleported myself over to it. The door didn't open as I reached it, so I hit the 'open' button. It slid back to reveal the same steel-eyed man who had jumped me in my room.

"Leaving so soon?" he asked.

I tried to push past him and escape, but ended up falling into him as my newfound strength and balance failed. He picked me up and carried me back into the room. I was too weak to mount an effective resistance. The door snapped shut behind him, cutting off my line of sight and any hope of teleporting away.

The old man walked over towards me and passed his hand in front of my face. I felt my consciousness fade away as he said, "I have what I need. Take him back."

———

I awoke lying in a hospital bed, connected to various machines which I assumed were doing something to treat or monitor me. To my left sat

Marcus, reading something on a datapad. I started to sit up, but pain shot through my eyes into the back of my head. I was sure there must be scorch marks on my pillow from the pain bursting out the back of my head.

Marcus looked up as I yelled out in pain. "Doctor!"

I took a steadying breath which sent pain down my throat. "Where am I?" I tried to croak out. Instinctively I grabbed the bed, willing the room to stop its incessant spinning.

"Easy, friend," said Marcus. He was trying to speak in a gentle, calming voice, but his vocal range was too gruff for that to be effective. "Try to stay still."

"Good plan. Hurts too much to move," I said. I didn't know why I was there but it was comforting to hear Marcus' voice, no matter how gruff it was.

Marcus was the closest thing to a friend I had on board. He was another robotics engineer, and we shared a repair shop down in the hangars. Before I came on board he was their only technician and simply couldn't keep up with the workload. We worked well as a team and, given that he was the social type, I think I saved him from going insane working alone all those hours in the shop.

"Then take the hint and stay put," he said firmly.

I decided he was probably right. I tried to reconstruct the events that had put me in this bed. It was a jumbled mess and I wasn't sure where one memory ended and another started. There was something about being attacked, a couch and a desk. I struggled to assemble them into something that made sense, but the memories just wouldn't behave.

"Ah! I see you're awake! Excellent!" said a new voice.

"He seems to be in a lot of pain," said Marcus.

"That is to be expected," said the voice.

I slowly turned my head, trying to avoid another flare-up of pain. The man who had spoken was an older gentleman wearing the uniform of a doctor. "Everything hurts," I said softly.

"Yes. I'm sorry about that, but we had to cut back your pain medication to start the detox," he said.

"Detox?" I queried.

"I'll explain in a moment. First, can you tell me your name?" he asked.

"Purwryn," I said.

He obtained a small cup of water from somewhere I couldn't see. "Here, sip this slowly. Your throat is probably rather irritated, but the water will help."

I remembered what had happened when I'd chugged a drink of water in the old man's office and contented myself with sipping this one. He had also asked me my name, but there was something strange about that memory. It didn't seem real.

"Do you know where you are?" he asked.

"I think – yes, this looks like the medical quarters on the *Paradise*," I said.

"That's correct," he said. "Do you know why you're here?"

"I was attacked in my quarters," I said.

"Attacked?" queried Marcus.

The doctor waved him off. "That's a common side effect."

"Being attacked?" I said. "How is that a side effect?" My mind might not have been fully functional yet, but I couldn't think of anything that would fit that description.

"Purwryn, tell me about this attack. What happened?" he asked.

"I was in my quarters and someone tried to take me prisoner. We fought but he was too strong for me. I managed to escape from the room and ran for the hallway, but then he shot me with a blaster or something."

"Did anyone see this?" he asked.

"Yes, there were several men in the hallway at the time," I said.

The doctor pulled back a curtain and I saw three more beds like the one I was in. "Them?"

"Could be; hard to tell from this angle," I said.

He closed the curtain again and said, "Everything you said fits. Are you familiar with tricholophate?"

"Yes, we use it in the robotics shop. Nasty stuff, but safe enough if you take precautions," I replied.

"Yes," he said. He sat on the edge of the bed and made a minor adjustment to some machine. "You seem to have your senses, so I'm increasing your pain medication a little. Hopefully that will make you more comfortable, but we need to keep it as low as possible."

I did feel a bit better and had to work hard to resist demanding more. "So, what happened?"

"Several people in your section reported being attacked. When security was dispatched, they discovered the entire section was flooded with tricholophate vapors. It seems a primary supply line ruptured and was leaking onto a heating element," he said.

"So everything I remember was a hallucination?" Tricholophate was used by addicts for just that effect.

"Yes, it seems that way," he said. "None of the security cameras show any attackers, and there were none there when the security forces arrived. It took a few hours to decontaminate the area before we could pull anyone out, but the only injuries we could find appeared to be self-inflicted."

"Then who did I throw a table at?" I asked.

"We did find your table overturned, but there was no one around and no sign that anyone had been in your room," he said.

"Makes sense," said Marcus. "Tricholophate is hallucinogenic even in small quantities. If the section was flooded with it, it stands to reason it would be intense."

"But the attack seemed so real. I mean, the fight really hurt," I said.

"Yes, the others report the same," said the doctor.

"But if it wasn't real, why am I in so much pain now?" I asked.

"Tricholophate is highly toxic and did extensive damage to your body. I'm sorry to say you will be here for some time until your body heals," said the doctor.

I wanted to believe him; what he said made more sense than what I remembered, but it didn't feel right. I was sure I had been attacked. It was the only really clear memory I had.

"How long?" I asked.

"I'm not sure," he said, "but at least a week, maybe two."

"Wonderful," I said.

CHAPTER TWELVE

Raquel led us up one final steep hill. This was much larger than any of the others and gave way to a flat summit. On the top of the hill was a large collection of stones that vaguely reminded me of a castle. Some parts looked as if they might once have been towers, others might have been wall segments, but for the most part it just looked like rubble which stretched out in all directions and seemed to cover the entire plateau.

"Zah'rak, Shira, welcome home," said Raquel.

"Home?" I repeated. A pile of rubble seemed an odd place to call 'home'.

"Yes, Zah'rak," she said. "Granted, ten thousand years ago when I was growing up it looked quite different."

I leaned against one of the rocks and was surprised to feel life in it. I stretched out my mind and could feel all the rocks. "The rocks! They're alive?"

"Not really, but they were heavily enchanted ages ago. This used to be a massive fortress: the headquarters of the Sac'a'rith," she said.

Shira gazed across it in wonder. "What happened to it?"

"It stood as an impregnable fortress for generations, until internal corruption caused it to fall," she said.

"But how?" asked Shira.

I leaned against the rock, letting it speak to me. I was thrilled to see Shira talking directly to Raquel, even if it was just because she was distracted by the view and the story. It was a start, and perhaps a sign of better things to come.

"Just as a person is born a magus, a person must be born a Sac'a'rith," said Raquel. "At first the order remained pure and only those born with the gift were allowed in. Over time exceptions were made, and some of those exceptions rose to positions of prominence. That weakened the group, and eventually external attackers overcame the damaged order."

I looked around at all the massive stones. "After all this time, the stones still have power?"

"Yes, but it's fading," she said. She climbed up on one of the stones and sat down. "There was a time when no evil dared venture for miles around this place. Now evildoers mock the stones as they walk past."

"But that doesn't make sense. Crivreen and Ragnar tell me the weave was torn or something and no magic was possible for ten thousand years. How could this place still have any power?" I asked.

"That's a good question," she said silently. "I don't fully understand how the whole thing works, but magic and life force are one and the same. The fact that life carried on beyond the rending means that not all power was gone. The rending was far from perfect, and isolated places like this remained. Some came and went with time, and others stayed. History is full of stories of odd events and unexplainable happenings that point to ripples in reality where some magic remained. Someday when I make it back to the Wizard Kingdom, I can show you the research that has been done on this, if you are interested."

I wanted to ask more, but Shira interrupted us at that point.

"Raquel," began Shira and then she hesitated.

"Yes?" asked Raquel in a gentle voice.

"Am … am I really one of you?" asked Shira.

Raquel sprang off the rock she had been sitting on and knelt before Shira. She put her hand gently on the smaller woman's shoulder and looked her in the eye. "Yes, my sister, you are."

"But – but – I was sure he was lying," said Shira.

Raquel smiled and joy filled her eyes. "You can feel the stones calling you. You're gaining strength and healing from the very trees and grass. You are one of the Sac'a'rith."

Shira inhaled deeply as tears began to flow. "I can feel them." Her shoulders shuddered a little but she kept her eyes on Raquel's.

"Shira, you are my sister, just as Zah'rak here is our brother. We may appear different from each other, but right here this castle is common to all of us. I can't explain how or why, but all of us are descended from the warriors who once called these halls home."

"But I tried to kill you!" Shira said and began to pull back. The moment seemed to have passed, all too soon.

Raquel didn't let her go and her smile didn't waver. "Hey, siblings fight sometimes. Narcion and I knew you were under the control of the necromancer and hold nothing you did against you."

"But – " she started and let the sentence hang.

"Shira, as one noble born, I formally invite you to join the order of the Sac'a'rith alongside Zah'rak as progenitors of the rebirth of the order. Do you accept?"

Shira gasped. Disbelief and amazement were written across her features. She slowly nodded.

"Then from this day forward you shall be known as Shira the Shadowmaster, of the Order of the Sac'a'rith!"

As she said that I could feel power build around them. I couldn't see it, but something powerful passed between them. Shira's complexion darkened, and a new strength grew in her eyes.

Before I could ask any questions, Raquel fell over with blood coming out of her nose. I rushed to her side and propped her up. She coughed heavily and seemed to drift in and out of consciousness for a moment, but recovered and leaned back against the rock.

"I'm okay," she said weakly. She pinched her nose to stop the flow. "Don't worry, I'll be fine in a minute."

"What happened?" I asked.

"I should have waited until tomorrow to do that," she said. Shira knelt beside her and handed her a canteen. Raquel took a deep drink. "Get some rest, both of you."

"We can't leave you like this," I said.

"I'll be fine until sunset. You'll need to be ready to fight later," she said.

"What?" I asked.

"At mid of night I will appear to die, and the magic which protects this place will fail for one hour. Then the nightwalkers who inhabit these woods will come for us."

"Wait, you're going too fast! What do you mean, 'you will appear to die'?" I asked. This was exactly the kind of thing she should start telling me in advance.

"I'm cursed," she said. "The more power I use the weaker I become. Sooner or later I use up my life force and I have to come here to recharge it. If I don't, I will truly die."

"But without us here to guard you, how have you done this before?" I asked.

"Narcion stood watch, and nothing that lives here dared challenge him," she said. "Look, you two are my only hope. I won't survive the night unless you stand guard."

"Tell me about the nightwalkers," I said.

"They are like the walking dead, but stronger, smarter and faster. The same power that gave you the strength to overcome the wraiths will work on them."

Shira asked, "One hour?" Shira was sitting by Raquel and had washed the blood from her face. I wondered if seeing the mighty Raquel collapse had touched her.

"Yes," responded Raquel. "One hour past mid of night my curse will pass and I'll be restored again. The rocks will once again protect this spot and the nightwalkers will flee."

"How did this happen to you?" I asked.

"It's a long story, and you two need to rest," she said. "Get some sleep. We can talk another day."

"Shira? Are you okay with this?" I sent privately. I was trying to get my mind around everything Raquel had revealed to us in the last few minutes. It was a lot of information and I really wished Ragnar were with us. I knew he would understand it all and help me make a decision.

"We can't leave her to die," she sent back.

I sighed, knowing she was right; I was just annoyed that she hadn't warned us ahead of time. I would have liked to have brought my armor and some better weapons. At the very least, it would have been good to have Crivreen and Ragnar with us for additional firepower.

"Okay, I'll take first watch. Shira, get some sleep," I said. There was no changing things now. All we could do was dig in and hope for the best.

Shira climbed up on one of the rocks and found a nook to nestle into. She seemed to be comfortable and even dozed off. I guess being so small had some advantages.

"You get some rest, too," I said to Raquel. "You don't look well."

"I'm fine, or rather I will be. I'm overextended, that's all," she said.

I gathered wood and kindling for a fire, and ate some of the jerky I had taken from the shelter. "Who maintains the shelters?"

"We do, or rather I have been doing so recently, but it will fall to you two next. This is holy ground for us, and someday I hope the Sac'a'rith will rebuild here."

I wanted to ask her more questions but she drifted off to sleep. She slept for the rest of the day and into the evening. To keep myself busy during my watch, I continued to gather firewood until it was my turn to sleep. I figured we could use it to restock the shelters, and the activity helped to keep me alert. As night fell, an eerie moan came from the shadows around us.

"Remember," I said. "She said they can't attack till midnight."

"Right, then we have to beat them back for an hour," she said.

"Yeah." I wasn't eager to go to battle with her by my side. In most of our raids she had only used her gates to move our team around. I feared she was too small to put up much of a fight. Still, it was too late to do anything about that. All I could do now was try to keep her out of the worst of the fight as much as possible.

I drew my swords as midnight approached. There were still no attackers within sight, but the moaning was increasing. I swung my blades through the air a few times to loosen up my arms and shoulders.

"We should move her up onto one of the rocks. That will give us less area to defend and the advantage of high ground," said Shira.

"Good idea," I said.

As gently as I could manage, I lifted Raquel up and placed her on top of what I assumed was once a section of a great wall. There was only one way up onto the wall, a narrow set of stairs, and unless the nightwalkers could fly it would be a good place to make our stand.

Standing on top of the wall segment I got an idea for delaying any attack. I climbed down and spread out all the firewood and kindling I had spent the day gathering. I made sure it was a meter or so from the wall, but completely encircled it. The pile was thinner than I would have liked, but it was too late to gather more.

"How long?" asked Shira.

"Not much longer, I think," I said.

Shira nodded and began to pace back and forth along the wall, peering into the shadows of the night. The wall segment wasn't very big, so she spent almost as much time turning around as walking.

For my part I stretched and worked through some sword drills, partly to pass the time and partly to loosen up.

"Look!" came a low cry from Shira.

Around us, humanoid forms were marching slowly towards our camp. "Seems it's almost time. Stay up here."

I sheathed my swords and ran down the steps to put myself between the dead and the only path up onto the wall. The wind brought a foul stench and I could feel ice flowing through my blood as they wailed.

Unlike the walking dead we had faced previously, these creatures were armed with clubs, swords and similar weapons. They stood just outside the circle of stones and stared at us with great intent. Raquel had said that we only had to hold out until one hour past midnight, so time was on our side. If possible, I planned to simply outwait them.

"Raquel has stopped breathing!" came in panic from Shira.

"She said she would appear to die. This must be it," I sent back. I really hoped I was correct. I had no idea how to get her breathing again if I wasn't.

The nightwalkers slowly began to approach, as if testing the boundary. I pulled out the fire starter that Raquel had packed in our bags and started lighting the kindling around the wall.

"Here they come!" sent Shira.

I looked back and saw they had started to run towards my position. The walking dead never ran; they were slow but persistent. These nightwalkers acted more like a pack of rabid animals.

I teleported up onto the wall as the fire spread through the kindling and wood I had laid out. Soon a wall of flame surrounded our position. It grew halfway up the wall and the ash and smoke made our eyes water, but the nightwalkers fell back from the fire. It seemed my plan might hold them.

"Clever," sent Shira.

"I don't know how long the fire will burn, but it should reduce the time we have to fight, at least," I sent.

The nightwalkers didn't seem to know what to do with the fire separating us from them. The fire slowly began to die, as the wood I had gathered was very dry and thinly spread, but it still kept them back.

An hour passed and Raquel had not moved. The fire fell to embers, and the Nightwalkers continued to wait.

"Now what?" asked Shira.

"I'm not sure," I sent. *"If she usually spends this time in a state like death, she might not have known it takes longer than an hour."*

"Your fire wall won't last much longer. We could gate away from here with her now. I could get us to the shelter," sent Shira.

"No, I think that would kill her. I think she needs to stay here till she recovers," I replied. It was a guess, but it seemed logical. At least as logical as someone dying for an hour and coming back fully recovered.

Shira sat down on the wall and let her legs dangle over the embers. *"There are so many of them. When they finally rush – "*

"They'll only be able to come up the path one or two at a time. At worst we only have to hold out till sunrise. We can do this," I interrupted.

She jumped to her feet. *"I think we're about to find out!"*

I looked and the nightwalkers were moving towards the path. I drew my swords, moved to the top of the steps and waited for them. *"Make sure they don't try to come up any other way."*

Shira nodded and stood over Raquel's body.

Then, with a loud cry, the nightwalkers rushed the wall.

CHAPTER
THIRTEEN

I had been lying in the hospital for five days when they finally started detaching machines from me and I could move without fear of setting off alarms. Following that I had two excruciating days of rehab before they let me return to my quarters. I was required to return to the medical department every day for an undetermined amount of rehab before they'd let me return to work.

"Purwryn," said Marcus. "Are you sure I can't get you anything?"

My legs weren't quite up to the walk back yet, so I rode in a hoverchair and Marcus came with me to make sure I made it safely. "Nah, I'll be fine. I just can't wait till I can get back to work."

"I think that will be a while yet." Marcus opened the door to my quarters and for the first time since the attack I was able to see for myself the aftermath of the fight. Most of the room was undisturbed, but someone had definitely thrown the table against the far wall.

"Want me to put that table back?" asked Marcus.

I hated to ask for help, but I knew I wouldn't be strong enough to move it once he was gone. "Yeah, that would be great. Thanks."

Once the table was back where it belonged he asked again, "Anything I can get or do for you?"

"Thanks, but I'll be fine. I plan to try and watch that movie that I never got to see," I said.

"Okay, but call me if you need anything," he said.

"Really, I'll be fine. Don't you have to get to work?" I asked. "I won't be an excuse for you to try and get out of demerits."

He chuckled. "I'm not late yet, but seriously, just call. Everyone will understand."

With that he left. Once he was gone, I moved my chair to the center of the room. I didn't accept the doctor's story that I'd hallucinated the attack; it was too real. I had done my share of recreational drugs before I wised up, and I know I wasn't high when that man appeared. Later, in the office with the old man I definitely had been drugged, but not before.

"If I threw the table to the left as I remember, and there was no attacker, then it should've been on the left hand side of the room," I said to myself. "So why was it on the right, unless there was an attacker who had to throw it off to get out from under it?"

I slowly stood and tried to walk a few steps. My legs were shaking under the stress, but I stubbornly wanted to stand for this. Turning around I looked at the wall on the far side of the room. It was completely unmarred. I had cast several mage bolts in that direction; they should have at the very least scorched the wall. Unless of course they hit something, or someone, before they could reach the wall.

As I looked around the room, everything matched what I'd expect to see if my memory was correct. I eased myself back into the chair and took a closer look at the table. It appeared undamaged from its ordeal. That was a shame; it was unrealistic, but I was almost hoping to have a face print on the table or something similar that I could point to as proof.

"Tricholophate," I said to myself. "Clever, but not clever enough."

I pulled out a datapad I had been using in the hospital. I was recording everything I could remember about the events. Every color, scent and sound. I spent the afternoon adding all the details about how my room was when I returned and correlating it with my memories. I knew as I got further from the incident the memories would fade, especially as my mind continued to heal from whatever drugs they'd used, and I couldn't allow that to happen. Someone was after me again, and I wouldn't be comfortable until at least I knew who and why.

That night I encrypted the datapad and hid it in my quarters. I knew it was best to go along with the doctor's story and not let anyone know my suspicions. The last thing I needed was for them to think I'd lost my wits and needed mental care.

The next morning I decided to try to take a shower. It had been at least a week since I had been able to wash properly. I slipped off my clothes and used the handrails in the shower to pull myself up. As I tried to wash myself, I noticed my back was tender.

Turning to look in the mirror, I saw a large bruise covering most of my back, complete with a new pink scar.

"Tricholophate didn't cause that," I said to myself.

I sighed and finished up in the shower. After getting dressed I sat at my table to eat breakfast. I'd be late for rehab, but right then I didn't care. I needed to figure out who captured me and why I was interrogated. They could come back at any time, and I wanted to be ready if they did.

After eating I slowly moved and sat in front of my terminal to do research. It was exhausting to move, but I was determined. I had barely gotten started with my plans when the doorbell chimed. I ignored it but then I heard, "Medical override," and the door slid open.

"Purwryn, you okay?" came a voice.

"Yeah, over here," I said.

One of the orderlies from ship's medical came into the room and said, "You're late for rehab." He didn't look happy with me. Not one bit.

"Sorry, showering and eating took longer than I'm used to," I said. I guessed there was no way out of rehab. I locked the terminal so he couldn't see what I was up to. I decided to make a play for pity to dodge his anger. "I was just resting my legs a bit after that effort before trying to get back into the hoverchair."

"Well, let's get you in your chair and take you down," he said. He seemed to soften at the idea that I wasn't being stubborn but had been unable to comply.

I slowly stood and uneasily walked to the chair. The orderly stood next to me the whole time with his arms out ready to catch me, but I refused any help. It hurt, made me lightheaded, and I had to go far too slow for my tastes but, by the Emperor, I did it myself. I wouldn't be an invalid; not now, not ever.

Once in the chair, he took over and brought me down to medical where the nurse made sure that I understood the importance of being on time in the future. She didn't seem anywhere near as understanding as the orderly, but I guess that wasn't her job.

After rehab, Marcus came by to escort me back to my quarters. "Hey, how about after my shift I drop by for a game of Pineman's Bluff?"

Pineman's Bluff was some card game that he had been trying to get me to play since the day I came on board, but I'd always had the excuse of being too busy with work. Unfortunately, I couldn't use that excuse now. Besides, I felt I owed it to him to try his game after all he had done for me. "Sure, but please bring dinner. Rations in my quarters are not very exciting."

Marcus left me alone in the room again. He really was turning out to be a great support through all of this. I wondered what his angle was. Did he think that someday I would be in a position to repay him for this kindness, or was he more like Crivreen, just an all-round nice guy? I hoped it was the latter. I hadn't met many like Crivreen, and it would be nice to know there were more good men out there.

I slowly made my way back to my terminal. It was time to get back to work on my case. The old man had wanted information about Zah'rak and his team. I had instinctively resisted telling him anything because I was trying to ditch that fake ID, but he kept pressing me. There must have been a reason.

"I have what I need," the old man had said, but I had never revealed anything, at least not that I could remember. I wasn't sure how much time had elapsed between the attack and waking up in the hospital, but surely long enough for them to do more than one interrogation.

It wouldn't be uncommon for interrogators to use drugs which cause amnesia. It would allow them to repeat the same line of questions many times, using information they'd learned that the subject didn't remember telling them.

I used the terminal to search for any information about other attacks or tricholophate accidents in the past year, but my search turned up nothing. I tried to find a way to pull up the medical reports from the others in this accident, or any news reporting on it, but failed. It was all locked down too tightly. I could really use Crivreen's skills now.

Late that evening Marcus came by as promised, with two big packages. "When I told the kitchen staff what happened and how you had no real food, they insisted I bring you all this." The packages contained enough dinner for several nights and various drinks and snacks. "And of course I got you some chocolate cake."

I had to smile at that. "You know me too well, I think."

He stowed the extra food and set up dinner. While we ate, he filled me in on the comings and goings of people we knew. Eventually he put down his cutlery and asked, "What really happened?"

"What do you mean?" I asked.

He pulled out a datapad and placed it on the table. "These three who were in the hall when you came out - they're dead."

"What?" I exclaimed. I picked up the datapad and looked at the pictures. "Those are blaster wounds." Actually they looked more like mage bolts, but I needed to be careful. I was pretty sure it hadn't leaked out that I was a magus, and I needed to keep it that way for now.

"Yes. The official story is that they shot each other under the influence of tricholophate," he said.

"They were in the hospital when I woke up," I told him.

"They died shortly after that from their wounds and tricholophate poisoning," he said.

"What are you getting at?" I asked.

"Tricholophate is a liquid at room temperature. You tell me: what happens when you overheat it like they said it happened?"

"It turns into a gas and – " I paused as I suddenly realized what he was getting at. " - becomes dangerously explosive," I said.

"Exactly. At least three blasters were discharged in the corridor, plus whatever hit you. There should be a gaping hole in the ship – yet there aren't even any scorch marks," he said.

"Look, I appreciate you looking out for me, but we both know that if I don't show that I'm well-adjusted and accept the official story I'll be thrown into a mental care facility," I said.

"Purwryn - " He took a deep breath and then continued. "Look, I know the risk, but I also know that you remember being attacked and the official story is obviously bogus. You might be on that mental watchlist right now, but I'm not. Tell me what you actually remember and let me dig."

I tried to size up his intentions. Was he working for some official group, trying to determine if I was really well-adjusted? Could he be working for whoever had attacked me, to determine whether I remembered anything that would cause a problem? Or was he truly concerned for my wellbeing?

"Very well," I said. "I guess there's no harm in telling you what I hallucinated while under the influence of the gas." I told him the story up to the time I'd collapsed in the hall, but modified it slightly to prevent discovery that I was a magus.

"Why can't you walk?" he asked.

"They had to grow a new spine for me. The bottom third of mine was extensively damaged."

"By what?" he asked.

"They don't know. They simply said I got hurt while under the influence of the tricholophate."

He cleaned up our dishes and served the chocolate cake. "Several hours are missing."

"What do you mean?" I asked. I took a bite of the cake; it was fresh, moist and wonderful. I hadn't had any since before the incident and it felt good to eat it, like a little bit of normality had returned.

"The timeline you just gave me indicates that you collapsed in the hallway several hours before anyone found you," said Marcus, drawing me out of my cake-inspired reverie.

"Careful," I said. "That way lie dragons."

"Look, I know the risks," he said. "If it's reported that I'm snooping around this obvious cover-up I could disappear, but someone attacked you and almost killed you. Let me help."

Marcus seemed like a nice guy and I didn't want to see him hurt, but it was obvious he wouldn't give up till he had something. "Yeah, there is time missing but my memory of those hours is sketchy at best. Even if there were no tricholophate in my system, something affected me, because my memory is disjointed and makes no sense. It's just a series of unconnected images and sounds; nothing that helps."

"What kind of images?" he asked.

"An office, a couch, a door and an old man: that's about it," I said.

"This man, have you seen him before?" he asked.

"No. Say, didn't you come over to teach me that card game?" I responded.

"Yes, in fact I did."

This time he seemed to take the hint and we began the game he so wanted to teach me.

CHAPTER FOURTEEN

The nightwalkers ran through the embers, not seeming to care when they caught fire. The stench of rotting flesh mixed with burning flesh was a combination I hoped never to smell again. For a moment I envied Raquel's unconscious state, as she would have no memory of the stench. They charged up the stairs towards us, but before they could reach me a thin blue oval appeared between us. The nightwalkers rushed right into it and disappeared.

"A gate! Smart thinking, Shira, but how long can you keep it open?" I asked.

"I'm not sure; I've never needed to know," she said.

The nightwalkers continued to rush the gate, apparently without realizing what it was. "Where are they coming out?"

Shira pointed up into the sky, where a steady stream of nightwalkers were falling from a great height. "I didn't expect them to keep coming like this."

"Keep the gate open as long as you can, but don't overstress yourself. We may need your spells to escape if things go poorly."

"I may have to close it soon," she said "Each one that goes through takes energy from me. It would be no effort to keep open if they weren't using it."

"Apparently they're not going to stop their charge. Close the gate and save your power," I said as I resumed my defensive stance.

The moment the gate vanished they were on me. I swung fast and hard to beat them back, but the push of their vast numbers was too much. I knew they'd overwhelm me soon. The battle was as good as lost already. "Look around, Shira, for another wall segment, one with no stairs, and gate us to it!"

"There!" she called out and opened a gate. "But Raquel is too heavy for me, unless I drag her."

I spun, swinging my tail hard across the front line of nightwalkers, sending several of them flying and creating a break in their attack. "Go!" I yelled as I sprinted up the remaining steps, scooped up Raquel and charged through the gate.

Shira, being closer, went through first and as soon as I was clear through the gate she closed it. "Okay, we should be safe for now."

After setting Raquel down I examined our new position. We were about ten meters off the ground on what may have been a support pillar for some gigantic building or perhaps a decorative column. It was hard to tell what it might have been, since all that was left was this single tall and wide column. The pillar was perhaps five or six meters in diameter, allowing us room to walk around. There didn't appear to be any way up or down from where we were, making it a secure retreat from our land-bound attackers. "Great choice. Now, eat and get some rest. Who knows what else this night will bring?"

"How's Raquel doing?" she asked.

Raquel lay where I had placed her, looking very dead. As far as I could tell she wasn't breathing at all. "No change. I think at this point it's safe to assume that we need to plan how to survive until daybreak."

Another hour passed with no change in Raquel's condition. The nightwalkers encircled our position, but there was no way for them to reach us. It was foolish of me not to have thought of a position like this sooner. I had been working under the impression that we only needed an hour, but this would have been a far superior position from the outset.

Shira sat with her legs dangling over the edge, chewing on some jerky from her pack. "Probably two more hours till dawn?"

"Yeah, that seems right," I said. "I assume they'll start leaving before then."

I closed my eyes and leaned back. Stretching out with my mind, I used my power of Sight to look around at the sky. It seemed unlikely that Night-walkers were the only thing out here, but I couldn't see anything else.

The stone below my feet was warm, and at first I assumed it was still radiating the heat it had absorbed during the day; when I stopped to examine it with Sight, however, it glowed softly as if it were alive. Crouching down, I placed my bare hands on the stone and tried to communicate with it like I did with the trees. I could almost hear a faint voice, but couldn't quite make it out. Unbelievably, the stone was trying to talk to me. I could feel it pleading with me, but I couldn't figure out what it wanted. I strained to hear its voice, trying to block out the rest of the world, but it was just too weak.

"Zah'rak!" screamed Shira, breaking my concentration.

I looked up and saw a group of wraiths flying towards us, too many for me to face alone. I hoped the little power in the stone would be enough to make me strong enough to overcome them. I kicked off my boots so my feet could embrace the stone directly and draw power from it. My claws sank into the hard stone just as if it were a soft mold, giving me a better grip.

Quickly drawing my swords, I called out, "Their touch is death!"

"Worse, those are collectors! Their touch means a living death!" shouted Shira. I don't know where it came from but she suddenly had a staff in her hands. She was standing with her back straight, holding the staff across her body. She seemed utterly fearless in the face of them, completely unlike the nervous and shy woman who hid in hydroponics.

Before I could say anything else they were on us. I swung my swords through the leader of the pack before rolling to one side. Shira swung her staff and spun away in the opposite direction. Her staff connected solidly and sent a wraith flying backwards into the group, scattering their formation. The creatures had no physical form, but Shira was one of the Sac'a'rith, and that made the staff in her hand just as deadly to them as to any normal creature.

Her spin put her on the edge of the wall as three more flew towards her. I rushed to her aid, but could only cut down the rearmost one before the other two reached her.

To my surprise, Shira leapt into the air and nimbly flew over them. She landed and launched her attack from her new position behind them by swinging her staff hard into one of them, driving it into the other. They screamed in pain as they hit and dissipated. She was proving to be quite resourceful in combat and not as helpless as I had imagined.

"You can fly?" I exclaimed, but had no time to discuss the matter as three more came at me. I spun out of their line of attack and swung my blades, cutting one of them cleanly in half. Each half drifted downwards briefly before dissipating.

"There are too many of them!" called out Shira as she once again leapt into the air to avoid being pushed off the wall.

"Do you have any spells that would help?" I asked.

"One, but I can't seem to get a chance to cast it!" she called back as she swooped low by me and swung her staff hard, knocking several away from me at once.

"Land, I'll cover you as best I can!" I called out.

She landed in front of me and I began swinging my swords rapidly and widely around her while she chanted. She was small enough to fit easily inside my reach. My swords formed a fence of deadly steel around her and the collectors hung back, waiting for an opening. I wasn't sure how long I could keep it up, but Shira didn't need long.

She yelled out the last command word and a beam of pure light came from her staff. She swept the beam through the wraiths and they screamed in pain. The entire force of them fell back and Shira called out another command word that stopped the beam, but her staff still glowed faintly, reminiscent of the early morning sun.

"Wow! What was that?" I asked.

She held the staff up high above us and let the light shine down on the rock and our position. "Sunlight. This is a sunstaff, an ancient artifact that my old master gave me in case the wraiths ever tried to challenge me."

"Why didn't you use that on the Nightwalkers?" I asked.

"I don't know how to recharge it and it only has a few charges left. I was trying to save them in case things got really bad," she said.

As the sunlight fell on the stone beneath us I could feel it gaining power. Its voice was getting louder. I couldn't yet make out what it was saying but one thing was for sure: it was waking up! "Shira, send a beam of that light at Raquel!"

"What? Why?" she asked.

I could feel the rocks reaching out, thirsting for the light. I could almost make out what they were saying, and I was sure they were begging for more. "I think it will activate the stone and wake her up!" I said.

She hesitated and then focused the light on Raquel. The stone continued to warm up and below us the nightwalkers were falling back. "It's working!"

The stone was soon glowing of its own accord, obvious even to normal vision, and the wraiths retreated into the night. I closed my eyes and used Sight to look around. The dead were fleeing and more and more stones were lighting up. "Keep it up!"

"The staff will be out of power soon," she said.

Raquel gasped deeply and arched her back. She began to cough violently. I went to her side and helped her sit up. Her eyes were vacant at first, but little by little she seemed to grow stronger and more aware. Soon she seemed to come to her senses, although confused.

Shira doused her staff and said, "Raquel?"

Raquel took a moment to shake out her limbs, stretch, and look around. "Where are we?"

"Are you okay?" I asked.

"Yes, I'm fine again, but it's almost sunrise; what happened?" she asked.

"You never told us how to activate the rocks," said Shira.

I told her what had happened while she was unconscious.

"I didn't know that needed to be done," she said to Shira. "May I see your staff?"

Shira hesitated and then said, "Sure, but it needs to be recharged and I don't know how."

Raquel stood up and smiled. She spun the staff over her head several times and then brought it down on the stone, calling out a word in a language I didn't recognize. The staff glowed dimly and slowly brightened until it was as bright as the midday sun. I had to turn away because it blinded my night-adjusted eyes. Blobs of light bounced around my vision for a bit but eventually went away.

"There, it's as good as new," said Raquel.

"You recharged it!" gasped Shira as she took back her staff.

"Yes, that's a fitting staff for you to have. Many of those were crafted here when this castle still stood. Anytime you need to recharge it, return here and repeat what you saw me do."

Raquel stretched out and said, "It'll be light soon. Once the sun is above the horizon we can travel back to the gate. I have my power back, so I can just gate us from here."

"Wait," I said. "Every time you cast a spell you use up some of your life, and have to return here to recharge?"

"Yes," she said. "But please keep this between the three of us."

"Of course, but Shira will gate us back when it's time. How did this happen?" I asked.

She turned her back to us and walked to the edge of the wall. "A choice, long ago," she said softly.

I started to press her for more information but Shira stopped me. *"Let it be. She'll tell us when she's ready."*

"Just how dangerous is this place?" I asked.

"If we leave the protection of this fortress before sunrise, it's unlikely we'd survive long enough to active the gate and get home." She paused and stared off into the distance. "Someday, Zah'rak, someday we must find a way to repair this world."

We sat in silence after that until shortly after sunrise.

"We should get going. All the activity last night is sure to have drawn the wrong kind of attention, and not all of it fears the sun," said Raquel. "I'm not confident the little power that remains here could hold up against some of the more powerful inhabitants."

I looked over the forest one last time, wishing we could stay here. Once this mission was over, we must come back and explore. I hoped to find a less dangerous place, so that we could spend some time among the natural life of the forests.

Shira nodded and cast her gate. When we were all through I asked, "If something were ever to happen to you, how would we get back here?"

"This is the home gate. Any Sac'a'rith can open it from any other gate," she said and unlocked the gate back to the Night Wisp. "Quickly; trouble can't be far off."

CHAPTER
FIFTEEN

Aboard the Night Wisp, I contacted Crivreen over the ship's internal comm. to let him know we were back.

"Get up to the bridge! We've got trouble," he said.

"Great!" I groaned.

The gate room was right next to the bridge so we were there in a moment. Crivreen was at the tactical station and Ragnar was at navigation. The ship was running in low power mode, and the main tactical screen was tracking multiple threats.

"What's going on?" I asked.

"With Ragnar's help, I'm hiding the Night Wisp as best I can," said Crivreen. "I didn't want to risk jumping until you were back, but we've got pirates sweeping the area looking for us."

Ragnar looked drained, and sweat soaked his shirt. I doubted he was scared, so he must have been exerting himself doing something. Perhaps he was using his runecasting to stay one step ahead of the pirates. I made a note to ask him later; first I had to deal with the pirates. "Can we jump clear?" I asked.

"Now that you're back, I think so, but I'm not sure where to jump to. The next jump will put us in a gravity well where we'll be trapped."

I pulled up a map of the region and was searching for options when Raquel asked, "Why aren't we fighting?"

"None of us has any real experience of a dogfight," said Crivreen. "Plus we're outnumbered four to one."

"Yes, but how do their ships compare?" she asked.

He looked over the tactical. "They're light cruisers. I think maybe we could take any of them one on one," he said.

"We don't have to fight," I said. "There's a jump route we can take out of here that they won't guess and will keep us clear of the gravity well."

"Fine, we can run - but is that wise?" she asked.

"What do you mean?" I responded.

"Narcion was never attacked like this because word had spread of how deadly he was," she said.

"Sure, but we're nowhere near as deadly as he was, and they know it," I replied.

"Then let's change their minds about that," she said.

"What are you proposing?" asked Ragnar.

"Shira gates Zah'rak and myself over to their lead ship and we take them down," said Raquel. "Then we contact the other ships from the bridge there and tell them to leave before we do the same to them."

"That does sound like something Narcion would do," I said. I hated to admit it but she was right. Narcion must have faced situations like this before he became known as deadly, and I suspected he'd left only a few survivors to tell the tale.

"We can walk away … no, fly away from this fight," said Ragnar. "I see no reason anyone should have to die today."

"They're pirates," snapped Raquel, obviously annoyed. "That's reason enough."

"Is that what a wizard would do?" asked Crivreen. "They don't seem like the type to go around killing people randomly."

"This isn't random," said Raquel. "They're trying to kill you!"

"Maybe we can deliver a warning?" came in Shira's timid voice.

"What did you have in mind?" I asked. I was surprised to hear her pipe up. Tempers were starting to flare, and even before Raquel came on board Shira would disappear when that happened.

"We could just throw some explosives through a gate into their ship and then send a message from here," she said.

"I still don't understand why we need to kill anyone. Let's just leave, and leave now," said Ragnar.

"How are you going to gate there, anyway?" asked Crivreen. "You've never been on the ship."

"Good question," said Raquel. She took a deep breath and regained some of her composure. "She can cast a site-to-site gate if you can align our ship so that she can have clear line of sight through the airlock windows."

"If we get line of sight I can just teleport over," I said. "Let's do that. I'll teleport over, place explosives someplace that will draw attention and teleport back. Crivreen, get close to the lead ship. Ragnar, you're in charge until I get back."

I quickly left the bridge before anyone could argue and headed to the mission room to put on my armor. Shira followed me down and started to suit up also. "What are you doing?" I asked.

"If you get in trouble you might need a gate out. I want to be ready," she said.

I wanted to send her away, but she was right; I might need her. Besides, last night she had proven to be pretty handy in a fight.

I pulled out some explosive grenades from the equipment locker. "Should be easy. I pop in, toss these grenades and pop out."

"It would be safer to throw them through a gate," said Shira. For the first time I noticed that when it was just us and no one else, she was much more open. Raquel said she saw me as family, and I was starting to understand that better. She obviously trusted me completely, but I wasn't sure what I had done to deserve that. I would have to be careful not to lose it, as such trust is not easily earned back.

"Yeah, but then we can't place them where we want," I said, deliberately switching to the plural so that she would feel included in my plan. I clicked on my helmet and teleported out of the ship via the airlock window. Once outside I secured myself to the hull and waited for Crivreen to fly into position.

Shira joined me and once I had a good line of sight she sent, *"Be careful!"* I could feel the worry in her mental voice. I guess what I was about to do was dangerous, but it was far from the most dangerous thing I'd done that week, or even that day.

I teleported over to their hull and worked my way around to their airlock. I set the delay on the grenades to give me enough time, and placed two of them into each of the three airlocks I found. Before they could go off, I teleported back to the Night Wisp's hull.

"You didn't go beyond the airlock," commented Shira.

"When I got there, I figured that blowing open their airlocks would cause all their air to rush out. They would have to seal blast doors all over the craft, preventing them from moving about. That should make the point without hurting anyone."

I watched as the grenades detonated and the doors flew off the airlocks in eerie silence. The cruiser pitched as the air rushed out and tossed them off course. The ship's stabilizing thrusters fired to counter the effect, but that would be the least of their concerns as their atmosphere was being emptied into space. *"Message sent,"* I sent.

We got back on board and headed to the bridge. "How does it look?"

"Well, you got their attention all right," said Crivreen.

"Open a broadcast channel and send this message," I said. "Pirates, as we have just demonstrated we can board your craft at will and destroy anything we wish. You cannot stop us. Do not attempt to follow us, and we will allow you to live. End transmission."

"Okay, message sent," said Crivreen.

"Jump then, but come up short in case we have to run." Once we were clear of the post-jump hangover I said, "Did they follow?"

"Doesn't look like it," said Crivreen.

"Okay. As discreetly as you can, get us out of here," I said.

Shira slipped off and presumably headed back to hydroponics. Raquel stood watching the tactical screens, but no threat materialized. Ragnar slumped into his seat, looking greatly relieved. I sent him to his quarters for some rest, planning to question him when he was rested.

"Now that that is behind us, I'm going to head back to the mess hall," I said.

"Wait, there's one more thing," said Crivreen. "That Phareon guy called, looking for you. He didn't seem happy."

"What did he say?" I asked.

"He just demanded that you call him on your return," he said.

"Really?" I was getting tired of his attitude and didn't appreciate the way he treated Crivreen like a second-class citizen. Dealing with him was just one more reason to retreat to the woods and forget this life for a while. "Well, put him up on the big screen and let's see what he thinks is so important."

"He's not going to like that," warned Crivreen.

"Good," I said, cutting him off. "Put the communication through."

It took Crivreen a few minutes, but eventually he was able to raise the commander. "Zah'rak, I see you're well," said the commander.

"Yes," was all I said.

"Then tell me, what in the Emperor's name is Felix up to?" he demanded.

"That's not really your business," I replied.

"He emptied all his accounts and disappeared while under contract with us. That makes it my business," he said.

"Commander, you haven't paid for the last two missions we completed for you. That means you are in breach of contract and Felix owes you nothing," I said.

"Look – " he began.

"No!" I interjected. "You are in breach of contract. There will be no negotiations until you pay what you owe. Is that clear?"

He cursed and closed the channel.

"I think we might be unemployed," I said.

Crivreen chuckled. "You think so or hope so?"

"He'll pay," said Raquel. "He has no choice."

"Why?" I asked.

"He needs you. I checked on current events before meeting up with you. Things are developing which would normally lead them to seek Narcion's help," she said.

"You mean more undead?" I asked.

"I don't know," she said. "All they know is that there are mysterious circumstances which other teams have failed to return from investigating."

"But why does he care about Felix?" asked Crivreen.

"He's a controller, and Felix just walked away from him," she said. "We'll hear from him again, but the last report I had was that he was sending a team of magi to check one of the stations in question. I suspect it will be another team like Criveen, Jasper and Felix."

"Crivreen, set best speed to Siden. I would like to have the supplies to make better armor before we accept any new missions."

CHAPTER
SIXTEEN

The flight to Siden passed without incident. Raquel worked with Shira, training her in the skills which Narcion had taught me at first, and Shira slowly accepted that Raquel wasn't planning to kill her. Crivreen and I studied the spell book that we had acquired from Master Dusty and his team. As time passed and I came to know Raquel better, my unease started to fade.

She was different from Narcion in some ways, but mostly she resembled him. Her instinctive behavior was to fight, and she was very cryptic when questioned on subjects she didn't want to discuss. It was obvious she was from a different time and a different world. Before waking up in our era, her life had been lived under the constant shadow of war.

"Okay, Zah'rak," said Crivreen, "we're in a geosynchronous orbit over the ruins of the necromancer's castle."

"Any sign of life?" I asked.

"Nothing on active or passive sensors, but we still haven't upgraded the sensor array."

I chuckled. Narcion had rarely depended on technology, so our ship was far from cutting-edge, a fact that bothered Crivreen no end. I didn't see the problem, since most of the time the Night Wisp was just a mobile home. We relied on other tools far more than on the ship.

"Everyone to the mission room, except Crivreen," I said. "Crivreen, I need you to take Felix's place and stay with the Night Wisp."

"I guessed as much," he said. An expression of relief passed over his face, as if he were happy to be left behind.

In the mission room we all suited up in our armor. Before clicking on my helmet I said, "Standard penetration formation. I'll go first and break left. Ragnar, you'll follow and break right. Raquel, you follow and make sure our rear is clear. Shira, once we give the all-clear you come through and close the gate. Everyone understand?"

"Yes," said Raquel. "But what are you expecting to find?"

"I have no idea, but we've jumped into plenty of unknown situations as a team. We can never assume a gate is taking us to a safe place."

She smiled and nodded in understanding.

I clicked on my helmet and disengaged the safeties from my blaster. Ragnar and Shira also engaged their helmets. They would depend on wands which Crivreen had crafted for them, but I still preferred the feel of a solid blaster in my hands. Crivreen's wands were just too small and flimsy for my taste.

I looked to Raquel, who nodded and pressed a button on the collar of her armor. A helmet automatically unfolded and surrounded her head. Once it was locked in place her armor deepened from its purple color to an almost perfect, flat black. No light at all seemed to reflect from it. Even in that well-lit mission room she was hard to see. It was like looking into a hole with no light. It was there, but you had to infer that from the blackness instead of seeing it directly.

"Ready," she said.

"Shira, open the gate, please," I said.

Shira cast her gate and I charged through. As I came out the other side

I dove to the left and rolled behind some cover. After a quick scan of the area I called out, "Clear!" on the comm.

Ragnar came through with a wand in each hand and found cover to the right. "Clear!" he reported.

I expected to see Raquel come through next, but no one came. I was about to say something over the comm when she called out, "Clear!"

Shira came through then and closed the gate, quickly running to my side.

"Hold cover," I said. After checking the environmental conditions with my armor's sensors, I pulled off my helmet and tasted the air to see if I could catch any scent of life around us. Closing my eyes I used my power of Sight to sweep the area and saw no threat.

Using Sight I was able to see Raquel crouched behind cover with her back to our position, watching our rear just as I had asked. I sighed with relief. "Looks clear."

"Where's Raquel?" asked Shira.

"Here," said Raquel, who shimmered into view as she walked up.

"Adaptive skin?" asked Shira.

"No," she said. "I don't have the concealment line of magic. This is a camosuit."

"What's that?" I asked.

"My armor automatically changes color and texture to match the environment, making me hard to see," she said. "It's an invention I picked up while traveling in another realm."

"Very nice," said Ragnar.

"Indeed. We may have to go there and buy ourselves some," I said.

"Oh, I doubt that would be wise. I barely got back with my life the last time I was there," said Raquel.

"Not exactly the prettiest place, is it?" commented Shira, bringing us back to the situation at hand.

The region had once been a thick forest full of life, but now it mostly consisted of burnt-out husks of trees and rubble, permanently scarred from our battle with the necromancer. There was nothing green anywhere to be seen and no trace of animal life. I knew from the orbital view that there was healthy forest not far from our position, but you would never have guessed it from our immediate area. We were close enough to see the remains of the fortress, which was also mostly destroyed.

"I've always wondered why Narcion didn't warn us about the aftermath of destroying the table," I said. "Was he afraid we wouldn't follow through?"

"No, nothing like that. We simply didn't know this would happen," said Raquel. "We assumed the power would have vented back into the Spirit Realm."

"We're being watched," said Ragnar.

"By whom? Where?" I asked.

"By – " he started to reply, but was cut off as a bolt hit him in the chest and knocked him down.

I grabbed him and dragged him behind cover while Raquel pulled Shira down behind some boulders. "You all right?"

"Yes," said Ragnar. "The armor absorbed most of the energy."

He was wheezing a little as he spoke, but there was no time to press him as another bolt slammed into the rocks near us.

"Where are they coming from?" I asked.

"I see him. He's behind those logs to the north. I need a distraction," sent Raquel.

"Go!" I sent and tossed a concussion grenade towards the logs. A thunderous rupture of energy shook the ground under us as the grenade went off. As soon as the shockwave had passed our position, I sprang up and was aiming my rifle when a human body went flying over the logs and hit the ground hard.

About to charge, I noticed something odd about the air above him, a sort of shimmer. Then a black hood appeared and pulled itself over the man's head.

Fire rained down on the area, and the downed magus screamed in pain. I closed my eyes and used my Sight to see Raquel in her image-shifting armor running for cover as a second magus cast fire down from the sky.

I fired my rifle at the invisible magus, but the energy from the bolts seemed to explode around him. *"Now what?"*

"He's shielded from energy-based attacks," sent Raquel.

"Shira, watch for the explosion and gate me right above it," I sent.

"Got it," she sent back.

Shira and I had used this technique many times now and she needed no further instructions. This would be the first time we used it against an invisible floating target, but the principle should work the same; at least, I hoped so.

I opened fire and elongated balls of tightly-packed, highly-energized particles flew towards the magus in the sky at the speed of light. As each blast from my gun slammed into his shield bright flashes of light were released, clearly marking his position for Shira.

Shira cast a gate in front of me and I sprinted through. As I came out the other side I was directly above the magus. Keeping my eyes closed, which allowed me to see him clearly despite his invisibility, I used my telekinesis to push against the ground and slow my fall. As I passed him I kicked him hard. My foot connected squarely with his chest, doubling him over and breaking his concentration. He fell quickly and slammed hard into the ground.

My kick had sent me flying backwards from him. I teleported to the ground, rolling a few times to use up my momentum, and came to a stop next to the magus. I raised the stock of my gun to strike him.

"Wait," called out Shira.

"Why?" I asked.

"I think he's dead."

Raquel appeared next to me and said, "They both are."

"Anyone hurt?" I asked.

"Ragnar had the wind knocked out of him, but his armor held," said Raquel. "Shira?"

"I'm fine. The fire magus was more concerned with you two than with me," she said.

I wondered if that bothered her. I knew I might feel slighted if an enemy never bothered to target me. It would imply that I wasn't enough of a threat to them. Shira's gate had won the fight, though, proving her to be a worthy target. It was impossible to guess what she thought of it all.

After making sure Ragnar was okay, I walked over to the corpse of the other magus. "What's with the hood?"

Raquel chuckled. "An old trick to keep a magus from teleporting away, or from using most of his spells." I noticed she had also tied his hands.

"Cunning," said Ragnar. "He can't use his hands to cast, and you allowed him no line of sight for aiming any spell that didn't need his hands."

"Who is he?" I asked. It struck me forcefully how easily a magus was disabled. A simple hood and rope eliminated most of his power. From a distance a magus seemed unstoppable, yet I'd just kicked one out of the sky and Raquel had stopped another with only a hood. Seeing how easily these two had been defeated was a strong warning for me; I would have to be careful not to overestimate myself.

"I don't know," she replied.

"He's a Korshalemian sorcerer," said Ragnar, "as was the other one. They must have been psionics, since one was levitating and the other teleported at least once."

"Not true," said Raquel.

"What isn't true?" asked Ragnar.

"This persistent belief that the basic powers differ between realms. They are in fact the same," she told him. By her tone it was apparent that she was fed up hearing that belief, but this was the first time I'd heard her address the issue.

"Look," said Ragnar. "I lived in Korshalemia for most of my life. I think I should know."

"The basic powers are a secret known only to the highest-ranking wizards. These abilities are deliberately suppressed and blocked because they're seen as impure. The sorcerers never cared about that so they were all trained in these powers, while the wizards saw the powers used by the sorcerers as evil and passed on this belief."

"But," argued Ragnar, "that would mean I could teleport and use telepathy, and I can't."

"You can," she said. "But we'll have to get help to remove the magical block that's preventing you."

"I don't understand why they would do this, and how would you know?" he said. "This theory of yours doesn't make any sense."

"This is very interesting," I interrupted, "but we are standing out in the open in what's becoming a battle zone. We should make for cover."

"Agreed. We're still being watched, but it's from a distance," said Ragnar with a sigh. I knew he wanted to continue the discussion, but we had to move before we were targeted again.

Raquel searched the bodies and recovered some wands and magic jewelry, leaving the bodies for scavengers. It didn't seem right to leave them there, but we had already stood around in the open far too long for my taste. If any of their friends were still around, they could deal with the bodies.

"Shira, which way?" I asked.

Shira led us to a section of the ruins which I estimated to be near the back of the castle. A stone trapdoor was still partly intact, but she needed my assistance to get it open. Once opened, it revealed a set of stairs descending down into darkness.

"My gate markers are gone, so I don't know whether the rooms are still there or whether they've collapsed," said Shira.

"I'm sure that once you were rescued the necromancer removed them, so that you couldn't gate people into his fortress," said Raquel.

"That makes sense," I agreed. As I took my first few steps down the stairs I felt a chill run down my spine. It was a sense which Narcion had told me was part of my Sac'a'rith nature: a warning signal that alerted me when I was approaching an area controlled by the undead. "We're not alone."

CHAPTER
SEVENTEEN

After two excruciating weeks of rehab I was finally walking and no longer needed the hover chair. I had a long way to go yet before I'd be able to return to full-time work, but I hoped I'd be put back on light duty soon. I was going stir crazy, sitting around my room all day. Marcus came by every night, which helped break the monotony, but I was itching to get back to being productive.

The ship's chief doctor had asked me to drop by and I was really hoping he intended to give me that clearance. "Purwryn, please sit down," he said as I entered his office.

He wasn't alone. There was a man with him whom I didn't recognize. He was tall, dressed in dark clothes and wore dark glasses which obscured his eyes. He had a presence about him that indicated he was not to be trifled with.

"This is an agent from Resden," said the doctor. "He is investigating the accident and would like to talk with you about what you remember."

"I can take it from here," said the agent, opening the door to show the doctor out.

The doctor wasn't happy about being made to leave, but went quietly. Resden was one of the most powerful trade consortiums in the region, not known for being magnanimous. Their agents were on the Paradise to ensure that Resden interests were being served. I couldn't think of a positive outcome from this situation.

I'd have to come across as completely loyal and useful in his eyes; anything else and I could easily disappear or have a 'tragic accident'. Things were really heating up here and it looked like I'd have to abandon this post at the next stop.

"Now, Purwryn, I want to hear what you remember," he said.

"The doctors here have informed me that all my memories are hallucinations, so I've done my best to forget and move on. I don't see how that can help," I replied.

"Let me show you something, then," he said. He placed a datapad on the table in front of me and played a video. It showed me running out of my room and a bolt of energy slamming into my back. He stopped the playback there. "Now, tell me what you remember."

"Well, okay. I can tell you the hallucinations and you can make of them what you will." I was beginning to get worried that this was a mental fitness check. If I couldn't show I was properly adjusted after the accident, I might be sent away for fixing.

"Yes, let's start with that and see where it gets us," he said.

"I was in my room getting ready to watch a movie," I started and then told him as much as I could remember, leaving out any parts that would reveal me to be a magus. "The last thing I remember is falling in the corridor as I got hit by a blaster from behind."

He sighed and restarted the video. "Watch and see." I saw three men running down the corridor with weapons drawn. They each fired a shot from their blasters, but there was no one else in the corridor. The bolts hit something invisible and seemed to be reflected back onto the men. A moment later my body disappeared.

"Right after that, the pipe ruptured and filled the section with tricholophate." He stood and walked around so that he was directly in front of me. "As you can imagine, everyone in that section started calling for help. Our teams were extracting people as fast as we could when this happened."

He started a new video on the screen that that showed the corridor by my room. "We had already removed everyone and marked that sector clear earlier in the response. Fortunately for you, someone happened to look at this camera and saw what was happening." My body suddenly reappeared right where I had fallen.

"But how?" I asked. It was clear that my actions in the corridor looked very suspicious to him, and I had to admit with good reason. He probably thought that I was either directly or indirectly the cause of the leak.

"You tell me. You were gone for hours. Where were you?" he asked.

I took a deep breath. "I don't know. Tricholophate does funny things to the mind, and I can't trust what I remember."

"Perhaps you didn't hear me. You disappeared before the tricholophate leak occurred," he said.

I didn't dare to resist him; that would just confirm his suspicions and land me in a whole lot of trouble. "I don't know about that, but I've worked around a lot of chemicals in my time and I know what it feels like to be affected by them. After I was hit in the corridor I remember waking up on a couch, but my head was very fuzzy. I couldn't think straight then, nor do I remember much of it now. I was definitely under the influence of something."

"Fuzzy?" he asked.

"Yes. It was extremely hard to focus, or form any complex thoughts," I said.

"You said you were on a couch? What else?" he asked.

"There was an old man there. He was asking me questions about my job, I think," I said. "I tried to run, but I don't remember why. Then I woke up here. That's all I remember."

"Would you say you were interrogated?" he asked.

"I can't say," I said, "because my mind at the time was clouded, and my memory of it is even less clear."

"The doctors only report tricholophate in your system. No other drugs were found," he said.

"Okay." I didn't like the direction things were turning.

"But again, you left the corridor before the tricholophate was released. You weren't exposed until your return," he said.

"I'm not sure where you're going with this," I said. Actually I was very sure, and I didn't like it one bit.

I was sure I could feel his gaze piercing me even through the eyeshades. There was something about that gaze that was familiar, but the glasses made it difficult to place it.

He sat on the edge of the desk. "Let's try this, then: describe the man you saw when you were on the couch."

"Sure. He was – " I began but a piercing pain interrupted my sentence. I couldn't see the old man in my memory through the pain. It felt like someone had poured ice through my veins and stuck my head in a vice. The harder I tried to remember what the man looked like, the more it hurt. I screamed at the top of my lungs.

The door burst open and the doctor and some orderlies rushed in. I tried to steady myself, but the pain was too much. I was vaguely aware that the doctor and the agent were arguing. The agent turned to leave and in that brief moment something inside me broke free; rage took over and I was overcome by a desire to kill the agent as the pain continued to escalate.

"It was you!" I screamed and went for his throat. "Traitor!"

He spun to kick me away but orderlies jumped on both of us. I fought with all my might to get free. The pressure building in my head had destroyed all reason. I only knew one thing: that agent had to die. The orderlies managed to drive me to the floor, where I writhed and kicked for all I was worth until everything went black.

I awoke back in the hospital bed. Marcus was once again sitting by my side reading, and I was hooked up to all the machines just like before. "No, not again!" I moaned. At least this time I wasn't in excruciating pain.

"Ah, you live," said Marcus.

"What happened?" I asked.

He signaled for the doctor to come over. "I'd better let your doctor explain."

"Hello, Purwryn," said the doctor as he came over and examined the readouts on the terminals. "How are you feeling?"

"Sore and tired," I said, "but overall much better than the last time I woke up here."

"What do you remember?" he asked.

"I was in your office and some guy was asking me questions," I said. "Something happened; we got in a fight and I woke up here."

"That's about right," he said. "Do you remember why you attacked him?"

"No." That was a lie, but I didn't dare share the truth. I shouldn't have attacked at that time, but the pain prevented me from thinking clearly. I would have to wait and bide my time.

"Well, if you remember anything else, let me know," he said.

"What happened?" asked Marcus.

The doctor looked at me questioningly.

"It's okay, Doc. Speak freely," I said, assuming he was concerned about revealing personal medical data in front of Marcus.

"You had a relapse," he said. "This is very common with tricholophate exposure. I suspect it was brought on by the questions you were asked, so I suggest you avoid thinking about the events of the accident for a while."

"Okay," I said. "How long do I have to stay in here this time?"

"Overnight for observation. Tomorrow you can go back to your rehab and perhaps next week return to light duty," he said.

"What are the chances of another relapse?" asked Marcus.

"Minimal, as long as he isn't interrogated again," said the doctor. "Now, you must excuse me to tend to my other patients."

After he left, Marcus started to ask a question but I cut him off. "Not now. I'm too tired to talk," I said, hoping he would get the message.

"Sure," he said. "I'll stop by your place and get you a clean set of clothes later."

"Thanks," I replied.

The rest of the day passed without incident, and in the morning I was given the okay to head back to my quarters. Marcus, true to his word, had retrieved me a clean uniform to go home in. We walked back mostly in silence, but as we approached the door he stopped me.

"You might want to prepare yourself," he said.

I punched open the door and looked inside: my place had been ransacked. All my drawers were out and cabinets emptied onto the floor. I sighed. "Did you call security?"

"No," he said. We walked in and he pulled the door shut behind us.

"Probably wise." I climbed over the mess and accessed a secret panel I had built into the wall my first day on board. In it was my sack full of money and the equipment I'd kept from my days as a special agent.

I pulled out a scanner and swept the room for recording devices. Once I was sure the room was clean, I put everything back. "Obviously, you never saw that panel." I realized too late that I should have waited until he was out of the room. I was slipping and that wasn't good, especially not with Resden agents after me.

"Who did this?" he asked.

"I was interrogated by a Resden agent at the hospital, but I didn't have any information for him," I said. "I assume that he or his cronies did this."

"Then I was right not to call anyone," he said. "Any idea why?"

"No," I said. It didn't make sense for them to search my room. It wouldn't have gotten them anything and they must have known that, so why do it? He helped me clean up the room and then left to get some food to restock my destroyed supplies.

I climbed into bed and rested for a moment. The one fact that I hadn't told the doctor concerned me greatly. In the midst of that pain, I'd had a moment of clarity: a memory of my attacker picking me up and carrying me while another man opened a gate. The agent interviewing me was the magus who opened that gate.

CHAPTER
EIGHTEEN

Z ah'rak, I should lead," said Shira. "I'm the only one who knows the way."

I wanted to argue but knew she was right. At least I could see easily over her head. "Okay."

We walked a few strides down the stairs, then Shira said, "Pull the door shut and lock it so no one can come up behind us."

From inside, the trapdoor appeared to be in far better condition and more than adequately sealed the passage. As the door closed we were plunged into darkness. I closed my eyes and reached out with my mind. My power of Sight meant I didn't need visible light in order to see. I looked back and saw Ragnar activate the night vision visor on his helmet, but Raquel didn't.

Shira activated her staff and a small amount of light surrounded us. "Is that enough for everyone?"

"Shira, douse the staff," said Raquel. "You don't need it to see."

"What do you mean?" she asked.

"Douse the staff and I will show you," Raquel replied.

Shira put out the staff and said, "I can't see anything." There wasn't even the slightest tremor in her voice. I would have been nervous in her position, totally blind in a crypt with the undead wandering around. I supposed that she might have become used to it over the years she had lived here.

Raquel slipped by me and knelt before Shira. "Shira, close your eyes and relax." Raquel reached out and took Shira's hand. "You can feel me and you can hear me. You know I'm right here. Focus on my voice. Push all other thoughts out of your mind. Can you feel my breath? Can you smell me?"

"I know you're there, but ... " she began.

"No 'buts'. Remember, magic works through willpower and belief. Put aside your doubts and concentrate on my voice." Raquel quietly and slowly coaxed Shira to use the power of Sight that all Sac'a'rith possessed.

"Wow," whispered Shira. "The whole tunnel is in black and white except for us."

"Yes," said Raquel. "You are seeing by the light of the weave. The weave is everywhere, so you can always see. Even if your eyes were destroyed, you wouldn't be blind.

"Things look different because of the way the light works. The stronger connection to the weave an object has, the brighter it will be. Rocks have no real connection, so they are indistinct and only appear because they absorb the light. Magi, like us, have a strong connection, so we should appear sharp and in full color. Mundanes will be someplace in-between and tend to look grey and fuzzy."

"So that's why I can see the dead. It's because they're still connected to the weave," I said.

"You can't see the dead. At least, they'd look no more distinct than these rocks," said Raquel. "I understand the confusion, and it's due to the unfortunate use of the term 'undead'. When a person or creature dies, they're dead. They don't come back as ghosts or zombies. Zombies are, as you know, just animated corpses, and are not people raised from the dead. Wraiths and other spirits were always spirits and never people."

"That doesn't make sense," I said. "What about that spirit we met on Nemesis, Nanny? Surely she was someone's grandmother once?"

"Nanny?" asked Raquel.

Shira giggled. "Nanny is a dinjini who serves on the Nemesis."

"A dinjini? Serving wizards?" asked Raquel. "How can this be?"

"Oh, she's the sweetest thing. Really, you'd love her," said Shira.

"Sweet?" asked Raquel. "Dinjinis are natives of the spirit realm, very powerful and extremely dangerous!"

"Not her," I said. "They call her Nanny and she takes care of the crew, pretty much like a grandmother would."

"Seriously, Raquel, you'd have to meet her to understand." Shira turned to me. "But she was never a person like you and I. Raquel is right; what we call 'undead' are really just animated corpses or natives of the Spirit Realm, for the most part at least."

I wondered if the others on Nemesis understood that. They seemed to love Nanny and saw her as a person. "Let's keep moving," I said, and Shira led us deeper into the catacombs. I wondered what she'd meant by her comment, 'for the most part', but Raquel spoke up before I could ask.

"So much has changed," said Raquel. "A grandmaster who is kind and forgiving, a wizard nation state, a master level spiritualist and now dinjinis serving among wizards. I'm not sure I can keep up with all of this."

"Tell me about it," said Ragnar.

Raquel chuckled. "I'm sure you have a lot to adjust to also."

"How far will we have to walk?" I asked.

"From this entrance, it'll be a good couple of hours," said Shira. "About halfway there we will probably start encountering the guards that my former master installed down here."

"Guards?" queried Ragnar.

"They never bothered me on my trips down here, but things are different now so we'll just have to see how it goes," she said.

We walked in silence for a while and then Ragnar asked, "It's the binding, isn't it?"

"What?" I asked.

"Yes," said Raquel.

"Raquel, how do you know?" asked Ragnar.

"What are we talking about?" I asked again.

Raquel sighed. "Let's stop here a moment. It would be good for everyone to hear this."

"Then go ahead and break out some rations and water," I said. If we were going to stop anyway, we might as well make good use of the time.

Once we were settled with our meals she continued. "In Korshalemia, things are very different to the way they are here. Their wizard's council rules the entire known realm and is much closer to a religious order than what we have. Here Grandmaster Vydor has set up the wizards as more of a nation state, contrary to what the Korshalemian wizards tried to create and much to their disapproval.

"In Korshalemia, the wizards are constantly watching for magi to be born and make a concerted effort to make sure that no magus is allowed to reach adulthood without first going through the binding. Kings and other rulers live in constant fear of the Wizard's Council, so they cooperate fully.

"Once magi become of age, they're sent to the wizards for evaluation. If it's determined that they are likely to become sorcerers, their powers are bound by extremely invasive psychic means, and they are forbidden under penalty of death ever to practice magic. Most of these magi end up trying to use their powers in defiance of the ban and are usually killed, unless they join the sorcerers.

"If they pass the test and may use their abilities, then certain power lines are checked for. For example, spiritualism is a forbidden art. If it's determined that theirs is one of those forbidden lines, they are likewise bound and ordered never to attempt to use it." She paused there to take a drink of water.

"What does this have to do with us?" I asked.

"Everything!" she said and paused for a moment before continuing. "As we rebuild the Sac'a'rith, we need to know the mistakes that were made before us so we can learn from them. The Korshalemian wizards are a perfect example of a good idea executed poorly."

"But why this whole ruse with the basic powers, and how do you know all this?" asked Ragnar.

"The basic powers are among the forbidden arts in Korshalemia. They're seen as profane and are believed to be a gateway to the darker arts. At this stage, the vast majority of magi don't even know anymore that the powers exist. It's primarily magi of elite level who know about them and are aware they've been blocked.

"One such elite wizard is Mantis, the primary benefactor who set up the Wizard's Council for this realm. He's well known for dissenting from some of the practices of the Wizard's Council in Korshalemia, and one of the practices he dislikes most is the binding ceremony, so he worked to make sure it wouldn't be repeated here.

"When the Wizard's Council discovered that, they worried about dissension in their own ranks, so they made up the story that basic powers differed between wizards. Grandmaster Vydor had no reason not to believe them and so never questioned it until much later.

"Not wanting to court disaster by sending over other wizards like Mantis, from then on the Korshalemian Wizard's Council carefully chose only the most loyal magi to their cause to send here, and instructed them to make sure the magi of this realm were brought up properly."

"And by 'properly' you mean 'loyal to them and their ways'?" I asked.

"Exactly," she said. "Grandmaster Vydor is no fool and realized what was happening, so he countered that plan by sending back their instructors as quickly as he could train up people to replace them, but in the end it was Mathorn who was first to fully reveal what was going on."

"Who is Mathorn?" asked Shira.

"Heir to the seat of Grandmaster in Korshalemia," said Ragnar quietly.

"Yes, he *was*." She paused there and took a bite of food. "Mathorn used his position and influence to take over the magi assignments to this realm. He gathered elite magi who weren't so tightly bound to Korshalem and convinced them to serve here in our realm. When most of them learned how differently things were being done here, and that things like the binding ceremony were not being performed, they chose to move here permanently. With their help, Grandmaster Vydor was moved into a stronger position where Korshalem couldn't simply force his hand. As for how I know all this, Mathorn told us of Korshalem's plans and through him we learned of the binding and other more despicable practices which they tried to hide from us."

Ragnar spat and said something in a language I didn't recognize. "Such deception and scheming hardly seems proper for a wizard."

"I agree, but the unfortunate truth is that when people in any realm are put into a position of power they tend to want to protect that position, often at any cost," said Raquel.

"What's to stop the same from happening here?" I asked.

"Ultimately, only those who keep the rulers in check; but the master wizards we currently have are all good people. I think we'll be fine, at least for the time being."

"How can we enable Ragnar to use basic powers again?" asked Shira.

"I will contact the Wizard's Council to find out when we're back in deep space," she said. "I'm sure it can be done, but it's beyond my abilities."

"Ragnar, are you okay?" I asked. He had a faraway look in his eyes.

"Yeah," he said. "It's just a lot to take in. There were hints about this kind of thing, and a general distrust of the Wizard's Council, but I never had any real facts before."

"Then let's get going again." I thought it best to give him time to process what he'd just learned. "I don't know what those sorcerers we killed were doing here, but I'd guess they had a good reason and more of them will probably come along at some point."

CHAPTER
NINETEEN

Walking in silence for a while, I was considering asking Raquel about the Wizard Kingdom when Shira sent, *"Hold!"*

We all froze and I asked, *"What's wrong?"*

"Zah'rak, around the next turn there should be a door and the last time I was here it was guarded by skeletal knights," she sent.

"How many?" I asked.

"At least a half-dozen, maybe. I don't really know. It wasn't important until now," she sent.

"Even if it's a dozen, Zah'rak and I should have no problem handling them," said Raquel.

"I agree, but watch our backs in case more arrive," I said. Shira and Ragnar nodded in agreement and fell back a few strides behind us. *"Ready?"*

Raquel silently drew her swords and nodded.

I drew mine and eased up to the corner to discreetly look around. *"I see ten of them standing in a tight formation in front of a closed stone door."*

"Rush on three?" asked Raquel.

"Sure," I sent and then counted down from three. On one I charged around the corner and barreled full speed into the middle of their number. The two out in front attempted to stop me, but lacked the mass to do anything but be thrown clear. As I got into the center of the group I swung my tail around in a full circle, sending more of them flying. Raquel charged in behind me and expertly used the opening I had created to move into position, guarding my back.

"When you say you're going to rush a line, you really mean it!" she sent with a laugh.

I wondered what she meant by 'rush' if it wasn't what I'd done, but there was no time to find out. Several skeletons came in at once, each with a sword and shield but no armor to speak of.

"They're skilled, but physically weak. You should be able to drive right though their blocks," sent Raquel.

As the first three closed on my position, I lunged forward and swung hard at the closest of the three. He raised his shield to block the swing, but too late. My blade connected with his arm, drove through to his chest, and the brittle bones crumbed under the blow.

The second skeleton swung his sword at my exposed side, but I was ready with my off-hand sword to parry. Pivoting on my rear foot, I brought my main sword around and removed his head. The third skeleton slammed into my side with his shield, but its strength was insufficient to move my mass. I continued my spin and brought my tail around. He attempted to block my tail with his shield, but I had too much force to be stopped. My tail drove his shield into his chest and sent him flying out of the fight and into the wall, destroying most of his brittle bones.

I sheathed my swords and charged the two remaining skeletons on my side, grabbed them both and threw them into the wall. Then I spun around to see how Raquel was doing.

As I looked over she removed the head from the final skeleton. "Clear," she said.

"Clear," I confirmed. All that was left of the guards was a pile of broken bones and their weapons. I saw Raquel searching the remains, just as she'd searched the bodies of the sorcerers. I hadn't seen anyone do that before as religiously as she did. "What are you looking for?"

"Anything that might be of value to us," she said distractedly.

"What could they have?" asked Shira as she and Ragnar walked up.

"I don't know. That's why I'm checking," she replied.

"Raquel is right," said Ragnar. "It always bothered me that we don't search bodies before moving on. I never said anything before because I was worried it might be some cultural taboo, and I didn't want to offend."

"I don't follow," I said.

"The rule is simple: we don't know what we'll face ahead, so always check bodies in case there's something you'll need later," said Raquel.

I wondered what a skeleton could carry that would be of value. Then Ragnar asked, "Where did you get your swords?"

"You were there; we got them from the remains of the skeletal army that attacked – oh, I see what you're getting at," I said. "I guess you never know what you might find that could come in handy."

"Exactly," said Raquel, "but I don't see much here, so how do we open this door?"

Shira walked up to it and asked, "Ready?" When we all nodded she tapped the door three times with her staff and said a command word. The door vanished, revealing a long dark corridor. "Go through so I can close it behind us."

Once everyone was through she tapped the air three times where the door had been, uttered the same command word and it reappeared. "It's just occurred to me: this door can only be opened and closed with a sun staff. That was an odd choice for a necromancer."

"What lies ahead?" I asked as we started down the corridor.

"Two more doors like this one with about the same level of security, then another fifteen or twenty minutes' walk to the storage room door," she said.

"Why so deep?" I asked.

"He was paranoid about all kinds of things, including someone finding this storage room. He took extreme measures in everything."

"Ten skeletal nights is not very extreme," said Raquel.

She nodded. "I'm hoping the storeroom guards are long gone, or we might be gating out empty-handed as fast as we possibly can."

"Perhaps now would be a good time to tell us about them," suggested Raquel dryly.

Shira inhaled deeply and slowly exhaled a few times before answering. "Soul-Witches."

Raquel stopped in her tracks. "Are you sure?"

"Completely," she said.

"What are they?" I asked.

"A much deadlier form of spirit than anything you've faced before," said Raquel. "Shira is right; we'll probably have to beat a retreat if they're still here."

That worried me, since I'd never heard Raquel consider retreat. I didn't know what Soul-Witches were, but I was very sure I never wanted to meet anything that scared Raquel.

We continued down the corridor and through the next two doors, easily pushing through the skeletons as before.

"It's just ahead," said Shira.

As our destination came into view it was obvious something was wrong. Instead of a stone door as we'd seen at the previous locations, there was a large pile of rubble and a gaping hole. I moved ahead of Shira and slowly looked through the hole. On the other side was a vast open room with many large stone containers. "Looks empty," I said. "Ragnar, can you verify that?"

"I can try," he said and cast his divination. It seemed like ages before he finally said, "I think we're alone. There are plenty of undead wandering the halls around us, but I don't think there are any in the room ahead."

"Okay, follow me and keep a look out for trouble," I said.

We searched the room for several hours and found very little left of the large stockpile that Shira remembered. There was a small quantity of gems and precious metals scattered throughout in dark corners, which could easily have been missed when the room was full.

"Is there enough here?" asked Ragnar.

"Enough to upgrade all our armor, but not enough to complete the order," I said.

"The sorcerers we killed must have been here cleaning out this room. There are traces of power everywhere. It must have been an incredible fight. Apparently the sorcerers came in a different way since the corridor we used was still guarded," said Ragnar.

"We came in what I like to think of as the back door. The main passage was shorter, but better guarded the last time I was here," said Shira.

Ragnar looked around at the vast empty room and exhaled slowly. "These materials are worth a lot back in Korshalemia. A stockpile of this size could fund a massive army for an entire war."

"Just how tough are these Soul Witches?" I asked.

"It would have been too much for one sorcerer, but if a group of necromancers fought together they could have handled it," said Raquel. "In time, with training and maturity, our little group could handle a few Soul-Witches; that time has not yet come."

"Do we gather what we've found and gate back to the Night Wisp?" asked Ragnar.

"Yeah," I said. "And come up with a new plan."

CHAPTER
TWENTY

"Welcome back," said Marcus as I entered our robotics repair shop.
"It's good to be back at work," I said. It had been a week since my fight with the Resden agent, and the doctors had finally relented and let me return to light duties.

My section of the shop was exactly as I'd left it, which was comforting. I had been worried that someone might have ransacked it also. I pulled up my repair queue to start prioritizing my work for the day. Marcus asked, "Is this room clean?"

"What do you mean?" I replied.

"Can we talk?" he asked.

I sighed. If it wasn't, he had just implicated himself. I had taken to carrying my old gear again, as it had become apparent that someone was watching me; presumably that meant that someone was still interested in making sure I stayed under control. I didn't know whom I had upset to draw this attention, but for now I had to play their game. When I found a way off the Paradise, then I could disappear again.

"Clear. We can talk," I said after scanning the room.

"My room was ransacked last night. I'm starting to become as paranoid as you are," he said.

"I'm sorry, man," I said. "Look, there's no reason for you to take the fall with me. I'll slip off the ship at the first opportunity."

"No," said Marcus.

"No?" I queried.

"Like it or not, I'm in this with you now. Even if you bail out, I'll still be under scrutiny because of our friendship," he said.

I stared at him for a moment, unsure what to say. I knew he was right. He was in too deep now; the fact that they'd ransacked his room made that clear. Yet there still had to be a means of escape without taking him down with me. I felt bad. He had only been trying to help me.

"Look, I'm here for you regardless of what happens," he said. "Now, listen. I couldn't sleep after seeing my room like that so I did some research and I think we need to get off the ship."

"Why do you say that?" I asked.

"I found orders for a security team to be installed at the next port," he said.

"But we already have one," I replied.

"Exactly," he said. "A whole new team will be installed. The current team, who happen to think very favorably of us, will be transferred to a new cruise liner."

"Are you sure?" I asked.

"Yes," he said. "I confirmed it this morning."

"How long until we reach port?" I normally paid no attention to the docking and sailing because I never left the ship. My goal had been to make it to the Phineary region without being spotted en route, a goal that I'd obviously failed to achieve.

"In a week we'll make our final jump. After that it'll be a few days to port," he said.

"These new forces - are they contractors?" I asked.

"No, Resden regulars," he replied.

That was both unusual and troubling. "So my grand plan to restart life in Phineary seems unlikely to happen."

"Yeah, it's starting to look that way," he said. "What are we going to do?"

"I'm not sure. If I bail out, they might come after you in order to get at me." I had once again fallen into trouble without intending to and dragged another innocent down with me. I didn't understand why things like this kept happening to me and to those around me. It was as if I were cursed, or brought bad fortune wherever I went.

"Then we both go," he said.

"But if you do, you'll be blacklisted for abandoning your post. You'll never work again," I said.

"No, I won't. The captain won't blacklist either of us."

"How can you be sure of that?" I asked.

"Because I know my father pretty well," he said with a grin.

"Your father is the captain?" I asked. "How come you never told me that before?"

"Because I'm not qualified for this position," he said. "All my certificates are fake. I only got this job because of him."

"You seem to know your way around the shop fairly well," I said.

"Well, I've been at this post a year now and have been training myself. When you came on board, I made sure you were assigned all the hard jobs."

I shook my head in disbelief. "I think you're understating your skill. If the captain is your father, can't he help us?"

He shook his head. "Against Resden? It would be suicide for him to mix himself up in this. I would only let him help if there was no way to trace it back to him."

"So we slip off and he covers our tracks," I said.

"Yeah," he said. "Then we get jobs on a different cruise line, one not friendly to Resden. You can list me as your apprentice and we just slip away from this mess."

"Until they come for me again," I said quietly, not meaning to speak aloud.

"What?" he asked.

I realized then that what I'd preached to Crivreen was right: you can never go back. I made a decision. I'd return to the Night Wisp and take up Raquel's offer. At least there I was with warriors who were looking for trouble, instead of dragging down random civilians along with me. I came to the conclusion that I wasn't destined to live in peace.

"Okay, you have a choice to make. I'm going to have to bail off this ship, maybe even before the next port. You can stay on board, report me as AWOL and behave as if you're completely loyal to Resden. If you do that, you might be able to escape blame and continue on with this cushy assignment you have.

"Your other option is to come with me, in which case Resden will no doubt mark you as a criminal, and you will probably spend the rest of your life on the run from them."

"Where are you going to go?" he asked.

"I have some friends that I can take refuge with," I said. "I'll be fine, but I can't promise that you will be. I can't even offer you shelter with them without checking, but I'm willing to ask."

"You'll need my help to get off this ship, and I'm not about to turn traitor and start licking the heels of Resden agents."

"What did you have in mind?" I asked.

"I have a small ship in the hangar," he said. "After the next jump, we launch it to do a routine check of the exterior robotics and never return."

"Okay." I had to admit his spacecraft would make things much easier. My best plan had been to sneak out at the next station. I was sure I could get off the ship, but after that I'd be stranded on a station where security would be looking for me. Using his ship meant I'd have a chance of escaping the sector without being spotted. "If you're sure you want to throw away all of this, for good."

"Look, I'm in this with you now, wherever it leads," he replied.

"Then we need to move our gear onto your ship as unobtrusively as possible before the jump," I said.

"I'll take care of that," he said. "You're on light duty, so it wouldn't be good for you to be spotted carrying equipment around."

"I really only need the things behind that panel in my quarters," I said. "Everything that I purchased after coming on board can be abandoned."

"Just that one big bag?" he said. "That'll be easy. I can stash that in an empty toolbox and roll it down there in plain sight."

"Great," I said. "But remember, the fewer people that see you loading the ship, the better."

"What about your therapy?" he asked.

"It's only exercises at this point. I don't really need medical care anymore. I'm not sure why they still have me on restricted duty."

"No one on board really likes Resden. Perhaps the medics are trying to frustrate their investigation?" he suggested.

"Hopefully," I said with a smile. "Then our plan is to lie low until the next jump and start moving supplies to your ship. I'll look over the local jump routes and see what our options are."

"Okay. Meanwhile, I have to get down to Section Thirteen again," he said.

"Now what?" I asked.

"The unit there that cleans the oxygen ducts is stuck. Again."

I merely shook my head. The path-finding algorithms on that model seemed to be especially bad, but it was the only model we had that could fit in the smaller ducts. Before this mess happened, I had planned to try and design a better robot. I was pretty sure I could modify the control unit from a more advanced model to work in that small frame, but now I would never know.

The rest of the week passed quietly and Marcus managed to get everything on board his craft, seemingly without raising any suspicion. When the morning came for our departure, I made one last sweep through my quarters to make sure I hadn't missed anything. Before stepping out of my room, I made sure to hide myself from the surveillance systems; anyone watching them wouldn't know I had left my room until it was too late.

Doing my best not to draw attention to myself, I made my way down to the docking arm where Marcus kept his ship and slipped on board. Marcus followed soon after.

"Ready?" he asked.

"Are you sure you want to do this? There's no going back," I said.

"Trust me, it's already much too late for that," he said and dropped into the pilot's station.

The way he said that made me suspicious; I was sure he'd done something, but being anxious to get underway I didn't question him. Taking my place in the copilot's chair, I said, "Launch when ready."

CHAPTER TWENTY-ONE

Shira was in hydroponics and the rest of us were on the bridge when the comm. beeped, indicating an incoming secure recorded message from the Phareon government. Before accepting the call, I checked my accounts and saw that our Phareon controller had finally paid for the last two contracts. "This could be serious," I said.

"You want me to play it on the big screen?" asked Crivreen.

"Yeah," I said.

A moment later the commander's face appeared on the screen. "Zah'rak, for your next assignment, proceed to MA-71. It's a secret testing facility, quite some distance from your last reported location. We've lost all contact with them and also with the team we sent to investigate. We urgently need your team to find out what's going on." Following that was a data stream with the coordinates and other information.

"This sounds familiar," I said, after the message had ended. "Send a reply. Tell him we're quite far away from that station and need to resupply first," I said. "There appears to be a military outpost not too far from us.

We'll stop there and get what we need, and then head to MA-71. If this is time-critical, we can join up with a larger fleet there to cut the travel time."

I knew he wouldn't like the idea of arming us, and I could obtain weapons from some of Narcion's former contacts, but that would take time and money; I preferred to make him pay for it all.

"Have we heard back from the Wizard Kingdom about Ragnar?" I asked. Raquel had sent a message a week ago when we left Siden.

"Let me check," she said and turned to her comm. station. "Yes; they want to send Mathorn out to talk with us."

"Fine. Crivreen, lay in a course and get us underway. Raquel, where could Mathorn meet us?" I asked.

"He can weavewalk to wherever we are, if Shira or I place a marker for him to home in on," said Raquel.

"A marker? Like Shira uses to gate?" I queried.

"Exactly," said Raquel.

"Okay. Arrange a time for him to come out and let's get Ragnar fixed," I said.

"You make it sound like I'm broken," said Ragnar.

"You want to be fixed, don't you?" I asked.

"I'm not sure yet," he said. "But I would like to hear what Master Mathorn has to say."

"Don't you want to be able to use all your powers?" I asked. The thought of not having full use of my faculties was something I couldn't entertain, and yet he seemed to be satisfied to remain in that condition.

"Because I don't know what that would be like," he said. "Besides, I want to hear this story directly from the source before I can accept it."

"We have two days before we can reach a jump point," said Crivreen. "Why don't we invite him for dinner tonight?"

"Raquel, what do you think?" I asked.

"It will take at least three days for the message to be relayed across the civilian network to Hospital Station, then for up to a day it will wait in the queue to be relayed through the gate to the Wizard Kingdom. That means six to eight days for a round trip message," she said.

I'd become so used to dealing only with the local government over their relay network that I'd forgotten that the Wizard Kingdom was over one hundred thousand light years from here. In theory a message could be sent to arrive right away, but the amount of power needed to send a message over that distance was well beyond anything we had yet invented.

Sending a massless message through jump space took a tremendous amount of energy, to compensate for the lack of gravity. Our little cruiser couldn't generate enough power to send a message directly from here to Hospital Station, so it had to be relayed across the civilian network. CivNet, as it was called, was basically a set of agreements between all commercial and many private spaceships that said if they received a message, their computers would automatically repeat it and send it as far along towards its destination as they could. Through a chain of such relays you could eventually get a message anywhere; it just took time, often a lot of time.

In the more populated regions, the Phareon government deployed a permanent network of jump relay stations that were capable of sending messages much faster, allowing for real-time and near real-time communications throughout most of its coverage area. We were far from that network, and had to rely on CivNet to slowly guide the message back to Hospital Station.

I was surprised to hear that there was a gate on the hospital station, but that at least explained how Raquel had traveled to the Wizard Kingdom and back in the space of a few months. "Okay, then set a date for dinner ten days from now."

"Sure," she said and turned back to the comm.

"Shira, if another wizard marks our ship for gating, can you remove it like your former master did?" I asked.

"Yes. There are a few on board; Raquel, Narcion, and Spectra have placed them," she replied. *"I should remove Narcion's at some point."*

"*I guess Spectra placed one so that she can pick up her delivery?*" I asked.

"*That was my assumption. Why do you ask?*" she sent.

"*We might be entertaining a wizard from the Kingdom to dinner in a couple of weeks. If he leaves a marker behind, I want it removed,*" I sent.

"*Who?*" she asked.

"*Mathorn. He's coming to fix Ragnar,*" I sent.

"*A wizard of his level could easily hide a marker from me, but I can check when he leaves,*" she sent.

"*That's a risk we'll just have to take. Raquel says you can put up a marker for him to weavewalk to?*" I asked.

"*Yes. Just let me know when,*" she sent.

"*Ragnar, Crivreen, Shira,*" I sent to get everyone's attention privately. "*Sooner or later we have to give Raquel an answer. Do you three have an opinion?*"

"*Zah'rak, I think there's wisdom in choosing a nation to side with. We've been just stalling, trying to figure out what to do next, since Narcion's death,*" sent Ragnar.

"*I tend to agree and I'd much rather side with the Wizard Kingdom than Phareon,*" sent Crivreen.

"*Shira?*" I asked.

"*Well, whatever you think best,,*" she sent. "*Is what she told us true? Is she our sister?*" asked Shira.

"*She seems to believe so,*" I said.

"*Then it seems to be the right thing to do, to stick with family – doesn't it?*"

"*Zah'rak,*" sent Ragnar. "*What do you think?*"

"*I don't know,*" I replied. "*I'd got used to it just being us.*"

"*But it never really is just us,*" sent Ragnar. "*Currently we are working for the Phareon government. As Crivreen pointed out, that's our other option. Sure, we could offer our services to Resden, or one of the other consortiums, but in the end we'd always be working for someone.*"

"*I suppose so,*" I sent. He was right, but I wasn't quite prepared to admit it. I liked our little squad. It felt safe. It was my family and my world. Raquel represented an upheaval of that world and I wasn't sure I was ready for that, but then I might never be.

"Crivreen, see if we have any good food left for that dinner," I said. We were too far from any station to pick up supplies en route before Mathorn arrived, so we'd have to make do with whatever we had on board.

He replied, "*Now* you think of it." Chuckling, he went down to the mess hall.

"*Shira, do we have any fresh vegetables to serve our guest?*" I sent.

"*Yes; not a big selection, but some of the faster-growing ones are ready,*" she sent back.

"*Great, let Crivreen know what we can spare for Mathorn's dinner,*" I sent.

Raquel leaned back in her chair and sighed. "I should tell you that proper etiquette requires you to refer to him as 'Master Mathorn'. That's how lower-level magi refer to those at a higher level. It's also how outsiders are expected to address wizards of importance, such as himself."

"I take it you're his peer, then?" asked Ragnar.

"Yes," she replied and went on to tell us about the structure of the government and ranks in the Wizard Kingdom.

CHAPTER
TWENTY-TWO

When the day came for Master Mathorn to visit, Shira placed a marker in our mess hall which he used to weavewalk to the Night Wisp.

On his arrival, I walked forward and extended my hand in greeting. "Welcome aboard the Night Wisp, Master Mathorn."

"Thank you, Zah'rak," he replied and grasped my forearm in the way Narcion used to. Narcion had called it a traditional warrior's grasp; it signified respect and honor between two fighting men. "Raquel has told me much about you all. I'm honored to finally meet you."

He was elderly and resembled the storybook version of a wizard more than any of us did. He wore deep purple flowing robes covered in strange symbols. A number of rings glowed on each hand, and he wore a pair in each ear. Around his neck was a chain with a large pendant. He had a full head of grey hair and a closely-cropped beard.

One of the skills which I had taught myself from the data Master Spectra had given us was an enchanter's ability to detect enchanted items. Using that skill, I observed that everything he was wearing was enchanted with very powerful magic, far more power than I'd ever seen attached to any item. I wondered whether I could make jewelry like that, or if my power was limited to clothing.

Ragnar came forward, bowed deeply, and said, "Master, I'm grateful that you came all the way out here just for me. If it's not an imposition, I would like you to explain to me about the basic powers."

"I'd be happy to tell you, Ragnar. I wish I could have told you at your binding. As I recall, you were quite excited that day. You have an older brother, I think? How is he?" he asked.

"Yes. He is, or at least was, Keeper of the Runes of Therin now. When last we were together he was doing well, but I've heard no news since coming here," said Ragnar.

"What a great honor! You must be proud!" said Master Mathorn.

"Aye, for him I am, but it meant I'd always be second string. That is, until I met Zah'rak and seized a new life."

Master Mathorn smiled and nodded at that comment. He might have said more, but Crivreen ushered everyone to the table to eat. When we were settled, Master Mathorn recounted essentially the same story that Raquel had told us. It seemed that the wizards of Ragnar's homeworld were a devious and controlling bunch. I wondered what that meant for the future here. Would our Wizard's Council turn out to be the same in the long run?

"Now, it's vital that none of you shares this information with anyone right now," he said. "The relationship between our realms is in dire straits. Grandmaster Vydor is doing all he can to save it, or at least to avoid the war that many of us are predicting."

"What does this story about the basic powers have to do with that?" I asked.

Master Mathorn took a deep drink. He continued, "There are many apprentice and journeymen wizards here who are still loyal to Grandmaster Korshalem. I believe that if they find out what I have just recounted. Once word of the deception spreads through the ranks of the Korshalemian wizards there will be an irreparable loss of trust, and that could potentially spark a civil war. I fear that the balance of power in Korshalemia is far too delicate to survive, and even if it does it would permanently destroy any goodwill that remains between the realms."

"What about Shea?" asked Ragnar.

"Shea knows, but she agrees with my assessment so she will say nothing as yet," he said. "In fact, she has asked us not to remove her blocks so that there is no danger of her accidently tipping people off."

"That makes sense, since she is constantly among the other wizards and I assume is well known," said Ragnar.

"Very much so," said Master Mathorn.

"So what does this all mean for Ragnar?" I asked.

"I can remove the power blocks," said Master Mathorn. "But I'd prefer to do that after he joins the Wizard Kingdom and we can update his files to list him as a native of this realm. That way no one will be suspicious if they happen to see him using the basic powers."

"Is that a condition or a preference?" Ragnar asked.

He smiled. "I'm not here to bribe anyone. The choice remains yours whether to accept our offer of citizenship or not."

"I'm being a fool, aren't I?" I sent privately to Shira, Crivreen and Ragnar.

"What do you mean?" asked Ragnar.

"I should accept the offer," I sent.

"That would be my advice," replied Ragnar.

"Master Mathorn, Raquel, our current commitment to the Phareon government might constitute an obstacle to our joining you," I said. "How can we work that out?"

"In truth, it might help to heal our relationship with them," said Master Mathorn. He told us how the Wizard Kingdom and the Phareon government had almost gone to war over Hospital Station just a couple of months previously. Phareon had apparently sent a fleet out to claim it, and Grandmaster Vydor had stopped them.

"Do you mean that the hospital station was wizard property all this time?" I asked. That at least explained why there was a gate there.

"Yes, and now the Wizard Kingdom's flag is flying over it openly," said Master Mathorn.

"Zah'rak," said Raquel. "I would suggest that we finish the current mission for the Phareon government and then tell them of the new arrangement. I suspect that the Wizard Kingdom will be very interested in the outcome of that mission. We can work out an arrangement with them after the mission."

"Seems reasonable," I said. "But what about Master Spectra's order?"

"Raquel told me about the order and your trip to Siden," said Master Mathorn. "I will be stopping there on my way out. I don't like the fact that the sorcerers got their hands on that stockpile, and I want to know what they are up to. In the meantime, I can have a sufficient quantity of gold and diamonds delivered to Hospital Station for you to pick up when you're ready. It was wise of Spectra to enlist you to make armor, and I suspect that you will have a permanent standing order to make armor for us as long as you are willing to make it. Enchanters seem to be much less common in this realm than in Korshalemia. This means we're sorely in need of all kinds of enchanted supplies, especially since the collapse of trade between the realms."

We talked a little while longer, until he was ready to take Ragnar aside to remove the blocks. He wanted to spend some time alone with Ragnar to make sure he understood the fundamentals of using the basic powers, and I was sure that Ragnar had more questions for him.

Crivreen left to answer a call on our comm system and Shira went back to her gardens, leaving me alone with Raquel.

"Zah'rak," sent Raquel privately, "everyone here looks to you for leadership – so the decision is more yours than theirs, in reality. They'll follow your lead, and I suspect you're the only one holding out."

"Yeah," I agreed.

"Look, I haven't been forthcoming about one matter," she sent. "Grand-

master Vydor has given me responsibility for representing the Wizard King-dom out here. That means I'll have to handle treaties, diplomacy and all kinds of government-related tasks."

"What are you getting at?" I asked.

"I can't do that and recreate the Sac'a'rith as well. I need you to lead that effort. I'll advise, train and offer what help I can, but it'll be up to you. Shira and any others we may find will look to you for leadership," she sent.

"What about Ragnar and Crivreen?" I asked.

"You know my opinion on admitting those who were not born into the order," she sent.

"If you're truly putting me in charge, then that's my decision to make, isn't it?" I sent.

"Zah'rak," she said. "My duties to Grandmaster Vydor have to take prece-dence now, but my real goal is to see the Sac'a'rith rise back up. I can see now that you're the best hope for that. Narcion saw it, and I'm beginning to see why. You will have to define the new era of our people."

I didn't know what to make of that. Until then, I was sure she intended to keep complete control over everything. I had to admit that was part of my problem with this agreement; I didn't want to give up control of my team.

I didn't have much time to think about that before Crivreen came rushing in.

"Zah'rak, Felix is in trouble!" he exclaimed.

"What? What happened?" I asked.

"I don't know. I just got a message from him that says, 'I guess you were right: you never can go back,' and it contains a coded location," he said.

"And by that you know he's in trouble?" asked Raquel.

"Yes!" he exclaimed. "He's a loner. Only serious trouble would lead him to send a message like that."

"How far is he from here?" I asked.

"Two jumps, maybe, but we still have to clear this Emperor-forsaken gravity well before we can do anything," said Crivreen.

"Lay in a course, and see if you can find out any more," I said. He ran off without another word, presumably back to the bridge. "Is that offer still open to Felix?"

Raquel smiled. "I suspect he could be a sorcerer for a decade and Grandmaster Vydor would pardon him and offer him another chance."

"You don't approve?"

"It's not that," she said. "Ten thousand years ago the wizards here were a military order, and discipline was fast and effective. I'm just having a hard time adjusting to this new reality."

"We all are," said Master Mathorn as he walked back in alone.

"Ragnar," I sent, *"are you okay?"*

"I'm fine. I just have some exercises to work on," he sent.

"Crivreen talks about the Wizard Kingdom in such idealistic terms, but the way you two talk about the other wizards belies that," I said.

"People are people," said Master Mathorn. "Wherever you go, that will always be true. Grandmaster Vydor and his masters are working hard to live up to the ideal, but they're still just people."

"Yet you gave up everything to follow them?" I said.

"Yes - because they are trying, where others have given up," he said. "Now, if you don't mind, I'd like to talk to Shira about that stockpile the sorcerers took. We hadn't heard of any movement from them out this way."

"Sure. She's over in hydroponics; right this way," I said and led him there.

When we arrived, Shira was tending the small section she had created to grow food. It was now pretty barren since we'd eaten a lot of it at dinner, but I knew she would get us more soon enough. Even if it was just vegetables, it was a real treat to have fresh food for a change.

CHAPTER
TWENTY-THREE

I had just sent a coded message to Crivreen when they finally found us. Blaster fire erupted all around our position, destroying our makeshift shelter and comm. station. Debris flew everywhere and the roof caved in right in front of us. There were too much smoke and dust in the air to be able to guess where anything was.

"Now what, Purwryn?" Marcus attempted to pile debris quickly between us and the direction the blasts seemed to be coming from.

"Run!" It'd been over a month since we had made our escape from the Paradise. The Resden agents were hunting us far more aggressively than either of us had guessed they would. I'd originally planned to put Marcus on a Phareon cruise liner and head off alone, but we never got that chance; they dispatched fighters almost immediately and we had been on the run ever since. It had been one close call after another, but this was shaping up to be the closest yet.

Marcus returned fire with his rifle, firing blindly through the smoke. "Obviously, but to where?"

"Anywhere but here!" I threw one of the sonic grenades I'd taken from a Resden corpse and ran deeper into the woods. We were on a small, forested planet where our ship had crashed after losing a battle with a Resden fast cruiser. I had hoped that Resden would have assumed we'd died in the crash, but that wasn't the case; they sent a shuttle down with a landing party. I thought we had lost them, but they found us again. They must have picked up my outgoing transmission.

Marcus ran behind me as the grenade detonated, sending a shockwave through what I hoped was Resden's position. "We should circle around and steal their ship."

"You're assuming it'll be unguarded and unlocked," I said.

"Locks won't be a problem. Guards, maybe," he said.

We were trapped on the planet, and without any cloaking tech we really had no place to hide. "A direct frontal assault would be suicide if there are any guards. We'd be caught between those guarding the ship and the ones following us."

"Right, so we have to draw them as far away as possible and then sneak back around them," he said.

A tree to my left exploded, throwing shrapnel everywhere. "Leading them doesn't seem to be a problem, but how are we going to lose them?"

Before he could answer we had to dive for cover, as Resden fired on our position. The ground and trees around us were shaking from the pounding. Marcus got into position and returned fire, shooting mostly wild but as fast as he could, forcing them to seek cover. He was much tougher than I had guessed while serving with him on the Paradise. I suspected he had more experience of this kind of thing than he'd let on; certainly having him along had saved my hide more than once.

I shouldered my rifle and drew a pair of blasters. "I have an idea. You slip away while I keep them pinned down. We'll meet back up at their ship."

"But how are you going to get away?" he asked.

"Don't worry about that. You just get that ship unlocked and ready to fly, or we both die here."

He nodded. "Good luck." He rolled over onto his belly and slipped away with unusual skill and agility, especially considering we were under fire. He was totally calm throughout this battle, while I could feel my heart racing at many times its normal rate. Sweat poured down my face, pushing dirt and grime into my eyes, but I didn't need much in the way of accuracy for this plan.

I kept my blasters firing as fast as I could. Resden kept their heads down. They knew as well as I that firing at this rate would overheat my weapons and soon leave me defenseless. All they had to do was wait me out: that's what I wanted them to think, and it was exactly what they were doing.

The guns got warm in my hands and I knew I'd have to stop shooting soon or risk damaging the weapons. I'd wanted to keep them from seeing that I was alone for long enough to give Marcus a head start.

Resden's position was well shielded from the angle I was shooting at, and if I stood to run they would cut me down. My own position was not nearly so well protected. I suspected it was only a matter of time before they broke through. I had done my best to avoid using any magic since leaving the Night Wisp, but there was no way to escape this otherwise. It was time to expand my combat options.

I teleported just behind their position. "Surprise!"

They turned to bring their guns to bear, but it was too late. I quickly finished them off and holstered my pistols, now dangerously hot.

There was a noise behind me, and before I could turn a blast hit my leg and sent me tumbling. I rolled over and saw another agent climbing out from his cover.

"Surprise!" he said with a smirk clearly visible through his visor. He had been hiding a little distance away from the group I had finished off behind a small hill. In his hands was a high-powered rifle and I was sure a direct hit from it would overwhelm what was left of my armor.

At this range I knew I didn't have time to draw my guns so I teleported again, this time off to the left. Predictably he turned and looked behind him as I leaned against a tree and drew my blasters, only to find out they had finally overheated and had shut themselves down.

Forcing myself to focus through the pain in my leg, I cast a mage bolt which slammed into his body, throwing him to the ground. Before he could recover, I unslung my rifle and finished him.

I couldn't see any other threats in the area, so I took a moment to check my leg. The armor had absorbed most of the blast, but it didn't look like it could sustain another hit. My leg was badly bruised, but nothing was broken. The armor Zah'rak had made for me would repair itself with time, as would my leg, albeit a lot slower.

"Focus. You have to get to the ship," I said to myself through gritted teeth. I broke a branch off of a tree to form a makeshift crutch and started hobbling back towards the ship. I didn't know if there were any others around, but I suspected … no, hoped that the rest were back at the ship.

As I approached the location, Marcus signaled me from a small shelter he'd found. "Are you all right?"

"I will be," I said. "What's our status?"

"Six guards are all I can see, well entrenched. I haven't been able to get any closer unseen."

I risked a fast peek over and saw them behind portable blast shields with what looked like rapid-fire rifles pointed in our general direction. "Did they see you?"

"Yeah, they know I'm out here, but not where," he said.

I looked over at him. The situation was still dire. Two mundanes couldn't survive this encounter, so it was either die or trust Marcus with my secret. "Do you trust me?"

"Fine time to ask," he said. "What are you going to do?"

"I'm going to create a distraction while you run for the ship. Get airborne; just leave the airlock open and give me clear line of sight to it."

"Okay, but if there are others in the area they might start shooting," he objected.

"Then go and leave me behind," I said. "You can come back for me later when things cool down."

He hesitated and looked like he was going to argue.

"Look, we don't have time for this; just get ready," I said and rolled out from the shelter behind a nearby fallen tree. It wouldn't stand up to any fire, but it shielded me from view.

I took a deep breath and prepared myself as best I could for the pain, then got to my feet. The guards called out, and I chanted a spell to bring fire down upon them. It was the only spell I'd had the chance to learn from the spell book before I left Zah'rak. I had practiced when I could, but hadn't actually used it in combat yet.

My pain and fatigue threatened my concentration on the spell, but I pushed through it. Over their heads a thin plane of fire appeared and hung for a moment. They looked up and, before they could react, I released the spell and fire rained down on them. Their armor protected them from my relatively weak spell, but the dry leaves they were kneeling in were not protected and soon flames erupted around their entire position.

Over to my left, I saw Marcus make a dash for the ship as the guards ran in a panic. Fire quickly spread through the area and I realized then that a fire spell in a dry forest hadn't been the wisest choice. Thick black smoke billowed out as the guards' equipment started to burn. My armor warned me that poisonous gases were being released, but filters in my helmet were sufficient to clean the air.

"Come on, Marcus," I said as I watched him disappear into the flames. "Just get her in the air!"

Heat from the fire was washing over me as the flames devoured the Resden position. I could no longer tell where they were, and the fire blazed between me and the Resden cruiser, completely blocking my view of it.

I was forced by the heat to hobble away from the flames. My armor was still holding up, but sooner or later it would be overwhelmed. If Marcus didn't get airborne soon, we would both be toast.

I did my best to circle around the flames, but they were spreading faster than I could move. The smoke thickened, completely blocking my line of sight and preventing teleportation. I gave up trying to reach the cruiser and headed away from the flames. I needed to get clear of the smoke so that I could teleport ahead of the fire, which was now a raging beast with a life of its own. The flames were devouring the forest around me and my wounded leg was screaming at me to stop. It wasn't the best situation I'd ever been in, and one I hoped to avoid in the future.

A sudden whoosh of wind came from behind me and stole my balance. "Arrgh!" I screamed as I fell on my wounded leg. Above me hovered the Resden cruiser with its airlock facing me.

"I sure hope that's you," I said and teleported into the airlock. As soon as I was inside, the outer door shut and I felt the cruiser accelerate away.

After taking a moment to catch my breath, I hobbled over to the inner door and onto the craft. Bodies of Resden agents were strewn about and there were blaster burns across most of the walls. I tried to wipe the grime out of my eyes, but just made things worse. Fighting fatigue and pain, I made my way to the bridge.

I found Marcus at the controls. He looked bad, really bad. His face was severely burned, he was bleeding from numerous wounds, and one arm was dangling lifelessly at his side while the other appeared to be wired to the controls to keep him from losing his grip. I had to admire his strength; most humans would have been dead, and he was still flying a shuttle.

"Hey, take over, will you?" he asked as he fell out of the chair, ripping his arm free of its makeshift harness.

The cruiser went into a dive as he slid across the controls. As quickly as I could, I pulled him out of the way and activated the autopilot. The computer quickly righted the ship, and I set it to take us into orbit. Thankful that I didn't actually have to try and steer in my condition, I turned my attention back to Marcus.

"Stay with me," I said. "Come on, Marcus." I stopped all of the bleeding I could find, but he had already lost a lot of blood. His wounds seemed to have a large amount of metal, wires and other foreign debris embedded in them. I didn't want to risk removing them and making things worse. He would need a real doctor as soon as I could get one.

I was too weak to carry him to sick bay, so I reduced the ship's artificial gravity to a fifteenth of a G and we mostly floated there. His breathing was shallow and his pulse weak, but he wasn't dead yet. Using the little medical knowledge I had, I got him into a hyberpod and activated its critical life support.

I felt my own strength leave me and collapsed against the wall.

CHAPTER
TWENTY-FOUR

When I awoke, I was still sitting against the wall in the medical bay. Every joint in my body ached from the awkward sleeping arrangement, not helped by the previous day's fighting. Judging by the ship's chronometers I had slept most of the night, but I didn't feel rested.

I pulled myself up and cursed as pain from my leg ripped through my body, reminding me that I needed to be more careful. The gravity on the cruiser was still set low, allowing me to hobble over to Marcus' stasis tube without putting much weight on my wounded leg.

The monitoring panels reported that his vital signs were weak but stable. They also produced all kinds of messages that I didn't understand but assumed were bad news. The tube hadn't gone into full stasis for some reason, but reported itself to be in critical care mode.

"That doesn't sound good," I said to myself.

Marcus looked a little better. Most of his wounds were covered with a metallic shine which I assumed had been applied by the machine to protect the vulnerable areas. He seemed to be peaceful, so at least he wasn't in pain.

I took some painkillers from the supplies and injected them right above the nasty bruise that had developed on my leg, granting a degree of relief. A quick check of my weapons showed that the blasters had reset themselves and were ready for action. In the fog of pain and fatigue earlier, I'd never checked the ship for survivors.

Sweeping through the small craft, I went from compartment to compartment but found no one else on board. It seemed that the only fighting on board had taken place by the airlock. Looking out through the airlock window, I saw we had achieved orbit.

I stripped the bodies of anything of value and loaded them all into the airlock. Using a nearby terminal, I rolled the ship until the airlock pointed down towards the planet and jettisoned the bodies into what would become a decaying orbit. They would burn up completely on reentry to the atmosphere. It seemed the most dignified method of disposal available to me.

Taking some food from their mess hall, I headed to the bridge. The autopilot had done its job perfectly and we were in a stable orbit around the planet. I set all the sensors to passive mode and turned off all the transmitters I could find.

Marcus had apparently disabled all the security on the controls, for which I was grateful. Had he not, we could have easily been stranded in orbit or worse; the ship could have set off an automated distress call and brought in allies.

Once I had given the ship as low an electronic signature as I could manage, I checked the logs. It seemed that the ship had come after me alone, and sent no distress signal. That was good, as it meant I had some time to figure things out.

"Computer, how long to Hospital Station at best speed?" I asked.

"Two months, four days, three hours, and twenty-one minutes," responded the computer.

I cursed loudly in response. There was no way Marcus could survive that long.

I kept searching the logs, hoping for some information that would be helpful. If I knew why they were after me, I might be able to find a safe harbor to head for.

"Crivreen!" I exclaimed. They had recorded a response to the message I'd sent for help. Crivreen was smart enough to have encoded it, and they hadn't yet broken the code.

"On our way. Please respond with your situation," was the entire message.

"Hang in there, Marcus!" I exclaimed. "Help is coming!"

I dared not risk a message yet, but hopefully Crivreen would take my lack of response as a reason to hurry. He had our coordinates, so now it was just a matter of time.

With Zah'rak's connections to the Phareon government and Raquel's to the Wizard Kingdom, surely a doctor could be found quickly. All I had to do was to prevent us from being found by anyone else until they could arrive.

I spent the rest of the morning searching the ship for transmitters or identification broadcasting equipment, anything at all that would give away not only our location but also the fact that the Resden cruiser was now stolen property.

Exhausted from my efforts, and sore from sleeping all night in sick bay, I took a break for lunch with Marcus. The medical monitors still displayed codes I couldn't decipher, but based on the little first aid training I had his vital signs looked a little better.

I wondered about all the debris in his wounds. The hyberpod wasn't likely to be able to do anything about that; it would probably require a surgeon to remove it. The real mystery was where it had come from. The ship was only superficially damaged, nowhere near enough to create that kind of shrapnel. I wished that I had taken a closer look at the wounds, but I'd been barely conscious at the time.

After lunch I checked my armor to make sure it was spaceworthy, and slipped out of the craft to inspect the exterior. The weightlessness of space was a relief to my battered body. I took a moment to look back at the planet below and saw the forest fire I had sparked off raging out of control. If any Resden agents had been left alive yesterday, they wouldn't have survived that.

I spent the rest of the day working outside the ship, removing or covering up logos to destroy any signs of prior ownership. It would be obvious that this work had been done, but for the moment at least it wouldn't be labeled as a Resden ship while we were deep in Phareon space.

It was late at night when I slipped back on board the cruiser. Even with gravity set low, it still felt heavy after those hours in space. I knew that I would have to return the gravity to normal strength if I wanted to avoid muscle and bone loss, but figured one more night of lower gravity would help me get a decent sleep without causing much damage.

Before turning in, I checked on Marcus again. His vital signs were weak but stable, which I assumed was a good sign. Looking through the window at him was less comforting. Most of his wounds looked as if they had metal plating over them, including half his face. I had never seen a hyberpod do anything like that before. It seemed to be installing Cyborg implants, but that should have been well beyond its capabilities.

I considered taking him out of the hyberpod but was afraid that would kill him; better to wait for the Night Wisp. Criveen had more medical knowledge than I did and would surely be able to figure this out.

I chose the crew quarters closest to the bridge and left the door open as I slept so I could hear any alarms that sounded. Nothing disturbed my slumber, and a good sleep in a proper bed did wonders for me.

The next morning there was still no sign of anyone else in the solar system, so I risked calling the Night Wisp.

"Felix!" came Criveen's voice as his face appeared on the comm. system.

"It's good to see you," I said. I didn't activate 'visual' on the comm., as I looked nothing like I had the last time he'd seen me. That issue could be dealt with later, as I had to keep the call short. It was difficult in my weakened state to make my voice recognizable to him and keep it so.

"What happened? Where are you?" he asked.

"Look, I'm still in hiding so I need to keep this short," I said. "I'm sending you my new location on a coded sub-channel. I need you as fast as you can get here. I have a friend who is badly injured, probably dying, but I can't even make out the displays on this medical equipment to know what to do."

"Okay," said Crivreen. "I'll send our ETA on the same coded sub-channel. We'll get there as soon as we can."

"Thanks. Felix out," I said.

It still hurt to put any weight on my leg and Crivreen had said they would be here in another day, so I left the gravity where it was.

"I'd better clean up the blood," I said to myself. With nothing else to do while I waited, I went back to the scene of the fight to clean up the aftermath.

CHAPTER
TWENTY-FIVE

Back in the Siden system near the ruins of the fortress, Henrick and Curetes seemed to be waiting for something. They were standing at a high point in the terrain looking at the ruins. The ground around them was smoking slightly and was pitted with large craters, as if there had been a recent battle. Curetes and Henrick were unharmed and unconcerned.

Nearby Mathorn suddenly appeared. He must have known where Henrick and Curetes were before he arrived, as he stepped out of the weave and into normal space calmly looking right at them.

"Well, I can't say I'm surprised to see you two here," said Mathorn.

"Ah, Mathorn the Mighty," said Henrick. "To what pleasure do we owe your visit?"

"I was wondering the same thing about you," he said. Mathorn looked over the battleground around them. "It seems that I missed some action."

"Had we known you were out this way, we would of course have invited you," said Henrick.

"I'm sure you would," said Mathorn.

"We came here to speak with Raquel, but when we arrived several necromancers from Korshalemia were already here, bent on harming her," said Henrick.

"Oh, really?" asked Mathorn.

"Yes," said Henrick. "Zah'rak's team had already killed two sorcerers, so I suppose these were sent to prevent a second failure."

Mathorn seemed to consider that for a moment. "Have you any idea why they came here in the first place?"

"No," said Henrick. "I had already removed anything of value from the caves below, so there was no reason for anyone from Korshalemia to come here."

"Yet you knew to look for Raquel here?" queried Mathorn.

Henrick gestured to a nearby pile of rocks. "That is the grave of her husband. Obviously she will visit from time to time."

Mathorn glanced briefly in that direction. "This story sounds awfully convenient."

"What are you implying?" asked Henrick.

"Nothing in particular," said Mathorn, "but it wouldn't be your style to actually fight or do anything for anyone. Did your little pet take care of these necromancers while you watched and critiqued?"

Curetes moved forward as if to attack, but Henrick placed a hand on his shoulder to stop him. "Relax, Curetes; he is merely attempting to provoke you."

Curetes begrudgingly took a step back, but his eyes never left Mathorn.

"Now, Mathorn, is that any way to treat an ally?" asked Henrick.

"No, it is not. So at least five sorcerers from Korshalemia came here for no reason at all, and out of the overflowing goodness of your heart, you killed the more powerful ones to protect Raquel?" asked Mathorn.

"Something like that," said Henrick.

"What does that mean?"

"The sorcerers had a reason; we don't yet know what it was," said Henrick.

"It's not a good sign to see them active as far out as here," said Mathorn.

"On that we agree," said Henrick.

"If you learn anything, be sure to let me know."

"Oh, I'll be sure to let Vydor know anything that pertains to him," said Henrick. "Tell me, Mathorn, when the chips fall and Grandmaster Korshalem foolishly decides to go to war - where will you stand?"

"Grandmaster Korshalem won't instigate a war without provocation. Are you planning to instigate one?" asked Mathorn.

"No," said Henrick. "You may despise me, but you must see that a war with Korshalemia would be devastating to all involved. I have no desire to take part in any such event."

"At least we know where you stand, then," said Mathorn.

"I think you always have," said Henrick.

"Then I bid you good day," said Mathorn, stepping out of normal space and into the weave.

"I don't like him in the least," said Curetes.

Henrick smiled. "Oh, I'm sure he thinks just as much of you as you do of him."

"Why deal with him at all?"

"Because, if there is to be war with Korshalemia, Mathorn is either our greatest asset or our greatest liability. It's in our best interests to make sure that, at the very least, he's not a liability."

Curetes seemed unconvinced but unwilling to challenge his master. "We have a probable destination for Raquel's next stop."

"Oh?"

"Felix sent a distress signal," said Curetes. "He's only a few days' travel from their last reported location."

"Excellent! They will definitely go there to rescue him," said Henrick.

"And Marcus."

"And Marcus," added Henrick with a smile.

CHAPTER
TWENTY-SIX

Z ah'rak," said Crivreen, "we've located Felix's ship."

"Excellent!" I said. "Where is he?"

"In a stolen fast attack cruiser, in orbit around the third planet."

"Get us there as soon as you can, but don't raise him on the comm. until we're close enough to help if there's trouble," I said.

"Okay," he replied and laid in our course.

"What's he doing way out here?" I asked.

"Looking for us, I assume."

"I thought he was finished with us," I commented.

"He thought so, too. He tried going back to life as it was before," said Crivreen. "He wanted to open a robotics shop and live life as a merchant. We used to talk about opening the store together when we got out of prison. For me they were just idle thoughts, but for him it was a childhood dream, one he lost when he became a magus."

Raquel was sitting nearby, paying close attention to the conversation but saying nothing.

"That's kind of sad," said Ragnar. "I wouldn't have guessed that of him."

"Prison changes you," said Crivreen quietly. "You have to learn to be hard or you won't make it. In there, you make deals and do things that you'd have never have thought you were capable of."

"I can imagine," I said. As a former slave, I could do more than imagine it. Life in the slave pits can't be much different.

"Zah'rak," said Crivreen. "I'd like to know: will you let him back among us?"

I hesitated before answering because I hadn't yet decided. I wanted him back, but he'd run away the first chance he got and had only called us now because he was in trouble. "That depends on him, Crivreen."

"What does that mean?"

"It means let's rescue him first and worry about those details later," I said. "He said his buddy was badly injured, so head to sick bay and prepare whatever you might need."

"Good idea," he said and took off.

It wasn't long before we were in orbit. We flew the Night Wisp above Felix's craft and lowered the docking hooks. Once the two ships were interconnected and the computers linked, we extended a pressurized gangway between the two craft.

"We're ready to come over," I said via the ship-to-ship comm.

"Okay, please send Ragnar first. I'll explain when you get here," Felix said.

I looked at Ragnar, who shrugged and climbed into the chute. It only took a few minutes for everyone to cover the distance between the craft, but when we arrived Felix wasn't there.

"I assume you're Marcus?" I asked the stranger who greeted us.

"No, that's Felix," said Ragnar.

"What?" I exclaimed.

"I can explain later. First, please help Marcus," said the man.

"Sick bay, I assume?" asked Crivreen.

"Right this way," he said.

Raquel and Crivreen followed him quickly down the corridor while I pulled Ragnar aside. "Are you sure?"

"Yes, that's Felix; no question about it," said Ragnar.

"How?" I asked.

"He wanted to disappear, so I guess he found a disguise," he said.

We caught up with them in sick bay in time to see Raquel pull Felix aside. She said, "We're losing him. I need you to make a hard choice. Leave him in there and we'll try to get a message out to Master Kellyn, who can save him, but he'll almost certainly be dead before she arrives. Alternatively, we can pull him out of the pod now, and I can try to save him with the few skills I have. If I fail, he probably won't last the hour."

"We have to try!" he said.

"Okay. Crivreen, prep that bed over there and get ready to open the pod when I give the word," ordered Raquel. She looked into the pod again and was quiet for a moment.

Behind her, a gate opened and Shira came through holding a couple of bottles I'd not seen before.

"Great! Stay by that table, ready to assist. We'll have to work very fast, but don't spill a drop of that. It's priceless," said Raquel. I was asking a question when Raquel cut me off and said, "Zah'rak, I'll need you to lift him out of the pod and place him on the table. We'll have to remove what's left of his armor so I can get at the wounds. He's heavier than he looks, but I doubt you'll have a problem."

"Understood," I said, deciding this wasn't the time for questions.

"Everyone ready?" asked Raquel. We all nodded, then she punched the controls on the pod and the lid popped open.

I reached in and lifted the inert body out of the pod. He was quite a bit heavier than most humans, and far too heavy for his size. Even with Raquel's warning, the weight caught me by surprise.

He was in bad shape, so I placed him on the table as carefully as I could. Once his clothes had been removed I could see the full extent of his injuries. There was little doubt how dire the situation was, and I was surprised that he was still alive.

His wounds were very strange. They were filled with some kind of electronic or robotic parts. I wasn't sure what I was looking at. Had he been too close to a ship which exploded, or had something else occurred?

Raquel said, "Shira, pour very small amounts into his major wounds."

Shira was holding a glass bottle containing a fairly clear, reddish liquid. I'd never seen the bottle before. She nodded and went to work, slowly tipping the bottle and allowing a few drops to fall. As the liquid hit the wounds the flesh around them slowly but visibly grew back, and the metal receded. When about half the liquid was used up, Raquel stopped her.

"Okay, we need to get the rest inside him." She lifted his head and tilted it back, forcing his mouth open. "Pour it all in. Don't worry, it's not possible to choke on this stuff."

As Shira poured in the rosy fluid, color started returning to his face and worked its way down his body.

"Crivreen, hook up the medical monitors and let's see what we've accomplished," said Raquel. "Shira, please help me splint this arm so the bones can grow back correctly."

The metal parts continued to recede and his skin continued to grow. It was the most amazing thing I'd seen in my life.

The three of them continued to work on him for another hour, using both mundane medical treatment and the potions. Finally Raquel said, "That's all we can do for now." She pulled a cover over his body and leaned back against the wall, obviously drained from the procedure.

"Will he make it?" asked Felix.

"I think so," said Raquel. "The damage was severe, and if he were a normal human there's no way he could have survived."

"What do you mean, 'if he were a normal human'?" asked Felix.

"You saw for yourself: he's a Cyborg," said Raquel. "That's why the pod wasn't working for him. His implants were attempting to regrow in the same manner as his body and were interfering with the pod. The problem was that his central nervous system had mostly shut down, so there was nothing coordinating the repairs."

"What would've happened had we waited?" he asked.

"The Cyborg implants would have continued to grow out of control and eventually destroy what was left of his body," she said.

"But now?" asked Felix.

"Now his brain is actively in control again and the implants are correcting their growth. Hopefully in a few days he'll be strong enough to wake, but for now we'll keep him sedated here in sick bay."

"What was that stuff?" I asked, pointing to the two empty bottles.

"Gifts from Shea. She's an alchemist, one of only two known to exist in our realm," said Shira.

"They're known as greater healing potions," supplied Raquel. "It's not as good as having Master Kellyn here, but far better than all of us combined could achieve. He should be fine for the moment, but we need an around-the-clock watch in case something changes."

"I'll take the first shift," said Shira.

"Great! In an hour, send all the data we have on his condition to Hospital Station and ask for advice, please," said Raquel. "My training is only in battlefield care, not long-term recovery; not to mention that I'm way out of my league with those implants."

"Good idea," said Shira.

With Marcus stabilized, it was time to get some answers. "Now, Felix, let's go to the mess hall and you can tell us what's been happening."

We gathered around a table in the mess hall and Felix told us how he had hired himself out as a robotics mechanic, but had been attacked and was now on the run. "So that's that. I still don't know why Resden is after me."

"Can you describe the old man at all?" asked Raquel.

"Last time I did it was very painful, so I'd rather not try," he said.

"What you've described sounds like a memory block," she said. "At some point when we're near Hospital Station, we can stop in and get that removed."

"But you still haven't explained why you look and sound different," I said.

"It's still me," he said. "Actually, this is the real me. The name I was given at birth is Purwryn."

"But you don't even come close to matching any biometric scans of Felix. How is that possible?" asked Crivreen.

"Zah'rak, how many fake IDs do you have?" asked Purwryn.

"I don't know; a few dozen, maybe," I said.

"And they all have the same biometrics associated with them. Correct?" he asked.

"Yeah. It's a big problem. Sooner or later they get matched up and we have to abandon them," I said.

"Right," he said. "Well, I was born with the ability to modify my appearance and voice. I don't know if it's related to being a magus, or a natural ability of whatever species my ancestors belonged to. Either way, that skill plus some tricks and technology allows me to completely change the way scanners receive me. The only problem I've always had is creating new IDs to match my new identity. Purwryn and Felix are the only two valid IDs I have, and Purwryn is suspect, since I disappeared decades ago and only recently reappeared."

"It would've been easier for you to have donned your Felix disguise before we boarded," said Crivreen.

"I thought of that, but if Marcus woke up I wanted him to see a familiar face and I knew Ragnar wouldn't be fooled," he said.

"So what're your plans now?" I asked.

"Raquel," he said. "If you'll still have me, I'd like to take you up on your offer to join the Wizard Kingdom, as Purwryn rather than Felix."

Raquel looked at me, then back to him. "What about Felix?"

He sighed deeply. "I thought a lot about him over the past couple of days while I was alone. As I mentioned, I even considered retaking his form to make the meeting with you easier, but in the end I came to the realization that Felix was a cold-hearted mercenary. I want him to stay dead and never be resurrected."

"And Marcus?" I asked.

"He has no place to go," said Purwryn. "I hope that you can extend him the same offer."

"Raquel, what are you thinking?" I sent privately.

"Grandmaster Vydor is very keen on second chances. I can't really turn Purwryn down," she sent. *"And, although it goes against my training and upbringing, I think in this case I agree. I suggest we give him the benefit of the doubt."*

I reached out, put my hand on Purwryn's shoulder and said, "Welcome back."

"Thanks," he said.

"I think we should make this unanimous, and all become wizards," I said.

CHAPTER
TWENTY-SEVEN

I was awake. After eons of sleeping, I had finally woken. A daughter of light had brought her staff and awoken me, but was nowhere to be found. Patiently I waited for her return.

The sun was setting over the hills when I climbed up out of the pit, which used to hold the building I called 'home' in ages gone by. My mind was sharp, but my memory was dull. I remembered that the end of the world as I understood it had forced me into hiding, but I couldn't remember what the problem had been or what action I should now take.

I stretched out my old joints and climbed up a section of wall near the tower I had been sleeping under when she came. When I first awoke, all around the field I saw signs of a great battle. It looked as if she had been forced to fend off an army of undead attackers in order to reach the tower. A section of the wall was blackened all the way around as if it had been set aflame, and there were piles of bodies wherever the eye could see.

A ring of debris around the wall told me that she must have cast a ring of fire in an attempt to defend her position there. I tried unsuccessfully to figure out how she could possibly have fought off so many enemies alone. She must be a powerful warrior of much renown.

In the sky overhead, a skeletal dragon flew by without noticing me. I could hear the nightwalkers stirring in the woods as the world came alive around me. This seemed wrong, but I couldn't remember why. Ever since I awoke the world had been the same. I had a vague memory that the ruins around me should be a fortress so, as I had every night since waking, I worked on cleaning out the debris and bodies.

Several more skeletal dragons continued their flight overhead, but these were watching me. They didn't like what I was doing, but I had no reason to fear them. Howls continued to come from the forest around me as the nightwalkers protested against my work, but they dared not approach the ruins.

For the past three months I had done the same and the work was slow and hard, but I had nearly finished clearing the ruins and was almost ready to begin reconstruction. While I desired to meet my savior, I was grateful for the delay so that I could get the place ready for her. I wondered what she looked like. I hoped she was big and strong like myself, but I couldn't remember ever knowing others like me.

As I dragged the final body out of the ruins into the forest, the nightwalkers attacked as they always did. They punched and kicked at my stone body, doing harm to themselves rather than to me. I ignored them and dragged the body through the forest.

After about an hour I reached a large pit that I had been filling with the bodies. I briefly wondered for what purpose it had previously been used. There seemed no reason to have a large open pit out here, but I was grateful for somewhere to dump the trash. I tossed the corpse in with the others, briefly disturbing the vultures and other scavengers, and turned back. The nightwalkers continued their stubborn but useless assault on me. I picked up a large boulder and rolled it down the path in front of me, knocking some of them aside so that I could make my way more easily back down the path.

I plodded through the forest back to the ruins, wondering when I might learn what had happened and why I still existed. As I approached the ruins, a group of skeletal warriors armed with swords and shields formed a line against me.

Batting aside the nightwalkers, who were still trying to stop me, I walked towards this line. I did not understand why they all kept attacking me. All I wished to do was to rebuild my home and make it presentable for the return of the light-bringers.

The warriors charged and swung their swords at me. Sparks flew as the metal blades scraped across my stone chest. I picked up one of the warriors and attempted to use him as a club, but he fell to pieces as soon as he hit the first skeleton, leaving me holding only a pair of legs.

The others pressed their attack, but their swords could not harm me. I decided to waste no energy on them and kept walking towards the ruins. One of them ran at me, pushing his shield in front of him, and slammed into my body. The shield held up, but he did not; he fell to pieces from the shock.

I walked through the line and finally reached the ruins. It was nearing mid of night and the undead were louder than ever. They were not happy that I was rebuilding this fort, but I knew not why. I wished they would climb back into their graves and rest.

When I had returned inside the ruins the attacks ceased, as they dared not enter the property. "I should make a wall first," I decided.

My princess, the one who woke me, had made a stand on the stone wall; therefore I started growing rock in that section. It would take a long time to grow all that was needed to encircle the property, but I did the best I could to encourage the wall to grow. Since I didn't know how much time I had before she came home, I wanted to work quickly.

I worked until the sun came over the hills. The light from it burned my stone skin, so I made my way back to my pit. It had been another good night of work. I liked working; it gave purpose to my life. I hoped the light-bringers would be proud of my work when they came, and that they would begin to reconquer this world and set things right again.

CHAPTER TWENTY-EIGHT

Three days after Purwryn rejoined us, Raquel said, "It's probably safe to wake Marcus now."

"Probably?" asked Purwryn.

"Well, I'm not a doctor, but his vital signs are strong and stable," she said.

"Why not wait till we hear from Hospital Station?" I asked.

"Zah'rak, they probably won't even get our question until tomorrow," she said. "It could be almost a week more before we get an answer. I know enough to realize that it's not good to leave him sedated like this for so long."

"How long until we're back in range of a government communications hub?" I asked. That would enable much faster communication, fast enough to have an actual conversation.

"If we stay on course, not for another week," said Raquel.

"Purwryn, it's your call," I said.

"I think we should wake him." He moved beside Marcus' bed. "He stayed by my side all that time I spent in the hospital."

Raquel and I were quiet while she set the computer to gradually bring Marcus out of his medically-induced coma. His heart rate, breathing and brain activity slowly increased as the drugs were filtered out of his blood. He looked far better than the first day I had seen him. His wounds were well on their way to being healed. He had a more natural color, and his chest rose and fell in a slow but steady rhythm.

"Purwryn?" came a weak voice.

"I'm here," replied Purwryn.

Marcus blinked his eyes and slowly looked around. "I guess it's my turn in bed."

"Yeah. You gave us quite a scare," said Purwryn.

"Us? Where am I?" he asked.

"You're on the Resden cruiser you stole, but we're hard-linked to the Night Wisp," said Purwryn.

"Night Wisp? Then we found them?" he queried.

"Yes, we're safe, for now."

Marcus tried to sit up but needed Purwryn's help. He looked at me and said, "You must be Zah'rak."

I smiled. "Yes, I do stick out ever so slightly." Gesturing towards Raquel, I said, "This is Raquel, who's been your doctor throughout your treatment."

"Well, thank you," he said. His voice was now surprisingly strong and clear, and his eyes darted everywhere as if looking for something. Was he searching the room for threats or just trying to take things in? It was impossible to tell, but I suspected a little of both.

"I'm not much of a doctor, and I have no real experience with Cyborg implants," she said. "Once you have your strength back you'll want to check them all for yourself."

He leaned back against the pillow that Purwryn had placed for him. "So my secret is out."

"It was hard to hide, since maybe half of your flesh was gone," said Purwryn.

"What's to happen to me?" he asked.

That seemed like an odd question, but I tried to answer it. "Happen? Well, I assume you'll continue to heal - "

"No," interrupted Purwryn. "He's referring to the implants. I'm fairly certain they're illegal out here."

"Illegal? Out here?" I repeated.

"Yeah," said Marcus. "Phareon passed a law saying all current Cyborg implants must be registered, whether they belong to someone living in Phareon space or merely passing through it. They also outlawed any future usage of them."

"When?" I asked.

"A few years ago now, I guess," he said. "I'm not sure of the date. I only found out recently when I was looking for parts for repair and almost fell into a sting operation."

"So I guess you never registered, and any Phareon citizen who finds out has to turn you in?" I said.

"That's the gist of it," said Purwryn. "At which point they'll take him in and remove all the implants that can be removed, leaving him a cripple. As if that wasn't bad enough, he'd serve jail time for failing to register. If a citizen doesn't turn him in and is caught hiding him, he'd also face jail and fines."

"*Raquel, I assume the Wizard Kingdom has no such law?*" I sent.

"*Of course not,*" she sent back, evidently surprised that I even needed to ask.

"It's okay. I can't ask you all to risk prison on my behalf," said Marcus.

I chuckled. "Well, you're in luck."

"How so?" he asked.

"We're not Phareon citizens," I said.

"You neglected to mention that," Marcus said accusingly to Purwryn.

Purwryn grinned. "Well, honestly, even if we were, it wouldn't matter. None of us would turn you in."

That was true. None of us was exactly the kind to blindly adhere to the rules. I was sure that not even Ragnar, who cared more about doing the right thing than any of us, would follow the law in this case. No, the Night Wisp was safe harbor, even for those on the run.

"Thanks," he said. "Doctor, most of my implants are reporting minimal functionality. I doubt I could manage to sit up fully, never mind get out of bed."

"What can we do?" asked Raquel.

"I don't know. This has never happened before," he said.

"Maybe they just need time, like any other body part? Or exercise?" I asked.

"No; they're not reporting any errors, just minimal functionality," he said.

I punched the button on the comm. "Crivreen, how long would it take if we altered route and headed to Hospital Station at full speed?"

"Over two months," he said.

I cursed and started pacing. There had to be another answer. "Any other ideas?"

"There really are none. All we can do is send an updated report and wait for their reply," said Purwryn. "We don't have any other options."

"Purwryn, you're a robotics whiz: can't you figure it out?" I asked.

"This is quite different," he protested.

"Is it really?" asked Raquel. "Look, it will take at least three or four days to get a message to the hospital over CivNet, and three or four days for a reply. That gives you plenty of time to study the situation and see what you can figure out."

Purwryn looked at Marcus, who was weaker than he'd let on and had drifted off to sleep. "Well, it can't hurt to investigate, at least. Maybe I'll get lucky and stumble on the answer."

Raquel and I left them alone in sick bay and climbed back on board the Night Wisp. Crivreen had rigged the two craft into a semi-permanent docking arrangement. Each of their onboard computers used their thrusters to keep both ships at zero relative to each other as we made our way to the next stop. Mooring cables connected both ships just in case the computers failed to calculate everything correctly, but it wouldn't be good if anyone was in the gangway between them when that happened. It was a dangerous arrangement, as there was nothing stopping the ships from crashing into each other other than a simple computer program managing their thrusters.

"Seems like a stupid law," I said.

Raquel nodded. "Cyborgs have become very active out here. Someone is uniting them and they're making an attempt to take over. That's one of the reasons communications are continuing to degrade here. Not only is Phareon too poor to build an adequate network, the Cyborgs and others have been destroying the jump space repeaters."

"So they are countering the threat by alienating their own people?" I asked.

"Phareon is running out of time. They have more enemies than they can possibly handle. Resden and Phineary have already taken over large regions of Phareon space, and others are vying for what's left," she said.

"Okay, so then their plan is to make more enemies?" I asked, trying to follow her reasoning. Political wrangling of governments had never made any sense to me. Narcion had been an expert at using their fights to his own advantage and had tried to teach me, but even he failed. I guess some things were simply beyond me.

She shook her head and said, "No. The Cyborg nation, or tribe, or whatever they are called is aggressively seeking to wipe out all life forms which they consider inferior. They're already everyone's enemy."

"What does that have to do with Marcus?" I asked.

"The Phareon government assumes that all people who have chosen to have cyber-genetic enhancements are either part of the great Cyborg collective or soon will be," she said.

"That seems awfully naïve," I said.

"'Naïve' is a nicer word than I would have chosen," she said. There was a bite in her voice when she spoke. It was easy to forget that she was one of the most powerful magi within a thousand light centuries, but there were times when a hint came through and that would turn a warrior's blood to ice.

"We'll help him get better and hide what he is while he's with us; then what?" I asked.

"I don't know. That'll be up to him. I'm sure he can become a citizen of the Wizard Kingdom with my assistance, and our laws would then protect him. But that would have to be his choice," she said.

"I thought the Phareon law said it applied to anyone passing through?" I asked.

She smiled at that. "Oh, it does; but they won't dare challenge us so soon after we showed them that we can deploy forces out here very quickly."

"Would the Wizard Kingdom really do that for just one person?" I asked.

"Yes. Even if Grandmaster Vydor himself had to come out here, they would."

"Wow." I couldn't imagine that. No one had ever done anything like that for me. I couldn't imagine how they could achieve it; we were so far apart, and even they must have limits to their powers.

"Yes, they're good people to the core. In many cases I find them hard to understand, but in this one I'm fully in their camp."

"What do you mean?" I asked.

"Nothing is more important than standing with your people. If any one of us is in trouble, all of us are," she said.

"Was that how it was ten thousand years ago?" I asked.

"Absolutely, and it's the same in Korshalemia and in every other realm I've visited. There's something special about being a wizard, even compared to being a magus."

CHAPTER
TWENTY-NINE

D r. Hawthorne came into my office and said, "Dr. Leslie, we've received a high-priority coded secure message."

This doctor was a kind, older gentleman who was always a pleasure to work with. His silver hair indicated wisdom, and the lines in his face spoke of a life of laughter. Before Grandmaster Vydor had officially made Hospital Station a wizard stronghold, he had run it and handled all the politics to keep it functioning and safe. When I'd been appointed he was more than happy to let me deal with the politics, but I still leaned heavily on his experience. "From whom?" I asked.

"A Master Raquel. It's coming over the civilian network, from deep space. Timestamp places it at four days old."

I hated that we didn't have solid communications out here. We were too far away from any population centers to have access to jump space repeaters, which meant all messages had to be relayed down the trade routes via local merchant vessels. "CivNet" is what the locals called it. *More like 'sieve net',* I thought to myself.

"What does it say?" I asked.

"It's the complete medical history of a patient. They're looking for advice. They used some of Master Shea's potions to pull the patient back from the edge of death, but they don't know what to do next."

"Put the records up on the screen, please," I said.

Once they were up, I saw that they'd sent reports of both the patient's original condition and his post-operative state. There was a wealth of data, far beyond what I would have expected. "Impressive work for people who claim to have no doctor aboard."

"Yes, it is," said Dr. Hawthorne.

"What's your opinion?" I asked.

"Well, they've done well and I think by now the patient is probably awake, but he's going to be in trouble," he replied.

"All his vital signs look good, but I have to agree. These status messages from his implants are troubling," I said.

"Yes. Assuming he's awake now, his implants have probably gone into cripple mode, leaving him helpless in bed," said Dr. Hawthorne.

"If we were there, we could easily reset them, but we're not. What options do we have?"

"We could reply, and in four days they'll have the information they need. As long as they wait for a reply, it won't cause any permanent harm for him to stay as he is," he said.

"If they wait. This report already shows they're willing to take chances with their minimal skills."

"The only other option would be to charter a large fleet which can travel that distance quickly, but I suspect that would take just as long if not longer to accomplish," he said.

I looked over the records again. They seemed to have some medical knowledge on their team, regardless of their claims of ignorance, and presumably understood the time delay in communications. Master Raquel had encoded the message in such a way that it would reach our level, so she must at least have been in control of his medical care, and judging by my brief encounter with her, she seemed to have a level head on her shoulders. There really were no other options. We just had to trust that she would keep things as they stood until our message reached them.

"Then gather up all the information we have that could be pertinent to the case, including several 'what if' scenarios, and let's get them sent as fast as we can. We'll just have to trust that they'll wait for us."

"What about that gate device we have?" he asked.

"Gates need exit points. If they happen to be flying around with a gate on board their ship we could link them."

"I suppose that's unlikely?" he asked.

"As far as I know, no one has ever attempted to put a gate on a space-craft," I said.

"It would be useful. We could put several gates on several ships and send them to key locations where they could be dispatched quickly in the event of a disaster."

"Perhaps someday it might happen. But even if they had a gate, that wouldn't help in this situation because we'd still have to communicate via normal means to arrange for the gate to be ready on both sides at the same time," I said.

Shortly afterwards he left to prepare the report to send to Master Raquel. I sighed and ran my fingers through my hair. It still felt good to have my hair back, and I doubted I'd ever take it for granted again. I still had nightmares in which Master Shadow had never rescued me and I was still a helpless, bald slave. There was no way that would happen again; I'd die fighting first.

An incoming secure message broke the silence in the room and the Resden ambassador's face appeared on my comm. "Hello, Doctor!" His voice had a sickeningly sweet, cheery tone to it, matching his face which was obviously medically enhanced and looked very fake. He should have presented a friendly appearance, but all I could see was the plastic face of a store mannequin.

"Hello, Ambassador. What can I do for you?" I asked.

"Right down to business, then?" he replied.

"Yes, I'm a busy woman. Now, what do you need?" He usually tried to flirt with me if I gave him any opening at all. I wasn't sure if it was genuine interest or just a political ploy, but either way I didn't care for it.

"Well, I can understand that, for sure! I just have a small request for you, unworthy of your brilliant mind. I'm looking for any information you might have on a ship named the Night Wisp."

"Oh? And why would you expect that I'd have any?" I asked.

He continued to grin, showing his teeth which were much too perfect. I thought that whichever doctor had fixed up his face should be fired; even his teeth looked fake.

"They have been reported at Hospital Station recently. I'm sorry to bother you with such a small request, but they're assisting a dangerous criminal to escape and we want to help them before they get hurt," he said.

"I see." *Yeah, right*, I thought to myself.

"So just transmit any data you have. No need to sort it or anything; we'll handle all that so you can get back to your work," he said.

"I'm not even going to check to see if we have any information," I said.

"Oh? Why not?" he asked. His smile wavered very briefly, but quickly returned, along with the assumed charm that went with his fake concern.

"Doctor-Patient confidentiality. If they were here recently, as you say, then they're patients of ours and we're duty-bound not to release any information," I replied.

He hesitated before responding. "Now, you know I have the utmost respect for your fine institution, but – "

"But nothing," I interrupted. "If the Night Wisp were your ship, you'd expect us to keep your visit private. That's how we've operated for decades, and nothing has changed."

"I see," he said. He was taken aback by my implacability, but I had no desire to play games with him.

"Good. Then, unless you have a request that I can actually fulfill, I have work to do," I said.

"Perhaps we can talk about this another time, then? Maybe over dinner?" he asked.

There he went again. "No, thank you," I said as firmly as I could manage. "Good day, Ambassador."

I disconnected the line and paged Dr. Hawthorne to return to my office. I got up and took a drink, trying to wash down the bile that the ambassador always brought up in my throat. I wished my job would let me pour one of my exploding potions down his throat and then kick him hard in the stomach.

When the doctor came in he asked, "What can I do for you?"

"What was the name of that ship that has the Cyborg aboard?" I asked.

"The Night Wisp. They've been here a couple of times. Very generous donors," he said.

"I should've guessed," I said and slumped down in my seat.

"Is there a problem?" he asked.

"Isn't there always? Resden just called asking about them, describing them as harboring a dangerous criminal."

"What did you tell them?" he asked.

"That slimeball? Nothing, of course."

"Let me guess, he asked you to dinner again?" he asked. I knew he found the whole thing a bit humorous. I suppose it was in a way, but that didn't make it any more enjoyable.

"Yeah. We'd better warn the Night Wisp of what we know. I'll send you a briefing to include with your transmission."

"I'd suggest that we stay out of this," he said. He had made a career from staying out of other people's fights, and had done well. He'd had to, in order to survive the decades since the fall of the Empire. Dr. Hawthorne had been defenseless until Grandmaster Vydor came out and claimed the station.

"Normally I would agree, but Master Raquel is on a mission for the Wizard's Council, so if that ship is in danger we need to let them know."

"Then the Night Wisp is one of ours?" he asked.

"It wasn't when last I heard, but if Master Raquel is on board then it is at least operating as one of ours," I said.

"I understand. I'll come back to you for that briefing once we have the rest ready."

"Thanks," I said.

CHAPTER THIRTY

Purwryn," said Marcus.

"I'm over here." I was behind his head, working at a terminal just out of his sight.

"What happens if we can't find a solution?" he asked.

"Then you're stuck in bed until we can get to Hospital Station. But we'll figure something out."

I walked around the bed to where he could see me and opened a door to the implant in his lower arm. A datapad lay next to me so I could follow the directions step by step. I spread out all the tools the instructions indicated I'd need. Perhaps unsurprisingly, they were the same kinds of tools I used in my robotics work.

"What're you doing?" he asked.

"Well, I've been doing nothing but reading about implants for two days now and I've had my fill of that. I'm going to start working through the basic diagnostics on each of your implants and see what I can learn," I said.

"But they're reporting no errors," he replied.

"I know that, but there's obviously something wrong and I need some hands-on time with these to learn enough about them."

I walked through the steps in the manual and it was as he said: nothing appeared to be wrong. Every motor responded to input and every sensor lit up when prompted. They were functioning as well as brand new prototypes in a lab, and yet he was still unable to stand up. It didn't make any sense.

The implants were well-engineered and designed to be easy to work on. It felt natural to be working on them, as long as I ignored the flesh around them. Perhaps someday I might become a doctor of sorts for Cyborgs. I moved up to the upper arm implant and started its checklist. "So tell me, Marcus, why did you get all these implants to begin with?"

"It's quite a long story," he said.

"Well, it's not like you're going anywhere soon, so start talking," I said.

"I guess you have me there. Well, the short version is that when I was little I was struck with a disease that destroyed the use of my legs. At that time I was given the most basic implants, just enough to enable me to learn to walk again."

"That must've been expensive," I said.

"Oh, I'm sure it was, but I was too young to be concerned with that kind of thing," he said.

"Well, if that were the whole story, I wouldn't be working on your arm right now, and you wouldn't be in breach of Resden's laws." I assumed that Resden would treat medically necessary implants differently from biological enhancements.

"True. It never stops with just one," he said.

"What do you mean?"

"It's addictive, in a way," he said.

"Body modification?"

"Yeah. I learned as a teen how to improve my running speed by overloading my implants, but I burned them out. My parents replaced them with a similar model, but I started shopping around. Eventually I found a doctor who would put in vastly superior leg implants at the right price."

"So you could run faster?" I asked.

"Run faster, jump higher, lift more weight and so on. Anything that you use your legs for, I could do better."

"Surely someone noticed?" I asked.

"Of course they did. I was too much of a showoff. It got me thrown out of school and all sporting competitions, but I didn't care. I left home and worked whatever jobs I could in order to raise money to buy more implants. Soon I was replacing perfectly good bodily parts with implants and selling those parts off to people looking for more traditional cures."

"Wow. I had no idea such a market existed." It was sickening to think there were people out there preying on addicts like Marcus. I didn't want to imagine what kind of person would get satisfaction from cutting off perfectly good limbs and selling them to the highest bidder.

"I suppose there's a market for anything. Well, you can guess how the story goes. I got into deep debt over the implants and eventually called my father for help," he said.

"I bet that was a hard call to make."

"Hardest call I ever made, but in the end it should have been the easiest." He was quiet for a moment and then went on. "My father paid off all my debts on the condition that I came to work for him."

"On his cruise ships?" I asked.

"Yeah."

"Do you still owe him?"

"No, I worked it off years ago; but until you came along I had no place to go, so I stayed and started collecting a salary."

"Is he going to be upset that you left?" I asked.

"No, I spoke to him about my plans before I left. Dad told me he was proud of me for taking a stand and sticking by a friend. He actually sent me with his blessing."

I finished checking that arm and found nothing wrong but, as I'd hoped, the information I was reading on the implants was starting to make sense. They were a lot like robotics, after all; many of the same parts would work. If we were back on the Paradise in my shop, I could have replaced or repaired a lot of the subsystems in each implant with spare parts that we had lying around - if I could have found anything to fix.

The temptation to improve oneself with robot parts was understandable. All robots were superior in some way. Some were faster, many were stronger, and most could survive environments which would easily kill organic life forms. It was hard not to be jealous of them, but in the end they were just machines with no free will or emotions and couldn't care what we thought about them.

"You had no new implants in all that time?" I asked.

"Nope … well, almost none. One of my implants failed and had to be replaced, so I took the opportunity to upgrade it at that time, much to my father's displeasure. He wanted me to replace it with exactly the same model or even downgrade it."

I moved down to his leg where, instead of just completing the quick test that I'd been doing, I began the full maintenance and testing procedure. I didn't think it would help to diagnose the problem, but it would help me towards a better understanding of the implants. "Did you have to borrow to pay for that one, too?"

"No, by that time I was earning a wage and paid for it myself," he said.

"Ah. So your addiction is broken?"

"A good doctor would tell you no addiction is ever broken, but yes, effectively it is," he said.

"Good. I'm glad you understand that." I knew too well the hold that addictions have over a person. No matter how much time had passed since my last hit, I still found myself from time to time thinking about just having one more hit. I couldn't allow myself to fall back into that trap, but I would carry the consequences of previous mistakes for the rest of my life.

As I finished checking the third implant, my disappointment was growing. I'd still found nothing wrong. There had to be something there, but I couldn't find it. I considered a forced hard reset of the implants to make them come online, but I didn't know the risks involved in that. Would they lose some critical programming and cease to function at all? Would they simply never come back online? There was no way for me to know, and I could find nothing in the manuals to answer my questions. If Marcus were a robot I'd definitely try it at this stage, but I couldn't risk my friend's life. I decided to wait until after we'd heard from Hospital Station before trying something so drastic. "I'm going to do the standard maintenance on all of your implants, and hopefully something will become obvious as I go."

"Are you finding them easy to work on?" he asked.

"Actually, I am. Raquel was right; they're a lot like robotics. I don't understand how they connect to the body, but the implants themselves are the same kinds of thing we worked on back in the shop."

I spent the next three days testing each implant one by one and performing all possible maintenance on them, but I could find nothing wrong with any of the implants themselves. Each one appeared to be fully functional. I couldn't tell if the potion had repaired them or if their self-healing circuits were responsible, but whichever it was had done a good job.

"Still nothing?" asked Marcus.

"These are the best implants I've ever worked on," I said with a grin. "Unfortunately, they're also the worst."

"Felix - " said Raquel as she walked in. "Sorry, I meant, Purwryn."

"It's okay. What's up?" I asked.

"The reply from Hospital Station has arrived," she said.

We brought the data up on the monitors. "Wow, they were thorough!"

"I noticed that also. They even have a section for what to do if we make mistakes along the way," she said.

"Even if we don't need it for this operation, this is a treasure store of knowledge," I said.

"Look here," she said, pulling up a record. "They predicted he'd have this problem and sent a procedure to fix it."

This message would be in reply to the first one we'd sent, so there must've been something in those results to make the problem clear. "Interesting: it seems that the implants put themselves in a cripple mode."

"'Cripple mode?'" asked Marcus.

"I would have thought you'd know more about your own body parts. Cripple mode is when they shut themselves down to prevent damage," I said.

"Why did they do that?" he asked.

"It appears that there's a specific set of operations needed in order to restart them after they've been in a hyberpod," I said, pausing to consider how to explain what I was reading. "In a sense they still think they're in the hyberpod, so they're not running."

"I don't recall reading anything about this in the manuals," said Marcus.

"Did you actually read the manuals?" asked Raquel.

"Yes; well, maybe not all of them. I mostly flicked through them looking for the interesting stuff," he said.

Raquel chuckled. "I say we shouldn't turn his implants back on until he's read all the manuals."

"A little help here, Purwryn?" asked Marcus.

CHAPTER
THIRTY-ONE

Hey, Zah'rak," called Purwryn as I was on my way to the bridge.

"Yes?" I said.

"Marcus is fully functional again. He'll need a bit of recovery time, but thanks to his implants he can get around just fine now."

"Excellent!" I said, although 'fully functional' seemed like an odd way to put it. "I take it that the message we received from Hospital Station yesterday was of some assistance?"

"Yes. Raquel is preparing a reply with all our new information, just to make sure we didn't miss anything else."

"Good. I was just going to the bridge to check out our progress. I believe we're less than a few days from the military base. From there, we should be able to establish an encrypted channel over the military network for a real-time conversation with the hospital."

"That would be great. Maybe we should hold the update until then."

"Good idea, since we might be able to contact them before they could receive that message." I had turned to continue my way to the bridge when he stopped me again.

"There was something else in the message from Hospital Station, and I think you should look at it right away."

I followed him back down the corridor and we met with Marcus and Raquel in the mess hall on the Resden craft. They played the message from Dr. Leslie on the hospital station warning us that Resden was hunting us.

"Since we're sitting on a stolen Resden cruiser, do you want to tell me what it was you did?" I asked.

"Nothing. I already told you everything I know," said Purwryn.

"I doubt they'd put this much effort into hunting you if there's no more to it than what you've told us. There must be something else," I said.

"I agree, but I really don't know what," said Purwryn.

"Marcus, do you know any more?"

He shrugged and said, "Honestly, I don't. Before we left I checked with my father, who is the captain of the ship we were serving on, and he didn't know anything either. He said he anticipated that Resden agents were going to take control from him at the next stop and sweep the ship."

"That could be it," said Purwryn. "Maybe they weren't after us specifically but, since we ran before they could search the ship, they're making the assumption we're part of whatever was going on."

Raquel frowned in thought. "That's a possibility. Any idea what they were looking for? Was it a person or a thing?"

"No. I wish I did, but I don't know what they were after," said Marcus.

"How did they know about the Night Wisp?" I asked. The whole thing stank. Someone knew something; whether it was Purwryn or Marcus I didn't know, but one of them did. I was sure of it.

"I can answer that," said Purwryn. "They intercepted the call from me to Crivreen, and his reply. The encryption code we used is a fairly simple one. If they transmitted a copy back home, I'm sure their computers could have cracked it."

"Makes sense," I said.

"Look, Resden is after one or both of you for some reason. If we're to protect you, we need to figure out why they're pursuing you," said Raquel.

They both remained silent. Despite everything, I believed Purwryn was telling me the truth, or at least the truth as he understood it. That left Marcus as a wild card. Had he done something and decided to capitalize on Purwryn's departure to make his own escape, or was he the innocent tag-along friend he claimed to be? I wasn't sure I trusted him fully. He'd done nothing to make me think he wasn't trustworthy, but there wasn't much he could do when paralyzed in sickbay.

"We're en route to a Phareon military base to restock weapons and ammo. From there we're heading into what is likely to be a hot battle zone. We can't have Resden making a move while we're already in combat, and we can't show up at a Phareon military base with a stolen Resden cruiser," I said.

"What are you suggesting?" asked Purwryn.

"First we have to ditch the cruiser. So, Marcus, you have a choice: you can come with us and potentially be killed in combat, or you can take this cruiser and try your luck alone," I said.

"Purwryn told me quite a bit about you all while I lay in sickbay," he said. "If I understood correctly, you're all citizens of the Wizard Kingdom?"

"Yes," I replied.

"Then I'd like to stick with you. The way I see it, the only way I'm going to be safe now is to move there. Resden certainly won't look for me there and you don't seem likely to cut me apart and remove my implants."

"*Raquel?*" I sent telepathically. "*What do you think?*"

"*Marcus knows more than he's telling,*" she sent. "*But ultimately he's right; the only safe way for him is to stay with us for the moment and later move back to the Wizard Kingdom.*"

"*So your advice is to help him?*" I sent.

"*I'm not sure it's the wisest course, but we should do it. I think Purwryn at least feels we owe him that much, and he may be right.*"

I sighed. It seemed I'd picked up a new team member. "Fine. Our next step is to gut this cruiser of everything that might be of value: armor plating, launchers, ammo, food, medical supplies, or anything else at all. I'll get Crivreen to lead the salvage operation. Once that's done we detach and blow her up."

"Let's get started, then," said Purwryn. There was relief in his voice. I wondered if he'd have gone with Marcus had we turned him away. Perhaps they'd have tried to make it to the Wizard Kingdom. That trip would have taken many years in the small cruiser, but for most of it they'd be out of Resden's reach.

They'd be out of everyone's reach. The inner galaxy was heavily populated in the controlled systems, but that was only a tiny fraction of the space; most of it sat empty. A ship making the trip would be completely alone without supplies or help should anything go wrong.

I left them to start salvaging and went up to the bridge. When I'd brought Crivreen up to date, I asked, "Is there anything creative we can do?"

"What do you mean?" he asked.

"We don't have any shuttles. Can we make one out of that cruiser, perhaps? Or - heck, I don't know; you're the engineer."

He shook his head. "We can probably cut off most of her armor and attach it to our hull, which would give us greater mass, which in turn would increase our jump distance. We'd need to compensate for that mass by adding in their engines, but all of that would take weeks in a space dock. Out here, without access to the tools we'd need, it'd be best to strip her of supplies and move on."

"All right. Head over there and take charge of that. I'll stand watch here."

"Okay, I'll keep my eye open for anything creative we can do," he said.

CHAPTER
THIRTY-TWO

Z ah'rak, our fearless handler is calling," said Crivreen.

We were approaching the military outpost, and once again were in range of the military jump space repeater network that allowed for re-al-time communications. "Did you send the list of supplies we need?"

"Yes," he said, "yesterday, so they should have it."

"Okay. You'd better put our friend up on the big screen."

"You enjoy poking the beast a bit too much," said Crivreen. The com-mander hated being on the screen before all the crew, but I wanted every-one to hear what he had to say. I refused to accept his arrogance and lack of respect for my crew.

"Hello," I said as he came on the screen.

"Where have you been?" he demanded.

"Around and about, handling another mission," I said.

"For whom? I didn't authorize any missions!" he exclaimed.

"This wasn't for Phareon. Now, do you want to tell us about this mis-sion or should we go on our way?"

"As special agents, you report to me; but we'll deal with that later. Dock, and the station staff will get you loaded up. As soon as you've restocked, you'll join with one of our fleets for immediate departure. They can get you to the target in two jumps."

"What exactly is the mission?" I asked.

"The fleet will stop within one jump of the station and stay there. You will jump in and find out what's going on. The setup is the same as before: this station is a secure military facility which was well-defended and suddenly stopped communicating with us. A team of five magi were sent in, but haven't been heard from since," he said.

"What was on the station?" I asked.

"Top secret weapons research. Do you think the necromancer could have returned?"

"No. Even if he could, he wouldn't come out here. The Wizard Kingdom has become active in this area, and he was here to hide from them. No, if he is active again it's elsewhere. This must be a new threat."

"Very well. Obviously we'd like to have the station back, but the primary objective is to identify this new threat and deal with it."

"Understood," I said and wrapped up the conversation. "Crivreen, has Raquel called Hospital Station yet?"

"Yeah. I helped them set up an encrypted channel once we were in range," he said.

"Okay, see to the reloading. I'm going to get an update," I said.

I found Raquel, Marcus and Purwryn in sick bay. I hesitated, feeling that it wasn't my place to barge in; however, before I could leave Raquel called me in.

"Zah'rak, they want to see Marcus for a full checkup," she said.

"We're months away and about to leave on a mission. How critical is it?" I asked.

"Zah'rak! Good to see you again," said Dr. Hawthorne. "It's not critical, but the sooner the better. Can you head here after your mission?"

"Sure, but it could mean months of travel for our little ship," I said.

"When you're ready, contact me and I'll see if any friendly fleets are nearby," he said.

"Will do. Oh, there's someone you should meet," I said, and then sent privately, *"Shira, please come to sickbay."*

"On my way," she replied.

"She should be here shortly," I said.

"While we wait for her," said a woman whom I didn't recognize, "did you get the message about Resden?"

"Yes. As you probably guessed, they're after Marcus, but we don't know why," I said.

"Dr. Leslie, Marcus has the full protection of the Wizard Kingdom," said Raquel. "I'll contact the Resden ambassador and tell them to stand down."

"Okay. Is it just Marcus?" asked Dr. Leslie.

"No, Purwryn also, but he's a citizen of the Wizard Kingdom with full protection," said Raquel.

"I don't envy you dealing with him, and I'm glad to pass on the task," said Dr. Leslie.

Shira came into sick bay and said, "I'm here, what's up?"

"Shira, I want you to meet Dr. Hawthorne," I said. *"Raquel, could you clear the room for a moment?"* I sent privately. I wished I'd thought about this sooner so I could have prepared the ground.

Raquel seemed taken aback but ushered Marcus and Purwryn out of the room.

"Shira! It's great to see you! How are you feeling?" asked Dr. Hawthorne.

Shira looked at me with obvious confusion.

"Shira, Dr. Hawthorne is the person who performed the surgery to remove your slave implant."

"Oh," she said, looking back at the screen. I couldn't judge her feelings. Human skin is much more reactive than Zalionian scales, which makes it harder to read. There was confusion there, and maybe some apprehension; whatever she felt, though, I was glad she hadn't run off right away.

I took my leave to let the two of them talk. Out in the hallway, I told Raquel what I was doing. "She never talks about the implant or the surgery, so I'm hoping this will give her an opportunity."

"Why do you think she'll talk about it now?" asked Raquel.

"Because Dr. Hawthorne will ask, and she never had a post-op check-up," I said.

Raquel considered the matter and said, "Maybe they'll talk, then."

"Was that a bad idea?" I asked.

"I don't know. It might have been wise to ask her about it first."

I sighed. All I wanted to do was to see Shira happy again, the way she'd been for a little while in the forest. "Okay; while we wait, I'll brief you on our new mission," I said and told them what the commander had said.

"Why doesn't the military just send in a boarding team to take the station?" asked Marcus.

"Because they're afraid this might be like the previous stations where their boarding teams were wiped out," I said, and summarized our earlier missions for him.

"Wow," was all he managed to say. His expression briefly showed genuine shock but quickly reverted to a more neutral look, as if a picture had changed in an internal slide show projected onto his face.

"Why are we still working with him?" asked Purwryn.

Raquel turned back from watching Shira through the window. She said, "We haven't told him yet about the new arrangement, partly because the Wizard Kingdom also has a vested interest in finding out about this station."

"Do you think the necromancer is back?" asked Purwryn.

"No, but he's not the only one from my era that I expect will waken. It's too soon to tell, but I anticipate more sorcerers waking up and operating out here," she said.

"Why out here?" I asked.

"When the wizards tore reality to end magic, the effect rippled outwards. Most magi fled ahead of the effect, hoping to find a safe place to wait out the spell. So all around the edge of this galaxy there are likely to be many sorcerers and wizards, those who managed to escape the impact long enough to slip into a timeless sleep as Narcion and I did, and I expect they will start making themselves felt soon enough."

Shira came out of sickbay and smiled weakly at me. She said, "Zah'rak, they'd like to speak with you."

"Okay," I said and went in to see them.

"Zah'rak," said Dr. Hawthorne, "thanks for arranging that meeting. Shira seems to be doing well, but when you bring Marcus, I'd like to give her a checkup too."

"Well, sure - but isn't that up to her?"

"Yes and no. She had an implant removed from her brain, which even in the best of cases can lead to impairment. Until we can fully evaluate her to make sure everything is functioning correctly, she needs a guardian to oversee all medical decisions."

"And that's me?" I asked.

Dr. Hawthorne nodded. "Yes. I assumed you had both discussed it already. We asked her and she named you without hesitation, and we thought it a good choice; unless, of course, you prefer to decline?"

"No, of course not," I said. She was my responsibility, and there was no way I would hand her over to someone else. "Whatever I can do to help her, just let me know."

"Excellent. We'll look forward to your call after your current mission," he said, and closed the channel.

Raquel came in and said, "While we have this opportunity for normal communication, I'll arrange everyone's citizenship of the Wizard Kingdom and call Resden."

"We probably don't have much time left. Our Phareon handler is in a rush to get us underway," I said.

"It won't take long."

"Okay, go ahead," I said and left her to do what she needed to. I almost hoped it would take too long, so that I'd get the opportunity to defy the 'good' commander's orders once more.

CHAPTER
THIRTY-THREE

As much as I had thought I'd prefer to get away, it was good to be back with Zah'rak and his team. Sitting once again as the primary pilot on the Night Wisp felt like coming home. Crivreen had taken Marcus down to engineering with him, figuring he would make a good backup engineer to Crivreen. Zah'rak hadn't give up any of his leadership when he'd joined the Wizard Kingdom, and Raquel seemed content to let him call the shots.

"This will be the last jump with the fleet," I said. We had been traveling with what Zah'rak called a jump fleet. It was a group of warships assembled specifically to get us to the primary mission objective as fast as possible.

"Purwryn, lock in for jump as normal, but don't use our jump drives at all," said Zah'rak.

"Okay," I said. Our mass was too small to matter on the scale of the fleet, so it was smarter to conserve our power in case we needed it. Once we'd cleared jump space I checked our status and said, "Zah'rak, we're well within jump range of the station and well within detection range of the station's sensors."

"How much time until they see us?" he asked.

"We're a little less than a light day away," I said. While jump drives allowed space craft to travel faster than light, and jump space repeaters did the same for communications, there was still a very real limit on passive and active scanning. Jump space allowed ships and messages to skip over normal space, but scanning needed to travel through normal space in order to do its job effectively and was therefore limited by the laws of nature. That meant we would have at least a day before passive scanners picked up the fleet, twice that for active scanners.

"Good. They'll certainly notice this fleet," he said. "Check with them to make sure we have the most recent data and then jump in. Let's try to stay ahead of their scanning."

"Do you want me to try to connect to the station's computers from here first?" I asked.

"No; that's sure to fail, and I don't want to tip our hand just yet," he said.

I wasn't so sure it would fail, but it would definitely give away our approach. When we jumped, we would go to the station alone. The fleet would hold back, ready to assist if we should call them. The Phareon government couldn't risk having another whole fleet eliminated; their recent losses were just too great.

"Zah'rak, the fleet has begun an active scan of the station," said Ragnar.

"What? How?" he asked.

Raquel moved to Ragnar's side and looked over the displays. "Clever. They're using the jump space repeater near the station to relay the scan signal."

That made sense, since we had a fixed point in space to scan and not a wide area. "Then our hand is tipped."

"No," said Raquel. "They can't know the origin of the scan beyond the specific repeater, and since it's coming via the jump space network they'll probably assume it's from a Phareon fleet and not a lone ship like us. Heck, for all they know it could be coming from anywhere in the jump space repeater network. If it were me I'd assume someone close by, but who knows how they think?"

"Should we jump now and try to get ahead of their response?" I asked.

"No. Let's wait for the results of the scan," said Zah'rak.

"It's coming in now," said Ragnar. "It looks as if the station is fully operational."

"That's not good. Any indications of a fight?"

"Nothing in these scans," said Ragnar.

"Zah'rak, the fleet commander wishes to speak with you," I said.

"Okay, put him on screen."

The commander was a Zalionian like Zah'rak but much older and his face was split in half by a large scar, making the normal hiss of a Zalionian voice much worse. "Special Agent Zah'rak, have you seen the scan reports?" he asked.

"Yes, sir. If it comes down to it, do you have enough firepower to take on a fully-operational station?" replied Zah'rak.

"No, and it will be at least a week if not longer before we can get sufficient forces out here to do that, should it become necessary."

"Have you communicated with Command yet?" asked Zah'rak.

"Yes, but it will be some time before we receive a reply. What are your plans?" he asked.

"Unless we're told otherwise, our orders are to find out what's going on. We can't do that from here, so we'll continue as planned."

"Understood. Good luck, and let us know if we can help," said the fleet commander.

When they had wrapped up the call, Zah'rak turned to me and asked, "What are our options for sneaking up on them?"

"We can go in under low power, but if they are actively scanning the area we'll be detected even if we turn the whole ship off. We're not a stealth ship by any means," I said.

"How did we hide from those pirates, then?" Zah'rak asked.

"What pirates?" I asked. I'd apparently missed a fight.

"That was my doing. I have a rune that causes misdirection," said Ragnar.

"What does that mean?" Zah'rak asked.

"It hides something by causing anyone looking for you to look anywhere but at you," he said.

"Interesting. So you're hiding in plain sight, then," commented Raquel.

"Exactly," he said. "It's very tiring to keep up for long because every time a person looks at you it uses power to redirect their gaze. It's not foolproof, either. A person can consciously override the subconscious prompt to look elsewhere, and if they do they'll spot you."

"Would it work against the station?" I asked.

"Sure, but I could only hold it up for a very short period of time against something like a fully-operational space station," he said.

Zah'rak thought about that for a bit and then he activated the ship-wide comm. "Everyone, meet me in the mess hall."

Once we were all assembled, he brought everyone up to speed and said, "We need a way to find out what's happening on that station. Any suggestions?"

"I could do it," I said.

"What do you mean?" asked Zah'rak.

Everyone was obviously surprised that I'd volunteered. As Felix I never would have; it was too dangerous. But as Purwryn I wanted to start a new life, to be a team player and support this ragtag group who were my family now. "We jump in and use Ragnar's cloak to hide the Night Wisp. Then I use my jump suit and fly over to the station while you jump out. In the jump suit I'll be too small for their sensors to care about, making me practically invisible even if I wasn't a magus, and I have plenty of experience with breaking into places."

"I don't like the idea of you going in alone," objected Zah'rak.

"I'll go with him. I might not be a magus, but I can avoid detection in my own way," said Marcus.

"But we'll have no way to get either of you out if you get into trouble," said Zah'rak.

"I can gate them out," said Shira.

"Don't you need a marker or something?" I asked.

"I can use you as a marker. It's a bit tricky, and I have to be quite close to do it, but I should be able to use your senses via a telepathic connection to open a gate at your location," she replied.

"Since your range is limited, we'd have to stay in the area for you to gate them out," said Raquel.

Shira was about to say something but Crivreen beat her to it. "I can solve that. If Ragnar can buy us even five minutes, we should be able to get into the sensor shadow cast by the station and park on its outer hull. We should be completely undetectable there."

"They would still see our jump exit," said Ragnar.

"Nothing can be done about that," said Raquel.

"So we jump in, disappear, and expect them to assume we left?" asked Zah'rak.

"What if two ships jumped in?" asked Marcus. His comment was met with general incomprehension and he continued: "We get the fleet to send a cruiser in with us; it jumps in, does a scan sweep and jumps out. If we jump in with it and hide, they should assume the cruiser was the only thing that came in."

I thought about that for a moment. It was a clever idea, and not one I'd heard anyone suggest before. "That might work, if we came out of jump space just a moment ahead of it and cloaked right away. They would still see us briefly, but if we got the timing right they'd assume the second cruiser was all they had detected."

"Ragnar, how fast can you cloak our ship?" asked Zah'rak.

"It will only take a moment or two, but I can't be more precise than that," he said.

"Okay. You work with Crivreen to get the best timing you can, and contact the fleet. Purwryn, you and Marcus get ready. As soon as we clear jump space, you go. That way, if we fail and leave you still have a shot at completing the mission."

CHAPTER
THIRTY-FOUR

Marcus and I were waiting in the airlock, preparing to deploy. The fleet commander thought the plan was brilliant and decided to send three cruisers with us, in slightly staggered jumps.

"Marcus, are you sure you want to do this? There's a very good chance one or both of us could be captured or killed," I asked.

"Purwryn, I'm a Cyborg. That makes me a bit of a superhero, and all I've ever used these parts for is winning bets and bar fights. It's about time I put them to good use," said Marcus.

I chuckled a bit at that. "I suspect you did very well in those bar fights."

"Yep, at least until the police arrived," he said, unconsciously rubbing his shoulders. "Those electrified clubs leave a mark!"

That they did, a mark I knew all too well. It was probably best that I hadn't known Marcus back in my bar days. No doubt we'd have gotten into a lot more trouble as a team than we ever could alone.

"Purwryn, are you ready?" asked Zah'rak over the comm.

I opened the airlock, made sure our tether was secured and looked at Marcus, who nodded. "Yes, we're ready."

"Okay. We'll be under communications blackout as we exit the jump, so telepathic communication only," he said.

"Understood." That posed a problem, since Marcus wasn't a magus.

"Jumping in three, two, one," came Crivreen's voice over the comm. before the azure of jump space wrapped around us. It always had a comforting feel to it. I didn't know why, but other magi said the same. It felt safe, like being home in a warm, soft bed that wrapped around you and held you tight.

"We're on," I said as I came out of the post-jump hangover. Our suits were programmed to put us on course the moment we cleared the jump, so we were already en route when we came to. The tether between us made sure we wouldn't get separated and allowed for communications that should not be detectable.

"Yeah," he said.

There was a slightly different tone to his voice which I couldn't quite place. I didn't have time to give it much thought, as just then the station opened fire on the three Phareon cruisers.

They quickly jumped out of the region long before weapon fire could reach them, and there was no sign of the Night Wisp. The jump suits didn't have much in the way of passive scanners, so I couldn't tell if the station was still looking for them or not. I just had to assume all was going according to plan.

"We should be entering the sensor shadow of the station shortly," I said.

"What's the plan for actually getting on the station?" he asked.

"I can teleport into any airlock with a window and open it to let you in."

"I suggest we head to the far right corner of the station. The power signatures there are the lowest; hopefully that means it's sparsely populated," he said.

"Good idea," I replied. We didn't dare engage our jump jets until we were in the shadow, but when we could we directed our flight over to the area he pointed out.

"It might be better if I open the airlock," he said, pointing to the access panel. "If you do, it might alert someone. I should be able to bypass any alarms."

"You're probably right," I said. Normally I wouldn't bother opening any doors, as I could just teleport through any place where I had a good line of sight.

He worked on the panel for a minute or so and then the airlock door slid open.

"That was fast," I commented.

"Let's just say I have some experience of bypassing government security."

"At a guess, I'd say that's probably connected to your bar fights?" I suggested.

"Maybe," he replied.

I shook my head and slipped inside, knowing well what that tone meant. We were more alike than not. Inside the airlock, we disconnected the tether. We could communicate verbally once we were in the air-filled station.

The jump suit engines and fuel tanks were bulky, so we elected to leave them magnetically attached outside the station near the airlock. If the mission was successful, we could collect them on the way out. If it failed, we wouldn't need them.

"Let's find a terminal and pull up a map," suggested Marcus.

In the clear air, I could clearly hear the quiver in his voice. He was nervous. I placed my hand on his shoulder and said, "Good thinking."

The station was dark, with only minimal bioluminescence lighting the corridors. That meant the power was off, and that could destroy our hope of finding a working panel. The air was fresh and the temperature was comfortable. "Environmental controls seem to be working, but everything else is off."

"That's odd. You'd think they would've cut those too," he said.

I agreed with him, especially since environmental control used a lot more power than lights did, but I put it down to the current owners of the station not being very frugal with their resources. It sure made things easier on us, so I wasn't going to complain about the conditions.

We worked our way through the dark corridors, heading in the direction that Marcus believed had a higher power signature than the rest of the station. The hope was that as we got closer we'd find a working access terminal.

"Alert!" he said in a hushed but urgent tone. "Maintenance bot coming."

I didn't know where the bot was, but followed Marcus as he ducked around a corner. He paused there as the bot sailed past our position with the single-mindedness that only a robot can achieve. It never looked to left or right and plowed right past us.

"That was close," he said.

"Might be on its way to check the airlock," I mused.

"It won't find anything. I cleaned up after myself," he said, sounding indignant at the assumption that he'd failed to cover his trail.

I hoped he was right, but anyway there was nothing to do now but press on. We eventually came to a better-lit section of the station and found a working access terminal in a secluded area.

"Okay, here's a map," said Marcus.

"Can you pull up current crew members? Not the crew who were here before it was taken over, but those running it now."

"Sure. They'd have had to add themselves to the system in order to operate the station. Who do you want to look up?" he asked.

"A security officer, specifically one who's off-duty, asleep, out sick or something of that sort. Somewhat close to me in mass would be good, too," I said.

"Here's one that might fit."

"Perfect," I said. I concentrated hard on the image on the screen and chanted a memory verse under my breath. My features melted and changed until I looked just like the picture. I wasn't sure how I did it; I just chanted that verse and focused, and the rest just happened on its own.

"Whoa," said Marcus.

"I need biometrics data and voice samples," I said.

"Here," he said, playing some clips of the officer's voice. I carefully mimicked them and then pulled out my Assassin's Guild-issued gloves which I programmed with biometrics Marcus had found in the system, completing the disguise. They automatically matched my skin tone and texture, making them invisible to the untrained eye. To all appearances I was now Sergeant Taylor.

I sighed, realizing it was this skill which had got me into trouble with the Assassin's Guild to begin with. My ability to get into places made me the perfect weapon; the only trouble was that I'd botched the one job they gave me. One tiny mistake was all it took to bring them down on me. Well, I wouldn't let myself botch this mission.

"Stay here and get all you can from that terminal. I'll be back in one hour. If I don't make it, get off the station with that datapad and head to the rendezvous. If I'm late, I'll do the same."

"What are you going to do?" he asked.

"Go in deeper," I said. I slipped into the corridor and got going before he could complain. As I got further into the station I came across more bots working on various tasks, but there was a distinct lack of people. The bots ignored me, as I expected they would. I looked like a valid staff member, and they were too simple to wonder why I was out here. Even the more complex ones were programmed to ignore normal staff movements, other than to stay out of the way. No one liked the idea that a robot could be used to spy on them, so they were deliberately designed not to.

I headed for the center of the station, hoping to find something out. I came to a secure door guarded by two robot defenders, but simply presented my gloved hand for a palm print and the door opened. My experience told me that everyone would expect this door to be impassable by anyone other than an authorized individual. It was that belief that made it so easy to get past. Had they had a more realistic sense of doubt, there would have been at least a second layer of checks.

Through the door I found myself among people, and did my best to find routes through the station that were lightly populated. I could pass myself off to a stranger easily enough, but if I bumped into one of Taylor's buddies that would be a significant problem.

A man yelling in pain drew my attention and I moved towards the sound. Two old men in dark robes were standing over a young human who was curled up on the ground in obvious pain.

"Don't fail us again," said one of the old men. His voice was deep and slightly raspy. It had a quality that sent a chill down your spine. They walked off, leaving the human on the floor, and stepped into a side chamber.

I slipped into a vacant chamber next to theirs and used one of my listening devices to eavesdrop on their conversation.

"What's the status of the fleet?" asked the first one.

"Still sitting out there," said a different voice.

"And the cruisers?" asked the first voice.

"They got away undamaged. Judging by their jump trajectory, they returned to the fleet."

One of them began to pace up and down. "They must be deciding whether they can take us or not; either way, our cover is blown. It's time to leave."

"But our experiments are not yet finished. The newest batch is still growing."

"Bring whatever you can, but we leave within the hour. Set the station to self-destruct before we go."

If the station blew while the Night Wisp was attached, we'd all die. I had to get back to Marcus and get off the station. As fast as I could move without drawing attention, I hurried back to Marcus. I would have liked to activate the suit comm. and alert him, but it was too risky.

CHAPTER
THIRTY-FIVE

I found Marcus where I'd left him. "We have to get out of here fast," I said and told him what I'd heard. "Just give me a minute to change back." I didn't want to risk getting shot by Zah'rak or the others if I charged onto the Night Wisp looking like Sergeant Taylor.

"That is seriously cool, Purwryn," said Marcus.

"I'm not so sure. I think more harm than good has come of that skill," I said.

"I might be able to stop the self-destruct – "

"No time to chance that. We have to move out," I interrupted.

"Back the way we came?" he asked.

I started to say, "No," but sounds from the hall cut me off.

"This way!" a voice called out as the sound of running got louder. "Check all the rooms along this corridor!"

"Run!" I whispered. We took off down the corridor with guards behind us, yelling at us to stop. I wondered how they'd found us, or if they were after us at all. It didn't matter; if they were searching they'd find us here soon enough.

"We have to lose them before they get enough help to trap us," I said.

Marcus stopped and turned towards the guards. As they ran at him, he pulled out a grenade and tossed it in their direction. There was a crack and smoke filled the air, moving quickly towards us. He had thrown it too close to us and we were about to be engulfed in the smoke. Marcus grabbed me, tossed me over his shoulder, and took off running faster than any human could ever achieve. He easily outpaced the expanding gas behind us and kept going until we'd left everyone well behind.

I don't know how far we ran, and I was slightly motion-sick from riding doubled over on his shoulder when he finally put me down. "You might have warned me you were going to do that. What was that you threw?"

"A knock-out grenade. In an hour or so they'll wake up, but until then they can't report in or call for help," he said.

"We need to come up with an escape plan," I said. My stomach hurt from where he had grabbed me, but I had to admit his ploy had worked perfectly.

"Our best bet is to go back the way we came and pick up the jump suit engines," he said.

"I guess you're right," I replied. I still thought taking a different exit would be prudent, but we had a very real deadline and I didn't want to waste time arguing. "Can you find the way?"

"Yeah, I have the map memorized," he said.

As stealthily as possible we worked our way to the uninhabited section of the station. It wouldn't be long before the sleeping guards were found, but there would be nothing to lead to us as long as we made no mistakes.

As we crossed from the inhabited section of the station into the uninhabited part, the blast doors slammed shut behind us. Over the loudspeaker one of the old men said, "You must have been very clever to sneak onto the station, but I doubt you'll be clever enough to survive in there."

"What do you think that means?" asked Marcus.

I pulled out my wands and said, "It means we'll have to fight our way out. Forget stealth: what's the fastest way outside?"

He unslung his rifle and said, "This way."

We started running, but it wasn't long before he stopped. "You hear that?"

"No? Hear what?" I asked. All I could hear was the sound of my own breathing.

"Something is closing in on us," he said quietly.

"Whatever it is, we don't want to wait for it."

"Too late," he said and spun in place, bringing his gun around behind us.

I turned to look as he opened fire on some bizarre creature. It looked as if it might once have been a person, but was now a twisted mixture of body parts, stone and metal. Marcus' rifle blew parts of it away but it kept coming, undaunted. It was right out of a nightmare or a mad scientist's lair.

"Take off the legs!" I called out.

He switched his aim and blew both legs off. The creature fell to the ground and starting crawling towards us. "Stubborn bugger," said Marcus.

"Can you hear any more coming?" I asked.

"Lots," he said.

"Find us a way out of here, now!"

He took off in a new direction and I ran hard trying to keep up. Several times he abruptly changed direction but eventually came to a stop.

"What's wrong?" I asked.

"We're surrounded now," he said.

"Which way is the shortest path to an exit?" I asked.

"That way, but … "

"Then we fight our way out," I said, pulling out more of Crivreen's wands to make sure I'd have easy access to them, enabling me to exchange them as I drained their charges.

He nodded. "I guess we don't have a choice."

We did have a choice, but it was risky. I could contact Shira and have us gated off, but that would expose the location of the Night Wisp to anyone who was watching. I didn't want to risk that just yet.

Marcus moved forward with his rifle at the ready, heading down the corridor towards what I assumed was an exit.

"They don't seem to be easy to kill. It'll be faster just to disable them," I said.

"That seems cruel."

He was right, and I didn't like it much. "Yeah," I said as the first creatures came into view. "But it won't be long till the station is destroyed, freeing them from whatever foul mind did this."

I aimed my wand and called out the command word. A bolt of lightning arced from my wand to the lead creature and its whole body convulsed. It fell over as a burnt husk and was replaced by more, marching over its remains. I was glad of my helmet, as I was sure the smell of burnt flesh was filling the corridor.

Marcus opened fire with his rifle, shooting faster than any mere human could hope to match. Between his rifle and my wands, we were cutting them down in great numbers, but they kept coming. They climbed over the remnants of those who came before them and kept coming, apparently with no concept of fear or disgust. Nothing seemed to faze them as they pressed their attack.

"We're heavily outnumbered," said Marcus.

"Time for our emergency escape plan," I said. I activated the comm. on my armor and said, "Shira, we need an emergency evac!"

"You're outside my range. We're moving closer," she replied.

I tossed aside my last two wands and grabbed my rifle. I couldn't fire as fast or as well as Marcus and the rifle wasn't as effective as the wands, but it was all I had. "Hurry, Shira! We'll soon be overwhelmed!"

Time passed. After what seemed like an eternity, Shira sent, *"Let me see the area around you."*

"Sure," I replied and hurriedly sent her what I was seeing.

As soon as she received the images, she opened a gate behind our position.

"Retreat!" I called out as Shira sent, *"Go!"*

I was between Marcus and the gate so I grabbed the back of his amour and pulled him through. We tumbled out onto the bridge of the Night Wisp and Shira quickly closed the gate.

"Crivreen!" I called out. "Overload the engines and get us out of here, now!"

Crivreen hesitated briefly, then jumped in the pilot's seat and did what I asked.

"As soon as you can jump, do it! It doesn't matter where, just jump!"

"Right!" he said.

There were a few tense moments as we flew away at high speed. Then Ragnar said, "The station is firing!" and the cool azure of jump space wrapped around us.

After we came out of the post-jump hangover, Zah'rak asked, "What happened?"

I described the plan for the station to self-destruct and the creatures we had fought.

"Crivreen, send a message to the fleet warning them that the station is about to be destroyed, and then rendezvous with them," said Zah'rak.

"How could they have known about the fleet?" asked Raquel. "The ships were still at least half a day away from being detected by the station's sensor array."

"Could they have used the jump space relays like the fleet did?" I asked.

"Maybe, but even if they acquired access that way they wouldn't know where to look," she said. "The array would only be effective if they could target the area to scan."

"There must be a spy on the fleet," said Marcus.

"Then we'll need to be very careful what we communicate to them," said Zah'rak.

"Marcus, did you get much from that terminal?" I asked.

He pulled out the datapad and scrolled through the contents. "Looks like it."

"Let's set it up in engineering and see what we can find," I said.

"Go ahead, but we won't mention it to the fleet for the moment," said Zah'rak.

"The fleet is reporting that the station has destroyed itself," said Crivreen.

"That was fast," said Zah'rak.

"The only way anyone got off that station was via a gate," said Raquel.

"And there's nothing close to gate to," said Shira. "So that means that whoever opened the gate is a far more powerful magus than I am."

CHAPTER
THIRTY-SIX

When we'd rendezvoused with the fleet, Raquel approached me and said, "Zah'rak, now that the urgency is over and we're still in range of the jump relays, I still need to contact Resden."

"About us?" asked Purwryn.

"Yes; in fact, it would probably be best if you two are not here for this," she said.

"Marcus, let's get this datapad down to engineering and see what we can learn," said Purwryn. Marcus nodded and they left the bridge.

"Okay. Let's get this over with," I said.

She nodded and opened a secure channel through the Phareon communications network. A human answered the phone but he looked fake, more like a mannequin than a real person.

Raquel moved to the center of the screen's viewport and said, "Greetings, Ambassador. I'm Master Raquel, the official representative of the Wizard Kingdom for this region."

"Ah, yes. Dr. Leslie told me to expect your call. What can I do for you?" he asked.

"I'm currently aboard the Night Wisp and wish to inform you that the Night Wisp is property of the Wizard Kingdom," she said.

He leaned back in his chair and said, "Well now, that complicates things."

"You should also know that Purwryn is an agent of the Wizard Kingdom, and we therefore request that you stand down your search and cease all attempts to kill him or Marcus, who is in his employ."

Raquel obviously hadn't studied diplomacy at any of the places where the diplomats I knew had studied. She was too direct, and it showed on the ambassador's face. He was unprepared for what he faced. Personally I liked her style, and I was glad to see that she wasn't the kind to play the diplomatic game.

"I see. Well, Purwryn and his accomplice Marcus are wanted for questioning in relation to the murder of many Resden citizens," said the ambassador.

"They have killed no one except the men you sent to kill them," she said.

"On the contrary, shortly after they left the Paradise it exploded, killing all on board. There were over a thousand tourists on that ship, and none of them had tried to kill anyone," he said.

Raquel didn't even blink an eye at that shocking news. "The Wizard Kingdom is sorry for your losses but, as you said, they weren't even there when it happened. You've made many attempts to kill them without a fair trial or hearing. That practice is not acceptable and will not be tolerated."

The ambassador actually smiled at that. "We formally request extradition for trial, in that case."

"The request is denied. Your previous actions indicate that they will not have a fair hearing," she replied.

He thought about it for a few moments. "Then I suggest that I send some agents to meet you and question them on your terms. If evidence is forthcoming, we can arrange the extradition."

"You can send one agent, and we'll keep them under guard while the agent questions them. We'll contact you again when we're near a star base for the rendezvous."

"Fine, one agent; but if evidence is presented, we expect extradition to be granted," he said.

With that they ended the call. Crivreen turned to Raquel and said, "You aren't going to let them take Marcus and Purwryn, are you?"

"No, of course not. I don't believe Purwryn had anything to do with that explosion, but it will complicate things," she said.

"What do you propose we do?" I asked.

"Ragnar," she said, "are you able to use a truth rune?"

"Yes," he said, obviously taken aback by the question. "That's fairly basic for a Runecaster."

"Good, then this is what I propose. We will ask both Purwryn and Marcus to issue statements about what happened while Purwryn was a member of the Paradise crew, and ask Ragnar to certify the statements as true. Then I can send all that up to the Wizard's Council, so they will be prepared in case the good ambassador tries to go over my head."

"What about their agent?" asked Crivreen.

"I'm not worried about him at all. Zah'rak and I will be there to prevent him from trying anything. We need to allow the interview to show some modicum of diplomatic courtesy. After all, Grandmaster Vydor wants me to make friends out here if possible," she replied.

The conversation was interrupted by our comm. indicating an incoming call from our Phareon handler. "Hello, Commander," I said.

He started to speak but then noticed Raquel, who was still standing by the terminal since her last call. "Ambassador Raquel Ravenwood?" he asked.

"Yes, this is Master Raquel," I said.

"I'm honored to meet you," he said. It was obvious by his face that he was not at all happy to see her, but he wouldn't be foolish enough to say that out loud.

"I expect you want to hear our report. Crivreen, can you verify point-to-point security on this connection?" I asked.

"Yes, Zah'rak, the line is secure."

"Thanks," I said and gave the commander a complete report of events on the station, including our suspicion that there was a spy in the fleet. "Right now, Purwryn and Marcus are working on the data to see if we acquired any useful information."

"Purwryn? Marcus? What happened to Felix?" he asked.

"Felix quit the team back when we stopped at Zenfar, and as you reported he ditched his identity and went underground. He talked about going home to his family. Marcus and Purwryn are new team members who have been traveling with us for some time."

"I see," he said. Strangely, he was being polite and respectful for a change.

"We believe that the sorcerers escaped the destruction of the station by using a gate, which means they could be anywhere by now. Have you any other stations which have dropped off your communications grid like this one did?" I asked.

"Before I disclose that … " He was talking slowly, with more deliberation than I'd heard him use before. "Master Raquel, if I may be so bold, what business does the Wizard Kingdom have with my agents?"

"With your agents? None at this time. However, there appears to be sorcerer activity out here, and that has our attention," she said.

"And you weren't concerned about the necromancer who was active some time ago?" he queried.

"Actually, Master Raquel fought by our side in the battle against the necromancer's forces. We couldn't have defeated him without her help," I said.

That made him very uncomfortable. I remembered that Raquel had said he had a controlling personality. He must have realized by now that he was not as much in control of my team as he had thought, and no doubt that was bothering him greatly. I wondered what dots he was connecting in his head and how this would affect our future dealings with him.

The commander took a deep breath and fidgeted with something on his desk. "Then let me be the first to thank the Wizard Kingdom for their help."

"It was an honor. Now, back to the situation at hand. I already know of at least two more stations and one planet-side base that you've lost touch with. The sorcerers could have headed for any one of those, or somewhere yet unknown."

"Is the Wizard Kingdom officially assisting this mission, then?" asked the commander.

"We're hunting sorcerers, and currently that makes this mission mutually beneficial," said Raquel.

"I'll have to inform my command about this before I can proceed," said the commander, continuing to move things about on his desk. "Zah'rak, send the information your team gathered as soon as possible. I don't much like the suggestion that there could be a spy in the fleet out there."

"Sure, Commander. After we finish here I'll start someone working on that," I said.

"Excellent. Meanwhile, stay with the jump fleet and I'll get back to you after I speak with Command," he said.

The commander was being unusually pleasant and accommodating so I decided to push my luck a little. I didn't really care if I upset him so I had nothing to lose. "Commander, since we're on hold anyway, may we utilize the jump fleet to get to Hospital Station? We have some business there."

He turned and pulled something up on his computer; after studying that for a moment, he came to a decision. "Sure, that would work out well. I'll send the orders."

"Thank you," I said and we wrapped up the call.

"He intends to send us to the planet outpost that dropped off the grid," said Raquel.

"Let me guess: that's near the hospital?" asked Ragnar.

Raquel went over to the comm. controls and brought up an image of the commander while he was studying his computer screen. She instructed the computer to enlarge the image and zoom in on his left eye. "There, see the reflection."

"A map," said Crivreen.

"And I'd wager those lines are jump routes," she said, turning back to the controls at her station. "In fact, I believe the computer can extrapolate the map he was looking at."

A few moments later a map appeared on the screen and Raquel walked over to it. She pointed to a spot and said, "This is our current location. Here is the hospital and there is the planet."

They lined up quite well. It was evident that Hospital Station wouldn't be much out of our way if we were going to that planet. "Excellent. Crivreen, contact Dr. Leslie and let them know we're on our way; then link up with the fleet so that we're ready when they are."

"I'll tell Resden we can meet them at Hospital Station once we have an ETA. I plan to give them a very small window of time to meet us, and I hope they miss it," said Raquel.

"Oh, about that," said Crivreen. "We had better be careful how we break this news to Marcus."

"Why, what's up?" I asked.

"Marcus' father was the captain of the Paradise," said Crivreen.

CHAPTER
THIRTY-SEVEN

As we docked with Hospital Station Shira sent, *"Zah'rak, I think I'm just going to stay in hydroponics until our business is finished here. I have a lot of work to do."*

I sighed. She was hiding again, but at least she seemed to be warming up to Raquel. Unfortunately I'd already made a promise to Dr. Hawthorne. *"Shira, you need a checkup."*

"I'm fine," she sent.

I wondered if we'd be repeating this conversation for the rest of time. *"Sure, but you had brain surgery not that long ago. That's not something to take lightly."*

"If my brain were damaged I wouldn't be able to use my magic, so there's no reason to trouble anyone," she sent.

There was certainly nothing wrong with her ability to come up with good excuses. *"Tell you what, why don't I see if Dr. Hawthorne will come aboard and do the checkup here?"* I sent.

"Oh, do you think he'd do that?" she asked.

"I have no idea, but it can't hurt to ask," I replied. I was surprised that it had worked, but I was pleased with the victory.

"Would you?" she asked.

Something clicked when she sent that: I realized it was crowds she wanted to avoid. I wondered if it was related to all the people whose deaths she had facilitated when she'd been enslaved to the necromancer. By her hand not only had thousands died, but they had then stood back up and fought as walking dead. Maybe she felt that she couldn't trust herself around people anymore, or perhaps she feared she wasn't worthy company; whatever her reasons, I was grateful to have a solution. *"Sure, I will."*

I watched the displays as the station's computers took control of the craft and brought us into one of the new maintenance hangars. "Why are we going inside?"

"Oh, they offered to repair some of the damage we've recently sustained and upgrade our equipment. They said it would only take a few days," said Crivreen.

"And you agreed?" I asked.

"Not yet. I told them I'd have to talk to you about it, but figured there was no harm in docking in the bay," he said.

I shook my head. I knew exactly what he was up to. He desperately wanted to upgrade the Night Wisp's equipment into something more modern and, as he would put it, more reasonable. He probably figured that it'd be easier to convince me if we were already in the bay, and if not it'd be easier for him to sneak in some upgrades. "Fine. If they're footing the bill, let them, but nothing big; we need to be ready to leave when Phareon calls."

His face lit up like a child's in a candy shop. "Don't worry, I'll oversee it all myself!" he said, and once we were docked he ran off, presumably to engineering. I was more worried about the station's engineers than the ship under his watch.

Ragnar was laughing, and Raquel chuckled.

"What? It'll be good for him to have some other engineering types to hang out with for a while," I said.

Raquel smiled and said, "I'd better contact Resden and see if they're going to show."

I turned to Ragnar and said, "What do you make of the Paradise blowing up?"

"I don't know." He paused in thought for a moment and continued, "We have Marcus and Purwryn's testimonies but they don't shine any light on what happened. All we know is that someone interrogated Purwryn, and then Resden was all over them."

"And you're sure both of them told us the truth?" I asked.

"I'm sure they believe they told us the truth, but whether it's actually so I don't know," he said.

"Interesting distinction," I commented, but it made sense and was worth noting. "Whatever is going on, I'll be happier once that's behind us."

"Then you're in luck," said Raquel. "Resden will have an agent here in a few hours to speak with them."

"Did you report all of this to the council yet?" I asked.

"Yes. They are up to date, and I was assured that they'd back me on this," she said.

"Great," I said. I left the bridge and headed for the station. I figured Marcus and Purwryn would probably already be heading for Marcus' check up.

On the two occasions I'd previously visited the station, I had stayed on the Night Wisp. It wasn't common practice for patients to actually come into the hospital unless their need was beyond what could be dealt with on the ship. Dr. Hawthorne had invited me to his office; otherwise I would have stayed on the Night Wisp as I had last time. I gathered that being citizens meant the station was now open to us.

The hospital was a very large station, and I quickly found myself lost in its twists and turns. I kept wandering around until I found what I thought to be an information desk.

"Excuse me, but I seem to be lost," I explained.

The woman behind the desk looked up at me and smiled. "That happens a lot. Where are you trying to get to?"

"Dr. Hawthorne's office," I said.

"Ah. Well, you're in the wrong section of the station for that. This is the maternity wing," she said and gave me directions to the correct section, which was quite a walk from there.

While I walked, I took some time to look at the staff and visitors to the station. Most seemed normal enough, but some really stood out: they were dressed in robes instead of more traditional clothing, and everyone gave them a wide berth. Most of them were physically unimpressive and none of them was armed, but it was clear that they were respected and possibly feared by most.

As I turned down the final corridor to the section with Dr. Hawthorne's office, two uniformed men stopped me. They were wearing battle armor and looked like warriors, apart from the lack of weapons. I wondered if weapons were banned on the station.

"I'm sorry, sir, but this corridor is restricted," said one of the guards.

"I have an appointment to see Dr. Hawthorne," I told him. I was surprised by their posture. It should have been obvious that even with their battle armor I could easily toss them aside, and their lack of weapons meant they couldn't stop me, but they had no fear of me at all. I was easily twice their bulk and that normally caused people to be intimidated.

"Wait here," said one of the guards as he walked off. The second guard stayed in position, blocking my path. It was so rare to see anyone stand before me completely undaunted by my size that I was tempted to test him, to see if he could back up that fearless stance with action.

I knew that would be foolish so I distracted myself with idle conversation. "I'm new here. What's the deal with the people in robes?"

A look of surprise crossed his face. "What do you mean?"

"Well, they seem to have some authority, but I don't think I've ever seen anyone dressed like that before," I said.

"You mean the wizards?" he replied.

"Wizards?" I repeated.

"Yes. The robes signify that they're wizards and the color indicates their rank," he said.

I wanted to hear more about that, but the second guard came back and said, "All right, follow me."

He left the other man alone at the entrance, which I felt was foolish, but maybe it was because there was no expectation of real problems on the station. That would be odd, considering that just a few months ago the station had come under attack and had a long history of living on the edge of danger.

We traveled down several corridors filled with offices until he finally stopped at one.

"He's in there," said the guard.

"Thanks," I replied.

He nodded and walked away.

On entering the office, I found Dr. Hawthorne sitting at his desk working on something on his computer. His office was neat and decorated with various paintings and sculptures which I couldn't identify. I assumed that they were valuable in some way or at least significant to him, but to me it was all just random decorations.

He stood to greet me as I came in. "Ah, Zah'rak! I'm glad you could make it!"

I was at a loss for a reply. Narcion had been much smoother at dealing with officials than I was; it was another thing I would miss about working with him. "Thanks for having us."

"Please sit down," said Dr. Hawthorne. "Can I get you something to drink?"

"No, thanks," I said. I found a chair that looked sturdy enough to hold me. "You wanted to talk about Shira?"

"Yes," he said, sitting on his desk. "Shea contacted us and sent on Shira's records just before they left the region. Last time we spoke I hadn't made the connection, but after further research into her case I identified her as Shea's patient."

"She met with Shea for a few hours when we crossed paths with the Nemesis," I said.

"Yes," said Dr. Hawthorne, nodding. "Shea's report is that Shira is suffering from depression and post-traumatic stress from her experiences. This is of course completely normal, given what she went through, but I wanted to let you know."

"What can we do about it?" I asked.

Dr. Hawthorne smiled and drank from a mug next to his computer. "Based on my last conversation with her, I'd say keep on doing what you're doing. You gave her a job on the craft, one that's solely her responsibility and is valuable to the ship. You also involve her in the missions; while they are dangerous, that means she feels she's doing penance for her actions."

"But it wasn't her fault! The necromancer had an implant in her brain. She has nothing to feel guilty about," I said.

"On a purely logical level you're right, but she still experienced it; she went through the actions. She heard the screams and saw the devastation. Logic has no sway over this," he said.

"What's my next step, then?" I knew he was right. All freed slaves dealt with negative emotions on some level, but I didn't know any who had seen the things she had. Shira refused to talk about that time, but I knew it haunted her sleep. I wished there was something more I could do, but nothing I had tried so far had worked.

"I think we should evaluate her psychological condition again, and see how it compares to Shea's report."

"She doesn't want to come on to the station to see you," I said.

"Why's that?"

"She didn't say, but I think she fears being around crowds. She did agree to see you if you came on board."

"Astute observation; I suspect you're right. Very well, then. Once I'm finished with Marcus, I'll get Dr. Leslie and we'll meet you at your ship."

"Dr. Leslie? Is she the doctor you had with you when we spoke last?"

"Yes, and she's a former slave herself. As she and Shira are both human females and former slaves, that may help to ease the tension a little. That's merely an educated guess, however, and we'll have to see how it plays out as we go. I assure you we will do everything we can for her, but not without your permission."

That seemed reasonable, though I hardly felt qualified to make any decisions about her mental care. "Okay. That seems like a wise plan. Could we schedule it for tomorrow, after the breakfast hour?"

He got up and checked his computer. "Sure, that will be fine."

CHAPTER

THIRTY-EIGHT

Purwryn looked pensive. He asked, "Marcus, are you ready for this?"

He and I were in the ship's mess as the Night Wisp docked with the hospital station. Thanks to my Cyborg connections to the ship's systems, I realized we were landing in a bay instead of docking externally. "Interesting. I wonder what's happening?"

"What do you mean?" he asked.

I had to remind myself that he couldn't hear or sense the things I could. "We're landing in a bay."

"Odd," he said. Then his face lit up with a smile. "I bet Crivreen is trying to get the Night Wisp some upgrades."

The Night Wisp was an older craft, but she was solid and reliable. Crivreen was too young to appreciate the advantages of tried-and-true stability over cutting-edge upgrades. "He might get them this time." My internal communications system was picking up unsecured traffic between Crivreen and the dock. He was excitedly talking over options with someone station-side and, despite his excitement, he was making very reasonable and sensible requests. The station engineers seemed to be enjoying his interest and encouraging it.

"You never answered my question," Purwryn said, interrupting my thoughts.

"What?" I asked, puzzled. "Oh, you asked if I'm ready. Ready for what?"

"To go openly onto the station as a Cyborg," he replied.

I struggled to understand his point. There was no sense in doing what he suggested. "Why would I do that? I'm just going to see the doctors as I've always done. They'll keep things confidential and no one will be the wiser."

"So you're going to keep your cover, then?" he asked.

Primitives like Purwryn were hard to understand sometimes. I couldn't fathom why he thought I would drop my cover; all that would achieve would be more trouble with the locals and more people at risk. I searched through my memory net for the most appropriate response in this kind of situation and went with a lopsided grin. "No reason to change now."

He shrugged. "I'll check with the station and find out the time of your checkup."

I didn't need a checkup. I knew the exact condition of every one of my implants, but there was no harm in getting one and it would allay everyone's concerns. It was important that I kept up my cover as someone who'd needed help and luckily fell among them. If they ever suspected the truth, my mission would fail.

They were a strange group, behaving like a family even though there were at least three or four races of primitives represented among them. I had even been treated like family, although they barely knew me. It was hard not to like them and want to be part of their team, but I had obligations to fulfill. I couldn't be drawn into caring about them; that might jeopardize my chances later.

"Sounds like we have a couple of hours," said Purwryn.

"Good. Let's go on board and check the station's vendors," I said.

"Marcus, this is a hospital, not a trading hub," said Purwryn.

"I know that, but hospitals sell medical supplies and I could use some spare parts. I had to leave mine behind when our ship crashed." I actually wanted to see the current top-of-the-line technology for implants. This hospital had a reputation for being advanced far beyond the rest of the sector; no doubt it was greatly exaggerated, but even allowing for that they should have some very interesting options. I might even ask for some upgrades while here, if I could think of a good excuse.

"Oh, sure. That makes sense. I'll download a map of the station onto my armor's computers," he said.

It was strange that primitives hated the idea of Cyborgs having enhancements wired into them, but they went out of their way to carry similar equipment on their person or in their pockets. Unlike most of the crew, Purwryn always wore his battle armor. This armor was amazing; I had not seen the like of it anywhere before. It looked normal to the untrained eye, but it was far from that. The armor fitted perfectly, almost like a second skin, and it was capable of self-repair. It was closer to an exoskeleton than anything else. If I could figure out how it worked and modify my own skin to work the same way, I'd be nigh unstoppable.

They all had armor like that, but the others only donned it when needed. Zah'rak was apparently making a set for me also but needed more supplies, which would hopefully be delivered to this station soon. Having my own set would be both a blessing and a curse. It would be great to have extra protection, but I'd be foolish to compromise it by trying reverse engineering. No, I'd have to get a second set somehow.

Purwryn had a small computer console on his wrist, and another in his helmet computer to control the systems in his armor. I had the same type of controls; they were simply part of me instead of separate. It was such a small step for a primitive to evolve by melding with the equipment they already used. I couldn't understand why they hated the idea so much. Shrugging off that thought, I downloaded the map to my local memory net and followed him off the ship.

We left the docking bays and headed towards the center section of the station where most of the visitor facilities were located. The station was very busy and apparently in the middle of a massive remodel. Everywhere I looked there were construction crews doing something.

Men and women dressed in full battle armor were patrolling, but they had no visible weapons. This worried me. If something went wrong I had a good chance against armed primitives, but if these guards were unarmed that meant they were probably magi. A quick search of public records for the region confirmed my suspicions. This was a wizard-controlled station, and that meant the guards were all battle wizards. That was far worse, as battle wizards would be combat-trained, unlike the local magi who were often more of a danger to themselves than anyone else.

Men and women in robes also came and went throughout the station, and these posed even more of a threat than the battle wizards. The battle wizards were a new order of wizard, according to my internal database; each was deadly, but still in early training. The station staff wearing robes, however, were a different matter. The purple and green clothes indicated that they were higher-ranking and far more powerful than the newly-formed battle wizards, most of whom wore red armor to signify their lower rank.

"We should be able to find what you're looking for around here somewhere," said Purwryn, interrupting my internal survey of the station.

I smiled at him while he worked on the map and tried to figure out where we were in relation to it. Gently turning him, I pointed to a sign that clearly indicated where we needed to go. "You could fight with that map, or we could just go that way."

"Sure, if you want to cheat, I guess we can," he said and headed towards the store.

I gasped as I walked inside. It was filled with implants far more advanced than I'd even heard of. The rumors about this place weren't exaggerated at all; if anything, they were understated. I moved excitedly through the aisles of holographic displays, reading each one and telling Purwryn what we were looking at.

"Wow, this one has a hundred times the memory of mine!" I exclaimed.

"Really?" he asked.

"And look at this: nano-rebreathers!" I said. On and on the aisles went, with seemingly an infinite number of options. It was overwhelming and beyond description.

"I thought we were here to look at spare parts?" Purwryn gently reminded me.

"Sure, but I've never seen anything like this stuff before," I said.

"Why would a hospital have all this? Much of this stuff would never be medically necessary," said Purwryn.

"True, but this station represents the height of medical technology for the region, and many people come here looking for the best of whatever they want. From what I'm told, it's partly how the station has funded its operations all these years."

I attempted to bring myself back to the task at hand, as I really did need to replace some of my tools and parts. I didn't bother to look at the price tags on the equipment; I knew it would be well out of my range, especially since I was now unemployed. I would have to talk to Purwryn about that at some point. If I was going to serve with this crew, I should receive some kind of payment.

I found an order station and punched in my list, gasping a little as the total came up. The prices were fair, but I hadn't realized just how much I'd lost.

"Hey, don't worry about the bill," said Purwryn.

"What do you mean?" I asked.

"Master Raquel gave me a credit account which will cover all your medical needs," he said.

"Why?" I asked.

"Your medical needs will be covered completely by the Wizard Kingdom as long as you are in active service. Now, before you get any funny ideas, a rebreather is not a medical need."

I chuckled. "No, I guess not, unless we can arrange an underwater mission."

"Is that everything you need?" he asked.

"Yeah, I think so," I said. I knew it was exactly what I needed, but I found that making uncertain statements instead of precise ones helped me to blend in with primitives more easily. I also worked hard to make sure any external signs of my implants were either disguised or covered by my clothing, so that no primitive could guess what I was. It was remarkably simple to blend in, but one tiny mistake would spell the end of my cover for good.

"Great. I'll have this delivered to the Night Wisp," he said.

Once that was done, it was time to head to Dr. Hawthorne's office for my appointment. I wasn't sure what to expect after seeing what was in that shop. Would they look at my apparently obsolete implants and pity me? Would they push all kinds of upgrades I couldn't afford but would desperately desire? I took some deep breaths as we entered the private office where the consultation would take place.

The office had several chairs organized in a semicircle around a small table. Another chair and terminal were close by. Behind the table was a large wall that seemed designed for a monitor but was empty. It was obvious by the layout where we were expected to sit, so we took our places in the chairs.

Purwryn looked over at me. "Do you want me to stay? This could get kind of personal."

I raced through my memory net looking for an appropriate response. I'd never had a primitive friend before, at least not since evolving beyond them, but I knew there were certain expected responses. Failing to find any, I went with my one of my default replies. "Oh, I guess so. I'm sure it's not going to be very exciting."

"Marcus, 'exciting' would be bad in this kind of meeting," he said with a grin.

We had no more time to talk, as Dr. Hawthorne had just entered.

When formal introductions had been made, the doctor said, "Marcus, I wanted you to come out here for this appointment because I'm concerned about some of your implants. I'm afraid I have some bad news."

I held up my hand to stop him. I didn't want a sales spiel. "Doctor, just as you know your hand is fine, I can tell my implants are all in good condition and operating within their tolerances. Mostly, at least."

He smiled. "I understand, but just as I wouldn't know that a cut on my hand was infected until it became bad enough to cause problems, you wouldn't yet see what we can observe."

"What are you getting at?" I asked.

"I'll show you," he said, pressing a button on his terminal. The wall behind him shimmered briefly and then changed to a diagnostic readout of my implants. It was easy for me to recognize; I'd seen the same chart many times over in my life. I could even pull up a version of it and overlay my vision if I so chose. The only difference was that the large scale of his display allowed the display of far more detail than I was used to seeing.

Dr. Hawthorne got up from his chair and walked over to the wall. "I'm sure you've seen this before, but for Purwryn's information this is a diagnostic readout of all Marcus' implants. With this, Marcus, we can tell the exact condition of every part of your body, even the unenhanced areas. As you said, everything is operating within reasonable parameters for devices of this age and type."

"I see," said Purwryn. He probably understood a lot of what he saw, as it wasn't very different to readouts from the testing gear he had used back on the Paradise to diagnose problems with the robots we maintained. "But if everything is within normal parameters, what's the issue?"

The doctor returned to his terminal and used the controls to isolate parts of the screen. "These implants are already beyond their life expectancy, and those are nearing the end of their lives." He changed the screen to bring up a network map of the wiring in my body that supported the implants. "Also, several main routes in this wiring show signs of being ready to fail. It's likely that in the near future some or all of them will fail."

"What does that mean?" I asked.

"It means you have three options," said Dr. Hawthorne, returning to his seat in front of us. "First, you can walk out of here and do nothing. I think you'd be fine for a while, but sooner or later some of these are going to fail, and you might not be anywhere near this facility when that happens. That could leave you crippled or worse until you could get help. Second, we could replace the failing parts, but that would require extensive work, as we'd have to upgrade much of your control network to handle the replacements." The doctor paused there.

"And the third option?" I asked.

The doctor smiled. "We could send you through the gate back to the Wizard Kingdom where, with the help of Master Kellyn, we could remove all the implants and make you a normal human again."

"That's not possible. Too much of my former body is gone; besides, I was a cripple before getting these implants." Even if it were possible, the thought disgusted me.

"It is possible. Master Kellyn could regrow all your missing ... parts, and you wouldn't be a cripple. You'd be a healthy human being with all your limbs fully functional," said Dr. Hawthorne.

"Wow." Medical science had really moved on in the years since I'd last been in the hospital. I'd never heard of a Cyborg being able to go back; it was always assumed to be a permanent upgrade. But, despite what Dr. Hawthorne said, I would be a cripple compared to my current state. It was inconceivable for a Cyborg to even consider it. "How long would it take to replace my implants?"

"We'd have to put you in sleep mode for a couple of days, and you would be kept on restricted duty for a week or so while we monitored the acceptance process. After that, we'd want to see you again in a few months to make sure all was still good."

"What do you think, Purwryn?" I asked. I knew we had a deadline, due to the upcoming mission.

"I could no more suggest you remove your implants and go back to being an ordinary human than I would consider going back to being a mundane. I think you should have the repairs done," he said.

I smiled. I hadn't considered that angle before; as a magus, he could understand how I felt about going back to being a primitive. I wondered if I needed to create a third class of people: Cyborgs, primitives and now magi. I needed more data to determine how different they really were. Powerful and dangerous, yes, but were they different where it mattered? Could they see beyond the here and now and comprehend a wider view of events, unfolding everywhere at once?

"Doctor, how much will it cost?" I asked.

"I deem this medically necessary, and you're currently deployed with the Wizard Kingdom on a military operation, so it will cost you nothing. Your medical care is covered completely."

Amazed, I looked over at Purwryn, who immediately said, "No, we're still not going to pay for a rebreather."

I couldn't help but chuckle. Why he was fixated on that specific part I couldn't tell, but it was entertaining. I was tempted to make a play for one just to see his reaction. "What about the mission deadline?"

"We'd better check with Zah'rak about that. Worst case scenario is that we come back after the mission and have it done then."

CHAPTER
THIRTY-NINE

I waited outside the room while the Resden agent was interrogating Pur-wryn. When he was finished it would be my turn, and then it was off to surgery. Zah'rak decided that, since Phareon had left us hanging, there was no reason not to have the surgery done right away. If Phareon tried to move up the timeline, he'd simply refuse until I was ready. I think he'd enjoy the opportunity to do just that. I wondered why he disliked them so much; there had to be some history there, but I hadn't discovered it yet.

To occupy myself while I waited, I reviewed my mission notes so far. Purwryn had all the marks of a maker. He'd quickly picked up on all the technology involved with my implants and expertly performed the maintenance, despite having no training in them whatsoever. I decided that I'd try to convince him to purchase some enhancements; maybe just a memory net or neural interface to start, something to whet his appetite. We could use more like him, and once he became drawn to enhancements he could probably design his own and advance the in-dustry as a whole.

I could hear everything going on in the interview through the walls, thanks to my enhanced hearing. The agent was pushing Purwryn hard. Purwryn didn't seem to have experience dealing with a professional interrogator and wasn't doing well under the pressure. Raquel jumped in several times and warned the agent to back off.

The agent didn't like being corralled, but Raquel wasn't a woman who could be pushed around. I couldn't see through the walls, but I was sure she squared up to him and enjoyed putting him in his place. Raquel was definitely a natural-born leader. She also seemed to live for competition, and was definitely showing the Resden agent that she was more than able for anything he could dish out.

I knew Zah'rak was in there, but he didn't say much. He was a warrior all the way through. Of all the kinds of primitives I'd discovered in my travels, his subtype was the easiest to understand: give him a weapon and a target and let him be. The warrior type didn't like management, and worked best when left alone. The only problem with them was that they fared poorly during peacetime. Warriors tended to get restless and often got themselves into trouble. He was more controlled than most of those I'd come across, but we were still on an active mission. It remained to be seen how he'd react to a time of peace.

While I waited, I looked through my memory net and tried to find anything that might give the Resden agent reason to force extradition, flagging it not to mention. I had no idea who was after Purwryn or why the agents were after him now. That much was the truth. If I just stuck to that part of the story, I should be fine.

Purwryn came out looking very shaken. He said, "Okay, you're up. Bit of advice, don't answer any questions unless Raquel gives you the go-ahead. He kept trying to trip me up with questions designed to trick me into saying things that weren't true."

"I've dealt with his type before, but thanks for the warning," I said. I ran a program I had stored in my memory net which kept my expression perfectly neutral. I usually let my face display a normal range of emotions, as it made primitives more comfortable, but this wasn't a time to risk giving anything away.

Inside the room were a table and several chairs. Zah'rak was there in full battle armor, including his swords and other weapons. He was physically impressive for a primitive, and even unarmed was more than a match for the human Resden agent, or indeed any other human. I was glad he was there because his sheer physical presence would keep the agent from doing anything stupid.

Raquel was in her body armor, which was by far the most impressive armor I'd ever seen. The nanotechnology it employed was centuries beyond anything we had out there. Like the battle wizards, she was completely unarmed. My file on her described her as perhaps the most dangerous person alive in this sector. She was a 'person of interest' on whom I was to gather as much information as possible, but so far she'd seemed fairly normal. There was no sign of her supposed power and strength.

The Resden agent was dressed in formal business attire and looked like the perfect clone of every other government agent. He didn't stand as I entered; instead, he gestured at the chair in front of him. I looked at Raquel who nodded, and I sat and waited silently.

"Marcus," the agent said, "your history shows many great debts which were recently paid off."

I kept my eyes locked on his and didn't say anything. I hoped my emotionless demeanor would frustrate him.

"Since the money was paid back, you haven't gone into debt. Why is that?" he asked.

"I learned my lesson about debt, and no longer spend more than I make," I said, keeping my voice monotone and to a precisely perfect rhythm. When he played a recording of this interview later on, he would struggle to hear any hint in my voice as to whether or not I was telling the truth and he would find nothing. I hoped he was not the type to give up easily and that he would struggle with it for days on end, even losing sleep over it.

"Your previous debt was all medical expenses. People don't normally have any choice about those," he said.

I said nothing in response. I had learned from previous interrogations that the secret was to say as little as possible. If they make statements, you don't respond.

"Tell me about the explosion of the Paradise," he said.

"Sorry, I can't. I wasn't there for it and know nothing about it," I lied. This was where I had to be particularly careful. When Raquel and Ragnar had asked me for a statement, I told them exactly what happened from the day that Purwryn was kidnapped until we joined their crew. They asked no questions about the explosion and I offered no information.

"Your father was on board. Correct?" he asked.

I was sure my father would have found a way off before the explosion. "I don't know; I wasn't there."

"Do you have any reason to think he wasn't there?" asked the agent.

"As I said, I wasn't there. I can't confirm or deny something which I know nothing about."

He leaned back in the chair and said, "This will go a lot faster if you just tell me what you know."

"You already have my statement," I said, gesturing to the datapad on the table.

"Yes, but it tells me nothing about the explosion," he replied.

I didn't respond to that. I could see Raquel in the corner with a big smile on her face. She was enjoying the agent's frustration with me and didn't care if anyone noticed.

I also knew that the agent wouldn't be happy and would persist. I kept a running log of all the questions he asked and every answer I gave, so when he tried to trip me up by asking the same question phrased differently I could repeat my original response. Just to be extra annoying, I pointed out when I had already answered a question and then told him my answer had not changed in the last few minutes.

The agent kept trying, hiding his frustration. He pressed questions about my medical history, previous money issues and so on, obviously trying to establish a motive for destroying the Paradise. No doubt he reasoned that if he could establish a motive he could then press for extradition.

After an hour, Raquel stepped forward and said, "I've heard enough. Marcus, you may go."

I rose to leave and the agent started to protest. Zah'rak stepped between the agent and myself and opened the door to let me out. As I left I heard Raquel say, "You had your chance, but you haven't convinced me you can establish a means or motive. Extradition is still denied."

Purwryn was waiting for me outside the room. "How did it go?"

"With a little luck, he'll be so angry and frustrated that he won't get any sleep tonight," I said.

He smiled and shook his head. "I wish I did know what happened. I mean, I was shot, kidnapped, drugged and interrogated by someone for some reason. It'd sure be nice to know why."

"Yeah." I sympathized with him but had no answers. As far as I knew, his introduction into the Paradise mission and the events surrounding it were a lucky coincidence for me.

"Any word from your father?" he asked.

I had told him I was sure my father had made it off the Paradise before it exploded, but I hadn't told him how I knew that. I suspected he thought me in denial as a way to cope, and maybe I was. "No, but he'd have no idea where to send a message. The last he heard, we were heading to Phineary."

"True," he replied.

We walked quietly through the station towards patient registration, and I remembered I needed to talk with him about something personal and important. "Purwryn, when I check in, I have to assign someone full medical authority to make decisions on my behalf if I'm unable to do so. I would be honored if you'd allow me to appoint you."

"Me? Wouldn't it be wiser to appoint Raquel? She's more or less your doctor," he said.

"But you're my friend. Besides, you can always ask her opinion; I'd just feel better if you had the final say." There was wisdom in suggesting Raquel, but I knew I could trust Purwryn to do the best by me, and Raquel to do the best for the team and the mission. Normally those goals would line up, but I couldn't count on that.

"Okay, I'll do it," he said quietly. "You just make sure you pull through this, you hear me?"

I thought that was an odd question. "Oh, my hearing implants are fine. They aren't even on the list to be replaced."

He shook his head and kept walking. When we got to the desk a nice primitive woman checked me in, her hands flying across the keyboard. It was such an inefficient means of entering data, but she was fast for a primitive. There was a time when no person was involved in the check-in process; patients just walked through a scanner and were automatically entered into the system, but it turned out to be surprisingly inefficient. Most patients had questions, special requests or other issues that an automated system couldn't handle, so people were reintroduced into the process. It was almost paradoxical that a slower primitive interface like this was a faster process than a pure, automated interface. It was yet more proof that the best way forward was to combine the two and retain the advantages of both.

When everything had been entered, a nurse took me back to a changing room with a safe. I was instructed to put all my personal belongings in the safe and put on a gown that barely gave lip service to modesty. The room was predictably chilly, but my internal systems simply adjusted my bodily functions to generate more heat in compensation.

While I waited, I received a message on my internal communications network.

"*Agent P2003, report,*" came the electronic-sounding voice. No one around me would be able to hear anything. It was all in my head.

"Operations progressing as planned," I silently replied.

"*Current status?*" asked the voice.

"I was heavily damaged and am going in for repairs," I replied.

"Dump mission report," said the voice.

"Initiating dump," I said and started the operation from my internal memory net. When it was completed, I said, "Dump complete. Mission still on track. Will be offline for repairs for one to two days."

"Acknowledged. Continue mission. Report back after repairs with new operational specifications," said the voice.

CHAPTER
FORTY

Two weeks had passed since we'd heard from the Phareon command-er and several days since Marcus had come out of surgery. Master Mathorn had finally been able to get us a shipment of gold and diamonds.

It was exciting working on the new type of armor for which Master Spectra had given us the formula six months ago. It was taking a lot longer to craft, but it should be much tougher and repair itself faster. I wondered if it would still be green, like the other armor I'd made. Was that green be-cause I'd made it or because of the materials I'd used? I must see if that was covered in the information they gave us. If I could make customized colors, that would be even better.

I had already begun a set of armor with the materials we'd been able to recover from Siden, but had run out of materials due to mistakes along the way. The new armor required a much greater degree of precision than that I had made previously. Thankfully this stop at the hospital had left me with a lot of down time, so I was able to focus on the armor. Even with the setbacks I should have Marcus' armor ready soon, as well as the experimental design for my own armor.

I went down to the cargo bay to get the supplies I needed for the crafting when Shira stopped me.

"Zah'rak!" she said.

"Hi, Shira." She had been seeing Dr. Leslie every other day since we docked. It seemed to be helping her, but she still stayed on the ship in hydroponics most of the time.

"I was wondering: can we use the gate and go back to that forest?" she asked.

"That forest wasn't very safe," I said.

"No, but if we go during the day, it's safe enough," she said. There was a wistful look in her eyes as she added, "I miss the trees."

"I do too," I said quietly. "Once we know something about our next mission, we'll see if we can schedule a time to go. I wonder how we can tell when it's daytime there?"

"I'm sure Raquel knows how to tell," she said.

"True. I'll check with her," I said.

"Could we also visit the other forest?" she asked.

"Other forest?" I asked.

"Yeah. Raquel told me about another place we can use the gate to get to. She said it's not in Vydoria or Korshalemia; it's a whole different realm, not marred by technology. It's sparsely populated with simple tribal people, living their lives in tune with nature."

"That sounds wonderful," I said. It sounded better than wonderful; it sounded like a place I could call home someday. "I'll tell you what: after this mission, we'll make it a point to go there. It'll be a good vacation."

She gave me the biggest hug her tiny frame would allow and ran off. It felt good to see her happy. As I watched her run, I wondered where her family was. I didn't want to ask her just yet in case there was pain associated with those memories. That might interfere with her recovery, but I would like to let them know she was free and doing well. If she were my daughter or sister, I'd sure want to know.

With a great sigh, I turned back to my mission to reach the cargo bays and get the supplies I needed to make the armor. It would be nice to get back to crafting. I wondered at the delay in getting new orders, but it suited me; it allowed us to get a lot of important work done.

I hadn't make it far when Purwryn crossed my path. He was just re-boarding the Night Wisp. "Hey, Zah'rak!"

"Hey. How's Marcus?" I asked.

"Doing well. The docs think the new implants will work well, and there are no signs of rejection. Of course, they still want to see him back in half a year or so, but he should be fit for duty if we ever get orders again."

I chuckled. He was anxious to get back to work. "Great! And I'm sure we'll hear soon."

Continuing on my way towards the cargo bays, I had almost made it to the hatch when Ragnar's voice came over the comm.

"Zah'rak, we have an incoming call from Phareon," he said.

I looked longingly at the hatch, sighed and turned back towards the bridge. "Ask Raquel to meet me up there," I said.

"Sure thing," he said.

Well, at least Purwryn will be happy, I thought to myself as I walked up to the bridge. When I arrived there, Ragnar was at the comm. station and Raquel was waiting for me near the command chair.

"Time to find out if Phareon still likes us," I said.

"Hardly, but they need us," said Raquel.

"Okay, Ragnar, put him on the screen," I said.

The commander appeared on the screen, but there was someone with him for a change.

"Hello, Master Raquel, Zah'rak," he said. "This is Ambassador Sarrin, and he will be joining us from now on."

"Probably to make sure the good commander doesn't start a war," sent

Raquel. Though her face didn't betray anything, her mental voice carried a chuckle with that statement.

She was probably right. The commander wasn't known for his finesse and it wouldn't be a surprise to learn that every one of his superiors expected him to cause a war. I didn't envy Sarrin's task of keeping him in line, but I expected it would provide some enjoyment to watch.

"Fine. Pleased to meet you, Ambassador. Now, what do you have for us?" Despite the potential entertainment value, I was annoyed at the addition. I had hoped to make this our last mission for them, but if they had assigned an ambassador then they were probably expecting long-term cooperation.

"I'll send the specifics in the data stream, but we need you to investigate a planet near your current location. We believe it to be the headquarters of whoever is behind the recent attacks," said the commander.

"What makes you think that?" I asked. It seemed that Raquel had predicted their next move correctly. She'd said when she joined us that there were several stations and a planetary base that Phareon should concern themselves with. Foolishly, I hadn't yet asked her for more information.

"We attempted to send infantry to reclaim a station, and found more of those creatures that your men fought on the previous station. That was all that was left of the crew of that station. Our casualties were very high, but we successfully reclaimed the station and were able to download the main database. That data, combined with the information you provided, leads us to believe that these stations are merely a distraction," said the commander.

The ambassador piped up. "A second fleet is on its way to you now. We would like you to land ahead of the fleet, learn what you can and then assist in the destruction of the planetary base. We assume the sorcerers will be there and unwilling to die without a fight, so we're grateful for any help that the Wizard Kingdom might be inclined to provide."

With that last comment the ambassador looked directly at Raquel, and she took the cue and responded. "Don't worry, Ambassador; if there are sorcerers there, we'll handle them. We'll need a copy of everything you got from that station, including all mission reports from the teams deployed to retake the station."

The commander started to say something but the ambassador cut him off. "Of course. We'll send that presently." That annoyed the commander greatly, but he held his tongue. I suspected that when this call was over there would be words between them. I found myself hoping they'd forget to cut the channel when those words started.

"When can we expect the fleet?" I asked.

"In about three days," said the commander.

"Excellent," I said. That would give Crivreen enough time to put the ship back together, I estimated. After that, we wrapped up the conversation.

Once the comm was secured, I told Ragnar to contact Criveen and tell him to have the ship ready to launch.

I was about to ask Raquel for more information on the Phareon stations when she said, "We need to get Shira and head through the gate to the Sac'a'rith fortress."

"Why?" I asked.

"Because it's almost sunrise there," she said and left the bridge.

I looked over at Ragnar who shrugged and said, "I guess that's as good a reason as any."

"I suppose so. Well, take charge till we get back," I said. I had to admit I shared Shira's desire to go back and welcomed the opportunity.

"And by 'take charge' you mean 'make sure Crivreen puts all his toys away'?" he joked.

I chuckled and said, "Yeah, and brief everyone on what we just learned."

CHAPTER
FORTY-ONE

Shira met us in the gate room with the black backpack Raquel had prepared for our last trip. "I can't wait to see the trees again!"

Raquel smiled. "Yeah, me too." She carried no technology on her at all, not even the purple armor that she usually wore into combat. Instead she was dressed in leather and animal skins, more like Ragnar's people.

I had wanted to take my armor but she insisted that I travel dressed as she was, more primitively. She also wanted me to leave my blasters behind, and all forms of technology - even my swords.

She walked over to the gate and said, "The sun should be coming up about this time. The last time we went through we made a forced run to the fortress, but we won't being doing that this trip. Later in the day Shira can gate us there, but this trip is more about learning what it means to be Sac'a'rith."

She turned to Shira. "Did you remember to leave all technology behind?"

"Yes," she said. "I rarely carry more than a datapad and armor, so no worries there."

She looked at me and I just grimaced in response. "I'll take that as a 'yes' for you, too. I think, as your training progresses, you will learn to lose your dependence on technology. It slows you down and hinders you; you're better off without it."

"I notice you normally still wear armor," I said.

"Yes, but remember I'm cursed and can't use my powers without great risk." Darkness passed over her face as she said that, and I wanted to kick myself for my gibe. It was unfair and hurtful.

She turned and opened the gate to the homeworld of the Sac'a'rith. As we stepped out, the power of the forest passed over me like a warm summer breeze. I felt stronger and more alive. I tasted the air with my forked tongue and picked up dozens of scents. I scented prey animals who were fleeing the area that we had just entered, predators cautiously pulling back and evaluating us, birds flying high up on the wind untroubled by our appearance and a dozen more scents that I'd never experience on a spaceship.

Shira's countenance was that of a small child given access to a candy store. Her eyes were closed and her head thrown back. The wind ruffled her dark hair and she laughed a little. "Oh, it's so good to be home." She inhaled deeply and held her breath for some moments before slowly releasing it. I could almost see her tension being released with that breath.

Even Raquel was a bit brighter. "In time, with training, you'll learn how to reach out to nature even in the vacuum of space; until then, forests like this one are so full of life that it becomes easy to understand what we are."

"Which is what?" I asked.

"Sac'a'rith – or in the common tongue, Warriors of Nature. Actually, perhaps 'Champions of Nature' is a better translation."

"Me?" asked Shira. "A champion?"

"Oh, yes, little one, very much so. You and Zah'rak are the progenitors of a new generation of champions. Centuries from now, stories will be told about you to upcoming generations. Families will name their kids after you and many will proudly boast how they are descended from you in some way, even those who are obviously not."

Shira was taken aback by that. "But, how? I'm not exactly – "

"No, not yet," Raquel interrupted. "But today, we'll begin to change that."

I leaned against a tree, feeling its power rush into me. A thought occurred to me that I was surprised I'd not considered before. "Raquel, didn't you say that this planet is where you were born, ten thousand years ago?"

"Yes," she said.

"Then this must be … Alpha World!" said Shira.

"Alpha World?" asked Raquel.

"A legendary world that no one really believed in," I said quietly. It was hard to believe I'd been flying around with a passage to Alpha World all this time. "The world where life first got its start before spreading out to the stars."

Shira continued the explanation in a very excited voice. "People of all species have been searching for it for generations, without success. Many times someone claimed to have found it, but they were always proven wrong. It became one of those reoccurring myths that everyone loved to pretend to believe in, but no one really does."

"Well, it very much exists," said Raquel. "I never thought about it that way, but yes: at one time all life got its start here."

"Where in the galaxy are we?" I asked.

"I'm not sure. I always use the gate to get here," said Raquel.

I looked over to Shira and said, "We should bring a datapad on our next trip and get an image of the night sky, then the computer on the Night Wisp can use the stars to locate the planet."

"No!" Raquel exclaimed. "Until we reclaim this world, we shouldn't let anyone find it. It's better that only true-born Sac'a'rith can get here via the gate for now."

I wasn't sure I understood her reasoning, but I knew she wanted to see the Sac'a'rith reborn as a pure order. There were only three of us, so I couldn't see us conquering a planet without help, however.

"So this is our world?" asked Shira.

"Yes, though it's currently occupied by the enemy and I have much to teach you. It's fall, so the days are getting shorter. Once you're trained it won't matter as much, but we need to fear the night, still," she said.

"Last time we were here, you said the forest was dangerous even during the day," I said.

"Oh, it is, which is why we need to get you a proper weapon," she replied. "This way."

I had plenty of proper weapons back on the Night Wisp, everything from knives to heavy anti-armor artillery and explosives. I couldn't imagine what we could find out here in the woods to match that.

She headed off through the woods down a game trail until she came to a clearing where a massive tree grew. It was wider around the trunk than my full reach could encompass and stretched upwards to what seemed like the edge of space, impossible though I knew it to be. Birds and small animals of all kinds lived in its massive branches, far above the ground.

The aura of life around this tree was the strongest I'd ever experienced from a plant; it seemed almost more than a tree, closer to a person than a plant.

There were tears in Raquel's eye as she touched the bark. "I planted this tree as a memorial on my wedding day."

I looked in awe at the majesty of life that it represented. This tree was ten thousand years old. It was still healthy and strong, and might last another ten thousand years for all I knew. I could only imagine what it had witnessed in all that time; the rise and fall of empires and nations, countless storms and beautiful summer days.

Shira walked over to Raquel and silently hugged her around the waist. I stayed back as they bonded. Eventually Raquel took a deep breath and turned towards me. "This tree will give you your first real weapon as a magus and a Sac'a'rith."

VINCENT TRIGILI

"How?" I asked.

"Ask the tree," she replied.

I slowly approached the tree. I had spent a little time reading about plants while Shira was learning hydroponics in case she needed help, and I'd heard of trees believed to be several thousand years old, but I didn't recognize the species of this one. That was hardly surprising since none of the plants here appeared in our database, but they all felt familiar. It was as Shira had said: somehow this was home.

I placed my hand on it to feel the bark that had weathered countless storms and received a sense of its spirit. Slowly my awareness drifted deeper into the tree and I felt it reaching out to me. As the sensation deepened, I could feel all the animals and insects that made the tree their home. A myriad tiny lives going about their daily business filled my thoughts.

Behind me I heard Raquel say, "Take the branch."

I looked up. Perhaps my eyes deceived me, but it seemed as if the tree had lowered a branch to where I could easily reach it. I grasped the branch it offered and it came off in my hand.

I stepped back and looked at the branch. It was long and strong, almost as long as I was tall. I turned it around in my hands a few times and it felt well-balanced. There was a power in the branch that connected to me as I held it. It grew and shifted slightly in my hands and became more comfortable to grip.

"Shira, draw down your staff," said Raquel.

As I watched, Shira reached into the air and pulled out the same staff I'd seen her use before. She spun it around with such grace and speed that it blurred into a disk. She stopped, stood up straight and planted the staff in front of her. It was slightly shorter than her, as the branch in my hand was just a little shorter than myself.

"A staff?" I asked.

"Yes," said Raquel. "Shira can teach you to fight with it, but first you must enchant it so that it truly becomes yours."

"But you use swords. Why can't I continue using mine?"

275

"I'm cursed, you aren't," she said quietly. "Now let us begin the binding process. You'll understand better when the staff is finished."

The staff had a much greater reach than my swords, but the lack of a blade struck me as a serious disadvantage. I doubted the wood could hold up if I swung it with any force against an armored target, but Raquel was here to teach me something and there was no way I could think of to protest which would not insult Shira as a teacher or rub Raquel's face in her curse.

Shira taught me the proper way to hold the staff and guided me through some basic moves. It seemed to make her happy to teach me something for a change, and I decided that I'd make an effort to learn to use this weapon, just for her. It would also give me another tool in my arsenal.

Raquel started to speak, but I sent, *"Let Shira do this first, please."* She smiled, nodded and wandered off out of the way.

After maybe an hour practicing with the staff, Raquel called me over. I was glad of the break, as my muscles weren't used to the movements required. I was sure I'd be sore in the morning, but the light in Shira's eyes as I successfully copied her movements made it all worthwhile.

"Now that you have the feel for it, let's begin the binding ritual."

CHAPTER
FORTY-TWO

Elsewhere, deep in an unknown forest, six magi gathered around a large sphere of pure tanzanite. The sphere was mounted on a large pedestal that looked as if it had been there for a thousand years. Surrounding the sphere were seven lampstands made of iron, each with a blue flame at the top, despite the fact that there were no candles. The flames danced in the light breeze, giving them the appearance of living things.

The six magi watched the sphere closely while chanting and weaving. They moved in a synchronized dance, slowly making their way around the sphere. Inside it, a scene was being played out which the magi were watching intently; a fleet of military spacecraft were gathering at a station.

Eventually their dance came to a halt, but they continued to watch the sphere as if it were of unsurpassed importance.

"They suspect our plan," said one.

"No, they have no idea. They are merely reacting to their bases being lost," said another.

"We must be more discreet," said a third.

"We have no time for that. We must build our army before the wizards realize what we are doing. If their idiot grandmaster ever learns to swallow his pride and obtain assistance from the other realm, we shall be ruined."

While they debated two more magi approached, both wearing pitch-black robes. They were wrapped in such evil and darkness that the very ground at their feet seemed to age and die as they walked towards the group. Energy crackled up and down their staves and wrapped around their forearms.

The six turned in unison and one of them, whose face resembled a skull more than a man, said, "Who dares disturb us?"

"I am Grandmaster, and you will not speak to me in that way!" called out the taller of the two approaching magi.

"Grandmaster?" laughed the skull-faced magus. "We shall see!"

With that he spun his staff and called out a command word. Fire leapt from his staff and engulfed the challenger and his partner. Neither of them even flinched.

"Is that the best you have, pyromancer?" asked the challenger. "Let's see how you fare against your own!"

The challenger chanted a spell, moving his arms and body as if he were pulling something out of the ground. Humanoid creatures of pure fire rose from the ground between the two opponents and cried out. The bravest of warriors would justifiably have run in fear from that cry, but these combatants ignored it.

The pyromancer had not been idle while the challenger was summoning; he also was chanting and pulling fire from the air around him, weaving it into a great ball. When he had finished, he launched the ball at the two challengers. The smaller one moved to intercept it, and the ball of fire hit him with a deafening crack as the superheated air rushed skyward at the speed of sound.

The summoned fire creatures marched towards the pyromancer, and the explosion from the massive fireball knocked the smaller challenger far back. His body skidded and rolled away. He did not rise to rejoin the fight, and smoke from his corpse carried the scent of burning flesh across the battlefield.

The remaining challenger took no note of the fall of his companion. He began to cast a second spell while his army moved towards the pyromancer.

The pyromancer began chanting and moving his arms in a ripping motion as the fire elementals approached him. The entire line of elementals dissipated as he finished his spell.

The challenger used that time to weave a dozen fireballs, which he launched towards the pyromancer in rapid succession. Each flew through the air with blinding speed and accuracy. Smoke trails filled the air between the two magi and sparks flew everywhere, threatening to start a forest fire. The combatants paid no attention to the forest around them. Neither of them could afford to risk diverting his attention from the fight.

The pyromancer danced around, dodging and using his staff to block the fireballs. He was occupied trying to avoid the danger and could not cast a counter-spell. It went well for him until he failed to block one fireball which slammed into his shoulder, breaking his concentration and dance pattern. As he stumbled back, another struck him and he fell hard on his back.

He rolled and used his staff to regain his feet, but the challenger was on him before he could recover. The challenger swung his staff heavily, hitting the pyromancer squarely on the temple. There was a sickening thud as the blow connected and the pyromancer dropped, dead before he reached the ground.

"I have defeated this contender to my title with his own spell line. My claim stands uncontested," said the challenger as he faced the five remaining magi. "Does anyone else dare to contest it?"

The five magi looked to the body of the skull-faced pyromancer and watched it turn to dust and blow away in the breeze. The challenger raised his hands as if to cast, and all the magi dropped to one knee and bowed their heads.

"No, Grandmaster," they replied.

CHAPTER
FORTY-THREE

The binding ceremony, as Raquel called it, took the rest of the morning and left me quite drained. I sat down and leaned back against the ancient tree with my new staff across my lap. Shira had climbed up into the tree and was sitting on a branch above my head. Raquel had moved a little distance away from us, lost in thought.

"Oh, Zah'rak, this place is so beautiful," commented Shira.

"Yeah," I said absent-mindedly. I was chewing on some beef jerky and wondering about Raquel. Something she'd said earlier had concerned me; I feared she might be dying, but she refused to talk about the curse or her health.

"Can I redesign hydroponics to be more like this and less modern?" she asked.

"What?" I asked, realizing she was looking for a response. I hadn't been paying attention, just enjoying the environment.

"Oh, I was just thinking that, with some work, we could make our hydroponics bay more like this forest," she said.

I looked up at her in amusement. "And how do you propose to achieve that?"

"We can start by gathering some soil and plants from this world to grow in the labs. Right now the bay is so sterile with vast tanks of oxygen scrubbing plants; it just seems wrong," she said.

I stood and stretched. "Take plants from here? How will you grow them and care for them? They've not been bred for life in space like everything we have now."

"Oh, we can figure something out, I'm sure. The plants that were brought along with the first space travelers wouldn't have been bred for space either," she said.

I doubted that was true, but since that had been thousands of years ago there was no way to know for sure. "Well, if you want to give it a shot, I don't suppose it would do any harm."

Raquel came over and looked up. "Shira, can you gate us to the fortress, please?"

"Sure!" she said and leapt from the branch she had been sitting on. It was too high for a safe jump but she slowed her fall, allowing her to touch the ground lightly. It was an advantage of being able to fly. I had to admit I was a little jealous of that power.

Shira cast her gate and we went through it, coming out in the center of the castle ruins. The place was no longer as we'd left it.

"What happened?" called out Raquel in shock. She teleported up onto a wall, one that hadn't existed the last time we were here.

Shira and I quickly joined her on the wall as she jogged along the top of it. She stopped when we got to the gatehouse, another new addition since the last time we'd been here.

"How is this possible?" asked Raquel.

I knelt and placed my bare hand on the wall. I could feel massive energy there, not unlike what I'd felt in the trees. "The wall is alive and growing!"

Shock crossed Raquel's face. "But how? This place was on the verge of death when we last visited!"

Shira was examining the gate, which was a massive structure in its own right. The gatehouse was at least ten meters high and twice that in thickness. There were two gates which created a passage not unlike an airlock. Both doors were currently closed and there was a pile of bones scattered around the path to the gate, which I judged to be fallen skeletal warriors who had launched a failed attack on the fortress.

"Where are the bodies?" asked Shira.

"What?" I asked.

"The bodies of the Nightwalkers you killed: where are they?" she asked.

Outside the walls of the fortress there were bodies strewn everywhere, but there were none inside; no sign at all of the battle in which we had fought for Raquel's life. Even the burnt section of wall had gone or perhaps been repaired and now formed part of the exterior wall. I tried to remember where it had been, but too many landmarks had changed and I was lost.

"On guard!" called out Raquel, and I looked up to see massive skeletal beasts flying overhead.

"What are they?" I asked.

"Dragons, or rather they used to be dragons; now they're foul undead creatures, perhaps some of the most dangerous creatures in existence," she said.

Shira swallowed hard. "They don't even fear the sun."

I watched as they circled over us. There were three of them, watching but making no move. "Will they attack?"

"No, we're safe for now, I think. The fortress has regained too much of its power. They might be able to break through, but I think the protection will hold," she said. She didn't sound as confident as usual.

"Might? You think?" I asked. That didn't hold out a great deal of comfort. I watched them as they circled and wondered what held them aloft. There were no visible signs of propulsion, and the skeletal wings surely couldn't provide much lift.

"Let's see what else has changed," she said and hopped off the great wall, landing lightly on her feet thirty meters below.

Shira followed her jump but I didn't risk it; instead, I teleported to the ground. I assumed they were using telekinesis to slow their fall, and I supposed I could do the same but I was more comfortable with teleporting. It seemed too much like tempting fate just to jump and hope for the best.

"It's probably best if we stay inside the new wall," said Raquel.

We explored the ruins but found little of interest. Grass and other plant life had started to come back, giving the fortress a more pleasant feel. Some of the rock faces had vines growing up them and there were plenty of traces of small animals.

We moved towards the centermost pillar where we had fought the wraiths. The exterior appearance was unchanged, but I could feel a fountain of power erupting from it and feeding the other rocks in the area.

The undead dragons continued to watch from above. They were too high up for me to get an accurate idea of their size, but I estimated them to be at least thirty meters long. They had no flesh, but their eyes glowed a malevolent red.

"When the fortress was young, this was a great central tower from which its defense could be coordinated. It was the command center for the Sac'a'rith," said Raquel.

"I think it's powering the regrowth in some manner. Power is flowing from it through the ground and into the wall," I said.

"I don't understand," said Raquel. She placed her hand on the pillar and looked around again in obvious disbelief. "At the height of its power the fortress could repair itself, but only under guidance; now it's far from the height of its power and no one is here to guide it. This should not be possible."

"Perhaps I awoke the fortress somehow with my staff?" asked Shira.

"Maybe; but even if you did, who's guiding the reconstruction?" she asked.

"That I don't know," said Shira.

"And who is defending the castle?" I asked. "Those bodies and bones we saw by the gate seem to indicate some kind of battle."

We wandered around some more but didn't find any more clues. Late in the afternoon, we took a break from our exploring to discuss the situation.

"Before this castle fell, there were three walls. The one that's growing out there now is the innermost," said Raquel. She took up a stick and drew a map of the castle in the soil. "Each of the three gatehouses was placed a little further around the perimeter than the previous one, in order to slow any rush into the fortress. That also made it difficult to get supplies in and out."

She continued drawing until she had completed a map of the entire fortress. "There, that's what used to be here. I remember running along the walls and around my mother's garden as a child, along with many more memories."

"I imagine that to you it only seems like a couple of decades since you were last here?" I said.

"Yes. I don't think this design would work as well with modern war machines," she mused.

She had a point. In the last ten thousand years, military tech had moved on. "True. We'd want some sort of anti-aircraft defense, perhaps on these towers," I suggested.

Together the three of us modified the map of the fortress, adding modern defenses, launch pads, food production and underground sections. It was an enjoyable exercise, but when we'd finished nightfall was fast approaching.

"Shira should gate us back soon before we lose all the light," said Raquel.

"It's a shame we can't take a picture of this plan," I remarked.

"We could leave it for whoever is rebuilding this place," said Shira with a grin. "Maybe they'll get the hint."

Raquel nodded in bemusement. "Sure, why not?"

Shira opened a gate back to the other gate to take us home. On the other side, she said, "We have around an hour of light left. I want to collect some soil and plant samples."

"How much?" I asked as Raquel activated the gate.

"As much as we can take in an hour," she said.

Raquel wasn't happy with that idea but I wanted to oblige Shira so, before Raquel could object, I took charge. I told Raquel to stand guard on the forest side of the gate and got Ragnar to help on the Night Wisp side. Shira pointed out what she wanted, I lugged it to the gate and passed it through to Ragnar, who placed it out in the corridor. From there, Marcus and Pur-wryn brought it to hydroponics. Through this teamwork we were able to acquire many different kinds of plants and buckets of soil from the planet.

As night fell, I ended the operation and everyone returned to the Night Wisp.

CHAPTER
FORTY-FOUR

The fleet had finally arrived and we were preparing to jump, so I joined my crew on the bridge. When I arrived I found Marcus manning our weapons, Purwryn in the pilot's seat and Ragnar handling communications and the science station. Raquel was in the captain's chair but vacated it when I arrived.

"Zah'rak, the fleet is ready when we are," said Ragnar.

"Okay. Lock in but don't engage our jump drive. The fleet is big enough to cover us, and I want to be able to jump out if need be," I said.

Something was really bothering me about this mission. I couldn't place my claw on it, but I had a really bad feeling about it. I had learned long ago to trust my feelings when they spoke this loudly, but in this case I didn't know what I could do differently. We'd just have to be careful.

"We are locked into their graviton field. We'll be ju… " Ragnar started to say, but the last of his sentence was cut off as the comforting azure of jump space wrapped around us. I liked the feeling and wished the transit there were longer. It was nice to relax in its embrace with nothing to worry about.

I sighed and basked in the simple comfort until we dropped back into normal space. Through the post-jump haze I could hear alarms going off and had a vague sense of Raquel taking command; by the time I'd recovered, she'd broken away from the fleet and activated all our defense systems.

I gave my head a good shake, trying to clear the cobwebs. "Report!"

"It's a trap," she said. "A Cyborg fleet has engaged the Phareons. I have us in a sensor shadow for now, but our cover won't hold."

"What! Why?" I demanded.

"No idea," she said.

My head was finally clear enough to process what was going on, and I realized that Raquel had acted long before any of the rest of us could respond. When we weren't in the middle of a battle, I'd have to ask her how she did that.

"What's the status of the fleet?" I asked.

"Their computers took over post-jump, so they're already fully engaged. Probably they're only now realizing the situation, just as we are," said Ragnar.

Raquel had put tactical up on the main screen, and I could see that the Phareon fleet was outnumbered and the Cyborg fleet was moving quickly to secure its advantage. The fight wouldn't go well, and I expected a swift victory for the Cyborgs.

"Can we jump out?" I asked.

"The Cyborg fleet has some kind of jamming tech," said Purwryn. "I've never seen its like, but somehow it's blasting out gravitons; as long as we're in its field, the jump drive is useless."

I looked at Raquel and knew how she felt about this. "Okay, start prioritizing targets. Primary targets are whatever is jamming the jump drives. Someone call Crivreen and tell him to get ready for emergency repairs."

"Cyborg fighters incoming!" called out Ragnar.

"Taking evasive action!" shouted Purwryn.

The Night Wisp lurched and turned, desperately trying to dodge the incoming attackers.

"Bring us about!" I called out. "Engines to full, target control to maximum rate of fire. Charge their squad, all guns firing!" It was a move born of panic, but I could not see what else to do.

Purwryn brought us about as Marcus' hands blurred across his command console. The Cyborgs hesitated at our approach, and that was all the time the Night Wisp needed with its recently-upgraded weapons. We passed through the heart of the squad, wreaking devastation all around us.

"Come about for another pass," I said. I doubted it would work a second time, but I had to do something.

"The Cyborgs are adapting. They're scattering into groups of two," said Marcus.

Not good, I thought to myself. "Pick the closest pair and destroy them. Ragnar, find us a way out of this jamming field."

"*Zah'rak, you're fighting like a mundane,*" sent Raquel privately. "*Let me show you how a battle wizard fights.*"

I turned to her and said, "Raquel, if you've got any ideas, don't wait for an invitation."

"Purwryn, come about to new heading 147 mark 90, and reduce thrust to twenty-five per cent," she said. Purwryn started to object but Raquel continued. "Ragnar, prepare an ECM cloud to drop on my mark. Marcus, I'm entering in new targets. The instant they are in range of our shiny new cannons, take them out."

Everyone moved to follow their orders. I noticed that the targets she picked were drone bays on a large carrier. That would've made sense, but we were a far distance from it and would be cut down long before we could reach it.

"Everyone ready?" she asked, as the Cyborg fighters switched from their scatter tactic and came straight at us.

We all replied in the affirmative, and she said, "Ragnar, in thirty seconds launch the cloud." The electronic counter-measures cloud was one of the upgrades that Crivreen had managed to sneak in while we were docked. It was a cloud of miniature drones that would broadcast out on all frequencies and would temporarily blind everyone's sensors to our presence by overwhelming them with input. For a moment while the cloud was operating nothing would be able to target us, and all weapons systems should lose their locks. We'd be like a supernova going off inside their displays. With luck we might even overload them, but that wasn't very likely.

Ragnar nodded and Raquel began to cast. I was annoyed because I knew what it cost her, but didn't dare interfere with her plan. I kept an eye on the incoming fighters.

Suddenly I felt the whole world shift and twist around us. It was nothing like the experience of travelling through jump space, nor was it like teleporting, but we definitely moved from one physical location in space to another without crossing the distance between. It felt as if we had suddenly turned to rubber and someone was bending and stretching us. I was sure that, wherever we went, my head and left shoulder arrived long before my feet did.

I watched in amazement as the tactical screens all updated themselves, showing our new location within range of the targets on the carrier. We had crossed hundreds of kilometers of space in an instant, leaving the fighters long and far behind.

"Firing," called out Marcus as our cannons ripped apart the drone bays on the carrier.

Raquel looked a little worn out from that spell, but called out new targets. "Marcus, for the next wave of targets use the new anti-matter missiles. I want to take out their jump drives."

"Okay," he said and, with a speed possible only for an enhanced human, his hands flew to target the missiles while still working the targeting for the cannons.

"Cyborg fighters coming in hot and fast!" called out Ragnar.

"Missiles away!" shouted Marcus.

I left the captain's chair and moved to assist Ragnar at the science station. He was learning our technology, but had still some way to go. "Raquel, my guess is that their carriers are running the jump jammers. They're the only things massive enough to generate so large a graviton field."

"Agreed," she said and punched the comm. "Shira, head to engineering. Crivreen, pull five warheads off the missiles and get them ready for simultaneous remote detonation."

"Confirmed hit!" called out Marcus.

"Excellent! Come about to new target and rip open a hole for me, as deep as you can," she said.

"Less than thirty seconds until the fighters are in range," I said. I had my back to the bridge and was focused on monitoring the battlefield. Phareon's fleet was not faring well at all. They were being pushed back as they attempted to counter the faster and more nimble Cyborg fleet. If something didn't change soon, they'd be wiped out.

"Four minutes till we're in range of target," said Purwryn.

Then everything shifted again and Marcus called out, "Target in range; firing!"

"Crivreen, have you got my bomb ready yet?" asked Raquel over the comm.

"Yes," he replied.

"Put it into an airlock. Shira, I'm going to get you a line of sight. I want you to send that bomb as deep as you can into the hole we opened in the carrier, as fast as you can. Then stand by to assist Crivreen in engineering."

"Okay!" Shira responded.

"Three minutes until the fighters are in range. A second squad of fighters is on its way, five minutes out of range," I said.

"Keep tunneling, Marcus," said Raquel.

"Ready!" called out Shira over the comm.

"Marcus, cease fire. Shira, send over our package," ordered Raquel. As they obeyed, she turned to Ragnar. "Transmit this message to the Cyborgs: We are ambassadors from the Wizard Kingdom; break off your attack on our vessels and leave this sector, or risk war."

"They won't care," said Marcus.

"Oh, they'll learn to care. We're no simple primitives." There was ice in her voice as she spoke.

"Package delivered," said Shira.

"Any response to our message?" asked Raquel.

"A third fighter group is headed our way," I said. I wondered what she meant by 'primitives'.

"Detonate the package," she said.

I'm not sure of the order of events, but the world shifted again as it had twice before and our makeshift bomb exploded, seemingly at the same time. The section of the carrier where the antimatter had been placed twisted and bent as the energy from the blast tore through it. The squads of fighters coming to intercept us were destroyed by the shrapnel and expanding wave front of energy. The carrier was badly damaged, but not destroyed; it was simply too massive for our small missiles to take down.

"Come about to 235 mark 15," ordered Raquel.

I studied the tactical display. "The jamming grid is broken! There are gaps now."

"Excellent," she said. "Marcus, drone bays on the second carrier, target them all and prepare to fire again. Ragnar, notify Hospital Station about what's going on out here and request assistance."

I looked back over at Raquel. "You mean to eliminate this fleet?"

"They'll retreat once they realize they can't win this round. They still think we're mere primitives and can be ignored. They need to know that we are not to be trifled with, or they'll make a move on Hospital Station," she said.

"Won't it seem like we're merely helping Phareon?" I asked.

"Most likely not. Remember, the Cyborgs hate everyone and everyone hates them, so even if Resden had a fleet out this way, they'd probably come to help too."

"Ragnar, repeat our message," she said. When the message was sent she cast, and the world around us once again shifted and bent. Marcus started firing at the carrier that was in range. Our antimatter missiles were tearing massive holes in its defensive armor, but we just didn't have enough firepower to cripple a target as large as a carrier.

"We're almost out of missiles," said Marcus without emotion. "Should we cut a hole in this one, too?"

"Save what we have left for now," said Raquel.

"Fighters will be in range in two minutes," I said as two more squadrons turned to intercept us.

"Ragnar, any word from the hospital?" she asked.

"Defense forces are amassing now and should be here in forty minutes," he said.

"Inform Phareon that reinforcements are on the way. We need to take down that jamming field," she said as she studied the display. "There! New primary targets!" She punched some keys on the command console and Marcus quickly eliminated whatever she had targeted.

"That did it! Graviton field collapsing!" I called out.

"Ragnar, find me another shadow to hide in. Zah'rak, get ready on the ECM. We'll need another cloud soon."

"Found one," called out Ragnar and he lit up a target on the display.

"Okay. Zah'rak, twenty seconds after I begin to cast, release the cloud. Purwryn, as soon as we arrive, bring us to zero relative so we can reassess our options."

"Fighters incoming!" I said.

I watched Raquel cast again and counted down from twenty seconds, as she had ordered. On cue, I released the ECM cloud and moments later we were elsewhere.

CHAPTER
FORTY-FIVE

We were sitting in the sensor shadow of one of the carriers while the battle raged on around us. I studied the display, trying to find something to be happy about, but Phareon was still being beaten back and there was little hope for them at this stage. If a wizard fleet didn't get here soon, there might be nothing left to save.

"I estimate the Cyborgs will guess our hiding location in seven minutes," said Marcus, still in a completely emotionless voice. He had used it when being interrogated. At that time I thought it was just to annoy the agent, but perhaps it was a way of dealing with stress instead.

"How do you figure that?" I asked.

"Easily, Zah'rak. It won't take them long to guess what we're doing, and once they do, they'll begin sweeping all the sensor shadows out here and eventually find us," said Raquel.

"Now what?" I asked.

"The Cyborgs still think that we're primitives and they need to learn we are more advanced than that, otherwise Hospital Station won't be safe from attack," said Raquel.

"The fleet is coming," I said. The wise course seemed to be to wait for them to eliminate the Cyborgs without taking any undue risks ourselves. That did mean Phareon would be in trouble, but they were already as good as dead. I was more concerned about my team making it out of this mess.

"Yes, and that's good. You all need training and this is a good time to show off the power of a Dragon Knight."

"A 'Dragon Knight'?" I repeated.

"It's the elite division of the Battle Wizards. They fight with completely unconventional means for a wizard and I mean to train you in their ways. Dragon Knights use a mixture of technology and magic and, unlike traditional magi, they prefer to fight behind enemy lines." She walked closer to the tactical display and examined the data. She was rapidly paging through the screens but not saying anything.

"Raquel, Phareon is wondering where we are and if we need assistance," said Ragnar.

"Don't respond. It'll give away our position," she said.

"Okay," he replied.

I wondered what she was looking for. She stopped at a large overview of the entire battlefield, her finger tracing lines on the screen, but I couldn't figure out the pattern.

"There! Computer, designate this as alpha target," she said.

I spun around to the science terminal and pulled up the data on the target. "The target appears to be a run-of-the-mill destroyer, upgraded with Cyborg technology."

"Yes, and we'll eliminate it," she said.

"How? We're almost out of missiles," I said.

"Master Shadow taught me a thing or two about weaknesses in military craft engine systems which can only be exploited from the inside. We don't have a spellweaver to do it the way he does, but I think I can manage it another way," she said.

"Spellweaver?" I queried.

"Inside?" said Purwryn at the same time.

"Yes, inside. Purwryn, Zah'rak and I will board the ship, destroy it from the inside, and bail out before they can do anything about it," she said. "Marcus, I'll need you to take over navigation in addition to tactical."

"Yes, ma'am," was the monotone reply. Purwryn and I turned in surprise. I asked, "How?"

"Come with me," she said, already exiting the bridge.

Purwryn looked at me. I shrugged and said, "Ragnar, take command until I return," then followed her off the bridge.

She headed for the mission ready room, turned to us and said, "Put on your full battle gear. Our goal will be to get into the engine room and sabotage the ship."

I started to ask for more details, but she raised a finger to stop me. Over the comm. she said, "Get ready for another transition. After we move, keep us at zero relative to alpha target, as close to the hull as you can manage."

"Understood," said Marcus.

The three of us donned our full battle armor and loaded up on wands, blasters, and other weapons. Once we were ready, Raquel cast her spell and I felt space twist again. The sensation was disorienting but something I was starting to get used to. Shira had said a traveler couldn't be caught, and seeing Raquel using some of her spells for the first time seemed to reinforce that. If she could bend the fabric of reality like this to change her position, what chance had any mundane of keeping up?

We moved into the airlock and teleported out of the ship onto the hull of the destroyer. Purwryn and I followed Raquel as she drifted through space, flying over the hull, always within reach of it. She finally grabbed a handhold and stopped herself.

She was overlooking what seemed to be the window of a private room. It amazed me that spacecraft had windows at all; they were much weaker than the armor around them, and couldn't give as good a view as a basic viewing screen. They also made it simple for a magus to board a hostile craft.

It'd be a good idea to cover the windows on the Night Wisp, I thought to myself, somewhat annoyed that the idea had only just occurred to me.

Raquel pointed to a window and sent, *"Teleport in through there. Alarms will go off almost immediately, so we'll make a mad dash for engineering. Use wands and staves at first; save your spell energy for the final push."*

"Staves?" I queried.

"Yes. Your staff will act as an extra large wand," she sent. *"Follow my lead."*

She teleported in through the window, and we followed. As she'd predicted, the lights in the room turned red and an alarm blared throughout the ship.

"Odd; Cyborgs don't need audible alarms. Must be left over from the previous occupants," commented Raquel. She drew her swords, opened a door and called out, "This way!"

We didn't get far before Cyborgs were marching on our position. I took aim with my assault rifle and blasted away, but they were using a combination of body armor and portable blast shields to render my weapon ineffective.

Purwryn had a pair of Crivreen's wands in his hands and sent bolts of lighting down the corridor, which was far more devastating than my trusty rifle. The bolts seemed almost alive as they arced from the walls to the Cyborgs and back. Used against creatures whose bodies were mostly metal and salt water, lightning was a truly horrific weapon.

"Use your staff!" sent Raquel.

I slung my rifle over my shoulder and drew the staff down from the air as she had taught me. *"How?"*

"Focus on a target and say the command word, just like a wand."

I pointed my staff towards the middle of the charging group who were trying to seek cover from Purwryn's insistent pounding. Speaking the command word, I carefully aimed the staff into the middle of the group; a green bolt of energy was released from the staff and slammed into the chest of my target.

The Cyborg was engulfed in a green-tinged explosion which killed him and several more around him. The effect was far more powerful than that of any wand I'd ever seen, and on a par with the heaviest of hand cannons.

"Wow!" called out Purwryn, who had paused to watch the carnage.

"Keep shooting!" called out Raquel as the fearless Cyborgs began to regroup.

Remembering my training with the wands, I mentally reduced the power level of the staff. I didn't know yet how to tell how much energy it contained, and figured I'd better conserve its power just in case. We blasted through that position of Cyborgs and charged on, meeting no resistance for the rest of the run; that bothered me. It was obvious where we were going, so they must have been digging in there, preparing for our arrival.

Raquel stopped us just short of engineering. As she sheathed her swords she sent, *"Assume they can hear and see everything we do, because I'm sure they can. They're expecting us to charge, firing our weapons, and they will have superior defenses and firepower ready to counteract that. I have no intention of making a suicide rush, but we're going to make them think we're doing that. So follow me on the dash, but when you see the gate open, dive through it. It'll let us out behind them in engineering. I'll open it as soon as I have line of sight."*

We nodded our agreement and she sprinted off down the corridor with her own pair of wands. As we came in sight of engineering, I blasted a hole through their defenses with a single bolt from my staff. Purwryn rained lightning down on them, and Raquel sent white energy bolts from her wands.

Moments after we began our barrage, a gate opened directly in our path. We sprinted through and, true to Raquel's plan, came out behind the Cyborg position. My staff and our wands made quick work of the Cyborgs, as they hadn't set up any defenses behind themselves. In their arrogance they never thought we'd get past them, so they hadn't prepared for it.

"Cover the corridor," she sent.

More Cyborgs were heading our way, but now we were entrenched behind cover and they had to navigate the corridor under fire. I switched to Crivreen's wands, as their smaller size made them easier to work with in the tight fortifications. I would have liked to use my grenades to force them back, but the narrow corridor would have channeled the explosion right back in my face.

I couldn't see what Raquel was doing, but I knew we couldn't hold out long. Purwryn had already burned through most of his wands, and the enemy numbers kept growing. I suspected they could run the ship as easily from the hall in front of us as anywhere else. We could soon have the entire crew bearing down on us.

"Okay, time to bail out!" sent Raquel.

I glanced over my shoulder to see her open a gate. No longer concerned about the narrow passage acting as a funnel for the explosion, I tossed two explosive grenades down the corridor and dove through the gate right behind Purwryn.

We came out on the bridge of the Night Wisp. Raquel said, "Purwryn, go back to navigation and set a course away from here."

He jumped in his seat and took control of the craft.

"Ragnar, send my warning to the Cyborgs one last time," she said and cast her spell again, moving the ship elsewhere.

"Okay, sent," he said.

She smiled and pressed a button on the comm. pad of her armor. Moments later a massive explosion ripped through the rear of the destroyer, throwing the remains of the vessel out of the battlefield.

CHAPTER
FORTY-SIX

Raquel, Zah'rak and Purwryn had been gone thirty-seven minutes when a strange blue oval appeared on the bridge of the Night Wisp. I searched my memory banks for a match and finally came up with one. *A gate*, I thought to myself; I had used one to get off the space station when Purwryn and I were grievously outnumbered.

Moving through them was like walking through jump space. It was a very odd sensation, and didn't have the hangover effect of the jump drives. This gate technology was something I needed to learn. The Great Core would definitely be interested in it.

They came running out of the gate moments later, and the blue oval disappeared behind them almost before Zah'rak had made his way through.

"Purwryn, get back on navigation and set a course away from here," ordered Raquel. "Marcus, watch for incoming fighters; if any move within our range, destroy them."

"Yes, ma'am," I said.

It was odd that she was running this battle, since Zah'rak was the captain, but it was obvious that she knew she was doing and Zah'rak did not. It was wise of him to let her lead, given her skills, but he seemed to be doing more than that; he was behaving as if she were the captain and he just another warrior following her into battle.

I listened as Ragnar sent her message once again, and I couldn't understand why she kept sending it. Did she think they hadn't received it the first couple of times? I was sure they had, and that it was stored in a memory bank somewhere. Cyborgs never forget anything.

Moments after we began to pull away from the destroyer, my tactical sensors were momentarily blinded by its destruction. I didn't know how they had achieved it, but somehow they had completely destroyed the craft. These primitives were extremely resourceful. *No, not primitives; magi,* I corrected myself.

"Alpha target destroyed," called out Zah'rak.

"Purwryn, prepare an evasive spiral while Ragnar finds us a new hiding-place," she said.

"Okay," he replied.

The Cyborg fleet was in disarray. The destroyer she had chosen was a lynchpin in their communications network, and it would take several minutes to reroute the comm. traffic to compensate for the loss. How in the name of the Great Core did she figure out that this one was the core of the fleet?

Raquel was the only trained wizard on the craft, as far as I could tell. Ragnar had some training, but he didn't seem very knowledgeable about current events or technology. Despite this, or maybe because of it, Zah'rak completely trusted Ragnar's input on any subject.

"*Agent P2003, report,*" came a call over my internal communications network.

"I am undamaged and on mission," I silently replied.

"*Agent P2003, the Night Wisp is a liability to the fleet. Eliminate the threat.*"

"I cannot without jeopardizing my mission."

"You will receive new mission parameters when the Night Wisp is gone."

"The Night Wisp is a minor inconvenience in this engagement, but its information value is irreplaceable."

There was temporary silence. I hoped I hadn't overstepped my bounds, but I knew it would be foolish to take down the Night Wisp at this stage. The magi had proven deadly in combat and, in order to compensate for their presence in this region, we needed information about them. No one was in a better position than I to do that. It had been a major stroke of luck teaming up with Purwryn back on the Paradise, and one I was eager to take advantage of for as long as possible. The Cyborg nation needed this desperately, even if they hadn't yet realized it.

"The fleet is jumping in now," said Ragnar.

I watched on my tactical readouts as a fleet of Class Three and Class Four tech. jumped into the battle, impressed by the show of force. The Wizard fleet by itself would have overpowered the Cyborg fleet, which was mainly Class Two technology. They had some Class Three, but Class Four was almost unheard of nowadays in these numbers.

When the Empire had fallen, there had been a general regression in the level of technology. Cutting-edge out here became known as Class Three tech, one generation of technology behind the Empire's last achievements, which had been arbitrarily labeled Class Four. Some of the more remote areas had fallen to the standard of Class Two or even Class One. The galaxy seemed to be losing ground as the constant wars continued to take their toll. Cyborg command predicted that most of the galaxy would fall back to Class Two before things stabilized enough to begin to rebuild. The Wizard fleet, however, seemed of a standard which called that prediction into doubt.

"Excellent," said Raquel. "The carriers won't be able to escape, and the rest of their fleet will be in a shambles for some time. Purwryn, head for the Wizard Fleet."

"Okay," said Purwryn.

"That fleet is impressive!" called Zah'rak.

"It's fairly primitive compared to what we have back home," said Raquel. "We had to buy all these ships out here and make do with whatever upgrades could be performed on them."

If this is what the wizards consider to be primitive, Cyborg Command was seriously overestimating their chances of victory now that the Wizard Kingdom had established a foothold out here. I wondered how I might convince them of that. Hopefully this battle would be enough to do so, otherwise our nation would fall.

"Acknowledged, P2003. Stay within current mission parameters."

"Understood," I said, not allowing my relief to appear across the connection.

"Send full battle report for retransmission."

I sent them the full report, including all logs of conversations on the bridge around me. The Cyborgs knew the battle was lost, but they didn't want to lose the information they'd gained during it. They would send everything back to Cyborg Command now, while they still could. My report would be added to the reports of every Cyborg out here, living or dead, and stored in the Great Core's database for analysis. Soon the fleet would begin to retreat, to save what was left of their physical assets.

"Three fighters incoming!" called Zah'rak.

My hands were already working the controls to target them, but they were still out of optimum range. "Targets will be in range of our primary weapons in two minutes."

My human emotions threatened to rebel every time I targeted a fellow Cyborg, but my programming was able to compensate by isolating all emotion and cutting it off before it could interfere with my ability to perform my tasks. Defending these magi was part of my mission parameters, and those fighters were attacking so that my cover wouldn't become suspect.

They understood they were flying to their deaths, just as I understood I had to terminate them. They had their part to play in the big picture, just as I did. We were tiny pieces in the larger puzzle that was the Great Core's vision, and it was that vision that mattered most, not us.

"Eliminate them as soon as they're in range," said Raquel.

"Yes, ma'am," I said. I knew my voice would sound strange to them, but if they questioned me I would say that I was running my implants in combat mode or something technical-sounding like that. I couldn't risk letting my human emotional response show through. The human mind was a powerful tool in its ability to deal with unknowns and unsolvables, but its emotional aspects were a major liability.

I let my hands deal with taking out the fighters and looked over at the tactical displays. The Night Wisp only had four cannons, so it was simple to let one of my sub-processors handle the targeting and firing while my organic brain kept an eye on things around me.

"The Wizard fleet is moving into attack formation," said Zah'rak.

"The Cyborgs are running!" said Ragnar.

"What?" asked Raquel.

"They appear to be cutting their losses and abandoning any disabled craft," said Ragnar.

"What about the carriers?" asked Raquel.

"They're staying put, but their bays are emptying fast," he said.

Raquel shrugged. "Head for a Wizard carrier and signal to them that we'd like to resupply before leaving. Then get me Fleet Command."

Moments later a man in purple battle armor appeared on the screen. Raquel told him all that she knew about the fleet and the fight.

"Master Raquel, I advise that we let them get away. I don't like doing it, but we dare not move more than a jump from our station until its defenses are fully operational," he said.

"I agree. We'll resupply and then rejoin the Phareon fleet. Thanks for your help," she said.

He bowed, said goodbye and closed the channel.

"Well done, everyone," said Raquel.

I had to agree. This little ship had utterly outperformed any logical prediction. As I looked over the crew, my eyes rested on Purwryn. He was becoming a good friend, and I knew that was a problem. It would have been a tactical error for the fleet to destroy the Night Wisp at this time, but I knew that at some future point it would become a necessity and I wasn't looking forward to that day. When the time came I would do it just as emotionlessly as I had killed the Cyborg fighters. At least I would try to; the truth was that I was not sure I could pull it off anymore. I was getting too close to everyone.

CHAPTER
FORTY-SEVEN

The Wizard fleet returned to Hospital Station, and we rejoined what was left of Phareon's fleet. I looked over the ruins of the fleet on the Night Wisp's tactical displays and was surprised at the extent of the damage. "Phareon is doomed, isn't it?"

They had lost at least a third of their number, and many of the remaining ships were heavily damaged. The Cyborgs were just one of many powerful enemies stalking the region. If a random ambush like this could wreak havoc on a fleet which was much larger than normal, then the region was practically lost already.

"Yes, Zah'rak, I believe so. My guess is that this region will become wild, probably in less than a decade," said Raquel. "Many will fight for it, but none will be able to control it for a long while."

"The Cyborgs seem to have sufficient might to take the region," said Marcus.

"No; if they think they do, then they have seriously underestimated some of the other players," said Raquel.

"What makes you say that?" asked Marcus. There was surprise in his voice, which stood out in stark contrast to the tonelessness of his speech during the battle.

"Since I woke, I've spent most of my time out here learning the state of the various powers that be, and those already active have enough strength to ensure that no one power can rule," she said.

"Are there others coming?" I asked.

"We're near the outer edge of the galaxy. All the magi who survived the Rending would have fled this far and then run out of options. Only the Weave knows how many yet lie sleeping and how many are already active," she said. "There's no way to guess the number of people who might be out here, or to what camps they might belong, but one thing is for sure: if they made it this far, they are among the most powerful."

"What of the wizards? Surely they could hold this region," said Ragnar.

"They?" asked Raquel with a smile. "Yes, *we* could. However, we have no plans to do that at this time. Our goal is to open trade out here and make friends."

"Still, they ... we could, right?" queried Marcus.

"Oh, definitely. There's no one out here who would dare try to match us other than the Cyborgs and, as you saw, we don't have much to fear from them. We could annex this region and have it as a second kingdom, but we're not seeking to expand out here, just to build relationships for a change." She went on to explain how the Wizard Kingdom's borders were always under threat, and that jealously and envy among what used to be the Empire had fueled hatred of the Kingdom. "We hope things will be different out here."

Our conversation was interrupted by the fleet jumping. Once we were clear, Raquel asked Shira and myself to join her in the cargo bay for magic lessons.

Raquel stood before us and said, "Now, as Sac'a'rith your powers will always be stronger the more you are surrounded by natural things, but that doesn't mean you're powerless on a space craft like this one. There are two spells which I think are the most useful for you to learn right now. The first is your bolt spell and the second is camouflage."

"Camouflage?" I repeated.

"Bolt?" said Shira with some excitement.

"Yes. The camouflage spell is nowhere near as good as what can be done by those with the concealment line, but it's good enough to fool most mundanes most of the time," said Raquel.

That didn't make sense. She had previously told us that it was her armor which allowed her to hide from sight. "Wait, I thought you said your armor … "

"Yes, this armor can camouflage also, but it works much better when I enhance it with my own spell," she said. "Speaking of which, change out of your armor for this. It will make it easier."

"But we need to wear it when we fight out here. What if there's a hull breach?" I wasn't at all comfortable about entering into combat with a modern foe without protection. It had become habitual for us to suit up when we were jumping into unknown space. It had only taken one hull breach a while back to show us that we needed to be prepared. When idling at a station, or even coasting between jumps, most of us ditched the armor, but even that was a bit risky.

"Of course, which is why I don mine for combat in space, but it will make it more difficult to learn to cast, so for the moment switch into natural clothing such as we wore on our first trip home."

What she said made sense based on the little experience I'd had of trying to use my magic while wearing the armor, so I reluctantly agreed and we went to our separate quarters to change. Shira and I arrived back in the cargo bay before Raquel did. "Shira, I assume you know this stuff already?"

"What stuff?"

"You know the spells. You've been at this magic business a lot longer than I have."

Her face flushed and she turned her gaze to the floor. "No. I was only allowed to study traveler spells."

Once again I wanted to kick myself. Of course her former master would have done all he could to keep her helpless. I was saved from further foolishness by Raquel's return.

"I think we'll start with a demonstration," said Raquel. She was dressed in armor that appeared to be made from animal skins and leather. She had worn it the time when we'd taken her to the Sac'a'rith ruins, but I hadn't paid much attention to it then. It covered her body as did modern armor, but seemed more flexible and much lighter. I was sure it was enchanted, but I didn't recognize the pattern of power; I guessed it was probably magic to make it tougher and lighter. What else would someone like her need? I wondered how it would fare against a good blaster. Leather alone would be useless, but I was beginning to understand that in the world of spellcraft nothing was as it seemed.

"Wait," I said. "You shouldn't be casting! The battle was one thing, but there's no need here."

"There is great need here!" she snapped, and got right up in my snout. "Don't you understand yet? I'm the last one alive who knows the old ways! If I don't teach you, our ways die with me!"

There was intensity in her eyes and an edge to her voice that shook me to the core. I had never seen her angry like this before. There was something deep inside her, barely showing in her eyes, which brought a chill down my spine and seriously threatened my bladder control. Involuntarily I took a step back.

"Hey," Shira said softly, "he's just worried about you."

Raquel turned on Shira, but caught herself up with a jerk. She walked a few paces away from us and breathed hard. Shira moved between Raquel and myself.

Just go along with the training. It obviously means a great deal to her, sent Shira privately.

After a few minutes Raquel turned and said, "Sorry."

"It's okay," I said quickly. I had no desire to see again what I'd observed in her eyes. I had witnessed enough violence in my time to recognize it: for a brief moment, they'd been the eyes of a killer.

"Look, I need to demonstrate in order to teach. I will already need to make a stop at home to recharge before we face the sorcerers at our destination, so a few more spells won't make much difference," she said.

"Okay, but please use only the minimum effort necessary," I said.

For the next several hours Raquel worked with me, trying to teach me the movements and command words for the spells. She could throw bolts of energy with such speed, precision and control that one might think her the equivalent of a cannon on a battle cruiser.

I, on the other hand, could do nothing; nothing but wave my arms about like a drunken fool, chanting gibberish. Sometimes it felt as if there was power building around me, but there was a barrier there; something was blocking me from reaching it.

Shira didn't try any of the spells. She just watched in silence, lost in thought most of the time.

Raquel was advising that we should take a break and try again later, then Shira said, "Let me watch."

That was a baffling suggestion from someone who had watched us for the entire session. "But you have been watching!"

"No." She stretched her tiny arm as long as it could go and pointed up at my head. "Let me watch from in there."

"That's a good idea, Shira. Zah'rak, will you let her?" asked Raquel.

I was inclined to refuse, but Shira had a pleading look on her face; I just couldn't say no to her. "I suppose so."

"Okay, go ahead and cast," sent Shira.

I could feel a deeper connection with her than usual. I didn't understand the sensation and did my best to ignore it. Crivreen had taught me how to force someone out of my head, so I knew I could break the connection if need be. Besides, I had to admit it was oddly comforting.

I set aside these thoughts and focused on casting, determined that this time I would get it. I focused everything I had on the spell. My heart was racing as it tried to send extra blood to my brain to compensate for the stress I was putting on my system. Energy built up around me and I could almost feel it on my scales, but as before something was blocking my access to that energy and the spell failed.

Cursing, I turned and slammed my fist into a nearby storage container, which sent it flying across the room, spilling its contents as it went. Pain arced up my arm and brought forth more curses.

Shira and Raquel backed away. Shira said, "It's all right. I think I can help you."

"How?" I asked.

She turned to Raquel. "Let's move this lesson to hydroponics."

Raquel's face lit up. "Of course!"

I nursed my throbbing hand as we made our way to hydroponics. I could hear them talking but my frustration had darkened my mood too much to care what they were saying. The Night Wisp was a fairly small craft and we soon reached our destination.

I hadn't been in there since our last trip through the gate, so I was unprepared for the transformation that Shira had wrought. Instead of sterile tanks of green goo, harsh lighting and rows of computer banks there were trees, bushes and plants. The lighting was different; less harsh and bluer than it had been before. The air was more humid and the temperature warmer than the rest of the ship.

The tanks were still there, but all around them and in between were the samples we had transplanted from the forest. The pots were connected to the water and fertilizer system, and the lighting had been rearranged to bathe them in its glow. She had even made paths through the plants so that you could visit each one should you so choose.

I could feel the life in there reaching out to me. Instinctively I reached out and used the power to heal my bruised hand. My heart rate slowed, and the pounding in my head receded. A calmness came over me.

"Shira, it's … it's beautiful!" I said.

She came up beside me and placed her hand on mine. "You really think so? I had so little to work with."

"Well, you worked a miracle in here," I said.

"It's impressive. Now I see what you had in mind for the plants you collected." Raquel walked around the room and touched a few plants. "We should try to bring more back each trip."

Shira was beaming with pride, and nothing could have made my heart happier.

"Okay, Zah'rak," said Raquel. "Try the bolt again, but be sure to aim it at me instead of one of the plants."

"At you?" I gasped.

"Don't worry. I'll be fine, and we don't want to undo all Shira's good work," she said.

I remembered watching Crivreen and Purwryn practice by casting spells at each other. If those two buffoons could do it safely, then surely Raquel could also.

I went through the movements again and said the command words, but something was different this time. My movements were smoother, my pronunciation was less forced, and I could feel my hands moving in and through some kind of energy field. The sensation helped me to focus and direct my movements more precisely than before. It reminded me of making the enchanted armor; if I just let myself flow with it, the power itself would guide me.

As I finished the spell I saw a green patch of something like plasma forming around my hands, and with my last movement it turned into a ball that flew across the room and slammed into Raquel's armor. There was a flash of green light and then everything returned to normal. Raquel was smiling, apparently unhurt, and Shira ran over and hugged my waist.

"You did it!" she said.

"But how? That was almost easy!" I spluttered.

Raquel walked over to me. "All magi, no matter what kind, draw their strength from what we have taken to calling the life force. Most magi tap the weave, which is the source of all life and all power. When you enchant your armor, you're pulling energy from the weave and intertwining it with the materials. When Crivreen tosses a lightning bolt, he's pulling power from the weave and converting it to electricity. Does that make sense to you?"

"Yes, but how does it answer my question?" I asked.

"The Sac'a'rith are magi, but we can do something no other magus can do: we tap the life force of nature around us. The weave is what gave life to the plants and to us; just as you can tap the weave, you can tap these plants. Think of them like batteries. The bolt you cast came because you instinctively conducted the power of life into your spell, the life surrounding you here."

"Then when I'm not around life, I can't cast?" I asked.

"No, you can cast even in the cargo bay. You can tap the weave directly like all other magi, but you're much stronger and everything is much easier when you're surrounded by life."

CHAPTER
FORTY-EIGHT

Raquel wanted me to stay in hydroponics until casting both spells became as easy as breathing. She said that once I could cast as well as she did, I'd be ready to try it in the cargo bay. It was much easier to cast in hydroponics, and after a week of practice I could at least cast both spells from memory without help, but Raquel's speed and smoothness was beyond imitation. In spite of my protests, she insisted that one day I'd have that too.

I doubted it would ever happen.

"Zah'rak, we are about a day from our last jump. This would be the best time to use the gate," commented Raquel.

"What time is it there?" I asked.

"Nearly nightfall. If we hurry, we should be able to get clear of the first gate and gate to the fortress before darkness."

I contacted Shira on the comm. and told her to change into her wilderness gear and meet us at the gate. Quickly, I suited up. We met in the room, Raquel opened the gate and we rushed through.

It felt good to be outdoors again. The trees, birds and other life around me were invigorating. I was disappointed that we would be gating directly to the fortress instead of walking this time. "Raquel, that first night we came, why didn't we simply gate to the fortress?"

"I was too weak, and Shira couldn't do it yet," she said aloud, but privately she sent, *"Shira needed that time in natural surroundings to begin to heal. When we get more time, we must spend more training sessions here so she can unlock her true potential."*

"Ah," I said. "That makes sense."

I wondered why the gate wasn't inside the fortress. Raquel said, "Looks like twilight is almost upon us. We'd better not delay."

Shira nodded and opened a gate to the fortress. Once we'd arrived, there was evidence of greater change than before. It had been a little less than two weeks since our last visit, but a lot of work had been done to the place.

"Odd," said Raquel.

"Yeah; it seems the place is still growing," I said.

"Well, yes, but look at the layout," she said.

I did but I wasn't sure what I was looking at. There were now thick walls, towers and buildings. An area had been cleared and leveled nearby, suitable for landing small craft. Another area seemed to have been cleared for gardens. The castle was really starting to take shape around us. I was amazed at the speed with which it was coming to life.

"The design is different," said Shira with a gasp.

They ran over to where we'd camped out last time and had drawn a map of the castle. I followed along to see what they were up to. At the campsite, we found that the drawing in the ground was gone and had been replaced by a scale model of our design. Suddenly the new castle features took on a familiar aspect: Shira's gardens, the landing pad for the Night Wisp and our other ideas had all been worked on. I gestured to the scale model of our design. "Someone is building this!"

"Apparently," said Raquel. She was lost in thought, looking at a particular building which had remained unchanged since our first visit, one of the few pieces left from the original castle. It wasn't much of a building; just a few walls and a slanted roof that might double as a door. I couldn't work out what it was that drew her attention.

The shadows lengthened around us and the wailing began from the forest as night fell. Wraiths gathered overhead and those great skeletal flying beasts circled, while the full moon gave an eerie grey glow to all.

"It seems more dangerous than the last time we were here," I said.

"Definitely. Whoever is behind the reconstruction has roused up the neighbors," said Raquel.

"What should we do?" asked Shira.

"Let's get back up onto the central tower where you made your stand last time," said Raquel. She led the way over to the tower; it was thicker and surely also taller than it had been. Looking towards the top of the tower, I saw it now had a roof and what might be windows. It matched the central control tower which I had added to our design. In my design, there had been a single door at the base leading to a large room with a single central staircase. I jogged over to the tower and found a door right where I had envisioned it.

"Perhaps we should take the stairs?" I asked.

"That should be interesting at least," said Raquel.

I reached for the door but as I drew close it opened by itself, like the doors on a spacecraft. I looked back at Shira and Raquel, who shrugged. So much power now flowed through the fortress that everything appeared to be enchanted. Even without focusing on using my Sight, I could see the power.

When the three of us had walked through the door, it slid shut behind us. The room we entered was vast. The ceiling was at least seven meters high, and the walls appeared to be made of polished marble. The floor was stone, perhaps slate, and also smooth and polished. The soles of our boots were padded, but our muted footfalls echoed throughout the chamber. In the center was a large spiral staircase which went both up and down.

"See any way to lock it?" I asked, looking back at the door.

Shira looked around and said, "Yeah, I think this latch here." She lowered a latch and there was a satisfying click. We checked to make sure we couldn't open it with the latch in place, then turned and headed up a staircase in the center of the room.

"Up, I suppose," I said. When we were envisaging our castle on the last trip, I had added a vast underground tunnel system. I thought that the stairs descending from this room led to a central hub, but I couldn't remember the precise layout we had come up with.

As we climbed the central stair, we passed many empty rooms. They looked freshly hewn from the stone and seemed to be designed in such a way as to use all the space in the tower. The walls themselves glowed softly in the visible light spectrum, illuminating everything with a cool omnidirectional light. I could feel the power of life all around me.

It took some time to climb to the top of the stairs. The tower had grown taller than it had been when we'd fought on top of it. We passed more empty rooms than I could count. Raquel felt that it would make an easy target if the fortress ever came under attack from the air; but if my design had been followed to the letter, it was much larger underground than above.

I heard Shira gasp as we entered the top room. The room itself was large, taking up the entire width of the tower, with windows on all sides. Unlike the others, this room wasn't empty. Three thrones made of stone were arranged along the outside edge of the room. They were spaced apart at equal distances, and situated so that there was no place in the room where all three of them were not staring at you.

On each throne was a figure. These were incredibly detailed and lifelike, dressed in regal robes, each with a crown on its head. They pulsed with life and power, but thankfully didn't move as we came into the room. Each seemed to be grown from a single block of stone, as there were no visible joints nor any marking that would indicate any kind of tool was used to craft them.

I swallowed hard as I looked at them. There was no mistaking their features, and nothing could have prepared me for what I was seeing.

"It's us," said Shira quietly.

I turned to Raquel, who was staring at her own statue. "Raquel, what in the Emperor's name is going on here?"

She turned to me and said quietly, "You awoke the fortress and it has accepted us as the Founders."

"The what?" asked Shira.

"The Founders: the first generation of the Sac'a'rith. We had a room like this, with seven thrones dedicated to them. It was the most holy spot on the grounds." She was visibly shaken.

"So you're saying the castle is building itself for us?" I wasn't even sure how to phrase my question. My mind was a jumble of thoughts that refused to untangle themselves.

"Yes, and it's no wonder the undead are so anxious. This," she said, waving her hands around the room, "represents the return of life."

"Where are they?" asked Shira.

"Who?" I asked.

"The builders. Someone must be doing all this work," she explained.

Raquel looked out the window and pointed to the one building that had not changed in all our trips. "There. That's where the caretakers lived ... live."

"But how could they know what we look like?" I asked.

"Zah'rak, I really have no idea. As far as I knew, all this was impossible," she said. She looked at her statue with tears in her eyes. "I don't understand," she said almost inaudibly.

I was about to suggest we check the builder's house when Shira asked, "Raquel, what do we need to do for you tonight?"

The reason we'd come here in the first place had been completely forgotten. Raquel regained her composure and walked over to Shira. "It'll be much easier now. The walls are strong enough to keep out danger, and I'm nowhere near as weak as I was. I should be able to recharge safely up here, and we can leave in the morning."

I decided I'd keep a watch on the caretaker's building while they worked it out. I wanted to see who was building this place and it kept me from having to see the massive statue of myself. I could feel it staring at my back and it made me uneasy, but that was less uncomfortable than facing it would have been.

As the full moon climbed into the night sky, the eerie grey hue seemed to deepen. This added to the creepy effect of the screams and wails from the undead, trying to breach the fortress walls but afraid to get too close. Overhead, the sky filled with foul flying creatures, most of which I couldn't identify; I was probably better off not knowing.

The night passed without any sign of the caretakers. Raquel collapsed again at midnight, but this time Shira knew what to do and Raquel was revived to her full strength by the end of the first hour.

The following morning, I went out to have another look at the scale model. In the long night hours I'd decided on some changes in the design of the fortress, and I wanted to update the model to see if things would be different the next time we returned.

Once that was done, I was planning to visit the caretaker's building but Raquel said, "We'd better go back and get some rest. We still have a battle to fight."

I sighed, knowing she was right. "Okay, gate us out of here; but when this is over, I want to come back and meet our sculptors."

CHAPTER
FORTY-NINE

Raquel had taken Zah'rak and Shira somewhere and once again left Ragnar in charge. I couldn't figure Ragnar out. He was obviously the weakest member of the team and the least knowledgeable, but everyone including Raquel respected him and his opinions on any subject. I would have to learn what part he played in all of this, but I had another task to complete first.

"Ragnar?" I said.

"Yes, Marcus?"

"Will you be okay up here? I'm going to jack in and run some maintenance before our final jump," I said.

"Yeah, go on. I'll call Crivreen or Purwryn if I have any trouble," he said.

"Thanks." It was nice to be among people from whom I didn't have to hide what I was.

I left the bridge and went straight to the cargo bay. I wanted to crash Purwryn and Crivreen's practice session before turning in. They met around this time every day to work on their skills. I knew that the others practiced regularly also, but my relationship with Purwryn should allow me the freedom to pry deeper.

Since coming on board I hadn't had a chance to learn much about how they worked their magic, and there was nothing helpful in the ship's computers. The computer records described what it looked like externally, and what motions to take, but gave no indication of how it all worked. I needed to talk to a magus to find that out, it seemed.

I slipped into the back of the cargo bay, careful not to disturb them. They were facing each other and focusing on something, but I couldn't tell what.

"Ready!" said Purwryn.

Crivreen nodded and moved his hands while chanting. His back was to me so I couldn't see much of what he was doing, but there was no question that his hands and body were moving in a pattern with a degree of precision I wasn't accustomed to seeing in a primitive. The movements were identical to one of the spells I had studied in the ship's database, and so perfectly matched I would have thought only a Cyborg could pull it off; but unlike a Cyborg's perfect but terse movements, these flowed naturally. There was no hint of working at perfection; it looked more as if he was moving his arms around randomly and they just happened to be in perfect sync with the pattern in the database.

As he completed the spell, a bolt of electricity arced from Crivreen's outstretched hand and struck Purwryn, who grimaced but held his ground. After a moment, Crivreen clenched his fist and stopped the flow of power.

A Cyborg with the proper implants could toss lightning like that, but it would quickly drain a power pack. A bolt like I'd just witnessed would probably eat up half its power, and I knew that they had already been down here practicing for hours. My study of the ship's library told me that magi had the ability to tap an energy store that they called 'the Weave'. It was that connection I wished to understand. At the very least, I wanted to find a way to block it and turn magi into primitives. Ultimately, the Great Core wanted the ability to tap this power for itself, but from what I had learned so far it seemed that only pure organics could do that. Magi refused implants of all kinds so that they wouldn't hinder their connection. This didn't seem to bode well for the Great Core's plans.

Purwryn, amazingly, didn't seem harmed by the lightning attack. I couldn't work out why that was, since there'd been enough power in that bolt to kill a primitive and seriously damage any unshielded implants. At the very least, he should have collapsed as the electricity overloaded his nervous system.

"Hey, Marcus! Think fast!" called Purwryn.

I turned towards him, and as soon as my eyes made contact with his he threw something at me. My automatic systems went into overdrive trying to understand the threat, but they were too slow. For the first time since becoming enhanced, someone had been able to get a jump on me.

Purwryn's fireball stopped a few centimeters from my face, just beyond the tip of my nose. I could feel the heat radiating from it and knew it was hot enough to have done serious damage to my organic systems had it landed.

It dissipated and Purwryn smiled at me. "You're going to have to be faster than that."

I replayed the memory of the fireball's flight and checked the timing. It wasn't good. "I would have needed half a second more to dodge that."

"You should have had that," he chided. "I know you have perfect memory. Replay the scene and look for the warning signs."

I did as he suggested and then saw it. Just before the fireball appeared, his hands had come together and mimed a push towards me. "You're right. I'll update my programming."

"Marcus, we're probably going to face sorcerers at this next encounter," he said. "You need to be ready. An attack like Crivreen's lightning bolts travels at the speed of light, but you should be able to dodge other attacks such as my fireball and the much slower earth bolt."

I didn't like being instructed like this by an unenhanced being, not one bit. "Try it again."

He cast, and as he did I noticed two things. The first was the laser-light focus of his eyes. No matter what his body did, his focus didn't waver. Secondly, he was casting slower than before and that angered me; he was going easy on me.

I saw the telltale cue and this time moved to dodge the fireball, but turned right into the path of a second one. It slammed into my armored chest and dispersed without breaking through. Once again he'd showed me up, and I wasn't happy. It took all of my programming to prevent myself from reacting.

"Marcus, are you okay?" asked Crivreen.

"Yeah, the armor held up well," I said. "Purwryn, what are you trying to prove? That you're better than me?"

"No," he said with genuine shock in his voice. "You're faster and stronger without a doubt, but you don't know our targets. You need to learn so you can use your advantages to overcome them."

I took a deep breath as I realized he was giving me what I'd come here to find out: a way to fight the magi. "Okay, sorry."

"I know you're a fast study, so what weaknesses did you spot in my two attacks?" asked Purwryn.

"Your eyes betrayed your target, and your hands betrayed your timing. Cast again," I said.

Purwryn nodded and cast. This time, a mere instant before his final gesture I moved with my Cyborg speed and dove behind a box, breaking his line of sight. The fireball whizzed by harmlessly.

Before he could say or do anything else I was moving again. This time I sprang up over the box and came down on him. I calculated the impact so he wouldn't get hurt, but I hoped it would shake his confidence.

As I came down, he looked up and saw me and then was gone. My sensors swept the room and found him on top of the box I had leapt over, pointing a wand at me.

"Bang! You're dead," he said, mimicking a gun with his fingers.

"What happened?" I asked. I replayed the memory and still couldn't detect his movements.

"Your plan was well executed," said Purwryn. "You dodged my attack perfectly, but you made too much noise with your own attack and gave me time to respond. Next time, come in absolutely silently and you should get the kill."

Purwryn was far better at this than had been apparent in our previous fights, especially the one against Resden. At that time I'd been hiding that I was a Cyborg, and he that he was a magus. Neither of us had been using our abilities to the fullest, and I was only now starting to understand how much he had held back. That had been a foolish risk on both our parts.

"Different spells have different gestures, so you'll have to watch and learn as we go. Pyromancy is one of the most common elemental lines, and the elemental lines are the most common power, so it's a good one to start learning the defenses for," said Purwryn.

"It seems I greatly underestimated you, Purwryn," I said.

"Everyone does," he replied with a grin. "I find it very helpful to allow them to."

I smiled. "Indeed it is." That was one tactic that I definitely understood. My camouflage as a primitive meant everyone always underestimated me.

I stayed with them another hour learning how to read their casting before I decided I really should jack in back in my quarters. I had plenty of power, but if we did have a fight on our hands tomorrow I wanted to be as ready as possible.

When I made it to my quarters and looked over the equipment the Wizards had provided for me, I was again struck by the difference between them and primitives. No ordinary doctor would have given me this equipment, and I hadn't ever seen this quality of workmanship outside the Cyborg ships.

Musing about the wizards, I was interrupted by an unusual displacement of air behind me and I spun round, ready to attack. Behind me I saw with my organic sensors a man who didn't belong on this ship. He was completely invisible to my Cyborg sensors and absent from my databanks.

I started to lunge towards him but he caught me by the arm and swung me around into the wall, pressing me up against it. I tried to break free and should easily have been able to overpower him, but all my implants lost their power and suddenly failed. I collapsed against the wall as my legs turned themselves off to save what little power they had left. I lost my connection to the ship's network and went mostly blind as the rest of my sensor array went offline. Somehow he had sucked the life right out of my batteries; I was literally powerless, my greatest nightmare realized.

"Now, Marcus, perhaps you will take a moment to listen," said the man.

He was wearing some kind of liquid metal armor that flowed over his body like a second skin. He appeared to be unarmed, but had already demonstrated that he needed no weapon. The most striking feature was his eyes: they were steel-grey and, despite being completely organic, seemed to bore right through me better than any sensor array. They were cold and hard, and in them I saw only death.

"Who are you?" I mumbled. My jaw was completely organic and continued to function correctly, but I had long ago replaced my vocal cords so that I could impersonate other voices as needed, and with my power so low they were struggling to operate.

"That doesn't matter. What matters is that right now your Command is analyzing all the reports you have been sending, and in a few hours they will come to a decision. They will tell you the crew of the Night Wisp is too dangerous and that you are to make sure they are killed in the upcoming fight," he said.

Something in his voice made me believe that he knew what he was talking about, but there was no way he could know what decision the Great Core would make. "So?" I wanted to say more but I had to conserve what power I had left; a single syllable was all I dared risk.

"You will disobey that order and make sure that all members of this crew survive. If any fall, I will come for you. Is that clear?"

He still held me pinned and I was powerless, so I did the only logical thing I could do: I agreed to his terms with a very slight nod. The vast majority of my systems were completely run down and I was unable to move enough even to turn my head to look at him. He lifted me up and placed me in my charging station, expertly hooked in the primary power coupling and then disappeared.

With the maintenance station connected, all my systems came back online. I did a full active sensor sweep of the Night Wisp with both my sensors and the ship's own internal sensors, but found nothing. Whoever he was, he was gone.

I wanted to report to Ragnar that we'd had an intruder, but I couldn't; if I did, they would start asking questions about the reason he was here and why he'd come after me. That could lead to them discovering that I was reporting to the Cyborg nation, which wasn't acceptable. No, I had to keep this to myself, at least until I'd figured out what was going on.

I was worried about shutting down without knowing the man's location, but then realized he could have killed me at any time. I suspected no one else on board would have stood a chance against him either. In the long run, it wouldn't matter whether I was awake or not. I sighed, settled in and activated my maintenance mode.

CHAPTER
FIFTY

It was late local time when we returned to the Night Wisp and I was tired from my long night vigil, so I had a few hours' sleep before heading up to the bridge. When I arrived, I found Raquel there alone.

"Good morning, Zah'rak. I sent Ragnar to bed. I think he stood watch alone the whole time we were gone," she said.

"That's not acceptable. What happened to the others?" With four people on board, there was no good reason for one person to have been stuck on watch alone for the entire time. It should have been easy to rotate their turns on the bridge, but I suspected Ragnar had never asked for help.

"Purwryn and Crivreen spent most of the time training, ran themselves ragged and collapsed. According to the ship's logs, Marcus had a power failure and was forced into maintenance mode."

"Any indication as to why?" I asked.

She hesitated. "Yes, but it's not good."

"Tell me," I said.

"When Marcus' systems failed it triggered a medical alarm, which was sent to my medical station. Ragnar didn't know he should monitor that station, so it went unnoticed."

That issue would have to be addressed also. Ragnar was from Korshalemia, which had a very primitive society. The people were far more advanced than we were in the ways of magic, but they hadn't even discovered electricity yet, never mind starships. The amount of catching up Ragnar had to do was immense. He had done well, but obviously there were still gaps in his knowledge; if he didn't know he should look for medical alerts, then those gaps were dangerously large.

"When the medical alert went off, the internal video surveillance in his quarters automatically started recording and tied itself to the alarm log. I think it would be best if you watched this," Raquel said and brought up the video playback.

I hadn't known that feature existed on this ship. It seemed that there were gaps in my knowledge, too, which I would have to fill. I was unsure how I felt about the presence of cameras in our personal quarters, but at that moment I was glad of them.

I watched as Marcus fell against the wall and slowly slid to the floor. There was something odd in the way he moved, but it was difficult to analyze. He was struggling to speak, but the audio was too low to make out any words. I wondered if he was trying to call for help, as fear was clearly evident on his face. Never having seen him scared before, I wondered what could frighten a superhuman like himself.

Suddenly he was moving, but obviously not of his own accord. He looked like a ragdoll being carried by a child, yet he was alone in the room. His body was lifted and placed roughly into his maintenance station. Once reconnected he quickly regained his mobility and jacked himself in the rest of the way.

Raquel stopped the playback there. "Once he was back in his station, he was able to use its power to reactivate his systems, but he wouldn't have been able to leave the station for a while. The ship's logs show he did a full sensor sweep of the Night Wisp, which found nothing, and then he dropped into maintenance mode. Though the logs won't show it, I'm sure he swept the ship with his own sensor array also."

"That would have been wise. What do you think happened there?" I asked.

She backed up the video to the point where Marcus was being carried by some unseen force. "What does a magus look like on sensors?"

"They don't show up. Are you saying a magus was in there with him?" I asked.

"Suppose a magus came aboard by teleportation, gate travel or some other means. Shira or I might have detected a traveler had we been on board, but no one else was likely to. Whoever this was, he surprised Marcus in his chambers and somehow disabled him."

I thought about that for a moment. "Since Marcus relies on his implants as his sensor array, he would have been just as blind as the camera."

"Something tipped him off. He spun round to attack but was too late," she said.

"Does anyone else know?" I asked.

"No. I waited till Ragnar was gone to check the alerts; I wanted to be sure he actually went to bed."

That was probably wise. Ragnar tended to be completely selfless in his service, and would have refused to retire had he known about this. "We will need his divination skills."

"Definitely, but first we should wait for Marcus to waken and get his report. We also have an offensive to plan, and the captain of the fleet will be calling soon to do it with us."

"I think it's best if we keep this incident to ourselves for the moment," I said. The last thing I wanted was Phareon demanding to come on board and 'help' with the investigation.

"I agree. Let's get the planning out of the way so we can focus on this," she said and started working the controls on the comm. station. Soon the captain from the Phareon fleet came on the screen.

After the appropriate pleasantries, Raquel asked, "Captain, to what extent is your fleet ready for combat?"

"We lost much in the Cyborg ambush, but most of what we have left is nearly back to full operational status."

"What are we facing in the system?" she asked.

"They took out the jump repeaters so we can't get any current information, but that leaves them just as sensor-limited as we are. At this distance we're too far to tell much."

"Sounds like they're better prepared than our last target." Raquel paced the deck in front of the screen, deep in thought. "Based on your educated guess, do you have the numbers to complete the mission?"

"It's hard to say. Fleet records show this to be an uninhabited and barren system, save for the outpost we had here. If they brought no additional equipment there would only be that one base to deal with, but they could have a full fleet in there and we couldn't tell at this distance, or not until their EM emissions finally reached us. Even that would be very old information."

"Since they're ready for us, we can assume that the trick we used last time won't work." She paused there as Marcus came onto the bridge and took his station at tactical. "Marcus, what are the chances that the Cyborgs will jump into the system and take advantage of the fight to take out both parties?"

"Huh?" His head came up. He must have been thinking hard, because he was never surprised like that. "Oh, I hadn't considered that possibility." His eyes defocused for a moment while he thought about it, or at least that's what I presumed he was doing. It was hard to tell with him.

I wondered what it was like to have a computer system in your head. I think it would be distracting dealing with all the status messages and suchlike that computers insisted on constantly providing.

"Raquel, why did you ask him that? How would he know?" I sent privately.

"For the same reason I'd ask you if we were facing a fleet of Zalionians.

He's a Cyborg and can think like them, just as you can think like a Zalionian," she sent back.

That seemed like a reasonable answer, but Marcus still hadn't responded. Just when I thought he'd fallen into a daydream, he said, "Unlikely. The most likely scenario is that they'll fall back to reorganize and rebuild their fleet before taking the offense again. The Wizard fleet beat them pretty badly, so they'll need longer to do that than this engagement should take."

The captain sighed deeply, obviously relieved. "Are you sure of that?"

Marcus paused before answering, but finally said, "Yes, sir. It's the action with the highest probability of long-term success, and the Cyborg nation acts solely on probability calculations."

"Excellent," said Raquel. "That leaves only the system itself as an unknown."

"Then I suggest we jump short of the system and launch probes to scout it out. That will give us an idea of what we're about to face," said the captain.

"That will delay our attack by at least a day, if not two," said Raquel.

The probes would have to fly into the system, being too small to have effective jump drives, and get within range of the target before they could begin scanning. Since the jump relays had been destroyed they would beam their message back to us at the speed of light; and while that was fast, it was slow on the scale of distance in space.

"Yes, and quite frankly my fleet needs that time. My men have been pushing hard to get repairs done, and I'd rather not head into battle with a tired crew if I can help it."

So the real answer to Raquel's earlier question about the fleet's battle readiness was that they needed more time. I sighed to myself. People really needed to learn to be more straightforward. Had we decided to rush in without knowing that, many more could have died needlessly.

Raquel nodded. "There is wisdom in that, and I doubt we are likely to surprise them at this point."

"Then it's agreed: we'll jump a couple of hours short of the system and send in the probes," said the captain.

I almost chuckled at that comment, remembering how confused Ragnar still was over the measurement of distance out here. Obviously, the captain meant light hours, or the distance light traveled in one hour, rather than a measure of time; that concept, however, was foreign to Ragnar. To him hours could only mean time. It would take the probes many hours to cross that distance, but they could travel much faster than the fleet.

"Sounds good. Please make sure I get the encryption codes so we can receive the data here directly," said Raquel.

The captain didn't look pleased by that request but made no objection. He had probably been told to cooperate fully, and warned that if he caused an incident it wouldn't be good for his career. Phareon couldn't risk losing this small chance of making friends with the Wizard Kingdom, especially if Raquel was correct in her prediction that they would fall within a decade.

CHAPTER
FIFTY-ONE

It was almost midday when my systems were fully powered again. I disconnected from my maintenance station and checked the ship's logs to see what I had missed. The logs told me that Raquel and company had returned in the middle of the night. Raquel and Zah'rak were on the bridge, and Shira predictably back in hydroponics. I was about to check on the others when my thoughts were interrupted by a message.

"*Agent P2003, report,*" said the voice.

"Mission continuing as planned. Night Wisp is approaching final jump before attacking a target of interest to Phareon and the Wizard Kingdom."

"*We are aware of the target. Make sure the Night Wisp does not survive the battle.*"

"Current mission parameters don't allow for that action. That would eliminate the possibility of success."

"*Your mission parameters have changed. The Night Wisp and her crew are too dangerous to us. Ensure it is eliminated and then report back for a new mission.*"

After that the connection was broken.

Every system in my body froze at that command. Whoever that intruder was, he had correctly predicted the Great Core's decision. That should have been impossible for any unenhanced being, even a magus. The Great Core makes all its decisions internally on its neural net, which is completely inaccessible to all but the elite among the Cyborgs.

Each decision it makes is carefully researched and vetted in an objective matter. Not even the Great Core itself could know of a decision it hadn't yet made. So how did the intruder know? It was obvious he was a magus of some kind, but not a type that I had found in the catalogue of magi on the Night Wisp database.

Those orders left me with an impossible set of choices. I had to choose between being deactivated by the Great Core for failing to follow orders, or being killed by the intruder for following those orders. I needed a plan quickly, but nothing came to mind.

I set all my spare CPUs to run various scenarios, trying to find a way out of this trap. It was risky dedicating so much processing power to any one task, as it would dramatically slow or prevent other operations from happening. My organic brain could handle basic life support, but all my implants needed guidance from my core processing units.

I distractedly walked towards the bridge as I allowed my CPUs to run on overload. Since the only two options before me would end in my death, and my will to survive was still strong, my internal network was stymied looking for a solution. What was left of me walked like a zombie to my station on the bridge. Had I been attacked in the corridor, I would have been dead before I had even fully registered the attack.

I didn't even particularly want to be part of the Cyborg nation. They had found me on the Paradise and recruited me because I could still blend in with the primitives. I was far less enhanced than the Cyborgs were, but that was advantageous to them at the time. Stumbling onto the Night Wisp was a stroke of luck that elevated my value in their eyes, but they had never given me anything other than the promise that I would be part of the ruling class when they'd conquered the region and wiped out the unenhanced. They hadn't even help to pay for the repairs I'd needed when one of my implants had failed some time ago; they just asked for a report on new operating parameters once the repairs were complete.

However, since everyone else hated what I had become, it was easy to let them sweet-talk me into their ranks. Now things were getting complicated, both because I had found people who cared and because logically their next move wouldn't work; it made no sense to take out the Night Wisp. I was gaining valuable information. After the last battle, I could see that they had good reason to fear this team, but I wouldn't expect the Great Core to act on something as base as fear.

As I sat there trying to think, I heard Raquel address me. I missed the question, but my audio sensors had recorded it. Quickly reviewing my lost logs, I saw that she had asked for my opinion on the chances of a Cyborg attack after we engaged in the system. It was a good question, and one I lacked the power to compute in my current state. "Oh, I hadn't considered that possibility."

I cycled through all my running processes and paused them, freeing up enough brainpower to answer Raquel. When enough cognitive functions had returned, I was able to calculate the odds. "Unlikely. The most likely scenario is that they'll fall back to reorganize and rebuild their fleet before taking the offense again. The Wizard fleet beat them pretty badly, so they'll need longer to do that than this engagement should take."

There was a man on the primary screen, to whom they had presumably been speaking when I'd walked in. "Are you sure of that?" he asked.

I paused and slowly recognized him as the captain of the fleet we were flying with. I had gone too deep with my calculations and realized I'd have to limit my processor use in the future. I should have noticed that a mission planning session was going on and paid attention but had been too deep in my own thoughts. "Yes, sir. It's the action with the highest probability of long-term success, and the Cyborg nation acts solely on probability calculations."

The conversation moved on. I looked over the scenarios I'd been running, and none of them looked good. My computers assigned a high probability of termination to all of them. I knew the Cyborgs considered all their members expendable, so contacting them wouldn't help. I doubted the intruder would want to help me even if I could reach him, and what was left of my birth family didn't have the resources to combat this problem. I had to solve this problem alone.

I had spent most of my life alone until I'd met Purwryn. Since joining up with him and his friends, I could finally relax. Everyone knew what I was and no one minded. They shared openly with me, and had even covered the cost of my repairs. I had never met anyone like these strange folk. Truth to tell, I was enjoying my assignment and didn't want it to end.

They ended the call with the captain, and I looked over at Raquel. I had yet to see her powers directly used in battle, but watching her manage the fight with the Cyborg fleet supported the information I'd gathered that concluded she was deadly. She carried herself with the confidence of an experienced warrior and had appeared fearless in any encounter I'd been able to witness so far.

Ragnar told me that she was over ten thousand years old. I was sure he had to be wrong, but he believed it. His personality type was not one to lie or easily be taken in so there had to be a good reason for him to think that, which meant that at the very least she was probably one of the oldest living primitives.

Watching her triggered a memory. It wasn't very logical, but this was a side effect of keeping my organic brain intact. It was another advantage of the organic brain: it could make illogical leaps and connect things that no computer would. Many among the Cyborgs replaced much of their brain, but I'd kept mine purely organic. It had disadvantages, but logic leaps like this made up for it.

The memory of Raquel dated from earlier in our travels. I remembered overhearing her saying, "The Wizard Kingdom is all about second chances." It was during one of the sessions when they were recounting the history of the Wizard Kingdom for my benefit. They, mainly Raquel and Ragnar, felt that I should have some historical context.

I remembered the selflessness that she had exhibited when saving my life before she even knew me, and the steady determination of Purwryn as he spent hours working on my implants. My organic brain couldn't recall the details exactly, but my system logs and the ship's logs had them all. I'd spent a lot of my time when lying around paralyzed doing nothing but reviewing the ship's logs and its database. I had learned quite a bit about the crew in those days and was impressed.

I looked over at Zah'rak, who'd gathered this ragtag group of misfits and turned them into a family, and suddenly I knew I had another option. I quickly ran the calculations and it had a very high probability of my survival. It would mean switching sides, at least for the present, but that was something I'd had to do in the past and probably would again. Besides, the side I was currently on was sending me to my death.

"Zah'rak, I have something to report. There was an incident while you were away," I told him. A look of relief passed over his face. That was not the expression I was expecting and it threw me off for a moment. I couldn't find any logical connection between my statement and his demeanor. I tried to rerun my scenarios to see if I needed to abort, but was unable to calculate due to the lack of information.

"Go on," prompted Raquel, drawing me back to the situation at hand.

With no better plan, I decided to push on. "I was attacked by an intruder in my quarters," I said and then told them everything that had happened. "When I awoke this morning I had a message from the Cyborg leadership, telling me to make sure the Night Wisp and all hands were destroyed."

"Do you often get messages from them?" asked Zah'rak.

"No," I replied. I took a deep breath and continued. "Please understand that before I met Purwryn, I was alone and hated by all. My father tolerated me, but I suspect that was only because I was useful on his ships. The Cyborgs discovered me and offered me the world if I would help them as an agent among the primitives. You see, I can do what they can't: I can blend in. They wanted me to be a spy, and in exchange I would be part of the ruling nation when they took over."

"And you agreed?" asked Raquel.

"Yes. I think anyone might have. I was alone, depressed and desperate," I said.

"When you joined this ship, was it as a spy, then?" asked Zah'rak.

"No. Purwryn brought me on board. My original plan was to see him off safely and then find a new place to blend in for the Cyborgs. That plan was derailed by my injuries and Raquel saved my life. The Cyborgs decided I should stay and ordered me to study the magi and send them information on how you work magic."

They were quiet for a while. I decided to let them think about it. It was likely that they were communicating via their telepathic link, something that I had no access to. I wondered what it was like. The ship's database described it as a direct thought transference. They could apparently exchange more than just words: memories, scents, emotions, anything that could be thought could be shared. It sounded much like downloading memories from other units and replaying them, but they could do it in real time.

This period was a little nerve-wracking. If my calculations were wrong, they might kill me or bind me in some prison until they could get rid of me. That would mark me as a failure and I'd be assumed defective by the Great Core, which would mean termination.

"During the battle, what were your orders?" asked Zah'rak.

"They wanted me to destroy you then because you were having too much success, but I refused and persuaded them it would be a tactical error. I don't expect they are happy with me right now, and by telling you this I have made myself an enemy of the Cyborg nation. There's no going back, but I don't think there ever really was after I came on board." I didn't know if that was actually true, but I suspected it was. Even still, I thought there might be a way around it if I was careful to keep my options open.

"Why *are* you telling us this?" asked Raquel.

This was the question I'd been waiting for; if I answered well, I'd live.

"Because I envy you. You're a family. Sure, you're not actually related, but I see Raquel going out of her way to help Shira heal, and Shira running to help Zah'rak understand Raquel. I watch Purwryn and Crivreen practice together with complete trust. I viewed the logs of Raquel saving my life. There's all that and much more. I want to be part of a family, and I can't be if I'm on a different side."

I waited in silence, assuming that they continued to confer telepathically. I knew from the stories I'd heard that both Raquel and Shira used to be enemies, not only of each other but also of Zah'rak's team. It was hard to imagine, but apparently at one time Shira had been doing all in her power to kill everyone who was now her friend. These stories gave me hope that switching sides as a means of avoiding deactivation would be a successful move.

Raquel smiled. "I could call home and ask Grandmaster Vydor, but I know what he would say."

Zah'rak walked up and placed his hand on my shoulder. "You're right, we're family. All of us have troubled pasts; yours pales compared to Shira's and you see how well she has worked out." He paused and looked at Raquel, who smiled again. I was sure some silent communication had passed between them. "Welcome to the team, Marcus."

"This intruder - did you get a good look at him?" asked Raquel.

"Yes," I said and sent a copy of this memory to the ship's primary monitor. "My implants couldn't read him but my organic mind had no problem, even with the lack of power." That was yet another reason I kept my organic brain. It could see and remember magi.

Raquel gasped. "Curetes."

CHAPTER
FIFTY-TWO

I awoke in my room on the Night Wisp, sore in a dozen places from the workout the previous day with Crivreen. I'd gotten much better at blocking his attacks, but he'd also greatly improved his attack skill. He must have singed off most of my hair; it had certainly smelled like it. I decided I wouldn't look in a mirror for a few days until it grew back.

The computer had woken me with just enough time to get ready and have a meal before my shift on the bridge, so I knew I had to get up, but trying to swing my legs over the edge caused pain to shoot up through my body and out of my eyes. I screamed a curse and tried to stand. *You idiot! You could be in battle today!* I thought to myself.

In the bathroom, I splashed water on my face and tried to pull myself together. The room spun around my head in a strange up-and-down fashion, and whoever was staring back at me from the mirror looked like he'd spent the night drinking. The gaunt face and dark shadows under the bloodshot eyes told the tale as clear as day. I had to grab the sink to keep from falling over. I cursed some more, realizing I'd overdrawn on my resource pools while training my powers. Then I reminded myself that I hadn't wanted to look in a mirror.

I fumbled around the room knocking over data pads and bruising my shins in a dozen places until I finally found a protein pack and ate it. I wasn't hungry until I started eating, but as soon as the bland paste hit my tongue I became ravenous. I sucked down the paste as fast as I could manage without falling over, and forced myself to let that settle before trying to eat anything else. Then I attempted to take a shower.

The shower was an ordeal, as I was sure the walls moved when I tried to grab them for balance. The water hitting my body felt like swarms of tiny bugs crawling on my skin, but I knew it was all in my mind; I just had to push through it and hope it didn't cause nightmares. I had read about this happening to magi, but I'd never been foolish enough to experience it myself until now.

Clean and dressed, I made for the mess hall to get something more substantial to eat. Rest and food were the only cure for this condition that I knew of. I found Crivreen there, holding his head and eating slowly. He looked disheveled, and I guessed that he had decided to skip the shower. I didn't blame him; it had felt very dangerous when I'd done it.

"Man, that was one great party you threw," I said as I took some food and joined him.

He cursed under his breath. "Purwryn, not so loud."

I nodded and we ate in silence. We had both overdone it in training and burned through all our illuminescence stores. Once a magus runs out of illuminescence he begins to tap his own life force, which is extremely dangerous and foolhardy. It would be a day or two before we recovered, and we could easily have killed ourselves had we gone much further. This was foolish at any time, and absolutely insane on the eve of a battle. Eating and drinking helped a little, especially the natural sugars in the fruit that Shira had grown for us, but not as much as sitting and letting our bodies begin to regenerate illuminescence.

"We'd better put some limits on these practice sessions," Crivreen said quietly. He was very pale and I doubted he would be much use today.

"You think?" I said.

The meal did help to relieve some of my symptoms, so I headed up to take my shift at watch on the bridge. I wasn't sure I could handle it if anything actually happened, but I could at least hit the alarm button if necessary.

I cleaned up after myself and stumbled up to the bridge. As I entered, I saw on the screen the image of a man who I'd hoped never to see again. I froze on the spot and a chill passed through my body.

I heard Raquel gasp and say, "Curetes."

"That's him!" I called out.

Everyone turned and looked at me. My mind was suddenly crystal clear as my heart pumped blood faster and adrenaline surged into my bloodstream.

"Who?" asked Zah'rak.

"That's the man who jumped me on the Paradise!" I said.

"Who's Curetes?" asked Marcus.

"He is," said Raquel as she pointed at the screen. "One of the most dangerous magi alive today."

"Who is he?" I stared at the image of my tormentor on the screen. I wanted to look away, but I couldn't. He was wearing the same liquid-looking metal armor, but it was the eyes that gave him away. It wouldn't matter if every other detail about him had changed; those eyes would give him away every time. The fact that this was merely a still image did nothing to lessen the effect. I felt that those eyes could bore right through me, stripping away my body and laying my soul bare.

"The right-hand man of Henrick, who is *the* most dangerous man alive, outside of the Wizard's Council itself," said Raquel.

I stumbled over to navigation and sat down. I was still tired and weak and the adrenaline rush was fading, leaving me shaky and lightheaded. I had hoped never to see him again, and I was in no condition to process the implications of the fact that he was on our screen.

"What do they have to do with anything?" asked Zah'rak, who was obviously taken aback.

"It seems our enemies are multiplying," Marcus said.

"Henrick is not exactly an enemy. We actually have a treaty with him, and he was involved with us in a recent war that the Wizard Kingdom fought for the survival of the realm. I wouldn't call him a friend either, though. He has his own agenda and his own nation of sorts," said Raquel. "If he's active out here, then we know something big is happening; really big."

"Wouldn't his attack on Marcus be in violation of the treaty we have with him?" asked Zah'rak.

"No, because he could claim it was in defense. And before you ask, when he attacked Purwryn he wasn't part of the Kingdom," she said.

"When did he attack Marcus?" I asked.

"Yesterday Curetes jumped Marcus in his quarters and left him completely disabled," said Zah'rak.

I didn't like the idea that my attacker could reach Marcus here. "How did he get on board?"

"A gate or teleportation, most likely. If Shira and I had been here, we would have noticed his arrival and acted, but I imagine he deliberately waited until we were gone," said Raquel.

I turned to Marcus and asked, "Why didn't you call for help?"

He hesitated and then said, "If your arm was cut off and you were bleeding to death, what would you do first: stop the bleeding or call for help?"

"Well, I'd have to stop the bleeding or die, so that answer is obvious," I said.

"When I was finally connected to power and could react on my own, he was already gone, so I concentrated on 'stopping the bleeding'; that is, I told my station to repair and recharge my systems."

I wondered about that; the analogy didn't seem to fit because being connected to power meant he was already stable. *He was probably embarrassed that he got beaten by an unenhanced human,* I thought to myself. I remembered how annoyed he'd been during our short training run in the cargo bay. He was used to winning any one-on-one competition and had a hard time dealing with failure. "Next time, call for help. There's no shame in it."

"I agree," said Raquel. "If Curetes returns, call me immediately. Don't try to engage him; all of you combined wouldn't even stand a chance."

"And you would?" I queried.

"Maybe, maybe not; but he can't attack me without risking the treaty, so it won't come to that. The important thing is that if he's here, then Henrick is at the very least interested in what's going on in this system. That means we are probably heading for something big. We'll all need to be at the top of our game, and I'd better try calling home. Grandmaster Vydor will want to know about Henrick's interest."

"When do we jump in?" I asked.

"Soon, but we'll be holding at the system edge until probes can get in and give us some idea of what we're up against," answered Raquel, and then she sent privately, *"So make sure you rest and get your strength back. No more practice sessions for now. "*

"Yeah, I know, and you don't have to tell me how stupid it was," I sent back. That seemed to satisfy her, as she didn't bring it up again. Then I sent to Crivreen, *"Hey, we have at least a day, so lie as low as you can and recover. When we get into the system we could have a very interesting time, to say the least."*

"Why? What did you find out?" he sent back.

I briefed him on the conversation. *"So Raquel figures we are heading into something big."*

"Great. Well, at least the Night Wisp is stronger than it's ever been before," he sent.

CHAPTER
FIFTY-THREE

Three days had passed since Shira, Raquel and I had returned from Alpha World, and the data from the probes had finally arrived. The captain of the Phareon fleet and his three advisors joined us via the comm as Raquel, Marcus, Ragnar and I tried to work out a plan of attack. Crivreen and Purwryn were still on mandatory rest after their foolish training session. Raquel figured they would be fully ready for combat in another day's time, and I hoped we could give that to them.

"Captain," said Raquel, "according to the data you sent, they have no interplanetary probes, no orbital defenses and apparently no anti-aircraft protection on the surface?"

"As strange as it sounds, yes. None of our probes detected anything of the sort on the way in, and all three are now safely in orbit over the target. As of last report, these appear to be undetected by the ground forces."

Displayed before me on our tactical screens was an image of the target. It was a modern military base with all the normal trappings, including the standard multiple perimeters created by blast walls, and patrol routes. There were numerous nondescript buildings throughout the complex which were

all designed to take a beating from above, and locations for artillery place-
ments. The one major difference was that the base had no artillery in the
mounts. There were places to mount them, and even mounting equipment,
but nothing actually mounted. There were no modern weapons of any kind
visible in the imagery. That didn't make sense, since this used to be a military base and would have been equipped with plenty of firepower. The only
logical conclusion is that they had taken down the weapons, but I couldn't
think of a reason to do that. Even if they couldn't work them, it would have
been simpler to have left them up.

Also clear in the images were the sorcerers' forces. These were made
up of some kind of creature which was a nightmarish mixture of man, machine and beast. They looked half-formed and ready to fall apart, but when
the Phareon military had fought them at the last station they'd proved to
be extremely resistant to damage and utterly fearless. They were milling
aimlessly around the complex and didn't seem to be serving any function
other than discouraging a direct ground assault. Looking at them made me
sick to my stomach. They were unnatural, and I couldn't wait to see them
destroyed.

"I don't get it. They have all the pieces in place to harden the target
against any assault, but they aren't utilizing them at all," I said.

"Zah'rak, you aren't thinking like a Korshalemian sorcerer," said Ragnar.

"What do you mean?" I asked.

"Remember, they don't have spacecraft or probes where they come
from," he said.

"Sure," said Raquel. "But they've been operating in our realm for a
while now, so it's not like they don't know about such things."

"Yes, but they wouldn't defend against them in the same way that a
Vydorian military force would. They have other tools," he said.

"What are you getting at?" asked the captain.

"I think I see," said Raquel. "They don't have artillery set up because
they won't need it."

"Exactly," said Ragnar. "If we try a simple attack from above, the sorcerers will reach out with their magic and destroy us in orbit. Failing that, they'll simply abandon the base and move the operation elsewhere. Either way we lose."

"I see," said the captain. "Then what's our plan?"

Raquel looked down at the map thoughtfully and said, "Captain, the only way we're going to take out that base is to eliminate the sorcerers. They know that as well as we do, so we'll have to put ground forces into play. I suggest that the Night Wisp lands here, and we move directly on the fortress. I request you to drop your ground forces about an hour behind us to land here and here. The goal will be for your attack to draw the sorcerers out from cover. When they show themselves, we'll engage them directly. When they are defeated everyone pulls out, and you bomb the base into oblivion from orbit."

The captain conferred quietly with his advisors and turned back to the screen. "What about air support?"

"You'll need it. I'm sure the sorcerers will have some of their own," said Raquel, "but I don't yet know what it will be."

"They will summon elementals, at the very least," said Ragnar. "Hopefully nothing worse, but they are sorcerers so it's possible."

"What are elementals?" asked the captain.

"Zah'rak, can you display some of the elementals from our database for them to see?" asked Ragnar.

"Sure," I said. Thanks to the datapad Master Spectra had given us, we had an extensive database of all the basic creatures elementalists could summon. None of us could summon them, but the information was great to have at times like this. I suspected our little ship contained the most extensive database of magic in the region, apart from Hospital Station.

The image on the tactical screens was replaced by a slide show of models of various kinds of elementals. Each image contained basic information about the creatures, but I suspected only Marcus could read fast enough to keep up with the ever-changing images. Surprisingly, he didn't seem to be paying much attention to the slide show; instead he was intently watching the interaction between the captain and his advisors. I wondered if he was able to read their lips, even at the poor camera angle. Perhaps he had a special lip-reading algorithm in that electronic mind of his.

In my musing I missed most of Ragnar's speech about the creatures, and only caught his conclusion. "As you can see, there are a large variety of them, but they are all constructed from natural materials of varying kinds. Your physical weapons should be effective against the more physical ones, and your energy-based ones should work well against the others," said Ragnar.

"Also," said Raquel, "they are summoned beings, but they have to obey the same laws of nature as you do; so a fire elemental is vulnerable to water, and earth elementals can be blown to bits. Using your basic knowledge of how things work to tune your attacks and defenses, you should do well against them."

"Okay. Ragnar said 'hopefully nothing worse,'" said the captain. "Could you expand on that?"

"Do you know much about the Great War?" asked Raquel.

"I was too young when it was fought to remember the war, but I studied it in school," he said. A look of fear passed over his face. "Oh, you mean they could call up creatures like that again?"

"Yes," said Raquel. "But those creatures take a lot of skill and power to cast, so we're much less likely to see them here. The Great War was a battle with the best the sorcerers had; this is just a random outpost. I'm counting on there being only a few sorcerers and those not being among their best. This is likely to be an expendable base in their eyes, but I can't fathom their purpose."

"I hope you're right, but what about their fear weapon? I remember hearing stories about crews being frozen at their stations, unable to fight." He visibly shuddered. "There was that destroyer, the Firebrand … "

He didn't finish that sentence and clearly didn't want to. The Firebrand had been part of the lead forces of the attack, and its attack group took the brunt of the sorcerers' fear weapon before the wizards made their move. It's said that the whole crew went mad and tore each other to pieces with their bare hands. I had no idea if that was true but, going by his expression, the captain believed it was.

"That takes even more concentration, which is why we must press the attack hard and fast," she said. "We can't let them focus on any one target for long. Truthfully, I'm guessing here; I don't know how many sorcerers are going to be down there or how powerful they are, so it's probably wisest to assume the worst until we know," answered Raquel.

"Raquel, what if there are too many of them for us?" I asked privately, not wanting to undermine her influence.

"Then we'll pull out and call for help. But despite my comments, I'm sure there are only three, maybe four, sorcerers, all fairly weak. We'll be fine," she sent back.

One of the captain's advisors said something to him privately, then turned back to the screen and asked, "Why are you going first, then? If we have to press them hard and fast, shouldn't we hit them first and then you come in when the sorcerers show up?"

Raquel shook her head. "If you go first, you won't survive the initial rush. We have to engage the sorcerers directly. You see, they aren't like us; they don't care if they lose every single person under their command or even the base, so long as they survive and you don't. Simply put, we need to get the sorcerers worried about us before you can attack."

"It's also the expected attack," said Marcus. "The Night Wisp often flies with fleets like yours and then attacks solo. If we land alone, they'll probably assume you aren't going to help."

"This is true," said Raquel. "That surprise should buy you some time in your initial attack run."

"All right, so you rush in and distract the sorcerers and we follow behind and pound them. When you've killed the sorcerers, we are to make a crater of their base. Is that correct?"

"I want the biggest and deepest crater you can make. Leave no survivors," said Raquel.

"That you can be certain of," he said. "But why does this sound like the battle plan for the Great War?"

"Because it is similar," said Raquel. "The sorcerers still have the upper hand with regard to deployment and numbers, and so long as that's true our options for battle tactics are limited to divide, distract and conquer."

"When do we attack?" he asked.

"It's currently mid-afternoon at the target, so I suggest we wait. The Night Wisp will land as the sun comes up tomorrow morning, local time to the target. Daylight will reduce their options, since many of their pets fear the sun," said Raquel.

"Agreed. Good hunting," said the captain.

CHAPTER
FIFTY-FOUR

Under cover of the early morning twilight, Marcus piloted the Night Wisp to the clearing that Raquel had chosen for our landing. It was closer to the target than I preferred, but it was the best landing site in the area. Ordinarily I would have preferred to leave one person behind to keep the Night Wisp safe, but we were about to go up against what Raquel believed to be at least three sorcerers and that meant we'd need everyone.

We were all suited up in the mission room waiting for Raquel to return from her scouting run. I hadn't liked the idea of her traveling alone, but she didn't wait around to argue; she simply stated her intention, activated her camosuit and left.

Being the only mundane among us, Marcus loaded himself up with heavy weapons and ammo. No normal human could carry the weight of all that equipment, nor could they wield the two heavy thirty-millimeter launchers. I was a little anxious to see what he planned to do with all that weaponry.

Marcus was wearing the set of armor I'd made for him. He had the first of the new enhanced line that I was making for Master Dusty's team. Since Marcus was the only mundane among our number, I figured he would need the most protection. I warned him that it hadn't yet been tested in combat and we didn't know its limitations but, as he pointed out, it was at worst far superior to his own armor.

Raquel insisted I should leave my normal weapons behind for this raid and rely on the new spells she'd taught me. After the fight on the Cyborg ship had shown me the ineffectiveness of my assault rifle compared to my staff, I had to agree with her. I took as many wands as I could carry, some grenades and my swords. My staff was always close at hand, thanks to the summoning trick Raquel had taught me. I didn't understand how it worked, or where the staff was when not in my hands, but that really didn't matter; what did matter was that I could pull the staff out of the air when necessary.

I was also wearing a new type of armor, chosen specifically for this environment. Those weeks spent waiting at the hospital station had given me time to experiment on some new designs. My armor wasn't spaceworthy, but it was made from completely natural materials that shouldn't hamper my ability to tap the forest around me. I was hoping that advantage would more than compensate for any loss of protection in the weaker armor. It was lighter and quieter to move in, which should also make casting easier.

Shira was in her own magical armor which she'd worn when she was a slave. It was far better than anything I could yet make, and also made completely from natural materials. Hers was sufficiently enchanted to protect her in the vacuum of space. She had somehow changed the color of it, too, and it was now as dark as her hair. She wore the pack Raquel had given her, but I didn't know what was in that.

"Zah'rak, lead everyone out northwards. You'll cross a wide game trail; follow that and it will take you around the rear side of the base," sent Raquel privately, interrupting my inspection of our team.

"Okay. Where will you be?" I sent back.

"I'll continue to scout ahead of you. We'll regroup at the base," she sent.

356

After one final check of my equipment I said, "We'll split into two groups. Ragnar, Shira, you're with me. Marcus, you take Crivreen and Pur-wryn and, when we hit the trail that Raquel found, take your team under cover on the far side and stay about thirty meters behind us. We'll take the closer side. That way, one ambush can't catch all of us at once."

We moved out into the woods, making our way carefully though the dense underbrush. I'd intentionally taken Shira and Ragnar in my group because they would both be very much at home in the forest. This would allow us to move with more stealth and speed and give us a chance to sur-prise any ambush, instead of the other way around.

"Here we go again," sent Ragnar, after we had been walking for a while. It was strange to hear his mental voice, but a relief also. Thanks to Master Mathorn's work with Ragnar, he could now speak telepathically on his own. That meant we no longer had to rely on the communications system in our armor to talk, which was good since I hadn't added that to my new armor.

I chuckled. *"Getting bored with this life already?"*

"No, I always enjoy a good blind rush into a sorcerer's stronghold!" he said. *"Having no idea what we're up against and a damaged fleet to back us up just makes it more fun!"*

I couldn't help but smile at his sarcasm. He wasn't a warrior at heart, but was invaluable on the battlefield despite that fact or even because of it. Either way, I wouldn't have dreamt of leaving him behind.

"Zah'rak, a big change is coming," he sent, with real concern in his voice.

"What do you mean?" I asked.

"I wish I knew. All I can say for sure is that the Fates have something in mind for us today, and I don't think we'll ever be the same afterwards."

I almost tripped over my own feet when I received that message. Rag-nar's domain was knowledge: present, past and future. His divinations and rune casting gave him insight and understanding beyond what any mortal should know. If he said a big change was coming, then there was reason to be concerned.

"Is this change good or bad?" I asked.

"I wish I knew," he said. *"I suspect a bit of both. All change seems to work out that way."*

Before I could respond to that thought, we came upon the trail Raquel had described. I reached out to a tree with my bare hand and used it to search the area. I found Raquel hiding farther up the trail but no one else. It was eerie being this close and still seeing no resistance.

"Why haven't they moved against us yet?" I sent. *"Surely they saw the landing."*

"Sorcerers tend to be cowards," sent Raquel.

I wondered if that were true or just a product of her feelings about them. "Marcus, cross here. It's clear," I said, remembering at the last moment that Marcus couldn't hear our thoughts.

He nodded and took his team across, and they disappeared into the forest on the other side of the trail. I knew I'd taken a risk putting him in charge instead of Purwryn, but I wanted him to know he was one of us now, and showing him trust by giving him this responsibility was the best way to communicate that to him. We waited under cover until I estimated they would be in place. Marcus' sensors should be able to follow us and stay within the planned spacing.

"Okay, they've had enough time. Let's move out," I sent to Ragnar and Shira.

"Why did we have to land so far away?" asked Shira.

I felt bad for her. Her short legs meant she had to take two, maybe three steps to every one of mine or Ragnar's. *"Because we want the Night Wisp to survive the fight."*

"You could've dropped me off and I could have gated everyone and saved a lot of time," she sent.

"We discussed that already. Casting a gate would be likely to tip our hand to the sorcerers, and we can't risk that at this early stage."

I knew Shira didn't agree with the plan, but Raquel had insisted that we use no magic until the fight started. She didn't want the sorcerers to have any idea what we were capable of. I felt there was wisdom in Raquel's plan, so I supported it. Shira felt that they probably already knew what to expect of us, and she might be right, but I'd rather leave them guessing than confirm their thoughts.

"*We're almost there,*" sent Ragnar.

Once the outer walls of the base came into view, I stopped my group and waited for Marcus and his team to catch up.

"*We have at most fifteen minutes before the troops are scheduled to land,*" sent Raquel as she fell back to join us.

"About fifteen minutes," I said out loud so that Marcus could hear. "Do we wait for them to drop in or do we charge now?"

"I suggest we move in as far as we can," said Marcus. "If we could get on to one of those empty artillery platforms, we could rain fire down on the enemy with some degree of safety."

I looked and we had clear line of sight to one of the platforms. "How about that one there?"

"Yeah," he said. "Not the best one, but it would work."

"We can get there easily and have Shira send a gate for you," I said.

Raquel nodded. "We should wait here for the ground troops to land, then head up there. Once we're there we can leap-frog to a better one if need be, but I suspect that once we join the fight, the sorcerers will come for us directly and we'll have our hands full with them."

"I thought the plan was for us to draw out the sorcerers ahead of the attack?" asked Marcus.

"It is, but our landing did that. By now they know that a group of magi have landed and are on the surface. It would be a simple matter for them to guess that we're moving on the only base on the planet. Until they can judge our strength, they will hold back their power. That was the goal behind our landing and approach, and as far as I can tell it's worked," said Raquel.

"The captain will jump the gun, and his forces will launch in a couple of minutes," said Ragnar.

Raquel spun round and asked, "What do you see?"

Ragnar took a stick and drew a circle on the ground, marking it as he spoke. "The troops will come in hard and fast, landing here, here and here. Troopers will unload first, running towards the walls, followed by armored vehicles. They will breach the outer walls in these three places, and the enemy will pour out through the breaches attempting to prevail through sheer numbers."

"What about air support?" asked Marcus.

Ragnar hesitated and then drew three wavy lines from the center of the base. "It's hard to see, but I think these are flight paths. They will arrive sometime after the wall is breached."

"And the sorcerers?" asked Raquel.

"They're hiding from me," he said. "But they will most likely wait for full engagement before moving. That's how they traditionally operate."

CHAPTER
FIFTY-FIVE

I watched in amazement as Ragnar sketched out the upcoming battle. My own probability analysis had come to similar conclusions, but through my Cyborg implants I had the advantage of being able to tap into and monitor the Phareon fleet's battle network. Ragnar couldn't have had that. I still had to guess what the enemy might do since I had no information on them, and they weren't using any network I could find, but he seemed to know exactly what they would do.

As he spoke, Phareon's battle net suddenly went active and the troop ships began their drop exactly when Ragnar had predicted they would. I searched their network for launch orders and found them; to my surprise, they matched exactly the plan Ragnar had laid out. I was very impressed.

"Drop ships are on their way," I said.

Raquel cursed. "Never trust a weave-forsaken mundane to stick to even the simplest of plans."

I had to agree with her on that one. Primitives, or mundanes as she called them, weren't trustworthy in that regard. The captain should have waited. On this occasion it didn't matter as we were in position and ready, but there had been no way for him to know that, and by launching early he could have caused major problems and needlessly lost many lives.

I looked again at Ragnar's drawing and traced his proposed flight lines back to a single location near the center of the base, drawing an X where the lines met. "Judging from Ragnar's report, that must be where they are launching from."

Raquel looked at the map. "Marcus – "

She was interrupted by the thunder of the drop ships' arrival as they came in hard. They had fired their braking thrusters at full strength at the very last instant, to decelerate enough to survive hitting the ground. I didn't envy the ride the troops had on those ships. They hit the ground with a very audible thud, sending dirt and rock airborne in a cloud around them. Troopers poured out of the ships followed by armored personal carriers and other armored vehicles. Everything was unfolding in accordance with Ragnar's predictions.

"Time to move," said Raquel. "Shira, gate us over."

Shira cast her spell and a gate opened. We all rushed through and came out on top of the battlement that Zah'rak had selected. It gave us a good overview of the battle and there were plenty of places to hide under cover. The location was a far better choice than I had previously thought, allowing me to set up my guns with a wide coverage of the battlefield.

"Crivreen, Purwryn, you two are on anti-air support. Take down anything that flies. Marcus, provide artillery support for the ground forces. Zah'rak, Shira, you're with me. We'll take on the sorcerers when they appear. Ragnar, guard Marcus and find me those sorcerers!"

Ragnar crouched down next to me and threw a handful of small rocks on the ground. They were each inscribed with a symbol I didn't recognize, but they must have had deep meaning for him going by the way he studied them. He picked up the stones and cast them a few times. I mentally overlapped the patterns they landed in, trying to understand what he could see, but nothing jumped out at me. The writing didn't match any I had on record, and the patterns that the stones landed in seemed random.

"Marcus, there will be a second front of enemies; much stronger ones," he said.

"Where?" I asked.

He traced a circle. "If we consider ourselves to be at the center of this, and the edge to be where the drop ships landed, then about here," he said, pointing to a location on the makeshift map.

I overlaid his map on the battlefield and adjusted it for size. "That will blindside the ground forces. How long?"

"Not long, maybe seven minutes," he said. "It'll be a large force, and it looks like their arrival will be very sudden. I see soil flying into the air, but no drop ships."

"Maybe from ground vehicles?" I suggested.

"No, I don't think so. The enemy doesn't appear to have any vehicles," he replied. "But they are definitely coming and they'll slam into the side of the ground forces, killing many before they can respond."

I made a snap decision and maximized my ability to fire on that location while opening a channel onto the Phareon battle network, a network to which I shouldn't have had access. Because of the news I was bringing, I hoped they'd be grateful enough to overlook the security breach.

"Phareon command, this is Marcus of the Night Wisp, over," I said.

After a hesitation, they replied, "Night Wisp, Phareon command, go ahead."

"Two more groups of enemy are incoming. Heavy ground forces will arrive in grid alpha three and enemy air support will come through grids beta six and seven. ETA on ground forces is six minutes. Air forces should arrive shortly after the ground forces."

"Acknowledged, Night Wisp. Phareon command, out," came the reply.

I watched as they quickly moved their armored vehicles to counter the attack that had yet to materialize. I was starting to understand why the team respected Ragnar so highly. He wasn't much of a warrior, but he could read a battlefield like no one I'd ever met. I wondered how he did it. It couldn't be those stones, as far as I could see.

I saw no indication of enemy forces on the way, but since his last predictions had come true I had no reason not to believe him.

Right on schedule, the ground burst open and massive creatures climbed out. I had already sighted my two guns on the general area and opened fire the instant before they appeared. Unlike assault rifles or blasters, the heavy assault line of weapons fired super-hardened slugs at hypersonic velocities. The recoil from the guns was such that even I had to brace myself to fire repeatedly. A primitive couldn't hope to control one without a tripod or other such mount.

I couldn't guess what kinds of creatures were coming out of the ground, but they were being shredded by my fire as the bullets imparted tremendous energy on impact. The roar of my cannon would have been deafening had I not worn full battle armor, including the thick armored helmet. As it was, I'd had to turn the gain down on my ears to dull the noise.

"Ragnar, how long till enemy air support arrives?" I asked. I had detected the launch of Phareon fighters, but it would be several minutes before they could reach us as they decelerated from orbit.

"Should be any moment now," he said.

Right on cue Crivreen called out, "Incoming!" and my sensors detected … life forms? Yes, large lizard-like birds or something resembling them. They each had a two-and-a-half meter wingspan, red scales and long snouts.

"Phareon command, Night Wisp," I said trying to match their choppy battle-speak.

"Night Wisp, Phareon command, go," they replied.

"Enemy air incoming now on predicted flight path," I said.

"Acknowledged. Phareon command, out," they replied.

As the creatures came in range, Crivreen and Purwryn opened fire with their wands.

Wands were interesting devices. The magi were able to store spells in them in some fashion for later release. It was like pre-firing missiles, but releasing and targeting them at a later time. It was hard to comprehend, but the creatures in the air didn't like getting hammered with them.

On Phareon's battle net I could hear troops requesting that the artillery fire be retargeted, and I figured they meant me. I retargeted without saying a word, as their channel was already busy. Whoever had asked sent thanks, and then I noticed a group of APCs moving to attack the flank of the enemy's heavy forces. I optimized my fire pattern to give this new deployment as much cover as I could.

The flying creatures reached us and opened fire on our position: literally. It seemed that the beasts could breathe fire, and that fire cut right through the metal and stone buildings in their way. Their breath was like the plasma from an engineer's torch, and I doubted if even this new armor from Zah'rak could cope with a hit from it.

Crivreen and Purwryn manage to keep the lizard-birds off our position, but the ground troops were not so lucky. The beasts strafed their lines with their fire and men were cooking inside their own armor. I couldn't think of a more horrible way to go. The human part of me wanted to help, but my guns were too slow to track the beasts.

A loud crack split the sky announcing the arrival of the Phareon fighters, braking hard and barely ahead of the sonic boom. They would have their work cut out for them, as they were outnumbered heavily and the birds were far more maneuverable. Their fire would be more than sufficient to cut through the fighters' metal exterior, and I feared that the fighters would have a hard time targeting the beasts.

Ragnar stayed crouched beside me with wands at the ready, but so far none of the enemies had targeted our location. Crivreen and Purwryn were putting up effective cover fire which kept the flying beasts away from us.

The dogfight between the fighters and the beasts was an interesting one. According to the chatter on the battle net, I'd been correct in my original assessment. They apparently couldn't lock their weapons on the creatures, so they were using their cannons in manual fire mode. The guns shredded the lizards effectively, but their accuracy was hit-and-miss without computer assistance.

"Ragnar, where are the sorcerers?" asked Raquel, sounding very impatient.

"They're still below ground, but beyond that I can't see," he said.

One of my internal alarms went off, warning me that my ammo stores were low. I had heard the ground forces calling for drops of supplies, so I decided to try it. "Phareon command, Night Wisp Artillery."

"Night Wisp Artillery, Phareon command, go," they replied.

"Running low on thirty-millimeter high-bond carbon. Got any spare?" I asked.

"Affirmative, Night Wisp. Sending a drop. Phareon command, out," came the reply.

Excellent, I thought to myself. I hadn't really expected it to work. "Heads up: Phareon is sending me an ammo drop and I would prefer if no one shot it out of the sky," I told them over my team comm.

Overhead the battle continued. The fighters had the beasts locked in combat with them. I feared that the fighters might not have the upper hand, but at least they were preventing the beasts from attacking the ground forces. Thanks to the ammo resupply that arrived shortly after my call, I was able to keep firing without ceasing. I had to be careful not to overheat my guns, but as long as I alternated between them and kept the speed down they should be able to take the abuse. I didn't know where Zah'rak got his supplies from, but all his weapons and associated supplies were of the highest quality.

I had settled to a good pattern when, somewhere behind my position, things suddenly turned violent. There was a loud crack, followed by Ragnar spinning round and firing both his wands at once as fast as he could call out the commands. I stopped firing and turned to see three men whom I assumed to be the sorcerers in the center of our position.

My position was exposed to a rear attack, and Ragnar had moved between the sorcerers and myself. His wands were pounding the closest target, but seemed to be hitting some kind of shield. They couldn't break through, which didn't stop him from firing at the same spot over and over with great precision.

I tried to bring my guns to bear but didn't have a clear shot. If I opened fire, there was a high probability of killing most of my team. I dropped the weapons and launched myself into the air at the closest target, but for the second time that week I was too slow. He pointed a finger at me and a pulse of energy flew from it; the blast hit me in mid-flight, square in the chest, and sent me tumbling back off the wall.

CHAPTER
FIFTY-SIX

M arcus is down!" shouted Ragnar.

The sorcerers had finally arrived and, just as Raquel had predicted, they teleported right among us. We had arranged ourselves in a fanned-out formation to make sure they couldn't appear and get us all with one spell. Various mounts and structures had been left over from the time when heavy artillery had been mounted here, and these provided cover and broke the line of sight needed to target a spell.

Ragnar had jumped between Marcus and the sorcerers, firing his wands as fast as he could, and Marcus had turned to attack. He didn't stand a chance head-on against a sorcerer, and he should have known better. I didn't know if he'd survived the hit or the subsequent fall from the roof; either could have killed a normal human, but he was made of tougher stuff.

"Everyone, target the sorcerer Ragnar is fighting! We need to overpower their defenses!" I sent.

Everyone except Raquel turned their wands on Ragnar's target, the third sorcerer, who started to fall back under the abuse. He was fully occupied trying to counter the attacks and could not cast a spell, which took him out of the fight for the moment.

"Stay on him!" I called out, considering grenades. I could have used telekinesis to bring them from where Marcus had placed his supplies, but we were all too close together and there didn't seem to be enough room. We needed to finish him quickly so that we could move to the next target and then help Raquel.

"Zah'rak, look out!" sent Shira.

I spun round just in time to see that the second sorcerer had teleported behind me. The fool was too close and I continued my spin, bringing my tail up to slam him hard in the chest, but he expertly teleported away and then charged back in with his staff, swinging it like a sword.

I pulled my staff from the air as Raquel had taught me, just in time to block his blow. Impossibly though it seemed, he had grown larger and now matched my size and strength. He kept pressing the attack with his staff, growing stronger and faster as we battled. I was totally unprepared for a sorcerer to use physical force, and that gave him even more of an advantage.

"Stay on that sorcerer; I've got this one," I sent. I wasn't sure I did, but we had to keep these two busy while Raquel battled the lead sorcerer. She was tied up in an all-out battle of magic with her opponent. Great energy flew back and forth between them, and it was impossible to guess who was winning or even to understand what was happening. I had to assume she would survive until I could try to help her.

I tried to press a counter-attack in between his attacks, but he was now definitely faster and stronger than I was. His reach even exceeded mine, and there was no question of his skill; since he looked like a normal human, I couldn't understand how that was possible. Not that it mattered, as he beat me back closer and closer to the edge of the tower.

As my rear foot started to slide off the roof, an idea struck me. It was crazy and foolish, perhaps even idiotic, but that should make it unpredictable at least. Just as we hit the edge, I sprang forward and grabbed him around the chest. He swung a fist and tried to bash it into the side of my head, but I didn't lessen my grip. I squeezed with all my might, forcing the air out of his lungs while springing back towards the edge and allowing myself to fall.

As we tumbled towards the ground he realized my plan and tried to break free, but it was too late. Just before we hit the ground I let go and allowed my full weight to slam into his body, using him to cushion my fall. My armor absorbed most of the shock, but he wasn't so lucky; I heard his ribcage break and collapse under my weight.

Extending my claws, I slashed across his throat, making sure he would never cast again. Once I was sure he was dead, I attempted to stand, and then I realized how bad the fall had really been. A wave of pain tore through my body, and my lungs screamed in protest with every breath.

I felt a strong hand on my back and heard Marcus say, "Let me help you up."

With his help I regained my feet. I was about to enquire how he'd survived the blast and fall, but then I got a good look at him: he looked worse than I felt. Half his face was gone, and he only had one functional leg. He'd splinted the other leg with some scrap metal, allowing him to stand, but it looked completely destroyed.

He spoke before I could and said, "No time for small talk; we have to get to the woods. Shira and the others are on the run."

I tried to take a deep breath to clear my head, but it brought on an agonizing coughing fit, which made me more lightheaded. I had to get to the forest soon to heal or I would do no one any good. I doubted I could walk all the way there, and even if I could the enemy ground forces would no doubt ambush me before I could get very far.

"Will you be all right? Can you find a place to hide?" I asked. I could see the forest from where I stood. If I could teleport there, then I could heal.

"Go. I'll catch up with the Phareon forces until you can come back for me." His voice was calm and controlled, despite how he must have felt with all those injuries.

Mustering what was left of my focus, I teleported to the woods and clutched a tree to prevent myself from falling over. I stood there hugging it for a moment, trying to regain some clarity of mind. I let myself mentally fall into the tree and drew on its great strength to clear my mind. I could feel the tree reaching towards me and lending its growing power to help me heal.

With its help, I was able to clear my mind enough to work my magic. I drew on the power of the forest to heal my body and felt my strength returning. I couldn't risk taking the time to bring about a full healing, just enough to dull the pain so I could focus on the fight.

Using the trees to search, I found Shira and Ragnar in battle with a sorcerer while Crivreen and Purwryn fought a group of those monstrous creatures. They were badly hurt, and I wasn't sure how much longer they could survive.

Raquel was still in the city, grappling with what I assumed was the most powerful sorcerer. Marcus was also in the city and the enemy ground forces had surrounded his position. They were moving in on him, and he couldn't move fast enough to get clear in his current condition.

That gave me three people who needed assistance; I couldn't help them all, so I had to make a fast decision. I ran towards Marcus in time to see him fall against a wall with the enemy pressing in on all sides. They had no weapons, but they would soon reach him and the foul mutations probably had ample strength to rip him limb from limb, especially in his weakened state.

Using my staff, I blasted an opening and charged in. As I neared him I had to stop firing or risk hitting him. I knocked aside the creatures closest to him, sending pain through my bruised and battered body.

When I was within reach, I grabbed him and tossed him over my shoulder. I was surprised again at his weight; he was much heavier than he looked, but still manageable. With him riding on my shoulder, I used my staff as an assault rifle and blasted my way out of the fight. I ran as best I could with his weight and my injuries until we were deep inside the woods.

When I felt we were far enough from the battle, I laid him down and said, "Find cover."

I didn't wait to see if he did; I had to reach Shira and Ragnar. I hoped fervently that the delay involved in helping Marcus hadn't cost me the chance to help them. Running through the woods as fast as I could, I drew on the life force of the forest to heal me as I went. I couldn't concentrate enough to make it as effective as it might have been, but it was enough to allow me to run despite my wounded condition. I could see through the forest that Ragnar was hunkered down casting his runes for all he was worth, countering spells from the sorcerer, while Shira pressed the attack with bolts from her staff.

Crivreen was down, but Purwyn was shielding him with his magic as the fight carried on around them. Surrounding them were an uncalculable number of the sorcerers' infantry.

I ran hard, not caring about the sounds I made or the damage to the woods, because one thing was clear: they were losing, and Ragnar was about to run out of runes.

As I burst into the clearing where they were fighting, I roared at the top of my lungs and lowered my shoulder to charge. The sorcerer turned to see me coming, but he was a fraction of a second too late and I hit him hard. A full-grown Zalionian weighs a lot more than even a brace of humans, and I'd been running fast when I hit him. Had he been a mundane human his spine would have shattered under that blow, and his meager body mass would have been thrown clear, but he was no mundane.

I hit something much harder than flesh and blood. The force of the blow sent him flying, breaking his concentration on his spells, but the recoil sent me flying back and I hit the ground hard on my left shoulder. I felt bones crumble and my vision turned red.

I screamed again and clawed my way back to my feet as the sorcerer also rose. Shira took full advantage of the momentary distraction and fired her staff at full strength into the side of the sorcerer, knocking him back down. His magical shielding held, but she pressed her attack and he struggled to keep his feet under the barrage.

I summoned my own staff back to me with my good arm and fired a similar blast. Ragnar stood and threw his explosive runes. The three of us poured on the firepower until he finally succumbed. The pain from my shoulder was overwhelming, and the wounds I'd received earlier were far from completely healed. I was paying for the punishment I'd put my body through to get here.

"Raquel, still fighting?" I sent, or tried to; it was hard to focus with the pounding in my head, the daggers in my lungs and a massive beast dancing on what was left of my shoulder. I couldn't even focus my eyes and gave up trying, letting the blurry world dance around me however it pleased. I collapsed, the last of the strength in my legs used up.

Ragnar was by my side with a bottle. I had no idea where he'd come from or how long he had been there. He was dancing and weaving with the blurry landscape. I wondered if he would get dizzy doing that; I was certainly getting dizzy watching him. I tried to reach out to stop his dance but kept missing.

"Here, drink this," he said.

He lifted the bottle to my mouth and poured it in. I didn't know what it was and I couldn't think clearly enough to decide if I should resist or assist. Warmth from the drink flowed through my body and my strength returned. Shaking my head to clear it, I saw Shira tending to Crivreen and Purwryn. The ground settled down and Ragnar stopped his dance.

"They're hurt too badly to deal with out here. We have to get them back to the Night Wisp," said Ragnar grimly.

"What about Raquel?" I asked, trying to get my mind back into the fight.

"As far as we know, she's still in the city. We were all supposed to gate away and regroup, but she didn't make it through before that sorcerer arrived," he said.

"We have to go back for her and Marcus," I said. I used my staff to climb back to my feet. Whatever it was I'd drunk had definitely helped with the pain, but I knew I wasn't nearly back to full strength. I began absorbing power from the woods to restart my healing. I wished I had the time to sit and meditate. I could be back to full health in a short while, but would be defenseless in the meantime, and I didn't know if Marcus or Raquel had that much time.

"I agree, but we have to take care of them first," he said, gesturing to where Crivreen and Purwryn lay.

Shira came over and said, "Ragnar, I can open a gate to the Night Wisp and drop off the three of you; then Zah'rak and I can go for the others."

"Splitting up doesn't seem wise, but I can think of nothing better," he said. "Here, Zah'rak, drink another healing potion."

I chugged it and asked, "How many more do we have?" I had full use of my arm and wits again, but I could feel a dozen more wounds crying out for attention.

"Not many," Shira said and looked in her pack. "Two. We used the rest to stabilize them."

"Save them. Marcus is in really bad shape," I said. "If he lives long enough, he'll need both of them and much more."

"Then you'd better get a move on," said Ragnar.

Shira nodded and cast her gate. I helped Ragnar get our unconscious friends onto the Night Wisp and then Shira opened another gate to take us near the outskirts of the city.

CHAPTER
FIFTY-SEVEN

We came out near where I'd left Marcus; he was lying quite still on the ground. I had left him propped up against a tree, but he had fallen over on his side.

"Marcus!" I called out as I ran over to him. He didn't respond at all. That couldn't be a good sign.

"Is – is he dead?" asked Shira.

"I don't know. I don't even know how to tell," I said. I turned him onto his back but he was completely unresponsive. Did Cyborgs have a pulse? Did he need to breathe? I assumed he did, but maybe I was wrong.

"Try to heal him!" she pleaded.

"Guard me. This will take a lot of focus." I lifted him back up and once again placed him against the tree. Placing one hand on the tree and the other on Marcus, I drew life out of the tree and pushed it into Marcus' body. I could feel a weak life force in him still; I focused on that and transferred all the power I could into it.

I heard Shira scream from behind and it broke my delicate focus.

When I turned, she and Raquel were fighting the last sorcerer, but he wasn't alone; behind him, slowly marching towards us, were more of those foul creations.

I stood and pulled off all the grenades from the sling on Marcus' pack and started to throw them into the advancing troops. Explosions ripped through their line, slaughtering large numbers of them, but they kept coming. I threw grenades until none remained.

"Shira, Raquel, we need to gate out of here or we'll be overwhelmed," I sent.

Shira broke off her attack and opened a gate. I grabbed Marcus and ran through it, followed closely by Raquel and Shira. On the other side I propped Marcus up by a tree. This time I grabbed the tree with both hands and drew power into myself. I knew the sorcerer would be along soon and I needed as much strength as I could get.

The sorcerer didn't disappoint and appeared moments later. Raquel was ready and launched a barrage of spells directly at him; Shira added bolts from her staff as quickly as she could.

The sorcerer used one hand to catch the bolts from Shira while sending power out of his other hand and into Raquel. Her first wave of spells failed to break through his shielding, and she was forced to break off her attack in order to block the incoming power from the sorcerer. He pressed her hard, mostly ignoring Shira.

Raquel looked bad. Her hair had gone completely white and her skin was heavily wrinkled. She seemed to have aged two hundred years since I'd last seen her. I had to find a way to help. Shira's staff didn't seem to be having much effect, so I doubted mine would either.

I slipped around behind him, using my camouflage spell to disguise my movements. I doubted it would have fooled him under other circumstances, but I was counting on his attention being taken up by the fight. The camouflage spell was just a little bit of extra protection.

Moving up behind him, I attacked in the way I knew best. I swung both of my swords down hard on either side of his neck. They would have cut easily through mere flesh and blood, but with a great shower of sparks they bounced off his magical shielding. His concentration faltered briefly but he continued his attack. So I swung again, and again, and yet again, each hit sending sparks flying and painful vibrations up my arms. I didn't know what kind of protection he had in place, but I was hoping to chip through it bit by bit.

Then my swords broke. Fire, light and sound erupted around me, tossing me away from the fight, but I roared and dug my clawed feet into the ground to halt my movement. For a brief moment the sorcerer was thrown off balance by the explosion, and I charged.

I came in low, putting my good shoulder low into his back and lifting as I hit him. He went flying over my back and slammed into the ground. Raquel was on him in an instant and kicked him hard in the temple. His eyes rolled around in his head and she leaned back and raised her hands, chanting in a language I didn't recognize.

The sorcerer started to get up, and I was about to pound him when I saw vines come up out of the ground and wrap themselves around him. He tried to break free of them but more and more came out of the ground and pulled him back down, squeezing him against the solid ground. He screamed and cursed in pain as the vines squeezed tighter and tighter around his body. I took a step back in horror, watching as his shield failed and his body was crushed under the pressure.

Out of the corner of my eye I saw Raquel collapse to the ground, looking even older than she had before. I ran to her side and scooped her up. At some point during the battle Ragnar must have arrived; he was propping up Shira, who looked exhausted.

"We have to get Raquel back to Alpha World," I said. "We can bring everyone; just get them to the gate room."

The adrenaline that had kept me going during the fight was fading and my legs were growing weak. My breath was ragged, and for the first time I noticed I was badly burned and my armor in tatters around my chest.

"Get yourself in there. I can handle these two," said Ragnar.

"Marcus is a lot heavier than he looks," I spat out between gasps. Fighting pain and fatigue, I forced myself to walk to the ramp of the Night Wisp and up to the gate room. Someone had already placed Purwryn and Crivreen in there. They lay there looking lifeless. I was too weak to reach out and see if they were still alive, so I decided to assume they were.

I laid Raquel down and saw Marcus float in while Ragnar helped Shira walk behind him.

"The engines are destroyed, and more enemy troops are incoming," said Ragnar.

"What happened?" I asked.

"As far as I can tell, while we were in the city wondering where the sorcerers were, they were out here blasting at our engines," he said.

"Was that the last of them?"

"Yeah," he said. "What's our next move?"

"Call Phareon and order the air strike. We'll all go through the gate and figure out our next move another day," I said. "After you make the call, gather what food and supplies you can. I don't know how long we'll be there, but it could be some time."

Ragnar left to get the supplies and I walked over to the gate and activated it. Shira stood up and walked through. I lifted Raquel and followed her. We came out deep underground in a tunnel I hadn't seen before, just as I had hoped. I laid Raquel down by the wall and got ready to go back for the others.

"Where are we?" asked Shira.

"Under the central tower," I said. "Last time we were here I updated our map and drew the gate there. Looks like the builders took the hint."

"Wow," she said and sat down next to Raquel to rest. "Do you think she'll make it?"

"I don't know," I answered and took a few moments to rest. I was battle-weary beyond words and none of my wounds had received the attention they needed. Eventually I forced myself back through the gate and found that Ragnar had all three of them floating, along with our supplies. "Ready?" he asked.

"Yeah, it's safe on the other side. Go through. I'm going to lock up the Night Wisp and follow you shortly," I said.

I worked my way up to the command station on the bridge and turned on the exterior sensors. It was as Ragnar had said: the enemy mutants were approaching the Night Wisp. I flipped the screens to show me the Phareon tactical network and saw their troops pulling out. They would start bombardment operations soon.

"Phareon command, this is Night Wisp," I said over the comm.

"Night Wisp, Phareon command, go ahead," they responded.

"Our ship is overrun with enemy forces, but we have another way out. Just make a crater out of what's left. Immediately." I hated to give the command, but I couldn't risk the gate falling into the hands of sorcerers, or indeed any of a dozen other enemies out this way.

"Acknowledged. Bombers on their way. Phareon, out," they replied.

I punched in commands to seal the craft and wipe its memory stores just in case anything survived, then slowly and painfully made my way back to the gate, which thankfully was next to the bridge.

It was sad leaving the first home I'd ever had, but I couldn't take the time to say goodbye as it would soon be a smoking ruin. The gateroom was empty and I walked through the gate. When I reached the other side, I closed and locked it.

Using a wall to prop myself up, I looked over what was left of my team. We were in sorry shape. Only Ragnar could still stand up straight, and I was fairly sure that he was hiding the effort it took him.

"Shira, can you gate us to the top?" I asked.

She nodded and used her staff to help her rise, then opened the gate and walked through without comment. Ragnar had everyone else floating now and he pushed them through. I followed him and hoped that I had gambled right that I could heal us all.

CHAPTER
FIFTY-EIGHT

I stood in the vacuum of space in orbit around the planet where Zah'rak and his team fought. I desperately wanted to go down there and help, but I knew that would be foolish. At the sight of the grandmaster wizard, the sorcerers would run and we would lose any chance to establish what was happening here.

Raquel fought her sorcerer to a standstill but did not push her attack. She was far more powerful then he, and could have defeated him if she had focused on the fight. As she was fighting him, however, she was using her power over nature to search the fortress. The toll of doing both at once was taxing her to the extreme; I could almost see her aging in real time before me. It made no sense. She should have killed the sorcerer and then searched, but for some reason she did not.

Zah'rak fought with another sorcerer and the others took on the third. I winced as I saw Marcus fall, but he was considerably tougher than he looked. He might have been able to rejoin the fight, but he was quickly set upon by many of the sorcerers' foul creations, managing to beat them off and go to help Zah'rak at great cost to himself.

"*Grandmaster, I have it!*" sent Raquel.

"*Good, then concentrate and finish the fight!*" I ordered.

"*Too late for that,*" she sent. "*I'll get the others safely home, don't worry.*" Then she sent me the information she had gathered when she should have been focusing on the fight around her. After reviewing this information I knew that some of it must have come from the minds of the sorcerers, which explained why she had kept them alive while searching.

"*I am worried about you,*" I replied.

"*I know, but it was too late for me before you were even born. Let me finish in my own way, I beg you,*" she sent.

I sighed. "*Very well.*" As she was in battle, I could not risk her being distracted by an argument with me. She had insisted over and over before the battle began that I should let her team fight. I relented, but had not realized the toll it would take on them. Now I regretted that decision.

I watched them fall back to the Night Wisp, defeat the last sorcerer and board the ship. I intended to call Kellyn and gate down there, but before I could I detected the ship's gate opening.

"*Safely home,*" Raquel had sent. They were gating out of there, but to where?

Just then I detected an energy shift that told me Henrick was on his way. I expanded the air pocket in which I was standing in to allow room for him. He did not need it, but I considered it the polite thing to do; besides, it would allow us to talk.

"Hello, Vydor," he said as he appeared.

"Hello, Henrick," I replied.

"It seems that Raquel's group did well down there," he said.

The Phareon forces were pulling out now and bombardment would begin soon. "Yes. There is nothing left to concern me now," I said.

"Yet you're still here," he said.

"Of course. It would have been rude to leave before your visit," I said with a smile.

He chuckled. "You know, it is camps like this one that Korshalem blames you for."

"Blames *us*," I said. "Yes. He fails to see the proverbial genie is out of the bottle already."

"It will be his downfall. Sorcerers like those below will continue to learn our technology and it won't be long before they take that realm," he said, "especially now that they are becoming more organized."

"Then you have heard?"

"Yes, they chose a grandmaster," he replied.

I nodded. "I feel sure that I will be blamed for that also," I said with a smile.

"Honestly, Vydor, I fail to understand why you fight to keep the treaty alive. You have already gained all you can from him," he said.

"I do not expect you to understand." He was not a wizard and did not understand the concepts of honor and integrity. I promised my friend Mantis I would try to keep the peace, and that was reason enough. Henrick would think it a foolish promise to keep, and perhaps he was right, but foolish or not it was a promise.

As we watched, the fleet began to release its bombs from orbit. The falling bombs passed through the atmosphere, heading for the planet's surface. As each successive wave hit the ground, a larger and deeper crater was created. They were being thorough, and I could see no way for any of the mutants to survive.

I sighed. "Well, it looks like that is over."

"For the present," he said and took his leave.

I considered the information that Raquel had sent. There were a dozen more locations like this one in which the sorcerers were actively trying to use our technology to breed a new type of soldier, one resistant to all kinds of damage and requiring very little in the way of supplies or support. They would be cannon fodder which could be dropped into the middle of enemy forces without fear of losses.

The sorcerers had always tried to avoid showing up in battle themselves, and these soldiers would mean they did not have to. When the sorcerers finally deployed these new forces into their own realm, they would no doubt arm them with blasters and rifles from this realm. The death toll would be horrific, but Korshalem refused to accept this and believed he could prevent this technology from reaching his realm by cutting off his only access to those who could help him counter that threat.

I understood his position, as it would mean the death of his people's culture. Once technology started to flow into their realm, life as they knew it would change dramatically forever. I would like to think it would be an improvement, but I have seen too much violence in my own realm to think that finer material things mean a better life.

Stepping out of normal space into the weave, I traced the route which the gate from the Night Wisp had taken. It had exited in this realm, about two-thirds of the way out on the far spiral arm in a completely unexplored section of the galaxy.

'Home', she had called it. I wondered what was out there, but without a precise endpoint I could not follow. I would have to wait until we heard from her again to know where they had gone. Meanwhile, I must see to the remaining camps that Raquel had found and at least delay the inevitable.

EPILOGUE

It had been many days since we'd left the Night Wisp, long dark days of sadness and mourning as we buried our friends Crivreen and Purwryn. Shira told me that they had used their bodies as shields so that she could cast the gate and get everyone out of the city. Then, when the sorcerer came to their new location, they spent all the power they had left holding back the creatures so she could focus on him. Had they not stood between her and the line of foul beasts, everyone might have been lost that day. They will be honored as heroes when the tale of our battle is finally told. I will make sure of it.

Ragnar, Raquel, Shira and I stood over their graves one last time. Over our heads foul undead creatures screamed their rage at our presence, but were powerless to prevent it.

The builder had done a remarkable job with the fortress, and it was back to full strength. As long as we stayed within its walls we were safe, which made it effectively a prison. A large and spacious one, but a prison nonetheless, and which I must admit I was anxious to leave.

Raquel ran her hands through her silver hair. We had returned her to the tower in time to save her, but for some reason her hair had never recovered. She looked older and wiser now. She had taken on too much at once in that last battle, but without her we would never have made it.

Crivreen and Purwryn had given their lives in that battle, and they were dead before I could attempt to heal them. In truth, they were probably dead before I had even rejoined Shira and Ragnar, but no one wanted to admit it at that time. After learning that they were already gone, I still wanted to try to heal them, but Raquel stopped me; she asked what I thought I might accomplish. Their souls had moved on and only the empty bodies remained. Nothing could change that now.

I sighed and turned back to the central tower where we have all been living. Marcus walked up to me. In a way, I think he might have preferred death to the healing I did on him. Most of his implants had been destroyed and were beyond my ability to replace; all I could do was to heal organic parts. I had actually considered letting him die, in the belief that he might be happier, but in the end I couldn't bring myself to do it.

All he had left of his former superhuman self were his core processing units, sensors and memory nets. With Raquel's help and the last of our healing potions, we were able to restore his body. For the first time in his life he was walking on two healthy, normal human legs, and I knew he hated it.

"I've checked and we're completely out of food now. Either we risk hunting or we leave via the gate; assuming, of course, that starving to death isn't an option on the table," he said.

I looked over to Raquel. "Does the builder know our situation?"

"Yes. I told him last night we would have to leave soon, but that we'd be back someday with forces sufficient to reclaim the world."

"How did he take it?" I asked. The builder was a large stone golem of some kind. He had slept for the last ten thousand years until Shira awoke the fortress with her sun staff on our first visit here. Since then, he'd been tirelessly rebuilding and protecting the castle. We finally met him this time on our second night back. I never thought I would see a walking, talking stone statue, especially one so excited to see us. I swear he would have bounced if he could have managed it. He had grown very attached to us even before we'd met him, especially Shira, to whom he referred as 'Princess'. She tried to pretend that she didn't like the attention he paid her, but I knew better.

"Oh, he'll be fine," she said.

"For a giant rock monster, he's a real softie," commented Marcus.

"So what's our plan, Zah'rak?" asked Ragnar.

"Raquel, do any of the remaining gates open to a place in our realm?"

"No," she said. "The network was originally intended to allow the Sac'a'rith to operate in many realms at once. The wizards maintained a network of gates in our realm, so there was no need for more than one here."

The rune that represented the Night Wisp gate had disappeared from the ring, so we knew that gate had been destroyed. That meant there was no way back from here, wherever 'here' was. Marcus had been unable to find a match in any of the databases remaining in his head which depicted the stars overhead. That put us in one of the vast uncharted regions of the galaxy, otherwise know as 'lost'.

I looked at my team and knew they needed me to make a decision about our future. I had made the decision for myself. Since the Night Wisp had been destroyed, this was the perfect opportunity to escape the life of a special agent and I planned to take it; alone if I had to, but I didn't think that would be an issue.

"Raquel, you can get back to the Wizard Kingdom, can't you?"

She hesitated. I hadn't asked her that before, but I thought it to be likely.

"Yes," she said. "I can leave the realm by the gate, and from there I can use my own spells to open a gate back into this realm at Alpha Academy."

"So can you get food and supplies? That way we could mope around for a while longer yet," said Marcus.

I waved away any answer that might be forthcoming. "Raquel, if you wish to return to your post, go with our blessing."

"Thank you," she said, without moving. "What are your plans?"

"Shira tells me of a forest world through the gate, one which is unspoiled by technology. I think we should go there. In a forest we should be able to support ourselves, and it will allow Shira and myself to study our art free from distraction." I paused to turn to Ragnar, and then continued, "I can send you back to Korshalemia, if you like; otherwise, you could return with Raquel or you can come with us."

He smiled. "I have no place to go back to, so you're stuck with me. Besides, I could use a break from technology."

Turning to Marcus, I said, "Well, I guess you really have the same choice: you can go back with Raquel or come with us."

He looked down at his completely human hands and sighed. "A fresh start would be good. I think I'll stick it out with you. There's too much temptation, too many memories of what I've just lost, to go back to civilization just yet."

I looked at Shira, but before I could say anything she smiled and said, "No need to ask; we all know I'm staying with you."

"Well, there you have it, Raquel. Sounds like we'll be moving on," I said.

She sighed deeply and looked around at the fortress. "I lived most of my first life here. There really is no place like it. Even with the foul beasts surrounding it, I could call no other place home. Not really." She paused and looked at us before continuing. "Zah'rak, I meant it when I said that the Sac'a'rith was for you and Shira to rebuild, but I would still like to be part of it. I need to go back and report in but after that, if you'll have me, I would like to join you and help with your training."

I nodded. "You're one of us now, Raquel; but don't you have to take care of the Phareon region for Grandmaster Vydor?"

She sighed. "Yes, I'll probably be sent back out there. There's still much to do to establish our presence in that region. They need me, but I will find you and stop in from time to time to guide your training."

"Will he be upset that we're not returning?" asked Shira.

"No, I'm sure he'll understand that everyone needs some time away to study and heal. He may wish to visit you in your new home someday, and the door will always be open for all of you to return," said Raquel.

"Then we are decided," I said. "Let's gather what we have left and move out."

A NOTE FROM THE AUTHOR

I hope you find as much enjoyment in reading these stories as I had living them. If you enjoy the books, please spread the word about them and please post a review to whatever store you purchased this book from. Thanks!

If you subscribe to our mailing list, you will receive access to our collection of free short stories! Plus you will get release announcements and access to other special promotions. Click this link to be taken to the sign up page: http://smarturl.it/LostEMail

You can also join the discussion on Facebook in our Lost Tales of Power Facebook group here: https://www.facebook.com/groups/LostTales/

Visit our website for news about the series, book reviews, and much more: http://losttalesofpower.com

Lost Tales of Power is on Twitter! Follow @LostTales for updates about the series, or follow @VincentTrigili for far more random tweets and information in addition to updates about the series.

Made in United States
Troutdale, OR
03/29/2024